First Kiss

A HEAVY INFLUENCE NOVEL

By Ann Marie Frohoff

AMF Publishing
Ann Marie Frohoff
heavyinfluencetrilogy@gmail.com

First Paperback Edition: December 2013

This book is a work of fiction. Names, characters, places, and incidents
are the product of the author's imagination or are used fictitiously.
Any resemblance to actual events, locales, or persons, living or dead, is
coincidental.

Frohoff, Ann Marie, 1971—
First Kiss : a novel / by Ann Marie Frohoff.—1st edition

Summary: About an up and coming teenage rocker on the verge of star-
dom, when the girl next door becomes something more; they're forced
to face the harsh realities on his road to fame and the expectations of
their friends and family. Sacrifices are made as everything changes as
they know it.

ISBN-10: 0615890822
ISBN-13: 9780615890821

...Art imitates life...

~ Oscar Wilde

PART ONE
SKID OUT

Chapter 1

JAKE

Have you ever wished you could take back a night? Wished you could at least forget it ever happened? That's how I felt, watching Rachel whiz around my bedroom. My head throbbed and I wanted to barf. Too much booze had me in a black hole and I'd hooked up with Rachel. After two years of keeping her at arm's length, she finally got to me. I wanted to fucking shoot myself.

"Do you see my shoes? Do you think they're in your car?" She chirped. Her mood was way too chipper for me and I hung my head, trying not to puke. "Aww baby. What's wrong?"

She sat down next to me, rubbing the top of my head. I stopped myself from pulling away, fighting the urge to be a dick. I wanted to blame the whole thing on her, but how lame would that be? What guy doesn't want a booty call? I shivered at the thought. What was I thinking? I didn't even like her like that.

"I wanna throw up, that's what's wrong." My head remained buried in my hands. I wanted to tell her it was a mistake. Maybe this would blow over and things would be like they were before. I could only hope. "What time is it? I have a meeting with a producer who came to the show last night."

She looked at her cell. "It's 9:30 AM."

Giving me a wet peck on the cheek, she got up and disappeared into the bathroom. I wiped her spit residue off my face with disgust and hoofed it out of my room to the kitchen. This could turn ugly, I thought. My mouth was as dry as the desert; I gulped down some Gatorade as I stood in front of the fridge. At least last night's show had gone well—we were on fire. I smiled, satisfied. It seemed like every one of my classmates had come to our show in Hollywood to kick off summer vacation. The place had been packed with familiar faces. We partied like the world was ending, even though it was really just beginning. We were all finally seniors.

Thankfully my mother wasn't home when Rachel finally left. I blamed our awkward goodbye on my hang-over. Her normally painted face was clean from the dark eye makeup and red lipstick. This was the first time I'd seen her without her war paint on. She looked odd without it. As pretty as she was, there wasn't anything extraordinary about her. She wasn't a natural beauty; cute, yeah, but nothing special. She didn't do it for me, simple as that. What was that saying– don't shit where you sleep? Was that the right phrase for this? Ugh. Rachel was such a big part of my band life, and now this was gonna seriously screw things up. I just knew it.

Driving to West Hollywood was the last thing I wanted to do, bad as I felt. The summer heat was just beginning and it made my wooziness worse. I tried to focus on the task at hand. When I got to King's Road Café on Beverly Boulevard, the outside tables were packed. Every hipster in town must have been eating there. You couldn't help but feel self-conscious walking up. Everyone watched everyone else, wondering who was who, if they were anyone famous. I chuckled to myself at how new-age-twilight-zone the scene was, everyone with their hip clothes and their cool shades, trying to look like they weren't trying. It was a joke. The fact was, we were all trying. At least *I* could admit it.

I spotted Jeff and made a beeline for him. I could literally feel the eyes poking me as I passed by.

"Hey, man, thanks for driving up," he said, holding his hand out.

I gave him a firm shake and glanced around. "I don't think I'm cool enough to eat here."

He shrugged. "Just think of it as a bad 3D experience."

We both laughed.

"I have to admit though, I'm a little jealous of all the tattoo sportin' mo-fos." I said, opening the menu. "I want a sleeve on this arm."

He nodded. "You're gonna have to wait until you're eighteen, unless you can talk your mom into taking you to Arizona."

"No shit?"

"No shit," he said with raised eyebrows.

"I'm all over that. Next tour, it's on." My mood buoyed at the thought. I'd wanted the same tat for the last three years. I was pretty sure of my choice.

"When do you leave?"

"In a few weeks," I said, gulping down the glass of water that was placed in front of me.

My stomach rumbled with hunger, making me more nauseous. Thankfully my breakfast burrito didn't take long. My mouth watered in anticipation of the first bite. We ate our food and talked about the band. Jeff was curious as to how we managed with all of us being in school. I explained that Bobby, Mike and I were toying with the idea of being home schooled our senior year if things kept going like they were. Dump, our drummer, was twenty—he didn't have to worry about school.

Jeff Arnault was a famous, Grammy-nominated producer. He was fairly young, in his late twenties, but he'd produced some of my favorite bands. I was beyond stoked that he felt us worthy of his attention. We made plans to record one song in his studio. I was on cloud nine when we got up to leave. We weaved our way through the closely arranged tables and chairs, trying not to bang into anyone. Once again everyone stared, watching us as we passed. I'd always gotten a lot of stares, mainly from chicks, but this was different; even the dudes were checking me out.

I stood next to my truck, staring back at the crowd outside, and wondered if I would ever be the guy everyone knew about. I didn't want to be famous for the sake of being famous. I wanted to be known for my music. I wanted to be the guy that these people pointed at and whispered about because of the songs I'd written. I could only pray, because there was no plan B.

I was finally feeling halfway human and continued to push Rachel from my mind. I hoped she wouldn't show up at band practice. I needed mass distance from that whole scenario. I tried to focus on thinking about the things I had to take care of before we left for tour as I dialed our manager. The call went straight to voice mail.

"*Hey, Notting, it's Jake. Just wanted you to know I met with Jeff and we're good to go. We're going into the studio next week, stoked. Call me back, wanna talk about the new merch and if it's gonna be done in time.*"

Driving down my street, I spotted my next-door neighbor in the distance, Alyssa. She and her friends hung out on the corner across from my house nearly every day there wasn't school. I looked for her again as I got out of my truck. Checking her out, it struck me that I'd been admiring her more often than I cared to admit. I wondered how old she was. She looked at least fifteen, but I knew she couldn't be because she didn't go to my school yet. She reminded me of my ex-girlfriend, Renee, a younger version, but not as dark. Aly was definitely prettier than Renee. Her figure reminded me of a doe—slender and timid. I honed in on her laughter as I stood in my garage trying not to stare at her. It brought me back to when I used to be friends with her brother Kyle. I used to tickle her until she peed her pants. That was fucked, I thought, laughing.

I perched myself behind Dump's drum set and grabbed a set of sticks. I banged out a new beat that'd been ricocheting around in my head and watched Aly to see if it would grab her attention. She didn't even glance in my direction. Living next door to me all these years, she'd probably tuned out my playing by now.

Rachel pulled into my driveway, adding fuel to my uneasy mood. Of course she had to show up, I thought.

"Hey babe," she said loudly as she slammed her car door shut. I cringed. I didn't want anyone to hear her. I

5

didn't want anyone to think she was my girlfriend. I looked out at the group across the street. No one seemed to pay attention.

"What's wrong with you?" she nipped. I quickly realized that she was wearing her bitch hat. Great, getting her to leave was not going to be fun.

Ignoring her, I banged hard on the drums, pretending that I didn't hear her. Finally, I looked at her. "What's up?"

I was being a dick and I didn't care.

Her face twisted. "Really?" She was ready to put me in my place, as always. She rolled her eyes at me. "You got an email with some dates and other things, so I just wanted to talk to you about it."

"You couldn't call?" I asked, agitated. "The guys are gonna be here any minute and I'm working on something. Can't this wait?"

Her mouth gaped open. "Is this how it's gonna be?" She folded her arms across her chest.

I sighed. She was right. I didn't have to be a douche-bag. "Look, I'm sorry. I'm tired. I still feel like shit from last night." I paused, deciding to put our hook-up to rest. "Rachel, I don't remember last night. I don't wanna be that guy, ok. I don't remember being with you, and I feel like shit about it."

I put as good of a spin on it as I could. The fact was I did remember flashes, enough to send the eebies running through me. What the hell was wrong with me? Rachel turned heads when she walked into a room. She was hot, as far as my friends were concerned. I was a fool for not wanting her.

She sighed and her face grew softer. "I see. Well, I don't remember much either."

"Yeah, not how I like to roll." I looked around uncomfortably and tapped on the cymbal.

Awkwardness began to creep in. I didn't know what else to say. I wanted her to get it. I wanted her to read my mind and leave. Thankfully, Dump arrived and I stood up. I stared at Rachel without a word, and she finally conceded.

"Ok. Hope you feel better." She stood for a moment, waiting for me to come around from the drums, but I was planted firmly. It was different now. Normally I would hug her warmly, thanking her for being rad.

"I'll call you tonight after I get through this and catch a nap. Thanks Rach," I said, giving her a crooked smile. She turned, flipping her blond hair without a word. She wasn't happy.

Dump stood quiet, looking at me with a bent grin. "Dude, you fucked up, didn't you?"

"Beyond, man. Why didn't you stop me?" I threw the sticks across the garage. "I just have to hope she doesn't take this like we're going out now."

"Good luck with that," he laughed.

"I wanted to chew my arm off this morning."

Dump laughed harder. "What, it wasn't with a boner that you woke up to her snuggled next to you?"

"Dude, I coulda chewed my arm off and beat myself with it." I grabbed my hair, groaning.

Band practice went along like any other. As soon as I confirmed that I wasn't into Rachel, Mike, our other guitarist, gave me a good ribbing. He began to strum an impromptu tune about what he'd like to do to Rachel and he drilled me for info. I don't think I'd ever wanna do a girl that my friend just did, but we're talking about Mike here. He was on a different planet.

The next few days I avoided Rachel as much as I could, and tried to ease back into the way things were. Thankfully, she didn't put any pressure on me, but I knew that wouldn't last. Sooner or later she'd wanna hang—alone—and talk.

Chapter 2

ALYSSA

Today was going to be different. I could feel it when I woke up. A strange excitement filled me—I couldn't put my finger on why. Maybe it's because I knew I'd be spending the whole summer with Matt. Or was it because I was finally gonna be in high school in a few short months? Nadine and I were the first to plant ourselves on the retaining wall across the street from my house. I wondered whose pool we'd infiltrate, or if we'd go down to the beach. I was antsy with anticipation of Matt's arrival. It was already hot. As ideal as Nicole's pool was, one of her older brothers could be such a jerk. He wasn't very accepting of us as a group. Our gang consisted of several guys. We were now a co-ed sampler of newly-minted high school freshman, and knowing him, it would just be one more reason to give us a hard time.

Greg Sanchez rolled up on his bike in all his plumpness. His jet-black hair made his fair skin look paler. His stomach spilled over his pants. Greg was interesting, his brothers had a huge influence on his behavior and he was always eager to share the going's on with them. It was gross and at the same time intriguing to listen to. Like the time he brought over his brother's video camera and showed us firsthand what'd gone down with a freshman in the boy's locker room. This one poor kid got all his clothes taken away behind his back as someone distracted him. He was left standing in his underwear and everyone was laughing at him. I guess they'd finally found his clothes in a trashcan across campus. That was the saddest thing to watch, and we all grew quiet with fear. In hushed tones, we wondered out loud how we'd get through our freshman year, especially the guys. Remembering their worried expressions made my stomach turn.

"What's up?" Greg said, nodding. I was happy to see him riding his bike; most of the time he had one of his brothers drive him over. He climbed off of his bike, letting it fall onto the sidewalk, and walked toward us. He stood there, breathing heavily, and lifted his t-shirt, wiping his sweaty face and exposing his pale white belly to us.

"Greg, you really need to get some sun on that thing. Your arms are super-tan and your stomach belongs some-where else," Nadine said, crossing her arms in disgust.

"Nadine!" I choked, trying to not laugh. She was so abrupt and embarrassing sometimes. Well, *a lot* of the time.

"Well, it's true. Tan fat is better than white fat."

Greg lifted his shirt again, rubbing his stomach. "My food baby likes being white."

"In all seriousness, Greg, I also used to be chubby in grade school, but I got my shit together. Tan that thing or don't flash it at me." Nadine turned away, mock-gagging, and Greg laughed. I laughed too, nudging his arm. He was such a good sport—always taking everyone's shit.

"So what's going on?" Greg wondered aloud. "I need a pool, or let's go down to the beach."

"Not much. Did you go by Matt's house?" I asked casually, not making eye contact, worried he would read my mind if our eyes locked.

Thinking of Matt Squire with his bold green eyes made me warm inside. I totally crushed on Matt. He was fast becoming Abercrombie status. He was the only guy who made me nervous. I wondered when he'd show up.

"Nope, they went to Vegas," Greg answered, kicking the rocks around in the flowerbed next to the retaining wall. "What's going on today?"

My fire went out. I slumped, kicking my feet hard against the wall. I was bummed I wouldn't see Matt, and wondered how long he would be gone.

"I don't know," I said, sulking, "Beats me. We should go to Nicole's." I hopped off the wall, frustrated.

That's the moment my world began to change. Jake Masters, the boy next door, pulled into his driveway. I'd known Jake practically my entire life. He's someone who'd spent the night at my house, sleeping next to me, piled on the floor in front of the TV. Nadine perked up instantly, fluffing her hair while glancing down at her chest. I then glanced down at mine, and back at hers. She pulled down on her tank top to show off her boobs a bit more. I looked back down at my chest. *What the?* I thought. *What's she doing?* I glanced in Jake's direction, I didn't think he noticed us.

When Jake was home, he was always out in his garage. He was either rehearsing with his band or tooling around with his truck. He never said anything to us besides a *"Hey"* or a head nod from time to time. Jake would small talk my dad when he watered the lawn. Jake and I would chat every now and then, but for the most part, we kept to ourselves. Jake was older than me. He was now a senior and he same age as my brother, Kyle. Jake and my brother used to be close, but Kyle went the nerd route and Jake went the wannabe rock star route.

I watched Nadine mess with her clothes and hair. "What are you doing?" I giggled under my breath.

"What?" she whispered loudly, tossing her hair to one side and puffed her chest out more.

I fluffed my own hair, mocking her. "This," I said. I puffed up my chest, looking over at Jake.

Then as we both stared at him, he took off his shirt, throwing it over onto the nearby lawn. Nadine and I stared in awe. Watching him hose down his truck half-naked made the world stop. I glanced back at Nadine, who had her mouth wide open, nearly drooling.

I looked at Greg, remembering that he was there. I was a little embarrassed. He glanced between Jake and us.

"Uh, you guys are weird," he said, uncomfortably, "I'm outta here. I'll meet you at Nicole's."

He rode away and I began to laugh, but Nadine didn't notice, her eyes were intently placed on Jake.

"Dude, what are you doing?" I murmured. "Do you like him or something? Do you want me to introduce you?" As long as I've known Nadine, she never acted this way towards Jake. I'd never realized she even knew he existed.

Nadine sat back on the wall and started to laugh loudly. I looked at her like she'd gone crazy and she leaned over to me, whispering, "Just go along with me."

I started laughing loudly, too. Sure enough, Jake looked over and smiled at us. I felt like an idiot.

"God, he's so freakin' hot," she said under her breath, nearly hyperventilating.

I laughed loudly, for real this time.

Jake smirked as he continued washing his big black truck, glancing from time to time at us. "You girls wanna share what's so funny?" he shouted. Nadine turned, eyeballing me, and I turned to face Jake.

"You want some help?" I shouted back. He stopped washing and offered the most brilliant smile I'd ever seen.

Jake shrugged his shoulders. "Sure, if you guys wanna help…that'd be cool."

Nadine nudged me with a wicked grin, striding ahead of me. I quickly followed behind her and we crossed the street without a word.

I awkwardly cleared my throat, introducing them to each other. "Jake, this is Nadine," I said, giving a weak smile. "She lives around the corner." I raised my arm and pointed, waving it around like a spaz.

He cracked a brilliant smile again. "Yeah, I've seen you before," he said. "You go to my school. What's up?"

Jake nodded his head as he examined us a bit more closely. His eyes parked themselves on mine and my stomach went nuts. I began to fidget with my shirt, looking away briefly. Jake looked around awkwardly too, and laughed a little.

"Wha'cha guys up to this sweltering morning?" He turned and walked into his garage, grabbing two rags and raised them up.

"Not much." I croaked out.

He threw each of us a rag and resumed scrubbing his truck. Nadine mouthed *"Oh my freakin' God!"* and turned, dipping her rag into the bucket. I stood there dumbfounded. This was new to me, the whole manipulating the situation thing. I'd only seen it on TV. Now we were the characters.

"So, Jake, how's the band doing?" I tried to make small talk as I diligently washed the windows on the other side of the truck; but at the same time I really did wonder. I glanced into the garage. "Looks like your garage has turned into a professional studio, what's that stuff on the walls?"

He looked up, wiping his damp brow with his forearm. "That's sound proofing foam. It's as sound proof as I can it get for now *and* the band is doing great," he explained, walking toward me. "We just had a show at the Roxy in Hollywood. You should come to the next one."

My heart began to race and my throat thickened. All I could do was gulp, trying to find moisture. He finally continued, taking the pressure off.

"We're a lot better than you probably remember," he said, coming closer to me. He tossed his rag back and forth between his hands while his eyes scanned my face. "Look at you, you've grown up."

Like a loud gong, Nadine's voice rang out. "Yeah, we'd love to come and see you play." She rounded the backside of the truck, standing a little too close to Jake.

He backed away, looking her up and down. "Uh, yeah, anytime, just let me know."

"Hey, would you like me to rinse the soap?" Nadine asked, grabbing the hose off the ground.

"Yeah, before it dries, that'd be cool," he said, flashing a wink at her.

14

What the hell? Was he flirting with her? I glanced at Nadine as she began to squirt the bubbles off of Jake's truck and I wondered if she saw what I saw.

"God, it's so hot," she said, holding the bright yellow nozzle over her head, squirting water straight up into the air. I squealed as it rained down on us and dashed over to the manicured lawn grabbing Jake's shirt from the ground, holding it over my face.

"Ahhh, shit," Jake shouted, laughing loudly. "Nadine, be careful of the garage!" he warned and jogged to the sidewalk, guiding Nadine's direction of waterworks.

Abercrombie, most definitely, I thought, staring at Jake's glistening wet torso. God, I'd never noticed how studly he was. His muscular build left me speechless. Covering my mouth, I giggled, and he took notice.

"What? You think you're gonna stay dry?" He shouted, running toward me. He grabbed my waist, twirling me around—then held me in a tight bear hug up off the ground.

"Nadine! Let her have it!"

The water rained down on us, and then fell directly upon me, stinging my skin. Jake held me tightly to his chest. I could barely move; squealing and laughing so hard I almost peed. I buried my face into his shirt, which I still held in my hands. Jake finally released me and I ran across the street, avoiding any more water games.

"You bitch!" I shouted through fits of laughter and leaned against the wall trying to catch my breath. I was soaking wet.

Jake ran after Nadine, grabbing the hose from her. He held her wrists together with one hand while he used his free one to soak her down. She didn't fight to get away like I did. She clearly liked the attention. Jake stopped and stared over at me. I was surprised to see how much taller he was than Nadine. Nadine had always been taller than me; I was already 5'8. I considered both of us pretty tall. Jake must be over six feet tall...— his voice shook me from my thoughts.

"Ok," Jake shouted over at me, "I promise we won't water fight anymore. Come back and help dry."

Sopping wet, Nadine futilely tried to fluff her hair. I walked back over, giving her a defiant smile, and she winked at me, satisfied. I was both relieved and feeling a little of something else I couldn't pinpoint.

"Be right back." Jake announced, going into his garage and vanished into his house.

"Oh my *God*, he is so to die for!" Nadine swooned against the truck. "When he was holding me back from squirting you, I wanted him to pin me against this truck and kiss me," she confessed. "You have to find out the deets on what's up with him."

My chin must have hit the ground. "What do you mean?" I said, pretending I didn't get where she was headed and dried my arms and then face with his shirt. I noticed how nice it smelled and took in a deeper whiff; my eyes rolled back into their sockets. "Dude, you gotta smell this!"

Nadine took a quick sniff and grabbed the shirt out of my hands, stuffing her face in it. Jake unexpectedly walked out his front door and we both spun around to face him. Nadine tossed his shirt onto the hood of the truck.

"Here ya go. I just pulled them out of the dryer." He handed each of us a warm towel. "After you're done drying yourselves, you can use them to dry the truck. Oh, and make sure you don't touch the tires. My mom'll kill me if I get black stains on them."

As he turned back to shut the front door, I quickly reached up and grabbed his shirt, tucking it into the back of my shorts.

We heard a shout from down the street. *"Nadine!"* and could see her mother wearing a bright red caftan and black leggings as she stood on the sidewalk, looking for her. *"Nadine!"* she shouted again.

"Shit! Shit! I totally forgot," Nadine said in a panic. "I forgot I have a dentist appointment." Glancing down at her watch she went on, "Now I'll have to change and we're gonna be late. She's going to kill me! I'll see you at Nicole's later." She threw the towel at us and turned, running home.

"OK," I shouted after her. I stood there in silence, feeling weird and suddenly self-conscious. I looked over to Jake, shrugging my shoulders. He smiled back and continued to dry his truck.

As watched Jake from the other side of the truck, his bare chest rubbed against the window as he dried the roof. The sight made me weak. I felt like a total perv, but I couldn't take my eyes off him. Then suddenly he opened the door and I quickly looked away, praying to God he hadn't seen me ogling his all-too-perfect frame. He stepped up into the cab and continued drying the roof. My heart raced. All I could see were his impossibly firm waist muscles shifting under his smooth, lightly tanned skin; I nearly jumped out of my own skin when his voice sounded.

"So, little Miss Alyssa Montgomery, what have you been up to all this time?" he asked. "You're nearly all grown up."

Laughing nervously, I fumbled for words. "Uh, well, just super stoked to finally be starting high school," I stuttered, walking over to his side of the truck. I inspected his work, as if I really cared. "I've been taking piano lessons, playing volleyball and just hanging out, really, not much else. What else is up with you?"

Jake was quiet for a few moments as his eyes searched my face. I felt the heat rising in my cheeks. I wanted to die.

Finally he spoke. "Besides rehearsing like a madman with the band and just barely getting through school, you're lookin' at it," he said. "Not sure if you knew, but we kinda been doin' little mini-tours. So I've been missing a lot of school, but I managed to eek out getting into the 12th grade." A proud grin stretched across his too handsome face.

"How does your mom feel about you eeking by?" I asked curiously, "my parents would kick my ass if I got anything below a B."

"By *eeking* I mean I'm not an A student, more like a solid B, some C's. I think with everything that goes on with the band, she's just happy I'm making it through." He shrugged. "You know, we have a pretty beefy tour lined up this summer, so I'm stoked."

His eyes sparkled when he spoke. I never noticed how blue they were, especially in contrast with his dyed-black hair. Jake used to have light brown, nearly blond hair. Then one day it was black, and he's never gone back.

"Wow, Jake, I had no idea. I feel bad for not paying attention," I said, shamefaced. "Does your band have a website?"

"Yeah, wanna come in and check it out?"

My insides tumbled around as I stared back at him. Nadine was right. He really was to die for. "Um, sure."

I knew his mom wasn't home. I assumed she was working and his dad had passed away when he was younger. I barely remembered his dad. Taking in a deep breath, I calmed myself. What the hell did I think would happen anyway? Stupid Nadine, this was all her fault. Ok, *breathe deeply*, I told myself. Desperately trying to stay calm. Like an out-of-body experience, I saw myself running across our lawns into my house.

"Are you ok?" he asked with concern in his eyes.

My frantic thoughts stopped in their tracks. "Yeah. I was just thinking if there was anything I needed to do."

"Alright, cool." He turned, leading the way into the house.

I continued to fight the voices in my head, trying not to look like a schizophrenic. Besides, whom was I kidding? I was no match for Nadine and her big boobs. Boys loved boobs. Not to mention all the hot chicks who were always hanging around Jake. *The Envies*, as we underclassmen called them.

I guess I'd been paying attention to a portion of Jake's life instead of Jake himself. But now that Nadine had shed light on him, my eyes were wide open.

Chapter 3

ALYSSA

I hadn't been inside of Jake's house in over two years. We walked through the foyer and into the living room. I was shocked by the change. I didn't recognize one thing from years ago. The inside was totally remodeled. Gone was the 60's-ish shag carpet, replaced with dark hardwood floors and the drab gray sofas had been replaced with dark tanned leather ones, they looked expensive and totally plush. A huge TV, the size of a bay window, covered the far wall. And an electronic stereo system stared back at me menacingly.

Note to self: Never Touch That.

The other wall, while once solid, now had windows allowing a view of the pool and backyard. The backyard appeared to be the same. It had always been landscaped like an oasis, with huge banana trees, ivy, and those sweet-smelling gardenia flowers. I loved his backyard—it reminded me of being poolside in Hawaii.

"The computer's in my room," he said, walking ahead of me. "Oh, take the slaps off. Kate doesn't want us grimmin'

up or scuffin' her shit. Like rubber will scuff, but whatever."
He shrugged, and a flash of irritation ran across his face.

I stopped just short of the earth-tone runner leading
toward the hallway. "Oh, ok," I said, kicking off my flip-
flops. "Hey, just curious, why do you call your mom by her
name?"

Jake looked at me with hooded eyes and a bent smile.
"Because when we're out doin' band shit, the last thing I
wanna shout out is—*Hey Mom*—so, naturally." He shrugged.
"And at this point, I prefer it."

Walking over the yummy rugs in my bare feet, I could
feel why Kate didn't want them messed up, I sank in an inch
they were so deluxe. We continued down the hallway until
we reached a door at the end of the hall. Jake had changed
rooms. He used to be in the closest room to his mom's; now
he was the farthest. The first thing I'd noticed was a French
door opened at the other end of the room and it led out to
the backyard. A hot tub was just to the right of it. *What a
guy*, I thought. Of course he'd want this room. I would.

"Wow, this is cool. When did you switch rooms?" I said,
marveling at how neat everything was. Matt's room was a
messy piece of shit compared to this. "I would die to have a
hot tub right next to my room." I fawned and turned looking around. "Dude, you have your own bathroom, too!" I
walked from one side to the other, scanning every inch of
every surface, twirling and landed on his bed, crossing my
legs up underneath me. I batted my eyes. "I'll trade you."

"Ha, I'm sure you would," he said, pensively. His eyes
locked on mine and my hands went numb. He flashed his
perfect smile at me and shook his head. "Is your dad still a
hard-ass?"

"Yep, the older I get, the more of a hard-ass he is. My poor guy friends don't even come to the door anymore. They just hang on the corner until I come out." I laughed at the thought. But it wasn't funny. He was way too strict, and because of it, my brother, sister and I always lied to him. "But he loves me, so what can I do?"

"You can't do anything, and I see why he's such a hard-ass." My hands tingled hearing his words.

Was that a compliment? Why would he say it like that? I felt the heat start to rise in my face.

"What?" A smile peaked at the corners of his mouth.

"Nothing." I laughed nervously, shaking my head. My spastic insides were getting the best of me, and I got up to look out into the backyard. Oh my God, I knew he totally caught me staring at him like an idiot. I scrambled to find anything to move me from my embarrassment and turned to face him. "When ya gonna pull up that music?"

"Hello, can't you see I'm booting up my computer?" He replied, playfully and gestured to me. "See, clearly this is why your dad is a hard ass."

Finally, in a more neutral mood I walked over to Jake and bent down, leaning over his shoulder as he pulled up his band website. I was impressed. It was done up professional, just like all the other hot bands out there. There was his picture, as big as life, staring back at me like someone I didn't know. He clicked on the music player and turned up the volume. Unfamiliar sounds streamed out of the speakers; a guitar riff and keyboard melody drifted out over the room. Drumbeats followed, and then a voice, a voice I didn't recognize. I really liked it. It had an alternative rock-punky vibe. I closed my eyes.

"So, who's singing?"

"It's me! Duh!"

My eyes shot open. "No!" I shouted, "Oh my God! You sound so good, like so old! I mean not like an old man or anything. Wow, you totally kill it!" I was completely floored. Nadine was going to shit a brick when she heard him.

Jake lowered the music and spun around in his chair to face me and I stepped away from him. I couldn't take my eyes off him. I kept taking in slow deep breaths to steady my racing pulse and without a word he got up and walked out of the room. I took this opportunity to look around more closely. The walls were plastered with posters of rock bands, surf shots, and bikini girls. The bikini girls were of all types. I couldn't tell what kind of girl he was into and I wondered if he had a girlfriend. I snooped around to see if he had pictures with any girls lying around—anything to identify a special someone. I only found party pics and band snapshots. Yes, there were girls, and two of them were in most of the shots. Hmm, I wondered.

I sat down on the bed just as Jake came through the door. My insides were tense, and it made me fidgety. He was carrying a bag and some water.

"You thirsty?"

I nodded my head *yes*. Why was I speechless? Come on, Aly, its only Jake, I reminded myself. Get over it.

He tossed me a small bottle of water and sat down next to me. I nearly drank the whole bottle of water in one gulp.

"Shit, you were thirsty! You want more?" he offered and pulled what appeared to be t-shirts out of the bag.

I licked my lips. "No thanks, this is good. I didn't realize how parched I was."

Jake stopped and stared at me with a crooked grin. We were only inches apart, and his blue eyes took my breath away. I wiped my mouth with the back of my hand. I swore I had to have been drooling.

"Parched, huh? Who says that?" he teased. "That's a word my grandma uses." I giggled. I was okay with him teasing me. It pulled any weirdness out of the room.

"I read a lot, for your information. English literature is my fave." I tried to think of something else to add, but nothing came to mind and I leaned into him with my shoulder, "so there."

The scent, his scent, from his shirt caught my attention. God that smell was going to be the death of me. None of the guys we hung out with smelled as good.

"I wanted to give you some merch," he said, holding up a black t-shirt with the words *Rita's Revolt* printed in bold white letters. "And some CDs. You can pass these singles out to your friends, and you can have these," he said, holding up hard CD cases.

I grabbed the t-shirt and held it up, staring at it more closely.

"Jake, I'm super impressed. I really had no idea. I know I keep sayin' that, but geez." I remarked, smiling at the t-shirt and a shock of electricity shot through me when he touched my knee and thanked me.

"Tell me more about what you've been up to." He asked and his hand remained on my knee. "You say you read English literature—like what?"

This time he wasn't being a smartass. I leaned back against the pile of pillows, putting my arms behind my head and he pulled his hand away. Relief washed over me.

"Well, I really like Jane Austen. I'm a little embarrassed to admit it, but I really like those old-time, long ago romance novels." I paused. "The kind where the guy is chivalrous. Guys seem to be such jerks these days. You know, our friend Greg, Greg Sanchez, the bigger one? The stories he shares with us about his brothers—it's like shock factor or something."

"Oh, I know exactly who you're talking about and yeah, I agree. Those guys are idiots, and they think their shit doesn't stink. A bunch of jock dorks." He shook his head. "Not sure what's up with Greg being so fat, knowing how his sporto brothers are built. I fucking hate sportos." He frowned. "So, what kind of stories has Greg told you?"

I pondered for a moment if I should tell him. What the heck, I thought; it would be nice to have someone other than a bunch of 14-year-olds to give perspective. I mean, Greg could be lying for all I knew.

"Well," I started laughing nervously. "I don't know." I squirmed, and his smile grew bigger.

"Look at you, you're blushing!" He grabbed my shoulder and his face fell flat. He leaned in closer, super serious. "What's tubby telling you anyway? I wanna know if he's feeding you a bunch of bullshit." Jake's intensity surprised me. He got up sitting back at his desk and leaned way back in his chair, waiting for my answer.

"Jake, don't embarrass me. I feel silly even talking about it with you." I looked down at my feet. "I mean, he just tells us stories about how they bet on how many blow jobs they can get—"

Jake interrupted me right away.

"Ok, so this is *really* what you talk about with the guys you hang out with? Blow jobs?" Jake was aghast. "Do you even know what that is? I'm no expert on when chicks start learning this shit. I never talked about this stuff with girls."

"Yes. I know what it is."

"OK, well let's hear it." He didn't smile or flinch.

I stared at Jake, completely horrified. I couldn't believe the direction our conversation had gone. My face must have said it all and we sat there in silence for what seemed like forever, staring at each other. Finally, he spun around to face his computer.

"Alyssa, don't always believe what you hear. Guys talk shit, they make stuff up and they lie," he said, while he typed. "Trust me. I used to make shit up all the time. I know it was only a few years ago."

"You mean you lie? About what?"

"No, not anymore, but when I was your age I did it to make me seem cooler. It's stupid, but whatevs." He spun back around to face me. "But this is just between you and me, of course. Your brother and I use to make shit up all the time."

"You're kidding!" I laughed out loud. "My nerd brother? Come on, you have to tell me, what did you guys used to say?"

"Dude, your brother isn't *that* big of a nerd, and I'm not telling you anything," he said, waving the palms of his hands at me. "I plead the fifth."

I was lost in his eyes again, along with his dashing smile. Contemplating his words: *I plead the fifth*, I tried to remember where I'd heard that and what it meant. "Plead the fifth?"

"What?"

"What does that mean?"

"It means that you aren't going to say anything because it might incriminate you, or be used against you at a later date. It's a law thing." He nodded his head and his eyes narrowed.

Just as he was about to go on, we heard Jake's name being shouted from the other room. Jake hung his head. "Looks like the guys are here to rehearse," he said, jumping up, "Don't forget the bag."

He waited for me to grab the bag and followed me out the door. As we rounded out of the hallway a group of *almost* equally good-looking guys stood staring back at us. They had bags of fast food in their hands.

"'Sup, bro," piped one with bleached blonde hair and intense blue eyes. He stuffed French fries in his mouth as he eyeballed me with a stupid smirk. I could only imagine what I looked like with my hair all rumbled and matted to my head.

"Alyssa, this is Mike," Jake said, pointing at smirk boy, "and that's Bobby, and Victor, but we call Vic 'Dumpster' or 'Dump'." Jake laughed. "But don't ask why we call him that."

"Sup, Alyssa?" Mike nodded as he chewed open-mouthed, looking me up and down.

I could tell right away Mike was a force.

"Hi," I squeaked out. I stood unmoving, like a statue and knew if I didn't get out of there pronto, they'd all notice I was blushing.

What the fuck, why was this happening?

"Uh…ok…Jake," I said nervously, "um, nice meeting you guys." I waved, walking toward the door, searching my pockets for my phone. "Oh, I left my phone in your room."

Of course I did, I thought, mortified that I had to be there even a second longer.

I quickly walked past everyone, practically running down the hallway into his room. The smell of him hit me like a baseball bat. What was that scent? I grabbed my phone from the bed and looked around for anything to give me a clue. I saw a bottle of whatever it was, but I couldn't read it. The writing was all in French. I sniffed the bottle. That was it, God it smelled good. I took one last big breath in and walked out as calm as possible. I was probably as red as a tomato.

Walking down the hall I could hear them talking and it was about me. I stopped to eavesdrop.

"So dude, ya doin' them younger these days I see."

"Shut the fuck up, Mike, she's my next-door neighbor," Jake *spat back.*

"That makes it convenient," Mike laughed. *"Yeah, clearly virgin territory."*

"I'm not doin' her, you fuck, get your mind outta the gutter."

I was even more mortified now and came out swiftly, not looking at anyone. "Alright, later," I waved. As soon as the door shut behind me, I sprinted across our front lawns, into my house. My sister was sitting on the sofa, watching TV. She didn't look in my direction. I ran up the stairs, colliding with my brother as he came out of the bathroom.

"Wow, man, slow down," Kyle said holding me by the shoulders. "Where's the fire?"

"Sorry, Kyle, I'm supposed to be at Nicole's right now. I got side-tracked." I explained, trying to squirm away.

"Hmm, what's in the bag?" he asked, letting me out of his tight grip. He grabbed the bag out of my hand and pulled out a t-shirt. "Ah, Jake's band…these are cool. Is there one for me?"

Kyle dropped the bag on the hallway floor and started pulling everything out.

"I'm sure there's one in there." I growled, stalking off to my room. I slammed the door. He irritated me.

I rummaged through my drawers until I found my bathing suit and gathered my stuff together. Taking off my shorts, Jake's shirt fell to the ground. I picked it up and stuffed my face into it. Gah, *that* smell. I collapsed onto my bed and firmly held it to my face as if my life depended on it. All of a sudden Kyle barged in, throwing the bag right onto my stomach, startling me.

"What are you doing?" he snickered.

"Nothing, just wiping my nose." I said, as my heart nearly sprung out of my throat.

Oh my God! What did it look like I was doing?

"Ugh, stay away from me!" he said, scowling and swiftly shutting the door.

After a moment of thinking *what the heck*, I put on my bathing suit and stuffed my things in a bag, along with Jake's shirt. I wanted Nicole to smell how yummy he was. Grabbing the bag of Jake's promo stuff, I bound down the stairs. I abruptly stopped before the door, staring at myself in the foyer mirror one last time. I didn't have a shirt on, only a bikini top. Should I put a shirt on? Ugh, why should I care? We live at the beach. Normally I wouldn't put one on.

As I opened the gate to leave my courtyard, my heart stopped. I felt lightheaded as soon as I saw Jake standing at the sidewalk, next to his truck. I didn't think I'd see him again so soon. Mike spotted me first and whistled. That made Jake turn to face me and he watched me walk toward him.

Why now? Why didn't I ever notice Jake like this before? I thought of Nadine. I could never admit that I was now crushing on Jake Masters. Nadine would beat my ass. I would be labeled as one of those girls who backstabbed her friends. She had first dibs. She saw him first. That was the rule. This was easy, though, because my dad would never approve of a senior, and me, even if it were Jake. I laughed at how quickly the fantasy rushed through my head. As if. I walked closer to Jake and his smile burned into me like a red-hot poker.

"Well, well, well, you comin' over to go swimmin'?" he asked playfully, holding his hands out at me. "Just another reason your father has become more of a hard-ass."

He made my knees go weak and my throat go dry. The cat calling continued as I passed by. All I wanted to do was run screaming down the street. I could still feel Jake's eyes on me the further away I walked. It was like an invisible string pulled at me to turn my head. I didn't dare to. *Don't do it*, I told myself—but I couldn't help it. When I looked over my shoulder, our eyes met and he gave me one last wave.

"Hey, I really want to know what you think of that music! Come by later," he shouted, giving me his heart-stopping smile.

What the hell was I going to tell Nadine?

As soon as I turned the corner and was out of Jake's sight, I sped up my pace. My heart raced and my thoughts swirled uncontrollably. The thought of him asking me to come back over sent my mind reeling. Why would he ask me that if he didn't want me around, right? Whatever it was, I could never admit my feelings to Nadine or any of the others. First, because of Matt, and second, all the others had big mouths. Nadine would find out in no time.

I hadn't notice that my pace slowed to a near standstill as I daydreamed about Jake in front of Nicole's house. There was no turning back.

Chapter 4

ALYSSA

I finally cleared my head enough to walk into Nicole's house. Nicole Hamilton and I had been best friends since the 4th grade. Her delicate, doll-like features and saucer-wide blue eyes were a contrast to my tall-thin build, brown hair and eyes.

I opened the front door and a blast of cool air slapped me in the face. I loved the air-conditioning. We didn't turn ours on throughout the day – *"It's too expensive"*, my mother would say. Nicole's family had lots of money. I had to admit, I was jealous. She got whatever she wanted.

Nadine wasn't there yet. Nicole's brothers, Stephen and Chris, were hanging out in the family room, watching TV. I crawled up onto the stairs, sitting midway up, which gave me a clear view of them and of the backyard, too. It was around 11:30 in the morning, and it was already 90 degrees. This was not normal Southern California beach weather. I looked through the sliding glass door, and Greg was chasing Grant, squirting him with the hose. I could see Nicole lying out, getting a tan.

"Hey Alyssa," Stephen said. Chris didn't look at me. Chris was the best-looking brother, and he knew it, too. Stephen had an offbeat good look and wore his hair longer, dressing like those eclectic hot Euro boys. Chris was sporty, the jock, and it was all about him.

"Hi." I smiled, holding the railing above my head with both hands. I leaned my head through the bars. "It's so eff-ing hot outside, and I'm not ready to go melt yet. Do you mind if I sit here for a minute?"

"Nope, feel free to sit as long as you'd like." Stephen got up and walked into the kitchen. My mother would sell her soul for their kitchen, with its grey granite counters and one of those industrial stoves. The fridge was one that looked like cabinets, and it was doublewide. "You want something to drink?" Stephen offered. "Cut the dust?"

"Yes, please."

"What's your vice?"

"Vice?" I tilted my head.

"Vice means—hmm, how do I explain this?" He placed both hands on the counter looking down. "It means what's your weakness, or what is it that you like the most. I think." He stared up at me, smiling.

"Ok, good enough," I laughed. "I'll take a Coke if you've got it."

"Yep." He walked over to the fridge.

I was now looking at guys in a new light. I noticed how muscular Stephen's arms were, and compared him to Jake. His t-shirt fit nicely over his biceps and chest—something I would have never noticed before. I admired his face as he turned around. I smiled at him when he reached up to hand me the soda. Our eyes locked for a second, and my stomach flipped.

What the heck?

"Thanks, Stephen." I was lost for any other words.

"Uh, yeah, of course," his lips curled slightly upward. He stared at me for a moment longer before he turned around.

I became self-conscious with that totally weird moment. What the hell was going on? Was I emitting some new vibe? I sat there drinking my soda, looking over the can, now focusing on Chris. Nadine crushed hard on Chris, too. I wondered how the Jake thing would play out because of that. Come to think about it, Nadine crushed on all the hot guys. She was completely boy crazy.

I never gave it too much thought until today, until the electricity had surged through me during our water fight. Why was I noticing guys in a different light now than I had before? I couldn't wait for Nadine to show up. I wanted to know when she first felt that intense attraction for a guy, if she ever felt what I was feeling. I ran through our fake conversation in my head. I'd play it off like I was envious.

I hopped down the stairs and through their family room. Chris finally noticed me and nodded a hello. I slid open the door leading to the backyard. Nicole laid face down across a lounge with her bathing suit pulled up her butt and her top untied.

"So, since when do you pull your bathing suit up your ass?" I asked playfully as I approached.

She lifted her head, squinting. "Since Stacey was over here laying out, and I saw what she did. She didn't have a lame big butt tan line or any lines on her back." Nicole buried her face back down in her towel.

"Shit it's hot out here." I pulled my towel out of my bag, and Jake's shirt came out with it. "Oh my God, dude, you have to smell this." I was giddy. I tossed the shirt near her head. She looked up. "Guess whose shirt that is?"

She took a little sniff. "Uh, yum!" she smiled and took another whiff. "This *is* yummy. Ok, I'm going to gross out if it's your brother's. Whose is it?"

"You know my next door neighbor?"

"Uh, yeah, how could I not notice Rocker Abercrombie?" she remarked.

Was I stuck in some sort of a bubble? I watched Nicole rub her face all over Jake's shirt again.

"Well, you won't be surprised, but Nadine is totally crushing on him." I reached over and grabbed the shirt out of her hands, stuffing it back into my bag. She gave me her pouty face. "Sorry, I'll have to give it back."

"Ok, spit it out, all the juicy details. How'd you get his shirt?" Her eyes flashed wide with intrigue.

I sat and told the story, giving her a play by play of every moment, with the exception of my feelings for Jake. I painted a vivid picture of how hot he looked dripping wet. I hedged a bit, not knowing if I should continue.

"Ok and…spit it out already," she said impatiently.

"Ok, ok." I giggled louder, covering my mouth. "Basically, I used his shirt to dry off my face and I kept it."

"And, tell me, how did Nadine act? You know, she kills me sometimes how she throws herself at guys." She rolled her eyes, shaking her head. *Boom*, there it was, another snide remark tossed at Nadine. Nicole had been tossing out subtle digs about Nadine more often these days, but I refused to bite. I didn't want to choose sides.

"No, she didn't throw herself on Jake. She didn't have a chance. Her mom came looking for her. She said she would be here after her doctor's appointment."

I finally laid down on a lounge. I was sweating from the heat. The sun burned at my skin, feeling kind of good, like a massage. Even knowing that I would pay for the sun damage later in life, I didn't care. I didn't use sunscreen. I loved having that sun-kissed look.

All of sudden, water came our way from Greg and Grant.

"Stop it, you a-hole!" Nicole roared. She didn't like to get her hair or face wet. In fact, when she swam, she only went in the water up to her chin.

"Calm down, sorry," Grant said, trying not to laugh. "What's up with you guys today, all secretive n'shit?"

"Let's go, they're talking about Jake Masters," Greg said, spilling the beans.

"What? Jake? That fucking wannabe. He sucks, and so does his band," Grant spewed as he climbed out of the pool. My blood boiled at the insult.

"Shut the eff up," I snapped. "You're just jealous because you can't play your stupid guitar as good as he can."

I was shocked at the harsh words that rolled out of my mouth and instantly regretted it. Nicole's mouth gaped open. Greg, with his usual timid self, backed away from our confrontation. I felt bad. Grant had tried out for Jake's band six months prior. I never gave it much thought until now. Grant didn't get picked, and I knew how badly he wanted it.

"You're a bitch, Alyssa." He picked up his towel and wiped his face. "I was only joking."

I realized at that moment he had to be kidding, because he would have never tried out to be in the band if he thought it sucked.

"Dude, I'm sorry." My stomach sank.

Grant hung his towel around his neck as he slipped on his flip-flops.

"Ok, you guys, just calm down. Grant, please don't leave," Nicole begged. She struggled to retie her bathing suit top, instead opting to gather the towel to her chest as she reached out toward Grant.

"I'll be back," he said to Nicole and threw me an angry glance. "I'm gonna go find Greg."

Grant went after Greg down the side of the house. We heard him shouting Greg's name.

"What the hell, dude. What was that?" Nicole glared at me. "You didn't have to say that shit."

"I'm sorry, I didn't mean it…"

"Uh, yes you did. I've never heard one mean word ever cross your lips, Alyssa. So don't tell me you didn't mean it. You shoulda seen your face. You know how bad he wanted to be in Jake's band. I can't believe you."

She got up and stormed into the house, leaving me sitting there in the blistering heat. My head spun. I felt panic rushing through me. Shit, now what? I'd managed to piss everyone off, all because of Jake Masters, in less than an hour. My thoughts went back to Jake. I wanted to be sitting in his room, lying on his bed, smelling his scent. If his friends hadn't shown up, I would have probably been doing just that.

I gathered my things and walked into the house. Chris and Stephen were no longer around. Nicole stood at the fridge leaning against it with a soda in hand, glaring at me.

"I'm really sorry," I said in a rush. "I don't know what came over me." I played with the handles of my bag. "I didn't get to finish my story. You wanna know?"

"Uh, yeah," she said theatrically. As if she'd forgotten my verbal bashing of Grant.

The lameness was instantly gone. I took a deep breath, smiling. "Ok. I was with Jake in his room, listening to his music…and, you know how close we used to be…" I paused.

Nicole stared off in the distance. She was no longer listening to me. She took a drink of her soda and set it on the counter, pulling her long hair out of her face. I admired how pretty she was, with her all-American, blond hair and blue eyes. No wonder Grant kissed her ass. He probably felt like he hit the lottery.

I sighed, totally not into saying anything about Jake any more until Nadine got there. "Hey, just so you know, I'll call Grant later to apologize and I'll just talk to you about Jake later. I'm gonna go home for a bit. Call me when Nadine gets here. I wanna hear what she has to say about Jake. Plus, she'll wanna know what we did after she left." I flashed a wicked grin, trying to lighten the mood.

She snapped out of her mood and whined. "Oh come on! There's gotta be more. I was listening, I swear, you have to share!"

I laughed. "It's nothing, trust me. Other than Nadine's slice on it—and I can't wait to hear it."

Chapter 5

ALYSSA

I glanced at the clock as I walked out of Nicole's house. Not very much time had gone by. I wondered if Jake was home and if he was still rehearsing. As I got closer to my house, I could hear the band playing. I arrived and stood in front of his house. I could hear his voice singing out, and it made me melt. He sounded older when he sang. I leaned against his truck. They played through two songs while I stood there in my dream state.

All of a sudden, the garage started to open, and I darted as quickly as I could toward my house.

"Hey, back already?" Jake called out and my knees buckled, making me stop. He opened the door to his truck, taking out a duffle bag and what appeared to be a camera tripod.

"Ha, yeah, I kinda got in an argument with one of the guys." I informed, throwing out my hands.

"Bummer," he said. He spoke again with his head down, muttering something as he struggled with the bag and the tripod. I couldn't hear his words clearly, as he gestured and smiled at me. He was too cute, and I couldn't stand it. Then he said, "Come by later if you wanna talk about it. The guys should be leaving in an hour or so."

My stomach fluttered as the butterflies slammed into each other. I looked past Jake and noticed Mike was staring at me smugly.

I slowly walked back to my house in a daze, thinking it would be cool if Nadine liked Mike instead. I wished so hard that it would happen. I had a lump in my throat the size of a grapefruit, and my mouth was super dry. Gross, I thought. I went straight to the kitchen and gulped down a glass of water, wondering if anyone else was home.

I shouted out, "Is anyone home?"

There was no response.

The only sound was the whirl of a fan someone forgot to turn off. I was a nervous wreck. I screamed out loud, throwing myself down onto the sofa. I was totally in la-la land. Thank God it was summer time and school wouldn't interfere with whatever was happening. My bag dropped to the floor and I leaned over, taking out Jake's shirt and draped it over my face. I lay on the sofa like that for an hour; peeking out every so often to see how many minutes had ticked by. Finally it was time to check if Jake's band mates were gone. I sprinted up the stairs to my room and stared at myself in the mirror as if my reflection would tell me what to do. I was a mess. Jake was more than *"just Jake"* now.

I ran to my parent's room, the only room in the house that had a view of Jake's backyard and of his bedroom window. When his window blinds were open, there was a clear view into his room, but I didn't see anyone.

I bound down the stairs and slowly opened the front door. I was happy we had a courtyard. No one could see me unless they were standing right in front of the gate. I crept over to the fence nearest Jake's house to see if I could hear anything. There was no longer any muffled music or voices. I pulled over a nearby chair and peeked over the fence to see if see if any of the guy's cars were still parked in front. They were gone.

I walked back into the house with my stomach in knots. I felt silly all of a sudden. Would he think I was a cling-on, a groupie, or whatever they called those fan girls? Finally, after talking to myself forever I made my way to his house.

"Hey," I said softly, approaching his garage.

"Hey, I was just wondering if you were gonna come back over. I was gonna wait a little bit longer and then head over to Dump's house." He flashed his thousand-watt smile at me. My hands began to sweat as my blood rushed to my head. "Are you ok?"

"Yeah, why?"

"I don't know. You look flushed." He looked concerned.

Oh my God! I was totally blushing! What a fucking freak. I had to get a grip! My thoughts smacked against each other as they ran around my brain.

"It's hot out here. Aren't you hot?" I said, fanning my face with my hand. Now I was light-headed.

"Let's go in the house. I'll get you some water."

He grabbed my hand pulling me toward him so he could put his arm around my shoulders. What he didn't realize was when he touched me it made my heart pump faster and my light-headedness even worse. We went into the house and immediately the cold air gave me relief. He sat me at the kitchen counter and handed me water from the fridge. I pressed the cold bottle against my cheek and closed my eyes. I breathed in deeply; telling myself it was no big deal. I could smell the faint scent of him, and I breathed in deeper. Opening my eyes, I felt an instant surge. Jake was still standing there, staring at me. His mouth was slightly open and he was watching me. My insides melted into my feet.

He cleared his throat. "Are you feeling better?"

"Yeah, thanks. I should probably go home and lay down." I got up and stumbled, grabbing the counter. "This sucks, I really wanted to listen to more of your music and…."

"You can lay down on my bed…come on," he interrupted, and grabbed my hand. "You probably just got a little heat stroke or something."

He led me through the house to his room and I thought I was dreaming.

He released my hand and fluffed his pillows. His gesture tugged at my heart even more. "Here, take a load off. Make sure you drink that water."

I collapse on the bed more dramatically than I needed to, but I wanted the smell of him to wrap around me. Just as I sank comfortably into his pillow, another voice came through the house. This time it was a female's.

"Jake?" the voice grew louder.

"Yeah," he shouted, "I'm in my room." He stood up walking to the door and stopped.

"Hey sexy," a raspy voice purred, then a short silence. *"What's going on?"* she asked as she came to the door. By the tone of her voice, it was apparent she'd noticed me lying there. I kept my eyes closed.

"That's my next door neighbor, Alyssa. She's not feeling well, probably from the heat."

"And you couldn't lay her on your couch?"

"Calm down," he said with annoyance.

I could hear their voices fade down the hallway. Then I heard another girl's voice, too. I could barely make out what Jake was saying.

"Look, we were gonna listen to some music, it's no big deal."

"No big deal? Jake, how would you feel if you walked into my room and saw a dude lying on my bed?"

"Rachel, if he was fourteen and your next door neighbor, I wouldn't care."

My stomach dropped. Fourteen, that's what he saw me as – fourteen.

What the hell was I doing? Ok, this happened for a reason. I needed to get a grip. He was way out of my league. He would always be "just Jake," my friend. I sat up and continued listening.

"She's only fourteen," the girl said dryly. *"She doesn't look fourteen."*

"Well, she is. She's gonna be a freshman this year."

"Great." The sarcastic tone continued.

"Look, Rachel, I don't know what else to say."

"You could tell her to go home. We were supposed to be hangin' today."

"Her parents aren't home. I'd feel better if she stayed here until she felt better."

There was long silence and another girl's voice chimed in.

"Rachel, you're outta control. Let's go. Jake, we'll see you later. Don't forget, Dump's expecting you. You might wanna call him."

Then Rachel's voice cut in. *"Call me when she leaves,"* her voice was laced with agitation.

I didn't hear anything else. I took a drink of water and stared at the posters of the hot chicks stuck to his wall. Those are the kind of girls Jake likes. Rachel was probably as hot as those girls hanging on his wall. I laughed to myself, shaking my head.

"Why you shaking your head?" Jake's voice took me by surprise and I jumped.

"I didn't realize I was." I stared back at him sheepishly. "I'm sorry, I didn't mean for you and your girlfriend to fight because of me."

"She's not my girlfriend," he said firmly.

"Sounds like she thinks she is."

"Well, she wants to be, but I don't feel the same way. Besides—"

"So you don't like her?" I interrupted, surprised at my boldness. But I wanted to know. I wanted to know him, every little thing I'd missed after all the time that had gone by.

"Kind of…." He trailed off. Then he laughed. "Only sometimes, after I've had a few beers. No, just kidding. I kinda dig her, yeah, but she's a little hard to handle. She's a spoiled brat, and I don't know if I can deal with that." He sat down next to me.

"What's going on with you, Alyssa?" he probed.

"Well, obviously not too much, since I'm only fourteen." I blurted it out without wanting to, like vomit.

He was silent and I couldn't look at him. I was embarrassed. I could feel him staring at me, burning a hole into the side of my head. I heard him breathe deeply and felt his bed move. He tipped back, lying flat. I glanced over and his hands were over his face, covering his eyes. His shirt came up, exposing his stomach, and all I could do was stare at his smooth skin. I wanted to touch him. He looked through his fingers and caught me staring at him, but I didn't move. Reaching over he touched my arm, tracing it with the tips of his fingers all the way to my hand and held it. I was frozen. My heart raced and tunnel vision took over. The lump in my throat almost choked me. I was worried he'd feel my hand starting to sweat.

"Look, I only said that to calm her down." He let go of my hand and sat up. "Alyssa, you're like family to me. I mean, come on, what's going on here?"

Did he really want to know that this morning he kick-started something in me I'd never felt before? Did *"family"* members do that to each other? I was grossed out at the thought.

"Jake," I said, standing up, "it's nothing. I just felt a little stupid—like I was a kid or something when you said that. I'm not a child. You know, I have feelings too. I'd better go. This was obviously a bad idea, me coming over here and hanging out. I didn't mean to cause problems."

What the hell was I doing? Fuck, I just kept puking all over the place.

"Alyssa, I don't want you to leave, I really want you to stay." He stood up, towering over me. His strong arms embraced me in a hug. "I'm sorry. I didn't mean to hurt your feelings. It was unintentional."

"But I heard you tell Rachel that you'd call her after I left. So she's probably waiting to hear from you soon…"

"Alyssa, I don't wanna see her." He sat down at his desk, facing the screen. "She just rubbed me the wrong way. I'll call her in a little bit to tell her it's a no-go."

He banged at the keys and brought up some music; it filled the air and took the edge off.

He continued to speak. "The cool thing about you is I know where you stand. You were always very open and opinionated, even if the timing was inappropriate." He smiled broadly at me with his perfectly white straight teeth.

"Your teeth are so white," I marveled.

"My mom makes me use those white strips," he said, rolling his eyes.

"Well, it makes you that much more *sexy*," I said, laughing at myself for emphasizing the word "sexy" with hand quotations. Jake's face bent with amusement. "I'm sorry, I shouldn't make fun."

He shook his head. "A little fire in you, I see. I can never underestimate you, can I?"

Chapter 6
ALYSSA

Jake and I sat in his room for hours, talking about music and his past tours. When I expressed interest in playing the guitar, he insisted on teaching me. When I finally looked over at the clock, it was 5:30 PM.

"Shit, the time!" I panicked. "Um, I should probably get going. I left my phone at home in my bag. The units are probably wondering where I'm at."

"Shit! And I forgot to call Rachel. Great. She's really gonna be happy now. Guess we're both in trouble, huh?" He slumped. "Now, don't get pissed, but I don't wanna hear it from her, so I'm not gonna tell her you stayed here the whole time. It's just easier."

He walked out of the room. I could hear his voice, but couldn't decipher his words with the music playing in the background. Then his voice grew louder. Were they fighting? I wanted to know more about this Rachel. I was going to ask my sister if she knew her and break out the yearbook so I could see what she looked like. Staring at the snapshots with the two girls again, I wondered which one she was.

Jake walked back in agitated. He threw his phone hard at the bed.

"You know, it's probably better it happened like this." He shut his door. He stood there shaking his head "Fuck, what a bitch. Oh, by the way, my mom's home now. I don't need her poking around here, that's why I shut the door."

"Why's your mom's a bitch?" I asked, shocked.

"No! Duh, Rachel." He plopped onto the bed. "She's too much. I'm glad it's out in the open, how lame she is. No matter what I told her, she still thought you were here."

"Well, I was...am...you know what they say about women's intuition."

He lifted his head from the pillow and leered at me. "Don't be a smartass. It's not like she's my girlfriend. She's been my friend for a long time and helps out with the band stuff a lot. We hang, but it's not like we're together."

"So, you don't think you could be leading her on? I mean, sorry to point it out, but you kinda acted like you cared when she came over earlier. You know, making excuses and trying to make her feel better about me being here."

His arms fell heavy against the mattress. "I see why she would think I like her like that, then. I mean I do, but not like that. That was a long time ago, when I thought I was interested." He sighed deeply, "Then with her freaking out about you and acting all territorial n'shit? I mean, she doesn't even fucking know you!" He gestured his hand at me. "She's lame."

"Tell her to beat it, then."

"Yeah, right. It's not gonna be that easy."

I looked out the back door and walked over to it. I stared at the far end of the backyard and wondered if the gate still worked. My dad had installed a gate so we could easily go from yard to yard when we were younger.

"Hey, is that gate still working?" I walked out the door. There were a couple of palm trees and other plants that blocked the path.

"I'm sure it does. We didn't do anything to it. I forgot it was there." He walked in front of me, rooting through the palms and unlatched it. He struggled with it a bit, and it finally opened.

"Yay!" I cheered and Jake raised his hand for me to give him a high-five. I squeezed through and was wedged against him for a moment. I felt that shock again when we touched and I loved it.

"Well, this is gonna make things interesting," he whispered.

What was that supposed to mean? My head spun. I turned back and hugged him. I couldn't help myself.

"Jake, thanks so much, fun times." I took in a deep breath through my nose to smell him one last time. His face pressed against my hair and neck. I could have stayed frozen there forever.

"Mmm, you smell good. Your hair smells like strawberries." He let me go and I almost passed out after hearing his words.

"I was just thinking the same thing. You smell good too. I'll talk to you later," I whispered loudly. I was numb from my excitement.

"Hey, if you're not doing anything later, you wanna come back and watch a movie?"

"Sure, if I'm not in trouble for something." I waved goodbye. "Probably sometime after nine."

I opened the back door and my mom smiled. "Well, hello." She came out from behind the counter to hug me, and then grabbed my shoulders, holding me at arm's length. "You have a nice glow. What have you been up to?"

She went back to chopping veggies. My dad brushed by me with a beer in hand without a word.

"Hi, Dad," I waved with false excitement.

"Hello, my dear." He collapsed into his chair and turned on the TV. That was the extent of our relationship.

"I've actually been hanging out with Jake today." I beamed.

"Is that right? And what's Jake been up to these days?" my mom asked, carefully placing each foil-wrapped potato in the oven.

"You know he has a band, right?" I said. "He practices every day, you must hear it."

"Yes, I hear it on the weekends. I suppose he plays before we get home from work." She turned, grabbing a bottle of red wine, filling her glass. I wondered what wine tasted like. I remembered Jake saying that he drank beer. I hadn't tasted any alcohol yet.

"Mom, can I have a taste of that? I'm just curious what the big deal is. I mean, you drink it every night."

With a wary eye, she handed her glass to me without saying a word. I smelled it, took a sip, and gagged. "Uh, thanks but no thanks. It's like fire going down my throat. Why do you drink that?"

I walked to the sink, sticking my mouth under the faucet.

"I drink because I like it; it's an acquired taste. All wines taste differently. It relaxes me after a long day of work, and it's good for my heart. That is why I drink it, in moderation."

"Including moderation itself," my father weaseled in. My mom rolled her eyes.

"What does beer taste like, then? I hate the smell of beer."

"I don't like it either. Go ask your father for a sip. Frank, give Aly a sip of your beer, she's curious."

My father held up the bottle of beer over his head, without a word, no fight, nothing. I walked over and took a sip just as my brother rounded the corner coming down the stairs.

"What, you let her drink, but not me?" he grabbed the beer from my hand and took a long swig.

"Goddammit, Kyle!" my father roared. "We know what you get into, give it back to her."

"Geez, calm down, sorry." He wiped his mouth with the back of his hand, handing me the beer. His eyes were wide. I stuck my tongue out at him and he flipped me off. "What's she doin' with it then?"

"She's not drinking, Kyle," Mom explained. "She's tasting, she was curious."

"Yeah, and I'm a girl," he guffawed. "I'm calling her bullshit."

I handed the beer back to my father and turned, punching my brother right in the gut.

"Ok, you two," my mom said dryly. "Stop it."

"What, you're not gonna punish her? If I woulda' done that, you woulda' grounded me!"

"Kyle, that's enough," my dad growled. "We were having a nice moment and you come down here, stirring the pot."

Kyle glared at me.

"Kyle, I swear I've never had one drink," I assured him.

He looked at me cautiously. "Whatever," he said under his breath, and mouthed *BEEEAAATCH* to my face. I flipped him off in return.

"What's for dinner?" he asked, shoving me out of the way as he passed into the kitchen. He opened the fridge and rummaged around.

"Close the door, Kyle. I'm making artichoke dip, and we're having steak and baked potatoes."

She poured a bag of corn chips into a bowl. Kyle walked over, took a handful and stuffed a few in his mouth. *What a pig*, I thought. I took stock of Kyle. Sure, he was cute, for being my brother. No wonder he and Jake grew apart; he'd become a total polo shirt-wearing nerd. A pang of guilt came over me for thinking that, but he was, plain and simple. One day he would find a nerd girl to share his nerd life with.

We sat down to eat, and my sister barely said a word. She was attached to her phone throughout dinner, like always. Which reminded me—I never called Nicole. "Mom, anyone, did I get any calls?" I looked around the table.

Finally Allison looked up as she took another bite of food, "No, but your chicks came over looking for you, and your phone kept ringing. Where were you anyway?"

"I was next door at Jake's. He was teaching me to play the guitar and we were talking about his music."

I said all those words on purpose. I wanted Allison to know. In my own way, I wanted to feel like I was one-upping her. I could feel her staring at me and didn't want to look at her. I looked at Kyle instead, but he was concentrating on his food and Mom and Dad were talking quietly. I finally looked at Allison and just as I thought, she was staring at me with an obtuse grin. You see, about a year prior she used to have the hots for Jake, until she got another guy to like her.

"Really, is that right?" Allison's condescending tone rang through my ears.

I didn't want to stare at her. She would see right through me and try to knock me down. Nope, I was going to eat my dinner, wait for everyone to go to sleep. Then I was gonna to go back over to Jake's house via the secret route and watch movies with him. No one would know. After 9 PM my mom and dad would be locked in their room. Kyle would be gone like usual, and who knows what Allison would be into. I was always locked away in my room after 9 PM, or at Nicole's house.

"Can I be excused?" I said loudly.

"Sure," My father said, glancing back at my mother.

I grabbed my plate and walked into the kitchen. I heard Allison ask to be excused too and I rushed to rinse my plate. I wanted to leave before she got into the kitchen, but it was no good. I felt her standing behind me.

"So, Aly. Tell me about Jake."

"What's to tell? You know what he's been into, right?" I didn't want to come off as too cocky, but I couldn't' help myself.

"Yeah, but he never asked me to hang out at his house and listen to his music, or teach me to play the guitar."

She wanted dirt, but I wouldn't budge. I would never let her know how I felt about Jake.

"Well, did you ask him to teach you to play the guitar?" I could feel her eyes raking me up and down.

"Uh…no." Her sarcastic tone returned. "Did you?"

"Not exactly, I only said it's something I've wanted to learn, and he offered."

"Oh, I see. I'm sure he felt obligated."

I really hated how she treated me, and I was glad she was jealous. Moments went by. I continued to do the dishes, hoping she would leave, because I was running out of dishes to wash.

"You wanna hand me your plate?"

"You know, Aly, you better be careful," her tone changed. It almost sounded like she cared. "Boys like Jake only want one thing, and a freshie like you is just what's on the menu."

My stomach sank. What was she saying? I thought of all the stories Greg would tell us late at night in Nicole's backyard about his brothers hooking up with chicks. It made my stomach turn. But I couldn't talk to Allison. She wasn't trustworthy. She would sell me out to our parents for sure.

"What's that supposed to mean?" I glared at her. My hand dropped to my side, dripping water onto the floor. She made me sick. What kind of sister would really be jealous of her younger sibling? But it was always that way. She would always try to be the best, to outshine me…to be a bitch.

She sighed, hedging on her words, choosing carefully what she would say next. Then she looked me in the eyes. "Aly, I'm serious. I'm not trying to be the mean big sister. Guys like Jake only want one thing, and once they get it, its dump city. There are other things you need to be concerned with, too, so just be careful."

I was finally alone in the kitchen. I looked at the clock. 8 PM. I went to the couch to get my bag and noticed Jake's shirt lying there. I picked it up and stuffed it back in my bag before digging for my phone. I dialed Nicole's number.

"Hey, it's me," I whispered. I dreaded talking to her.

"Where the hell have you been? We've been waiting for you all day. Nadine is freaking out. We hung out on the corner, waiting for you to show up. Jake never came out of his house. We knocked on your door at 4, and your sister said you weren't home."

"I was home, sleeping. I didn't feel well." I didn't want to lie, but I felt like I had to. I wanted to tell her, but I just couldn't.

"Oh, I'm sorry. Are you feeling better?"

"Yeah, I'm fine now. I think it's just the heat."

"Okay, are you coming over tomorrow? Matt's gonna be home, so you know he'll be over here."

This perked my interest. "Yeah, I'll be over."

"Ok, see you tomorrow. Oh, and call Nadine, she's comin' outta her skin to know what went down with Jake."

"Sure. See ya tomorrow." I hung up the phone, unsure of what to feel. Matt was going to be home. Normally, I would be excited. But I only thought of Jake and watched the minutes tick by as I waited for my parents to tuck in.

I decided to take a shower. I normally took showers in the morning, but since I was going to Jake's, I wanted to feel good. As I got ready for my night, I reasoned with myself... Why should this be any different than all the other times Jake and I watched movies together? Yeah right, whom was I kidding? I liked him now; that was the difference. This wasn't the same—at least not for me.

9 PM rolled around quicker than I wanted it to. I was nervous. I heard my parents disappear into their bedroom.

I brushed my damp hair and went into the bathroom to brush my teeth. My sister was just getting out of the shower.

"What are you doing tonight?" I asked, trying to sound casual.

"Like you care?" She sniffed.

Why did she have to be so lame? Kyle was gone, thank God. Back in my room I closed the door behind me. I stared at myself in the mirror once more. I wore black cotton shorts and a black tank top. Simple but flattering enough, I thought. I put on lip-gloss and I stared at my chest. I pulled down my tank top a little lower, just like Nadine did. Ugh, what was I doing? There was no way I'd ever look that big unless I got a boob job—and that certainly wasn't going to happen.

I heard my sister shut her door and she immediately started talking loudly. I turned off my light and turned on my TV. I messed up my bed and gently shut my door, making my way down the stairs and out into the warm night air.

Jake must have heard me struggling with the gate, because he was standing at the door, waiting for me. I felt like I was dreaming.

Chapter 7

JAKE

When I watched Aly go back into her house while I hid at our "secret entrance," it really started to hit me that she was unlike any of the girls I knew. I dug her—completely. Making my way back into my room I sat in front of my computer and opened my email. I glanced over the messages Rachel told me about. More dates for local shows before we were to leave on tour. I wasn't sure if we could pull any of them off. I brought up my calendar in attempt to figure out the timing of everything, but my mood was strange.

I felt empty inside and I couldn't focus. I knew right away it was because of Alyssa. Liking her was the last thing I needed. I didn't need any distractions in my life. The thing with Rachel was gonna be enough for me to handle, but there I sat, wondering if *Aly* was really going to come back.

I wasn't in the mood to work. I lay on my bed and watched the time tick by before finally turning on the TV, which did nothing to distract me from my thoughts of her. I should have gotten her phone number. What if her parents caught her sneaking out? I wondered if she really had the balls to go through with it. Who knew what girls tried to get away with at that age? Ugh, that was another thing—her age.

As always, my acoustic guitar came to my rescue. It stared at me from the corner of my room, perched perfectly in its stand, calling to me. Grabbing it, I sat on my bed, tracing my fingers across its smooth wooden contours. I thought about Rachel and Aly, comparing them to each other. Thoughts flooded my brain and I grew anxious. I felt bad about Rachel, regardless of her personality flaws. I told myself not to waste my time worrying about her. What would be would be. My mind twisted back to Aly, and thoughts began to get the best of me. I wondered what it would mean if she *did* show up. I thought about how soft she felt when I hugged her at the gate, and the way her hair smelled. I liked how clean she was. She wasn't sticky and made up like all the others.

I pictured Aly creeping down the stairs, out of her house, and into my room. For a brief second I wondered if she'd want to make out. I quickly pushed it from my mind, reminding myself what she was to me. She was my kid next-door neighbor, or at least she used to be; the few years' age difference shouldn't matter now. Besides, I told myself, she probably wouldn't show.

I began to strum a tune and the words began to flow—grabbing a pad of paper, I had the whole song written in less than an hour:

<u>TRANSPOSE</u>
Sleepless nights aren't new to me
All these thoughts are killing me
Someone come and put me to ease

First Kiss

All of my anxiety
There's no cause that I can see
What's this scratching at my brain

And I can't stop
even if I wanted to
It's up top
Maybe I'm simply deluded
That's right
Here I am just wasting my time
All my time
And it's hard to justify what you can do
I'm so sick and tired of falling through
It's true, maybe I've been wasting my time
All this time

Come creeping, no one can hear you now
I listen, so you can show me how
There's something that I'm missing here
Softly, stab my evil dreams
Faster, help me fall asleep
Come close, I don't wanna see you again

From time to time, we fall in line
But now it seems that we are blind
No one knows, that's how it goes
all the thoughts that we transpose

And I can't stop
even if I wanted to
It's up top

Maybe I'm simply deluded
That's right
Here I am just wasting my time
All my time
And It's hard to justify what you can do
I'm so sick and tired of falling through
It's true, Maybe I've been wasting my time
All this time

Just as I hit the last chord, I heard the gate make noise, at exactly the same moment my phone began to ring. It was Notting. My heart sprung up into my throat. She fucking showed. Now what? I had to take Notting's call and answered the phone. I would have to tell him I would call him back. What the hell was I getting myself into?

Smiling to myself, I realized that I didn't even care.

PART TWO

FIRST KISS

Chapter 8
JAKE

I could still feel the warmth from her body on the sheets when I reached over, searching for her, and for a moment I wondered...had it been real? Bleary-eyed, I stared at the clock. It was only 7 in the morning. The sound that woke me must have been the door shutting—Aly sneaking away. We must have fallen asleep sometime after midnight.

She shouldn't have stayed over. She'd kept trying to leave, but I'd keep pulling her back into the bed. Not that anything had happened. We'd just talked and hung all over each other, horsing around. Kid shit. I sighed, rubbing my eyes as I sat back down on the edge of the bed. What did I expect? She *was* a kid. Alyssa Montgomery. What the hell was I doing, hanging with a girl her age? If her parents caught her sneaking back in this morning...

I swore and tripped on the sheet tangled around my leg as I hopped from the bed. I opened the door to the backyard to see if she was still visible, but I was too late. It was quiet and cool. I shivered, standing there, wondering when I'd see her again. As I reached for my phone, I saw that three texts had come through. They were all from Rachel Schaffer.

I didn't read them—I just tossed my phone to the foot of my bed. I seriously didn't even wanna deal with that shit right now. One drunken hook-up and what, she thought she had dibs on me? Yeah, she was an old friend, and she helped out with our band stuff…but I'd seen how she plays hot and cold with other guys; she should know what's up. And it's not like I'd ever shown even the slightest interest in her. But still, I just *knew* that it was gonna rain shit-balls once she realized that I was into Aly. I pushed the looming issue from my mind and tried to go back to sleep. This was my last summer vacation, and I wanted to go into my senior year with my future in music secure.

I could smell Aly's strawberry-scented hair lingering on my pillow and closed my eyes, reliving our night. When she'd first arrived, I'd sat down on my bed while she paced back and forth in front of me. I recalled how she looked in her little black cotton shorts. Her long legs were tan and smooth. It'd taken everything in me not to reach out and touch them. When I finally did, I think she had the softest skin I'd ever felt on a girl.

I guess I finally drifted off to sleep, because I was startled awake by a knock at my door.

"Yeah, what?" I groaned.

"Rachel is here. It's eleven o'clock," my mom's muffled voice informed me.

Shit. Are you kidding me? "Alright, tell her to come in." I threw off the blankets, sat up, and before I knew it Rachel was standing there, glaring at me.

"What's up, man? What's so important that you had to wake me up?" I stood, grabbing a shirt off the back of my chair and pulled it on.

"Really? Man?" she huffed, shoulders slumping.

"Dude, what is up with you?"

"Me? What about you?"

"Are you kidding me, Rachel? I was up all night…writing." I turned, holding my arms out, pleading. "Come on. What's up? What's this all about?"

"You totally blew me off, Jake. You fuck around with me, and then you ignore me?"

"Ok, wait a second." I scoffed. "I could say the same thing about you. You fucked around with me too, Rachel."

I knew trying to put it on her was a dick move, but I didn't even care. I'd had enough of it.

"Yeah, but I'm not blowing you off."

I stood there, mind racing to find something to smooth over our exchange.

"Look, I don't mean to blow you off. Come on, I'm just doin' my thing. You have no idea the shit that's about to go down—I have to focus."

She stood silent as her eyes searched me up and down, then they roamed around my room. Slowly, she began to walk around, searching as if she finally sensed that someone else had been there. My stomach sank. I could still smell Aly's scent on me, and Rachel could probably smell it too. I backed away and went into the bathroom, turning on the water. I rinsed my face. I didn't want to deal with the drama of it all. I walked out, drying my face as I waited for her to say something.

We stood there, silently staring at each other. She was trying to read me. I didn't know what to say.

She broke the silence first.

"I don't want things to change, Jake." Her voice was void of her usual bitchy tone, which only made it harder. It'd have been easier to ignore her if she was being her usual overdramatic self.

"Rachel, nothing's gonna change if we just move past what happened."

"What am I supposed to do with that?"

She moved close to me, taking my hand. Her fake nails raked against my palm. I looked down at her perfectly painted red lips and could only think of Aly. I laughed at the absurdity of the moment, gently pulling my hand away from hers and grabbing her shoulder.

"We're gonna chalk up that blurred night to something that just happened and chill. I don't want things to change."

"Then don't ignore me," she said, standing on her tiptoes trying to kiss me. I turned my head away, and she stiffened.

I could hear her breath escape her.

I backed away. "Rachel, I'm sorry. I have a million things on my mind, and it's got nothing to do with you."

Her eyes flashed with disappointment. I waited for her to berate me, but she surprised me once again with silence. Sadly, I knew it would never be the same between us and it was only gonna get worse.

"I'm sorry, too," she said quietly and kept looking around my room, walking toward my bed. Panic filled me. My eyes dashed around the bed and floor, looking for any trace of Aly. I didn't see anything.

"Look, Rachel, I don't' mean to blow you off, but I gotta meet with Notting. Apparently we got some sort of a licensing deal for a movie or something."

Her eyes lit up. "Wow, that's awesome. Which one? What's it all about?"

"I don't know anything yet," I said, maybe a little too harshly.

"Geez. Ok. Grumpy." She shook her head. "I'll just talk to you later then. Um, and just ignore those text messages. You obviously didn't read them yet."

"Yeah, ok," I replied, grabbing the back of my neck and rubbing it. The tension was giving me a headache.

"Is there anything I can do to help?"

"No, Rachel, there isn't." I sighed deeply, deciding just to lay my thoughts out there. "Don't worry about helping with anything right now. I don't have it in me to deal with it. Just chill, ok?"

I could see her swallow.

"Alright, then," she replied, obviously trying to play it cool. "Whatever. I guess call me later. Or not."

She left with her sarcasm hovering over me. I just stood there, unable to say anything. I felt like a jerk. It was weird seeing her like this; all vulnerable and unsure of herself. I pushed it from my mind.

It seemed that every other thought throughout the afternoon was about Aly. I sat talking with Notting, my manager and father figure, and tried to focus on what he was saying. A production company had commissioned us to write an original score. Even though the movie was a low-budget flick, it had some well-known actors attached. I was stoked. After Notting left, the guys and I sat around the garage, tinkering with our instruments. I got up and hit the switch to open the door.

"Dude, it's fucking hot out there—you're gonna let all the cold air out," Mike whined. I ignore him.

"What are you doing?" Bobby chimed.

"I'll close it in a sec." I said, and walked out to my truck pretending to look for something. I glanced over at Aly's house, hoping she'd miraculously appear. I didn't have her phone number and wondered if she'd surprise me by coming back over later. I thought back to our conversation the night before.

"You don't think this is weird?" She'd asked in a whisper.

"Don't be silly. We're just watching a movie."

Our legs pressed against each other's, and I recalled how hard it had been not to be all over her. I wanted it to be chill—but it was far from that for me.

"It's nice to have someone different to hang with, you know," she said quietly. "And it's cool that you're next door."

"Yeah. If you see lights, come over anytime."

"Really?"

"Yeah, sure."

I thought about how the light from the TV had made her eyes sparkle as she'd smiled, clasping her hands, pressing them under her chin before she rolled over onto her side. Her reaction was so endearing it pulled me in even more. With her back facing me, I pictured myself running my hand gently over her arm, down to her side. I wanted to touch her legs so bad. Just thinking about it made me tug at my pants.

I hoped she'd take what I said to heart and come over later.

Dump's drumming and Bobby's baseline pulled me back to reality.

"Hey, that sounds good," I shouted over the music. "Start over."

I needed to focus on the music.

Over the next hour we hashed out something pretty clever for the film, though I was so distracted that my shit was rough around the edges. Dump and Bobby's parts were solid. Mike would draft off me when I was finished. But no matter what the other guys did, my mind kept drifting back to the song I'd written the night before about Aly as I'd waited for her to sneak over. It'd come easier than any song I'd ever written before—like magic. There was something about that girl…

Finally, I gathered the courage to say something. "So I wrote a new song the other night and it's a little different, kinda, and I wanna know what you think."

"Shoot," Dump encouraged.

I took a deep breath and began. I couldn't look any of them in the faces for the entire song. After it was over though, I looked up, steeling myself for their reactions. Bobby wore a huge grin. Dump nodded his head and tucked his tatted arms to his chest. Mike's mouth hung open.

"Interesting lyrics, where'd you pull those from?" Mike remarked.

Again, I ignored him. No one else said anything.

"So?" I asked. "Any other commentary?"

"Nope. I dig it," Bobby approved.

Dump still sat there, nodding his head with his eyes closed. "I'm bumpin' some shit around. All right. It's a little lighter, but I gotcha. The lyrics are cool."

I smiled, satisfied.

Later on, I sat at my computer watching random YouTube videos. The day had flown by; it was already 8:15 PM. The bright light from my computer screen cut through the gray haze of fading sunlight that consumed my room and reminded me to turn on the lights. The code now set. Would Aly remember that I told her if she saw my lights on to come over anytime? I got up and opened my back door.

A rush of adrenaline coursed through me when I heard the faint rattle of the gate outside in the distance. I jumped up, going to the door, wondering if I was hearing things. Euphoria overcame me when I saw Aly's darkened figure come through the bushes.

With a grin, I stepped out to meet her.

Chapter 9

ALYSSA

I must have been hallucinating, because he looked like he was glowing, backlit from the lights behind him. He didn't have a shirt on and his broad shoulders dominated my vision. I didn't know what to say other than "*Hey*". He winked at me and I felt that intense electric surge when I brushed past him into his room. He stood in silence, and a smile spread broad across his face.

"I was wondering when you'd wanna hang again." He beamed, and my mouth went dry.

"Yeah, I was wondering if you'd mind. So I thought what the heck, I'd see." I shrugged and sat down on his bed, waving around the movie cases I held. I'd taken them from my brother. He and Jake used to be best friends years ago and would certainly have a lot to say if he knew where I was. "I borrowed these from Kyle."

Jake came and sat down next to me, grabbing the movies out of my hand. I went numb. *Really though, what the hell was I doing here?* I couldn't take all the questions bouncing around in my head. I'd barely eaten anything since the night before. I concluded I had to ask him about his relationship with that girl Rachel 'cause it was eating at me big time, not to mention the feelings that swarmed through me. Yesterday, when I'd first gone to his room, she'd come by and caught a glimpse of me lying on his bed. He made innocent excuses when she gave him a hard time about it. It was obvious that there was *something* between them…but what? My gut was telling me that there was more to them than just her crushing on him, as he made it out to be. Oddly enough, I wasn't nervous about our impending talk. I would still be his friend no matter what his response. I would still want to come and talk music, and have him teach me to play the guitar. At least, that's what I told myself, but with those thoughts, the truth came fast behind. I also didn't want to think something was happening between us if it was only happening in my head.

I kept thinking about poor Matt Squire. He had been my main crush for so long, and now Jake? Matt would be returning from Vegas the next day, and I wondered what I would feel for him now. I was completely and utterly confused. Or was I? All I knew was that I loved the way Jake made me feel.

I was fidgety, and Jake immediately called me out on my mood. He reached over and grabbed my hand and I froze. I wanted to curl my fingers around his, but I stopped myself. I didn't know which way was up. Finally, he spoke again lightening the mood, and our conversation drifted to the new song he'd written. I begged him to play it for me, and when he did I wanted to die. The way he looked, sitting there strumming his guitar without his shirt on, left me speechless. Everything about him was perfect. He was so talented. When our small talk ended, I decided to go for it.

My stomach did cartwheels.

"Jake, I have a question." I breathed deeply, trying not to hyperventilate. "I'm just going to ask, because I don't know how else to do it." I paused for a long moment. Our eyes were locked.

His cheerful expression turned to concern at the seriousness of my tone. He froze, speaking slowly. "Okay."

My heart raced.

I paced back and forth what seemed like a million times. Finally, Jake grabbed me by the waist and drew me onto his lap. When he touched me it felt like I was plugged into an electrical socket. He held me snug, placing his chin on my shoulder and spoke softly into my ear. His tone was measured. I thought I was going to faint. My heart raced and my hands started to sweat, again and I gulped for air.

"What's up? Something's obviously on your mind."

I closed my eyes. "Do you feel it?" I breathed heavily.

"What? Feel what?" he asked, holding his breath, in an attempt to feel *it*.

"The electricity or whatever it is," I tried to explain. I held my breath too, wanting it to last.

"The electricity," he repeated slowly. He moved me off his lap, but my legs remained draped across his thighs. "What are you talking about?"

I was instantly mortified. "Never mind. I'm just going crazy, that's all. This was a bad idea."

I knew it was only I feeling anything at all—whom was I kidding, anyway? I was just a stupid girl with a stupid crush. I was embarrassed, and I deserved it. I threw myself back onto his pillows.

"Hey, don't stop," he said softly. "I wanna understand."

Holy crap. What else did I have to lose? I'd already completely embarrassed myself. He could take this back to his stupid friends and have a laugh. I covered my eyes with both hands, wanting to rip my eyes out of my head. I breathed in deeply, trying to come up with something to say, and kept peeking out between my fingers. The seconds ticked by and Jake stared at me tenderly, shaking my knee. My words came out like a bursting dam.

"Jake, when I get near you, it's this feeling I've never felt before. I'm embarrassed to admit it, but the only way I can describe it is, electricity. It's like this weird energy that passes from you to me." I wouldn't look at him. A long moment passed and his cell phone began to ring. "Now I feel stupid," I blurted out. Thankfully he ignored the call.

"Don't feel stupid." His voice soothed my frayed nerves. He sat quietly, contemplating his next words, nodding his head. He placed his hands on my thighs and I seriously thought I would die. I still wouldn't look at him for any longer than a second. "I guess that's the way you could describe or explain it. It's also known as sexual tension," he said flatly. My stomach dropped. So he thinks I've already had sex? I was shocked. What the hell? The shift of my emotions was too much, and they ran up my spine and out of my mouth.

"I've never done that!" I spat, jumping up. "I've never even really kissed a boy!" I wanted him to know I wasn't some slut. There were girls my age who were already known for hooking up with guys, their reputations tarnished by their easy, teasing ways.

"Alyssa, calm down, that's not what I'm saying. It's just another way to describe the energy that flows between the opposite sex when they're attracted to each other," he explained. "It's also known as chemistry."

My warning bells were going off as I remembered what my sister, Allison, had said to me just the night before: *"Guys like Jake only want one thing, and when they get it, it's dump city."*

Jake was gonna try and get in my pants, wasn't he? I started to panic.

"I should probably go." I tried to walk past him, but he grabbed my arm and I flinched, blurting out, "You're not gonna try to have sex with me, are you?" I pressed my eyes tightly closed. I wanted to cry, feeling the sting in my eyes and the burn in my nose.

Jake laughed nervously and immediately let go of my arm.

"Whoa, whoa, no, absolutely not. I wouldn't just take that away from you." He paused. "Or force you to do that."

His face maintained a serious expression, his eyes searching mine.

A few silent seconds passed. My brain fought to catch up, deciphering his words. "Take what away?" I asked, not immediately understanding what he meant.

"Your, your," he stuttered and paced around. He grabbed the top of his head and looked at the ceiling. "Whoa, warp speed, all in a day. I guess we're making up for lost time."

He forced a smile, but didn't look happy.

"Jake, I'm sorry, I didn't mean to…"

"Alyssa, don't be sorry." He shook his head. "Let me explain something to you. Guys and girls, sometimes this is how it goes." He gestured between us.

We stared at each other for a long moment until something came to my mind.

"Like love at first sight?" I couldn't help myself. I sounded so naïve.

"I'm not sure about that, to be honest. But I can tell you that you're not misreading anything. There's something here."

"So, you've felt this with someone before?" I asked, even though I knew what the answer would be and didn't want to hear it.

"Yes, I have."

I was disappointed. *There goes my schoolgirl dream of finding true love—of being the one.* It was ridiculous, and I knew it.

"You have." I confirmed. My voice was barely audible.

"Take Rachel for example. I was attracted to her at first, but then after I got to know her and what she was really like, that feeling vanished into thin air, like it was never there."

"But you don't feel it with me. It's just a one-way thing, then," I stated. I was exhausted from my emotions.

I plopped over onto the bed, rolling onto my side to face him. He was so perfect and I was so foolish. To think I was anything special was idiotic. I pushed his pillow under my head and closed my eyes, breathing in his scent again. I swear, I'd never get enough of the way he smelled. When I opened my eyes, he was staring at me curiously from across the room. I mustered a little smile and croaked out a question.

"Do you want me to leave, Jake?"

"No, I want you to stay, if you wanna stay." There was sincerity in his voice. He turned around, fiddling with the

DVD player, and started the movie over again. I wondered briefly about his mom. I never saw her anymore.

The next thing I knew, Jake hopped in bed behind me and stuffed a pillow under his head. I was paralyzed. I could feel the heat radiating from his body even though he wasn't touching me. The sensation was electrifying. I was completely captivated by the way I felt when I was around him. The peaks and valleys of everything he exuded enamored me. It was there, that *tension* again. I could feel his breath on my shoulder. I flinched as he moved my hair away from my neck.

"I'm sorry," he whispered. His hand moved down my arm, giving me the chills. He tucked his arm around my waist, pulling me closer to him. My heart skipped a beat. I could feel his breathing speed up, too. "Alyssa, let's just not read into this whole thing. I *do* feel what you feel. I enjoy being here with you, and that's the way it is."

"I'm–"

"And I'm not going to do anything that would ever hurt you," he interrupted. "You can trust me on that. I promise." He squeezed me tight. I could feel him burying his face in the nape of my neck, and it gave me butterflies. His promise echoed in my head, mingling with the butterflies fluttering around every inch of me, lulling me to sleep.

———

I was dreaming the most awesome dream; I was still in Jake's bed and my head lay on his chest. He had me safely tucked under his arm. My consciousness returned, jolting me awake. It wasn't a dream at all. I sat up in a near panic, thinking about my parents. I was lying with Jake and he *was* holding me. Dawn was barely shining and the clock read 6:12 AM. Jake's eyes fluttered open at my movement. His dark lashes framed his bright blue eyes, mesmerizing me. I wanted to stay right there, forever, staring at his face. He squinted at me, smiling softly.

"Shit, we're no joke with that sleep," he said, sitting up. Still shirtless, his hair was all mussed. He looked amazing for just having woken up. I wondered what I looked like. I walked to the mirror, attempting to brush my hair with my fingers, and I immediately got self-conscious.

"Do you have to leave?" he asked, grabbing a thick comforter at the foot of the bed. We had only slept with a thin blanket and the warmth of the night, and now a morning chill had consumed the room from leaving the back door open.

"No, I can't go home yet, my parents are up getting ready for work. They're probably in the kitchen, drinking coffee." I laughed. "Yeah, hey mom, hey dad...I was just sleeping in Jake's bed."

He flashed a lop-sided smile. "Come lie back down then. Go back to sleep. It's too early," he said, slapping the pillow next to him.

I crawled back in next to him. There was no way I was going back to sleep, not lying there so close to him. He held me just like he did during the night. I started to daydream about what it would be like to have Jake as a boyfriend. We would be going to school together soon. He would be able to drive me, and I wouldn't have to depend on my brother or sister.

I could see us pulling in the parking lot together and him putting his arm around my shoulder as we walked across campus. Wouldn't that be a dream? I was crazy to think it would ever happen; my father would never allow it. And of course, there was Rachel and the rest of The Envies. Now *that* was reality, I thought as I closed my eyes, hoping ninth grade would be easy.

"You know," I mused, "technically these aren't the first times we've stayed together. We can just add this sleepover to all the others."

"Nope, we've done this a million times. But this is the first time we've been at my house, and we're teenagers. Not sure our parents would agree."

"Oh sure they would, no big deal right? If I get caught, I'll just act stupid. *"Oh, mom, dad, I didn't think you'd care, we used to have sleepovers all the time."*

"Aly," he said firmly, squeezing my waist. "Zip it, go back to sleep." His voice was tired and raspy.

"I'm sorry." I whispered. I lay there wide-awake, feeling his breath get heavier on my shoulder. He fell back to sleep.

I must have fallen back to sleep quickly enough, too, because I couldn't recall any more of my daydream. Now it was 9 AM and Jake was standing in front of the TV brushing his teeth, still shirtless. I marveled at him and immediately got up. I was wishing I had someone to share my fabulous night with, but I was alone in my deeds.

"Ok, I gotta go," I announced, standing by the door. He turned around smiling, mouth full of toothpaste.

"Hold on," he mumbled. I could hear the water in the bathroom turn on. He was back in no time, opening a drawer and pulling out a t-shirt, tragically covering his brilliant naked torso. I smirked without realizing it.

"What?" he asked half laughing.

"Oh, nothing," I giggled. "It's nothing. I'm just laughing at myself."

He smiled, opening his back door, walking out into the cool morning air. He shivered, crossing his arms to his chest. We looked over and up at my house. Everything was still and quiet, with the exception of the sound of cars whizzing by in the distance. It was sunny and bright already. A cool ocean breeze whipped my hair in my face. He reached over and brushed it out of my eyes. His touch sent bolts of lightning through me.

"See ya later," he said.

Was that a question or a statement?

"Yeah," I mumbled, smiling weakly, not sure what else to say. I went through the gate, heart pounding, wondering if someone would see me come from Jake's yard. I reminded myself that I needed to act normal. I needed to get ready for my day and meet everyone as I always had. Nadine would be waiting anxiously. Matt would be there, too. I wondered how I would feel about Matt when I saw him later and anxiety filled me at the thought.

I had unlocked the office door before I left just in case the slider got locked and it was. I crept in, looking around quickly. Standing still, I held my breath. I didn't hear anything but the faint sound of a TV. I strolled down the hall toward the kitchen, where our family portraits stared at me accusingly. My brother was on the sofa watching TV. He didn't even acknowledge my presence. This was good. I poured some orange juice and walked upstairs. My sister's door was closed. She was probably still sleeping. Once again, no one noticed that I'd been gone the whole night. I was giddy with excitement.

I stared at myself in my bedroom mirror, and for the next couple of hours I was lost in the haze of Jake. I finally returned Nadine's text messages from the day before, telling her to meet me. I was sure everyone would notice me glowing like a light bulb. How was I gonna keep a lid on this? The fact that Nadine noticed Jake first and made it known that she wanted him had me reeling. I was sneaking around, behind my best friend's back, professing deep like for Jake to his face.

I was sick at the thought of it. How was I to know that I'd be overpowered by the chemistry Jake spoke of? I quickly picked out a new bathing suit, a shredded jean mini-skirt and white tank. I smelled my shoulders, and they smelled like him. I didn't want to shower. I wanted to smell like him all day long.

Chapter 10
ALYSSA

I sat on Nadine's porch, overwhelmed. Nadine was talking a million miles per hour, but I wasn't really paying attention. I kept staring in the direction of Jake's house. From where we sat I could see a portion of *the corner*. His house and mine were out of view.

"Hey, Aly!" Nadine said loudly, snapping me back to attention. "What else did Jake say? Anything about me?" She was coming completely unraveled.

"Sorry to say, but no, nothing. I mean, you were only there for a little bit before you took off." The excitement vanished from her face and the gleam in her eyes dulled. I felt bad, sort of. I would have felt worse if she didn't get attached to every cute guy that came along. It would only be a matter of time before someone replaced Jake. That's what I hoped, at least. Then I'd be home free.

Nadine took out her makeup bag and began inspecting her face with a MAC compact. She had beautiful green eyes. She was cute, in a childlike way, with a round face. Unlike me or our other best friend, Nicole Hamilton, Nadine had curves. She was 15, but her curves made her look 18 or older. She had the boobs we all envied.

My mind wandered back to Jake. His smell, how he looked without a shirt on, and the song he played for me the night before...

"Wait until you hear Jake play," I gushed. "You're gonna die."

"So other than all that, nothing else, not one other thing?" She sighed.

"Well, I went back over there and had, like, a heat stroke or something, and when it happened he took me and laid me down on his bed."

Her mouth hung open. I tried to be nonchalant about it, but hearing myself say it out loud, no wonder she was looking at me like I was nuts.

"Don't look at me like that, you know how long I've known him," I said, ignoring her doubtful expression. "He's like a brother. *Anyway*, let me finish without you looking at me like I have shit on my face." I sighed heavily. "So, I'm lying there and some chick shows up. I think it was his girl-friend. Her name is Rachel. He said she isn't his girlfriend, but I don't believe him. She certainly acted like she was." There, I said it. It came out smoothly enough. I only had to lie a little bit. No big deal, I told myself.

Nadine stood up and began walking.

"All right, enough. Let's go and see what'll happen today," she said, turning back to me with a devilish grin. "Maybe one of his band mates will be interested. You know they're all super cute."

I was relieved to hear those words fall from her over glossed lips. "How long have you noticed them?" I asked, sincerely curious. "I mean, dude, I've known Jake forever and I've never even paid much attention."

I really was flabbergasted at how quickly she could turn off her like switch and move on to the next guy. Our short walk to the corner had me freaking out about seeing Matt sooner than I wanted with Jake being in the vicinity.

Nadine waved her arm at me obnoxiously. "I've noticed all of them for a long time. Now come on."

We arrived at the corner, and Matt was there with Grant and Nicole. I'd had a crush on Matt Squire for a long, long time. We were all best friends, really. When I laid eyes on Matt, to my surprise I got butterflies. Wait, were the butterflies for Matt or Jake? I wondered painfully. Jake and his band mates were hanging in his garage across the street from us.

"Hey Matt," I said cheerily, waving to him. Matt skated around doing tricks with his board. His blond hair flipped and waved around with each maneuver. I tried to focus on just him and the endearing little heart-shaped scar right above his left eye. Angels must have been watching him that day, and thought him too cute to leave an ugly gash. Matt's eyes looked especially green this morning; they were shining. They used to draw me in, but not so much today. I thought back to Jake's intense blue eyes and the way he looked at me when I was lying next to him. Those were the eyes I wanted to look into.

"What's up, Alyssa?" he greeted, as I walked up to meet him. He looked over at Grant and Nicole sitting on the retaining wall, as if wondering if he was being watched. "What's been goin' on?"

"Not much, the usual. Thinkin' 'bout goin' to Six Flags. We talked about it, remember?"

"Yeah, that would be cool. When should we go?"

I shrugged, unsure of anything at the moment. "I don't know, whenever, you choose. We just have to find a ride."

I was having a tug of war in my head when a welcomed distraction came into view. My neighbor and classmate, Marshall Lawrence, was walking up the sidewalk toward us. Marshall was a pretty-boy, with his fashionably cut hair, unlike the other guys in my school. He would definitely be hot someday. His brothers were all good-looking too, with their almond-shaped eyes and perpetually tanned skin. Marshall was different than his brothers, though. He was slight and thin, not big and bulky.

I'd always wondered if he were gay. It seemed obvious to me ever since I'd learned what gay was. I'd never talked to him about it, but he was flamboyant in his dress and his mannerisms were feminine; it seemed it couldn't be denied. I'd always liked Marshall. He was soft-spoken, kind and funny. He took all the teasing from kids in stride, and never lashed out when being bullied by anyone.

"Hey, Marshall," I waved happily. "Wha'cha doin'?"

He waved back timidly. I could see his eyes dart from person to person around me. He finally spoke when he stopped in front of us. "Hi, Aly." He paused, looking down at his painted blue toes sitting in white flip-flops.

"Nice toe-nails, Lawrence," Grant teased.

I instantly shoved at Grant's shoulder and glanced at Marshall for his reaction. He just smirked at Grant. Grant only wore black; a uniform of black board shorts, t-shirt, shocks, and Vans tennis shoes, always, with the exception of different t-shirt graphics.

"Um, where you comin' from?" I said, trying to move past Grant's lame remark.

"Work. Um, I gotta get going though. I'll catch up with you later." He smiled softly at me and quickly moved past, waving good-bye.

My breath escaped me and I yanked my stare to Grant. "What's wrong with you?"

"What? I can't admire his paint job?" He snickered.

"Stop being an asshole." Nadine scolded, shaking her head at Grant. Their bickering continued as Nicole watched on in amusement. Matt poked at my elbow and moved away, leaning against the wall farther down from everyone else. He tossed his head at me to join him.

Then out of nowhere there was an urge, a pull. I wanted to look in Jake's direction, but I didn't. I ignored the sensation.

Scooting up next to Matt, I wondered what he wanted. "What's up?"

"Um, you wanna go to the movies tonight?" Matt asked quietly.

My heart hit my stomach. "Why are you whispering?" I whispered back.

"I don't want them to hear." He jutted his chin towards the others. "I don't need them tagging along."

The butterflies started swirling and my mouth went dry. A little breathless, I responded. "Yeah, I'd love to. I have to check with my mom though, she might have something planned I don't know about. What time were you thinking?"

"I don't know, like seven or eight. We can grab a bite, too, at the mall." He kept tossing his skateboard with his foot and glancing at me, a bit bashful. I thought it was cute. We were both nervous. This was the first time he'd asked me out without the rest of the crew. It was a big deal. I was stoked and torn.

As we all sat and leaned against the retaining wall across the street from Jake's house, out of nowhere, a white convertible BMW full of girls tore around the corner and stopped in front of Jake's house. All any of us could do was stare. I looked back at Nadine and her face fell, her hopes of flirting with the band diminished. I finally looked at Jake and he was staring right at me. He didn't look at the bright white spectacle. I thought I would faint. I looked at Nadine and she was staring at me, too. I looked at Matt, and he was also staring at me. I decided to stare at the shining arc of Envy status to take the attention off of me.

"Well, I guess we finally have something to aspire to," I muttered, irritated.

Nadine was sour too. "Yeah, if my parents had the kind of money theirs do, it would be easy." She hopped off the wall, walking over to Matt and me. Matt took off on his skateboard, doing tricks when she got too close.

"So, Jake keeps staring over here. It looks like he has eyes for you," she snarked.

I tried to laugh it off. "Ha, yeah right, shut up. I'm sure he's just wondering who Matt is. You know, the *big brother* thing."

This was all just too much for me. Now Jake wasn't *just* my next-door neighbor anymore. I sat there pretending to be into Matt's skateboard tricks, trying to come up with what to say to Nadine when she started in on me.

"So, you know…all this time Jake never paid attention to what was going on over here. Now he's watching and can't take his eyes off us, especially you," she said perceptively.

"Maybe he's watching you?" I evaded.

"Oh, yeah right, I saw him *staring* at you," she insisted under her breath. "Are you going over there? Let's go over there."

"Are you crazy? Matt's here, and those girls are there and the band…and we've never gone over there like that before." I blurted out all the reasons I could think of. "I don't wanna embarrass myself. One of those girls is probably Rachel."

"What are you talking about?" Nadine snapped. I about died. She said it so loud that Nicole and Grant looked over at us. I immediately glanced in Jake's garage, and thankfully no one looked our way.

"Shush, you spaz," I pleaded. "Calm down already. You're like freaking out for nothing. I'm talking about Jake's girlfriend. I just told you about her at your house. I just don't know which one she is yet."

Nadine slumped. "Oh, that's right." She pouted, and I didn't blame her. I felt the same way. "Yeah, I've seen them together at school. She's the one with the blond hair. I thought she was just a friend."

"You're killing me." I shook my head, agitated. "I'm not going over there."

"Calm down. What's going on with you, you're acting like…like, not you," Nadine said, glowering.

I huffed, pulling my arms to my chest. "Nothing, never mind."

Nadine just stared at me like I had two heads. It was pointless to complain. I looked back in Jake's direction. That Rachel girl was near him, and all I witnessed for the next half hour was her all up in his face. It made my insides churn.

"All right you idiots, what are we gonna do?" Grant asked. Matt skated up to me, placing his arm around my shoulder. I froze and the butterflies swarmed.

"We could go to my house," Matt offered. "My parents aren't home."

Now my stomach really flipped around. I quickly turned to face him so his arm would fall. I casually glanced in Jake's direction, but he wasn't there any longer. Only Mike and Dump remained. To my surprise, Mike acknowledged us and waved. I smiled and returned the gesture.

"Who's that?" Matt asked.

"That's Mike. Jake's guitarist, I guess. I met him yesterday," I explained.

"Ah," he said softly, looking in Grant's direction. "That's the guy that Jake picked instead of Grant."

I was reminded how defeated Grant was the night he found out Jake hadn't chosen him as his new guitarist — how I'd seen him wipe tears from his eyes, even though he tried to hide it. He'd wanted it so badly.

I sat back on the wall taking in the scene and turned to face Matt, but my eyes kept bouncing back to the garage. Mike played with his guitar, and a loud trill bounced around, echoing off the neighborhood facades like a pinball machine. He glanced over at us now and then. He was a good-looking guy, with his spikey bleached-blonde hair and tattooed arms. He always seemed to have a cigarette hanging from his lips, lit or not. I wasn't sure what color his eyes were, but he had good form. Tall, a little thinner than Jake, but, I suppose, just as good looking. There was no reason Nadine shouldn't be interested in him.

Finally, Jake and The Envies came back outside. Rachel was hanging on Jake until one of her friends, a gorgeous raven-haired chick with bright red lipstick, tried prying her away. She had a punky vibe for sure. I really liked her look. I was completely and utterly captivated by the whole spectacle. Finally they boisterously walked to their car. They looked like they were drunk or on something. Maybe they were.

"Hey, Nadine, check out that girl with the black hair," I pointed out quietly, "What do you think? I think she's cool looking."

Nadine nodded slowly, deciding. "Yeah, she's got a great look."

"And what do you think of Mike? I think he's Abercrombie status," I said, hopping off the wall nonchalantly. I planted the seed and now she was staring at him. "I think he's hot, more edgy, you know with his tats and all. I can't believe his parents allow him to get tattoos."

"I think it's hot. I can't wait to get one as soon as I move out." Nadine informed me.

That surprised me.

———

Matt was attentive, and it made me feel worse about leading him on. Watching the videos of him competing in skateboarding events blew me away. After all these years I had no idea he was so avid about it, let alone that good. No wonder he had such roughed up knees and elbows. He was sponsored by some pretty popular skate brands, and had already won several contests. He proved his insane capabilities video after video. I was impressed with how high he went in the air on ramps and half pipes, and by all the tricks he was capable of.

My phone kept making that pinging sound, telling me I had new text messages. I'd ignored it long enough. I knew it was my mom, since I was with everyone else who would be texting me. I grabbed my phone to see what she wanted. When I viewed the name on the screen, it lit up with the name *JAKE*. I almost passed out. My head immediately began to spin from the blood rushing to my brain. How could this be? I excused myself, trying not to run into the bathroom. Shutting the toilet lid, I sat there with a stupid grin on my face. I was worried it was someone playing a joke on me. I replied back:

- *IF IT'S JAKE, TELL ME SOMETHING THAT NO ONE KNOWS, LIKE WHAT YOU DID LAST NIGHT?*

I hit send and stood up pacing the tiny bathroom. I waited what seemed like five minutes, then the ping:

- *SLEPT NEXT TO U*

My heart raced. Oh my God. I didn't know how to reply. In those few seconds of thought, another text came:

- *SMELLING UR STAWBERRY SCENTED HAIR*

My hands trembled. I couldn't wipe the smile from my face. Looking into the bathroom mirror the person looking back at me was flushed. I took a deep breath:

- *HOW'D U GET MY #?*

Jake replied:

- *WHILE U WERE ASLEEP THIS MORN I PRGRMD UR PHN. U SHLD RLY HV A CODE.*

The texting continued:

- *WHERE R U?*
- *MATT'S*
- *IS MATT THE GUY W/THE SKATE?*
- *YES*
- *IS HE SITTING NXT 2U WHILE U TXT?*
- *NO*
- *MISSIN' U. WHEN R U COMIN HOME?*

I stood there with my heart in my throat and my blood pounding against the back of my eyeballs.

- *SOON, BUT I'M SUPPOSED 2GO2 THE MOVIES W/HIM*
- *OH, OK*

I sat on the bathroom counter waiting for a reply and I didn't get one. My heart sank. *I shouldn't have admitted anything about Matt. I bet he thinks I'm a fake.* I had to go. I had to go home. I opened the door and floated into the living room. I was numb, which added realism for my fake sickness I was going to continue to lie about.

"Guys, I'm still not feeling right, I'm gonna go home," I said weakly, for better effect.

Matt immediately got up coming over to me. "Ok, do you want me to walk you home?" he offered, concerned.

"No, I'll be ok," I assured him. "I've felt weird all day. Yesterday too. I'll be ok."

The next thing I knew, I was knocking on Jake's door like a maniac talking to myself. Jake finally opened the door, noshing on an apple. Astonishment sparked in his eyes. I guess he hadn't been expecting me.

Chapter 11

ALYSSA

Jake's eyes danced and a smile peaked at the edges of his mouth as he stood holding the door open for me. I wondered what he was thinking. I was definitely, officially losing my mind. I should be admitted to a psych ward. Every inch of me wanted to hug him, but I refrained. I moved to walk past him, and he draped his arm around my shoulders, pulling me close. My reaction was instantaneous. I returned the gesture, wrapping my arms around his waist, not saying a word. Unexpectedly, his mother came in the house through the garage door, catching us mid-hug. We awkwardly released each other, putting some room between us. Her expression was warm and her eyes crinkled at the sides when she smiled.

"Alyssa, my goodness, it's good to see you," she said, throwing us a sly grin. "Come in here and talk to me. Tell me what you've been up to."

Jake and I shrugged simultaneously. As his mom turned away, I shook my head *no*, silently pleading with him.

He looked at me sideways, shoving me forward. I sighed, reluctantly walking ahead of him into the kitchen. I sat down on a stool perched next to the counter and swung my legs back and forth.

Jake cleared his throat.

"Um, Aly came over the other day with one of her friends and helped wash my truck," he explained. "Then we got to talking…"

I chimed in. "Yeah, my friend Nadine wanted to meet Jake. So I introduced them." I gulped, wondering what else to say. Then the words came flying outta my mouth before I realized it. "Mrs. Masters, I had no idea how awesome Jake's music is. I mean, I knew he liked to play, but the sound coming from your garage was always muffled, you know."

Stop blathering, I told myself. Jake had moved out of my view. Even though he wasn't touching me, I could feel his energy behind me.

"Aly, you don't have to call me Mrs. Masters. I'm no longer a Mrs. and I've known you far too long. Kate will do."

Kate Masters was a stunningly beautiful woman, with long, honey-colored hair. I marveled at her eyes. She had the same intense topaz blue eyes as Jake. Her face showed hardly any signs of her true age, no deep lines, and barely any wrinkles. I wondered how old she was. If you didn't look too hard, you'd think she was Jake's older sister.

"Are you kids hungry?" She flipped her hair off her shoulder as she turned toward the fridge.

"Yeah, actually, I am." Jake said, looking over at me and I shook my head in agreement. "Aly is, too."

"Ok, I'll make a pizza. Do you like pepperoni?" she asked me.

I nodded. "Yeah! That sounds yummy."

Jake walked over to a small TV mounted underneath one of the kitchen cabinets and turned it on. Kate stacked the counter with what appeared to be ingredients for the pizza. I was waiting for a box to come out of the freezer. She quickly explained how bad frozen food was for you.

She schooled us about sodium and the amount used to keep frozen food edible, which was way more than anyone needed for an entire day. She went on— *"if you just take some time for preparation, your health will be much better in the long run."* She preached lightly about organic food, acupuncture and natural remedies for modern day ailments. I sat there, listening, fascinated by this new information.

Jake was trying not to look bored—he'd probably heard it all a thousand times, but I asked a plethora of questions. Each time I glanced in Jake's direction, he nodded at me approvingly. I was exactly where I wanted to be.

It was cool making pizza dough. I attempted to toss mine in the air like those pro Italian pizza guys.

"Oh, you think you're fancy like that, do you?" Jake teased.

With one toss, Jake's dough launched across the counter and landed on the floor.

"I'm obviously fancier than you," I snickered.

Jake cursed under his breath, laughing and leered good-humoredly at me. I was proud of my lop-sided dough canvas. We finished our pizzas and put them in the oven. Kate disappeared into the other room.

"You can relax now, Chatter Box," he chided, moving in closer to me. "I'm not gonna lie. I'm glad you ditched skateboard boy."

I threw him a cross look for his smart remark.

"Don't forget I told Matt I might go to the movies with him tonight."

There was silence. Jake held a bag of pepperonis, tossing them one-by-one into his mouth. The anxiety grew inside me with each silent second. He walked to the fridge, grabbed a bottle of water and took a long swig. Finally, he looked at me.

"Yeah, well," he said, standing there leaning against the counter staring at me with a blank expression. I was dying inside. I didn't want to always be the one pouring my guts out. "I guess the one thing I can always count on is that you'll tell me the truth, right?"

I stood there frozen, thinking about all the lies I'd told to everyone *but* him. At the moment, his statement was true. I didn't know how to respond, so I just shrugged and he asked, "so, what's up?"

I could feel the heat rising in my face at warp speed and turned away without a word. I walked out of the kitchen to find solace alone in the bathroom. In the midst of my brain hemorrhage, I didn't hear Jake walking behind me. When I turned to close the bathroom door, his arm extended above my head, pressing into the wood, holding the door firmly in place. I'm sure he could read my face like a bright red stoplight.

Looking up at him, I wanted to kiss him. I wanted to grab his face and kiss him, like I'd seen in the movies a thousand times. His face was so close to mine, and I could smell his perfect scent. Closing my eyes, I took in a deep breath and felt both of his hands cup my cheeks. My heart stopped. He rested his forehead on mine and I felt his breath warm on my lips.

"Don't be embarrassed," he insisted, his voice was low and velvety. His hands left my face, prompting me to open my eyes. I brought my clenched fists up under my chin and considered my next words. Before I could speak, he pulled me close, hugging me, and led me toward his room. "Come on, let's talk. I'll go first, but you have to promise me you'll be honest, too. I'm probably just as nervous as you are."

I sat there on his bed, petrified. My breathing was shallow. I needed to find relief or I'd pass out.

Jake continued. "Ok. So…I've been thinking about you all day, ever since I saw you with… *Matt.* I thought about you all morning, too." He paused, getting up to pace back and forth in front of me. "I was stoked to know that we'd be hanging out, you know, getting to know each other again. I thought you felt the same way, especially after last night. Then I saw you and Matt hangin' on each other and I found myself getting… jealous, which isn't normal for me. I'm not *that* guy and it made me …uncomfortable."

I was tripping out on how open and honest he was being. Were all boys like this?

"Jake…." I reached out and touched his hand. He held it in return. He remained standing, playing with my fingers, and continued to speak.

"No, wait, let me finish," he said firmly, taking a seat beside me. "I wanted to know if you were still with him, if you were alone with him. I wanted to know what you were doing. That's why I sent the text. When you told me you were going to the movies with him…I felt stupid or whatever. Like, did I misread you? I thought we were on the same page."

I interrupted, "Jake, there's no confusion…."

He squeezed my hand. "Look, I know better than anyone that someone can be attracted to another person even when they're attached to someone else. That's why people break up most of the time; because they meet someone else they like better. Kinda like what happened with Rachel the other day. If I didn't like being with you, I would have walked you home and hung out with her."

His confession made my heart swell with excitement. I couldn't believe what I was hearing. No one in the history of my life would ever compare to him. He finally looked over at me, resuming his thoughts on the matter.

"So, you know, when you admitted you've liked Matt for a long time, it just brought to mind that maybe, while you felt attracted to me…our time these last couple of nights might just be fleeting, because of your stronger connection to Matt."

I couldn't comprehend his words quick enough to reply. His speech was a complete masterpiece.

In my stunned state I barely eeked out my next words. "You know all too well, huh?"

Jake looked at me oddly. "What? This is for you more than me, Aly. You're the one that's having this thing with Matt."

"I just feel bad, you know. Don't you, about Rachel?"

"No. I don't. Rachel has her own issues. She's a big girl. She'll get over it, eventually."

I gulped. "Ok. What else? What else makes you know all too well?"

Jake sniffed, and a reluctant grin peeked at the sides of his mouth.

"Sometimes people stay in something, even when they know it's not gonna end well, and…and some people don't ever get into anything because they're waiting on someone else, with the hopes that *that* someone will eventually come around."

"Wow. That's deep." I chuckled uncomfortably.

"Yeah, sorry, didn't mean to go all Dr. Phil or whoever." He paused, sucking in a deep breath. "So then I threw my phone down after you said you may go to the movies with him. I was bummed."

Jake looked sheepish and shrugged his shoulders.

"I guess there's your answer," I said leaning into him. I was embarrassed to look at his face any longer than a few seconds.

"I trip out on how fast this has all come on, you know, but realizing I've known you my whole life, I guess it's not so strange," he confessed.

Before I could respond, Kate shouted out that our pizzas were done. We both stood up, a bit uneasy. He put his arm around my shoulder, nuzzling me warmly as he led me out.

We ate quietly, and I chose my next words as I admired his long lashes. "The difference between you and I is," I said, decisive. "You've already been where I'm at, now. You understand what you're feeling." I knew he'd probably been there and done *that*, and every other thing in between.

Jake considered my statement and finished chewing. "Yeah, but…I can talk to you. I've never had that with anyone before. No matter how much I liked someone…" He trailed off. "I'm always boxed in. I don't know...sometimes I feel like there's this image thing I have to uphold."

Jake's voice grew quiet and he stared at the pizza crust in his hand.

"What image?"

"You know, like nothing bothers me. I don't know… it's stupid. Put it this way, sometimes I don't always do what I want to do because of what people might think. I shouldn't give a shit, but it just happens. Like this voice inside telling me—*that's not cool, everyone will think you're a pussy if you do or don't do this or that*—So I don't always do the right thing."

"I see."

I certainly did see...every perfect contour of his face that stared back at me. I repeated his words in my head and wondered what it must be like for him. I felt like I could tell him anything.

My phone pinged with a new text message.

Jake glanced in its direction. "I wonder who that'll be," he said sarcastically, bobbing his head. "I'll bet it'll be Matt."

"Shut up. It's probably my mom." I picked up my phone, and lo and behold, it *was* Matt. My stomach sank. I didn't want to admit it was him, but I couldn't lie to Jake, not ever. Not even about the smallest thing. "Ding, ding, ding, you were right. He wants to know if I'm feeling better, and if we're still going to the movies."

"What, you weren't feeling well?" Jake swooned, mocking me.

"No, I wasn't. I *was* sick. This whole thing with us has completely thrown my whole universe into a black hole. The last 24 hours? I feel totally rattled." I paused when I saw the confusion on his face. "Ok. I mean, how do I tell my friends? *Oh, I don't like Matt anymore, I'm into Jake now; and by the way Nadine, I'm sorry, I know you wanted him to like you, but he likes me now*—Really, how do I do this?"

"Wow, I didn't realize all that," he said. "So, Nadine's the reason you came over?"

"Yes, and don't look at me like that," I huffed, gathering my thoughts. My next words came out slowly. "You know, I'm totally blameless in all of this. I didn't know I would react the way I did, and feel the way I'm feeling. It's like I've been living in black and white and you're the color, the vibrant bright outline to everything grey."

I was embarrassed about my honesty, but I couldn't help myself. I stared down at my pizza crust, feeling my face get hot again.

"So, where do we go from here?" Jake said, smiling softly at me and taking another slice of pizza. "I mean I have to ask, right?"

"Like you said last night, not to read into anything? Besides, my family would die if they knew I was hanging out with you like this. You're the only one who knows."

"What were you gonna do about going to the movies with Matt if they won't let you date?"

My stomach tumbled.

"What do you think? I was gonna tell my parents we were going as a group."

"Of course you were," he said dryly, rolling his eyes, not surprised.

I sighed deeply. "What am I gonna do about Nadine?"

"Why don't you just tell Nadine how it is? She'll get over it," he said, a bit annoyed.

His solution sounded simple enough, but there was no way I was going to tell her.

"Jake, it's a girl thing—and she's my best friend, and even though she likes to flirt with everyone, she rarely *quote unquote* makes dibs—meaning she told me straight out that she likes you," I explained, pausing. "It just has to run its course, I guess."

"What are you gonna do about Matt?" Jake asked again, more firmly this time. A surge shot through me.

"I'm thinking about it, and in all honesty, I really care about Matt. We've been friends since kindergarten. He's always been there for me." Jake shook his head in understanding. "I don't wanna hurt his feelings."

"Ahhh, I guess *I'll* just have to get over it."

Jake reached over grabbing my empty plate and placed it under his. I noticed a tiny little tattoo on the side of his left ring finger, an *R*. My stomach sank. Was that for Rachel? Was he lying to me about everything?

I cleared my throat.

"You know, when I saw Rachel hanging all over you, I didn't like it either." I admitted, agitated. "What's that on your finger?"

I pointed at his finger, but only stared at his face. I watched for any indication that he was calculating a lie, something I'd learned from dealing with my sister. I recalled how easily he'd lied to Rachel about me *not* being at his house, when I was. He looked down, staring at it and then rubbed it. He shrugged and half-laughed.

"A stupid drunk night, that's what this is. It's the initial of my first real girlfriend, Renee. That night was actually the first night I ever drank, see, and look what happens."

I could only hope he was telling the truth, for truth's sake. Not that it mattered whose name it stood for. I didn't want him to lie to me to save me from bad feelings like he'd done with Rachel.

I stared at him blankly.

He tilted his head, reading me.

"Aly, I'm not lying. I'll call her and hand you the phone if you don't believe me."

Now I felt stupid.

"No. Geez. I was just wondering. I mean it *is* an R, after all." I said fiddling with the placemat. "What do you think Rachel will do when she realizes we're actually hanging out?"

"It's gonna be hard getting rid of her. Her best friend is Dump's girlfriend, Sienna Barnes, the girl with the black hair. They're inseparable, her and Rachel that is."

After more small talk about how Jake and I felt about each other, I finally sent Matt a text apologizing, telling him I still didn't feel well. I felt bad about lying, kind of.

Jake and I continued talking for hours.

Chapter 12

ALYSSA

Getting my wits about me was nearly impossible.

"By the way, you have to really teach me how to play the guitar. That's the only way I'll be able to come over here so often without anyone wondering. Just my luck, my bitchy ass sister will ask me to show off my new skills," I told him.

We were sitting in Jake's living room and he picked up a guitar, handing it to me. Being too close and feeling the warmth of him, I didn't know how I would focus on learning anything. He began playing a familiar tune that I couldn't place. I marveled at how easily his fingers navigated and plucked away at the guitar strings. He strummed the melody as I searched my memory, trying to place the song.

After the first few hand contacts and body brushes, I finally calmed enough to pay attention. I didn't have to admit I was nervous—Jake could tell; he reminded me more than once to breathe. *"Aly, don't hold your breath, breathe slowly."* His voice remained smooth and even, soothing my nerves until they were completely gone.

He told me about what my first lesson would entail without ever looking down at his playing. He made it look too easy. He explained in a gentle voice that we would focus on basic chords and add in very simple strumming.

"There you go, see, it's not bad." He released his hold on the guitar. "I think you're gonna be picking this up pretty quickly. You're a natural."

"Ya' think?" I chirped with excitement. "I was so nervous my fingers wouldn't get it."

A knock came at the front door, and my mood plummeted. It seemed we were always being disturbed. I hoped it was a sales person or one of those Jehovah's dudes. I heard the familiar voice and my heart stopped. I took in a deep breath and stood up, pacing a bit. Then I sat back down waving my hands in front of face as if they would help cool me off. Soon enough, the voice grew louder, and there she was. Nadine. WTF!

"Hey, it's Nadine," Jake announced. I imagined myself bopping him upside the head. Didn't he get it? Didn't he hear what I said about Nadine liking him? We were supposed to keep our hanging out under wraps. What an idiot. What the hell was she doing here anyway? I wondered, silently fuming. My stomach acids were raging. I composed myself, making like I was out of it, since I was supposed to be sick. I hoped Jake didn't forget about that too.

"Hey, what's up?" I said weakly.

"I just went to your house. Your mom said you were over here having a guitar lesson, so I thought I'd come over and check it out," she said, looking around curiously.

"Yeah, well, since I'd blocked this time with him I didn't wanna cancel, since it was only for an hour."

"Yeah, sit down, take a load off." Jake gestured to the lone chair next to him.

When Jake chimed in he eliminated the negativity. Nadine's eyes lit up when he spoke to her. I wanted to slap her upside the head with the guitar. I reminded myself that she didn't know how I felt about him. She should be the one slapping me around. That guilty feeling crept in again. Ugh, I hated myself. What was I going to do?

"So, Nadine, do you know how to play any instruments?" he asked.

"I use to take piano lessons ages ago," she answered, smiling. "I know how to read music, and I think it would be easy for me to learn."

"Yeah, well that'll make it much easier for you since you have an ear for the notes." Jake nodded his head. He looked over at me and winked. I was afraid to look at Nadine in case she caught that. "So, you interested in lessons?"

I almost passed out when I heard the words hurl out of his mouth. I immediately excused myself and went into the bathroom without looking at him. I didn't shut the door all the way because I wanted to eavesdrop. I could hear him back-pedaling. He was stammering. *Good*, I thought, *that'll teach him*. I laughed silently, triumphant.

Nadine was prying:

"So, how long has Aly been here? I mean, how long ago did her lesson start? Are you almost done?"

"We actually just started. My mom was here, and hadn't seen Aly in a long time."

It was killing me! He was sharing too much information! I could only imagine what she looked like, with her tits hangin', spilling out of her tank top. I had to keep reminding myself that this wasn't her fault. She was just being herself. I was the one that was the backstabber. I berated myself for the mean thoughts going through my head like a roadrunner on crack.

"Why don't you come back in an hour? We should be done," Jake suggested.

I couldn't believe my ears! What the hell was he thinking? I leaned against the door in disbelief and strained to hear more.

"I can call Mike over and I'm sure he would be glad to make a schedule for lessons; besides, he owes me. I would offer, but Aly is enough for me right now. I shouldn't even be spending the time with her."

"Oh, sure, yeah, I understand. If Mike could do that, it would be awesome."

I could hear the disappointment in Nadine's voice.

"I'm sure it'll be no prob. I just have too much to prepare for with the upcoming tour and all."

"Oh, I totally get that. Sorry, I don't mean to put any pressure on you."

She sounded sincere. Now I really felt bad.

"Hey, don't be sorry. Come back in an hour and I'll have more info. Ok? Let me go check on Aly."

Oh shit! I gently shut the bathroom door and locked it. I ran the water and wet my face. My heart raced. Even though I anticipated his knock at the door, my heart still lurched into my throat.

"Aly, you ok?" he asked gently.

"Yeah," I said opening the door, peeved. I wanted him to know I was upset. I dried my face with a hand towel, my words muffled. "Did she leave?"

He shook his head *no* and I gave him a tight, evil eye. He grabbed my arm tossing me into the hallway. He practically shoved me along the way. I put on a pathetic sick face as we rounded the corner back into the living room. I walked slowly, moving my hair from my face, which I matted wet against my forehead.

I sat on the sofa, giving a frail smile. "Hey, sorry I didn't call. I'm feeling a lot better than I did yesterday, but still not quite right." I knew she didn't care. She was probably pissed as shit at me that I crept in on her territory.

"It's ok, I hope you feel better," she said sympathetically. "Jake's gonna have Mike come over to teach me to play the guitar too."

She glittered with excitement. By all appearances, she didn't seem to be mad at me. I was cautiously relieved. I'd certainly know the truth when she had me alone.

We sat there quiet for a moment and Jake pulled a metallic blue and black pack of gum out of his pocket, offering up a piece as he popped one into his mouth. He prompted Nadine to leave by standing up and touching her shoulder. Nadine bounced out of her seat and practically danced out of the room.

"Alright, I'll see you in a little bit! Aly, I hope you're still here when I come back." She disappeared out the door. I reminded myself to tread lightly with my assumption that she'd be okay with this arrangement and considered my options while I chewed my gum.

Jake sat and put his arm around my shoulders, pulling me close. I melted into him as he leaned back, sinking into the cushions. My head bounced around on his chest when he began to chuckle.

"Why are you laughing?" I asked, miffed.

"I'm laughing at you. You have to trust that I know how to play the game, Aly."

"Oh, do you?" I said sarcastically. "Please share with me what you know about game playing, with girls."

He smiled thoughtfully and his eyes roamed my face. My insides bubbled. I tried to pull away, but he held me in place.

"Relax Aly, the Nadine thing will work out. I have a plan."

I closed my eyes relaxing, slightly. I suddenly felt his lips brush lightly against my temple and a bit of breath escaped me. As much as I wanted him to really kiss me. I was scared. My mind reeled—*what if I kissed like shit? What if I drooled all over him? What if I couldn't control myself?*

"Jake?" Our faces nearly touched. He leaned down and softly kissed the side of my mouth. My breathing instantly became shallow and erratic. The *energy* was pulsing between us. "Jake, I don't think…" As I began to speak, he gently kissed me full on the lips, and it took my breath away.

His warm, minty breath washed over my face. His lips brushed against my cheek and pressed softly onto mine again. My heart thumped a million miles per hour and I pulled back. Sensing my hesitation, he released me. My chin dropped to my chest, my eyes averted his. I was embarrassed. He lifted my chin to bring us face to face and placed his forehead against mine.

His voice was low and silky. "I'm sorry, I should have asked," he whispered, pulling me close once more. I buried my face into his neck.

"Jake, I'm the one who's sorry, I'm not…" I had trouble spitting it out. I didn't want to sound like a baby.

"Why are you sorry? Don't be sorry, that's ridiculous." He rubbed my back tenderly and moved, making room between us.

I sighed deeply, and my words came out in a burst. "Maybe I *am* too young for you. I'm not what you're used to. I know about guys like you…"

He put his finger to my mouth stopping the avalanche of dialog. "Wait, what? Guys like me?" he repeated, sounding offended. "Guys like me, what?"

"I know you're used to being with girls, and you know I wanna be there too, but…" I giggled nervously. "Wait, that came out wrong."

He laughed, throwing his head back.

"So, you wanna be what?" He teased and his eyes glimmered.

"You know what I'm trying to say, Jake, don't make this harder for me than it already is." I begged, shoving at his knee.

"Please continue. I wanna know more about guys like me." He grinned and enjoyed watching me squirm.

"You know what, never mind. I'm not gonna continue humiliating myself." I pouted.

He hugged me, sniggering. "Alright, I'm sorry. I get it, but check this out. You don't know guys like me, Aly."

Wait, what was that supposed to mean? Is he agreeing with me?

"What?"

"This thing with you isn't the same as it would be with someone I just met at a party, or someone at school, or some fan girl." He released my shoulders and placed his elbows on his knees. His head hung low and his lush hair waved over his forehead. After a long moment he continued, looking at me. "I'm in no rush with this. I don't wanna be anywhere else other than being on tour. I totally dig hangin' with you. It's comfortable."

"I still feel lame. I'm sorry I keep bringing it up."

"Don't be. I'm perfectly fine kissing you like we're still in 6th grade." His smirk grew more pronounced.

I could have been insulted or embarrassed, but I wasn't. I was relieved. The thought of French kissing him made me nervous beyond belief. Even though I'd dreamt about doing it more times than I could count. Actually doing it with *him* was another story.

Chapter 13

ALYSSA

I continued with the lies, kind of, texting my mom explaining I was with Nadine, which would be true soon enough. I tried to keep things on the up and up—for the most part. Jake finished his call with Mike and was all smiles.

"What? You wanted a solution, now we have one."

God, he was beautiful. I was enthralled. Words couldn't describe how much I was taken by his entire...*everything*. I gave him a sideways grin and he reached over and took my hand. His skin was so much warmer than mine. He played with my fingers, tracing my nail beds, giving me the chills.

"You have nice hands, and nails, real nails—not those fake lame ones," he remarked, pausing. His eyes roamed my face. "So you don't wanna continue your lesson?"

I groaned. "No, I don't. I don't feel like it now. When is Nadine coming back? Is Mike coming over now too?"

"Yeah, in about forty-five minutes."

I was resigned. The plan was set in motion, and I couldn't change it.

"So, what's this thing you'd promised to do to get Mike to commit?"

"We're gonna play at a house party."

I had heard about these house party drunk-fests. "Keggers," my father called them. They were off limits to my brother and sister—supposedly. I knew they still went when they stayed over at their friends. I would overhear my sister crafting her plan. Nicole and I would sit with our ears pressed up against the wall, listening to the gossip of high school life. Finally, we were going to be a part of it.

"Where's the party at?" I inquired. Like it really mattered, but I was curious anyway.

"You're not gonna wanna hear this, but it's at Rachel's place. I'd already been going back and forth about playing there. Now I'm locked in." He motioned, resigned, brushing crumbs around the tabletop. "It's basically a summer kick-off party. She's always had them, since, like, seventh grade."

I pictured The Envies at the party, standing out in all their perfectness...how was I going to measure up? I felt an inch tall and totally insecure. I focused on the fact that I was holding Jake's hand and that he was gently rubbing the inside of my palm with his fingertips.

"Do you think Rachel would let us come to the party? Or are we too young? Like is this only a senior thing?" I tried to sound nonchalant.

"I'd say come. I'll just tell her you guys are coming. Fuck it." He shrugged. My mood buoyed. "She knows who you are to me, so whatever."

"Really, and what's that?" I asked, surprised at my boldness.

He stalled. I knew what he meant, but I wanted to hear him say it because it was apparent she still thought herself as his girlfriend.

"She knows we're close, that we grew up together," he stated, leaning over and kissing me warmly on the cheek. A million thoughts rushed through my head. I pictured myself grabbing him by the neck and pulling him back to me, when he backed away. All the while his bright blue eyes burned a hole in my head. I was speechless.

He went to the TV, tapping at some buttons. Wii Sports popped up brightly on the screen. A smile spread across his face as he held up two remotes.

"Since you're not into continuing with your guitar lesson, we can battle it out on Wii until our fronts arrive."

"Fronts?" I asked, cocking my head.

His lips curled up. "This is why you pull at my strings." He wagged the remote at me. Clearing his throat, he continued. "Fronts, meaning us using Nadine and Mike to our benefit, to throw people off our trail; like in the those old gangster movies, when they would have a store front and then in the back there was a secret gambling hall."

"Ah, right." I nodded, understanding. I feared this was all a dream and I would wake up at any moment.

———

I felt dutiful, now having a mission: the quest of getting Mike and Nadine together. I watched Nadine and Jake play Wii and my insides froze like a glacier each time she stroked his back in encouragement. I reminded myself, again and again, she'd liked him first. That he was only being his cool, kind self when she playfully hung on him, tossing her head back and forth like a brainless Barbie doll. He kept flashing his radiant smile at me, warming my stone-cold insides like electric white heat. As the scene played out, I tried to calm my growing disdain at what I was witnessing. The next time we made eye contact it was as if he'd read my mind, and he distanced himself from her.

Finally Mike came through the front door and he smiled broadly, nodding his head at me. "Hey, Aly."

I hoped he was over making snide, distasteful remarks about me behind my back.

"Hey, Mike," I greeted casually, walking into the kitchen.

"Hey, Bro," I heard Jake acknowledge.

I stood with the fridge door open, deciding whether to have a soda or water when Mike appeared in my peripheral vision and I became blinded by the blood rushing to my head. Why did he have to come in here, and why did he make me so nervous?

"Hey, any beer in there?" he asked, practically breathing down my neck.

"Uh, yeah…" I barely choked out my answer before he grabbed one from over my shoulder. I wanted to say something like *I don't think that's a good idea*, but I didn't want to sound like a baby. I was in disbelief. I'd never been around anyone who blatantly drank alcohol, underage, in my face. My sister and brother would come home in what appeared to be an intoxicated stupor from time to time, but I'd never witnessed its progression.

Regardless of it being a bad idea, it was rebellion at its finest and I wanted to be a part of it. I grabbed a soda, popped its top and stepped back, leaning against the counter. What must it be like? Getting drunk? I recalled the horrid taste test from the other night. I wondered what the big deal was. My mother's words, "*Acquired Taste*," echoed in my head. No thank you, nothing about acquiring that taste appealed to me.

I watched Mike thoughtfully as he swigged his beer, staring back at me. It seemed as if time stalled. I admired his spikey blond hair and his build. Mike had a tough guy demeanor. He was standoffish in an appealing way that made you want to crack his code. If only the words that came out of his mouth weren't so douchey all the time. There should be no reason Nadine wouldn't want to date him.

"So, I hear you and your friend wanna play the guitar?" he asked, finally breaking the awkward silence. He took another long swig of his beer.

"Yeah, it just kinda came up, you know," I said nervously. Our eyes remained tied. I couldn't stand it anymore and looked away as I continued rambling. "Jake offered. I hope you don't mind. Nadine jumped on board after she'd heard about it."

"What? Naw man, it's cool, you and her…what's her name? Natalie?"

"Nadine."

"Yeah, Nadine, you guys wanna learn to play, we'll teach you," he said, tipping his head back and pouring the last bit of beer down his throat. He brushed past me too closely and gave me a sly smile that woke my sleeping butterflies. He opened the fridge and grabbed another beer, holding it out toward me. "You want one?"

"No tha…" I was interrupted.

"What the fuck dude, don't be offering her beer," Jake snapped. I nearly jumped out of my skin. "Don't fucking offer her anything anymore…got it?" Jake glared over his shoulder at Mike as he led me away by the elbow.

We walked past Nadine briskly. Jake practically knocked her out of the way. She frowned at me and mouthed *what the hell?* I shrugged my shoulders.

"I'll take one." I heard Nadine laugh uneasily. Their conversation grew inaudible as we walked all the way into Jake's room.

He let my arm go and walked in a small circle in front of me, round and round.

"What, what's wrong? I wasn't going to take it."

He sighed deeply and walked up to me, grabbing my face and kissing me hard on the lips. My head spun. His lips grew softer as he kissed me lightly a few more times.

I was breathless. I wanted more.

Chapter 14

JAKE

I'd never felt completely at ease chilling with a girl, as I did with Aly. I'd always felt like I had to be *on* with other girls. I never gave it any thought until now. I'd come to the conclusion it was some sort of a weird alter ego that took over, but with Aly it simply wasn't there.

Aly pretty much knew most things about me, other than the band stuff. She knew I'd lost my father and how screwed up I was about it for a long time. Remembering how she sat quietly off to the side as her mother and brother, Kyle, consoled my mother and me in those early days after the burial. Not that guys don't cry, but I hadn't shed one tear since then.

I wasn't an emotional person, until now.

So I took her face in my hands and kissed her. For a quick second she stiffened, but I didn't let go. I felt her cool hands and arms wrap around my neck. I kissed her softly while I searched for what I should say.

I was lost.

"I'm sorry," I paused for a long moment. I was agitated and fighting my feelings. "I just…I saw Mike…him looking at you the way he looks at girls he's interested in, and then offering you beer. That's his M.O, you know, get girls drunk to make it easier. I have to tell him about us, or he'll keep hitting on you."

"Jake, don't be sorry…and you know, that was totally innocent back there." Aly laughed in earnest.

"No, no it wasn't. I know him. There's nothing innocent about him, trust me."

I was adamant about Mike. He was one of *those guys* that her sister warned her of. Was I blowing it outta proportion? Was I just being overprotective? I sighed, frustrated, and began pacing again.

"These people don't know my sister, do they? Jake you can't say anything. If my sister finds out I'm coming over here for anything *other* than guitar lessons…."

Her eyes pleaded with me.

I walked to the door and looked back at her. "Trust me, this'll work itself out. None of them know Allison or Kyle, at least enough to say anything, and to tell you the truth none of them give a shit. But I have to say *something* to him or he'll keep at you. Everything's a game to Mike."

I turned and called out Nadine's name.

"Why are you calling her in here," she asked anxiously.

"Because, I need to talk to Mike without her in my face. I can't have him offering you guy's beer, or anything else for that matter. If my mom were to come home she'd shit herself, and my whole gig here would be ruined."

"Jake? Where are you?" Nadine shouted.

"Back here, in my room, come in here," I called.

Nadine skipped down the hall, stopping all puffed up and doe-eyed, in front of me. "What's going on? Is everything ok?"

"Yeah, just have to take care of something. Stay here."

My adrenaline rushed through me as I approached Mike.

"Hey man, you know I can't have you offering Aly beer, so just cool it. Don't do it again, got it? I'm responsible for her, and I don't need her going home with beer breath and her dad coming over here ripping my head off…."

"Damn, dude, relax, it wasn't any different than me offering Rachel a beer."

"She's not Rachel, alright?" I snapped, exasperated that he didn't get it.

"All right, step off already. What's going on with you and her anyway? You've been checked out all day, and bam, she's here again and you're all fucking lame." He chuckled, knowingly, throwing his hands up. "I got it, you like her."

"Of course I like her… I care about her. I've known her my whole life. I already explained that…"

"No, but you dig her, like wanna get in there." Mike laughed, convinced by his assumption. "Aw man, you should've just said something."

He continued to laugh obnoxiously, and I wanted to punch him.

"It's not like that…"

"Yeah right, I got you, buddy," he retorted.

"Look, just halt on the booze offering…or anything else for that matter with Aly, I could give a shit about anybody else."

I stormed off thinking maybe having Mike there was a bad idea. Walking back in my room, Nadine stared at me all steely-eyed, her lips curled upward.

"What?" I smirked. I felt like she could see right through me. Aly was right, she had a sixth sense.

"Oh, nothing," she sang out, retreating to Aly's side.

Aly's face began to glow. Nadine must have looked at her strangely or transferred some crazy telepathic chick vibe. Why else would she be blushing? I got hot under the collar, too. This was ridiculous.

I cleared my throat.

"Alright, let's get this started. Nadine, why don't you go and begin with Mike?"

"Mmhmm," She hummed tilting her head, looking us both up and down and spun out the door. "I got ya."

Nadine vanished and I reluctantly looked back at Aly.

"She knows." Aly held her palm to her forehead, obviously distressed.

"Yeah, I got the impression she suspects something. We're not doing anything wrong, Aly. Who gives a shit what she thinks?"

I was agitated by all the girl-dancing-around-eggshells bullshit.

"I do, for all the reasons I stated earlier. I'm sorry. I can tell you're irritated."

Now I felt bad.

"I'm not," I said, regretting my shortness.

"Yeah, you are. I can tell by your mannerisms and the look on your face."

"My mannerisms?" I smiled curiously and Aly shifted. I loved watching her squirm.

"You grab the back of your neck when you're frustrated. It's something you've always done. You used to do it all the time when you and Kyle would fight or whatever." She giggled, embarrassed by her assessment, but she continued. "It's cute. It's just one of those things you do that makes you, well…you."

If she didn't already have me, she did now. I wanted to know what else she knew about me. She had no idea that her little explanation had such an impact on me.

Back in the living room Mike immediately acted up when we appeared. "Yeah, buddy," Mike sang and he grabbed his guitar, strumming it as we walked back in joining them. He nodded deviously looking at Aly. Nadine was more than astute with her stare. "We're gonna get the rhythm started up in here."

Aly yanked me into the kitchen, mortified by Mike's melodic assertions. "See, I told you, did you see the way she looked at us? She eavesdropped on your convo with Mike," she whispered. "And what's up with Mike and his little stupid song?"

"Aly, it is what it is, seriously."

We faced each other from across the counter. I could see the wheels turning in her head. I wanted to take all her angst away. I leaned down onto the counter, holding my palms out to her, wiggling my fingers at her to come closer.

"I told you it would work out," I said, reassuring her.

The sweetness of her filled me, and I couldn't hold back from kissing her again. Suddenly, the moment shattered when abrupt coughing interrupted us. Aly jumped, standing straight, and gasped. It was Rachel. I seriously wanted to punch someone. I barely moved. My elbows remained stuck to the counter. I looked at Rachel, then back to Aly, rolling my eyes. I really didn't give a shit if Rachel noticed. I stood slowly, beyond irritated that she was there. She certainly had a knack for showing up unannounced. I could see Aly gulp, frightened by Rachel's presence.

Rachel spoke first, barely suppressing her disgust at seeing the two of us together.

"Well, um, did I interrupt something important?" Rachel said with forced cheer. I could see the fire in her eyes as she seared Aly up and down with her heat vision. She smiled tightly, lifting her eyebrows waiting for an answer.

An awkward moment passed.

"Yes, as a matter of fact you did. Did you ever hear of knocking, or better yet, *calling*?" I responded harshly. I looked back at Aly and laughed softly, trying to smooth out the wrinkled mood. Rachel's mouth fell open and she tried to compose herself. "Nah, just kidding. Relax. Aly and I were just talking about…well, it doesn't really matter what we were talking about, now, does it?"

I couldn't give one shit about what Rachel thought. I knew all too well how she treated other girls when she felt they were trespassing on her territory.

"Are you alone?" I looked past her to see if anyone else was around.

"No, I'm here with Dump and Sienna," she said too quickly, peeved. "I see you have a little party going on." Rachel nodded her head toward Mike and Nadine.

I sighed loudly. Again, words escaped me, so I sauntered to the fridge and grabbed a soda. I wasn't even thirsty, but I didn't know what else to do. I stood close to Aly, so close our arms grazed each other's, a statement of solidarity. I'd wanted Aly to know I meant what I'd said.

"Rachel, this is Aly. Aly, Rachel."

"Hi," Aly waved her hand innocently and squeezed out a weak smile.

"The pleasure's all mine, I'm sure," Rachel responded dryly. There was a standoff. Sticky silence filled the room and I remained anchored at Aly's side. I couldn't take it anymore, but I didn't know what to do.

"I wonder how Nadine's lessons are going," Aly said, walking past Rachel.

I could practically see the heat of Rachel's stare searing the side of Aly's skull as she passed. Aly was a whole head taller than Rachel and physically opposite in every way. I looked at the clock—already 7 PM.

Aly would be leaving soon.

Chapter 15
ALYSSA

As I moved into the living room where Nadine and Mike were still playing with the Wii, I ran my fingers through my hair to shield myself from Rachel's laser vision. Mike and Nadine appeared to be enjoying each other, especially Nadine, who was wearing a mile-wide smile. She didn't realize that Rachel had arrived unannounced.

I looked out of place with my cuffed denim shorts and white V-neck tee shirt. My unkempt hair looked wild compared to the other girl's stylish blunt cuts. Sienna wore fishnet stockings under her ripped jean shorts and laced-up boots. Her jet-black hair was so perfect that it looked like a wig. She wore her signature red lipstick and cat-like black eyeliner. I had a full-on girl crush for her.

Nadine threw her hands in the air, fussing about losing to Mike. She proceeded to grab her adult beverage and looked around. Finally, to my relief, she walked over to me.

"Looks like the band's all here, along with *her*," Nadine said quietly, taking a mouthful of beer. She leaned against the sofa. "Holy shit. Uh oh, Blondie's staring us down. Watch out."

"Give that to me," I said, grabbing the beer bottle out of her hand, taking a long swig. I pressed the bottle to my lips; rubbing its smooth surface against them as my thoughts swirled uncontrollably. The taste was disgusting. I gagged. "Gross. How can you drink this stuff?"

"Right on, Aly, it'll help you relax," Nadine whispered, encouraging my bad behavior as her eyes darted around the room. "Why is Rachel here anyway?"

"I know, right? Maybe we should leave?"

"Hell no!" she hissed, her face animated with defiance. "That's just what she wants, to vibe us out the door. Sorry, it ain't happening."

Jake startled me by gently taking the beer out of my hand. His body pressed up against my back. I felt his breath brush my ear. "I don't think this is a good idea," he whispered. "Just what I need is for my mom to walk in and find you holding this." I could have melted into a puddle at his feet. He squeezed my hand and walked away. Nadine looked bemused.

I shrugged. Words escaped me as I stood there, pretending to be innocent.

"Rachel just followed Jake into the kitchen. She was watching us." Nadine sniffed. "What a crazy bitch. You better be careful."

"What are you talking about?" I said, uncomfortable.

"Oh, come on, Aly—it's obvious he's totally into you," she said, not sounding too put off.

It was now or never. I was standing at confession's ledge and I'd decided to jump.

"I have to talk to you. Let's go to my house—better yet, let's go to Nicole's, so we can fill her in on the drama." I just prayed my sister wouldn't find out about Jake. Nadine said goodbye to Mike and he jumped up from his seat.

"You're leaving? Why?" He stared directly at me. *Why me?* "You're coming to the party tonight, right?"

"Where's it at? Can I text you? We need to take care of something," Nadine took out her phone with its glitter pink case, punching in Mike's number.

I could hear Jake and Rachel arguing. We passed by the kitchen as we headed towards the front door, and Jake called out my name.

"Aly, wait!" Jake shouted. I could hear Rachel calling to him—*"Jake, come on"*—but he was quickly at my side. "Let me get rid of everyone and I'll text you."

The touch of his hand on my elbow made me stop in my tracks. I was unconvinced he would text anytime soon.

"Isn't there some party tonight?" I reminded him, standoffish.

"Yeah, Mike said there was a party and invited us." Nadine remarked and hope filled her eyes that we would be able to join in.

"Uh, yeah, there is. Let me get rid of Rachel and figure things out."

An outburst of laughter and ruckus came from back inside the house and Jake hung his head in frustration. My insecurities flared, thinking the laughter was about me.

"She's like a bad rash, you know," I said, slumping.

"Good luck with that," Nadine laughed.

"We'll be around," I sighed.

Stupid Rachel, she's going to be a pain in my butt, I thought to myself. Just as that thought rolled into my mind, she strolled into view. If looks could kill, I'd be lying on the floor hemorrhaging.

I glanced nervously at Nadine and she returned Rachel's evil glare. Nadine tugged at my shirt and we turned simultaneously and walked out the front door. Jake followed us out onto the porch and watched us walk down the street.

Nadine was too quiet, and it spurred me to say something. "Nadine, I'm sorry." I hopped in front of her, stopping us in our tracks.

"For what?" she said, looking confused.

"You know *what*, Jake being the way he was with me."

"Don't worry about it," Nadine said, waving me off. She didn't sound mad, so I just left it alone. She'd probably let me have it once I told her about what was really going on.

We burst through Nicole's front door, finding her hunched at the computer. Grant and the guys weren't anywhere to be found, thank goodness. We blabbered in unison and she grabbed our hands, dragging us upstairs to her room. Her brother Chris stood in his bedroom doorway watching us, amused.

"What, did Zac Efron drive by and wave?" he laughed, teasing. "Lookin' good Nadine. Nice shorts." He smirked and walked down the stairs.

"OMG, did your brother just notice me?" Nadine looked at Nicole. She could barely contain herself. She blushed with a smile from ear to ear.

I shoved Nadine's shoulder and we tripped into Nicole's room.

"Ok, we'll get back to Chris," I interrupted, holding my hand up in her face, glancing between the two of them. I began to explain myself. "I haven't been completely honest. Nadine, I kinda knew that Jake liked me because he asked me to hang out and watch movies last night. He was kinda flirty with me."

"You hooker!" she smiled wildly, shoving my shoulder. "You should have just told me!"

"Well, it wasn't like that. I'd gone over there to talk about you, and we got to talking about his music and then he started teaching me to play the guitar and he was just really sweet, and really touchy feely with me…"

"Where did he touch you? Did you kiss him?" Nadine asked breathlessly, throwing her arms in the air, spinning around. "You're effing kidding me! I can't believe you didn't tell me!" She paced around, looking bemused.

"Shut up, Nadine. Let her finish," Nicole barked, sitting at the edge of her bed with her hand covering her gaping mouth.

I continued in a roundabout way with the story of last night. I didn't mention our sleepover. I painfully contemplated whether or not to divulge the more intimate details.

"Ok, ok, let me," Nadine interrupted, looking at Nicole with her hands together, as if in prayer. She turned to me. "Let me tell her the rest."

Nadine weaved her web for Nicole exactly how I recalled it. It was as if she was never interested in Jake at all. She also threw in tidbit rumors about Rachel's mean girl antics, and my heart sank deeper into my gut. "Rumor has it, she only went out with one guy to make Jake jealous and it didn't work. I also heard she drugged a girl's drink at a party." Nadine's eyes were wide. She nodded seriously at us as if we didn't believe her.

I sucked in a deep breath, closing my eyes.

"Aly, dude, are you ok?" Nicole asked, concerned. "You look pale."

"Yeah, I'll be ok, but I'm worried. What if she messes with me?"

"Try not to worry about it," Nicole said. "Hopefully Jake doesn't mean that much to her."

"Yeah, right, you should have seen her face." Tense laughter escaped Nadine's lips. "When Jake came up and took that beer out of Aly's hand and whispered in her ear—and by the way, he practically licked her in the process—Rachel shit herself. *You should've seen it, it was classic!*"

"A beer? So when did you start drinking?" Nicole teased, surprised.

"I haven't, it's gross. I was just freaking out. I needed a distraction." I stalled, thinking. "Let's find Chris, I wanna know more about Rachel."

The sun hung low, casting golden tones over everything it touched. It was a luminous late afternoon and the intense heat was finally subsiding. Staring at the water, I wanted to go swimming. I was overwhelmed with mixed emotions, and the water would be a soothing remedy. I moved, quietly, to an unoccupied lounge. Nadine hopped up, taking a seat next to Chris.

Hearing my name called out shook me from my cloud.

"Dude, Aly! Turn on the music," Nadine shouted. "Hello, you there?"

Chris looked quizzically at me, mouth half open. "So, Aly…Jake Masters? Really?" He clearly didn't believe what Nadine had told him, whatever it was. My mouth hinged for a few seconds. "Ha! Aw, Aly, you're pink. Does that mean I'm right?"

He continued to chuckle and Nadine punched him in the arm.

"Don't tease her, you jerk," Nadine scolded.

"Ouch!" Chris winced and playfully shoved her back. Nadine grabbed his muscled-up bicep and rubbed it apologetically. "This time I swear I'm not teasing her."

Chris continued to observe me. We all silently glanced back and forth at each other. Chris shook his head. "Wow, little Alyssa and Jake Masters. Who woulda thunk it?"

I was insulted. "What's that supposed to mean? And besides, we're friends. We just started hanging out again, that's all," I said defensively.

Nadine and Nicole came to my guard as well. "Yeah, and why not Jake Masters?" Nicole piped in.

Nadine punched Chris again and he yelped, getting up and took a few steps away.

"Hey, man, I don't mean it like that." He smiled. "I mean, shit, man, I guess I could see it. Aly, growin' up n'shit." He looked at Nadine and then to me. "It's just hard for me to think of you any other way than my little sister's annoying friend."

"Oh, now I'm annoying!" I chided, half-laughing. "You're a dick, keep digging yourself a hole, douchebag."

"Oh, douchebag, am I?" he exclaimed and dashed over, scooping me up into his arms. I fought him, knowing he was about to throw me into the pool. I heard Nadine scream as she flew into the water in the arms of one of Chris' sporto friends.

Chris held me tightly as he jumped towards the water and just then, in mid-air, I glanced up, seeing Jake come out of Nicole's house into the backyard. Chris held me firmly as we hit the water. I opened my eyes to a million little bubbles as I struggled against his tight grip. He didn't let go of me until our heads popped out of the water.

"Next time you'll think about calling me a douchebag." He laughed, taunting me with a little splash to the face. Chris effortlessly climbed out of the pool. The muscles on his back flexed and shimmered in the late afternoon sunlight. Hopping to his feet he turned, surprised to see Jake. "Oh man, speak of the devil," Chris said loudly. I could feel my face getting red. "We were just talking about you. What's up, bro?"

Was this really happening?

Chapter 16
ALYSSA

I wanted to scream. I now stood at the shallow end of the pool and stared dumbly at everyone. *What the hell was Jake doing here anyway?* Nadine waved eagerly for me to get out of the pool, but my feet were stuck to the bottom as if encased in cement.

"Yeah man, Aly said she'd be over here," Jake explained.

"Hey it's cool," Chris said, awkwardly looking around. "Your girl was teasing me, so I had to let her have it."

I wished I were a mind reader. Jake glanced over at me, giving a nod and lop-sided smile. Chris continued with his nonsense and I wanted to stuff a sock in his mouth. Jake stood there, glancing between everyone.

"So, you and Aly, huh?" Chris asked, snooping—like it was all a lie or something.

I wanted to sink to the bottom of the pool. I pictured myself hurling one of the nearby plastic dog toys at his head.

"Somethin' like that," Jake remarked, validating the rumor.

My head must have exploded. I only heard ringing in my ears. Did I hear him correctly? Searching for Nicole, she'd moved to a lounge, sitting down with a towel up to her mouth to hide her expression. Our eyes met.

"You got a towel for her?" Jake asked.

"Oh, yeah." Chris readily bolted over, grabbing a fresh towel from a large rattan basket near the fire pit.

Jake stood poolside in all his hotness, holding a towel open for me. I emerged fully clothed, sloshing over to him. His brilliant smile broadened across his face. I was mesmerized and breathless. Awkward silence hovered like the L.A. smog as they all watched us. Nadine came to the rescue, clearing her throat.

"So Jake, did you work out the sitch with the party?" she prodded, moving closer to Chris. She killed me! She was a piece of metal and a good-looking guy was the magnet— she was always makin' moves.

"Yeah, I did. That's why I came over. Nine tonight. Two-thirteen Circle Court, Hermosa."

With a towel draped over my shoulders, for a brief moment I felt at ease. My friends and Jake were all in one neat little box. The fear of Nadine freaking out – *Woosh*, it was gone. If Jake didn't care about Rachel, neither would I, for now.

I dried myself, rubbing the towel up under my eyes. I knew I looked like a drowned raccoon with mascara melted underneath my eyes.

"So…what are you doing here," I asked softly, surprised that I was embarrassed by his presence.

"I had it out with Rachel and I told everyone to leave."

"So, what does that mean?"

"It means I'll see them later and Rachel will get over it." He wrapped the towel more tightly around my shoulders and gave me a squeeze. "Walk out front with me."

I trembled inside. "I'll be back," I called out.

Jake and Chris exchanged nods.

"So, when you playin' next? I hear you're going on tour soon," Chris asked.

"Yeah, we leave in a couple of weeks, back before school starts," Jake informed.

My stomach sank. He never mentioned he would be gone the entire summer. Chris finally finished ooo'ing and ahhh'ing over Jake's impending tour, while I had a nervous breakdown, waiting.

I sulked, leaning against Chris's beat up SUV parked in the driveway. That's one thing I could give Chris, even though his family had money, someone would never guess it with him driving that piece of shit around town. I liked that quality in a guy. Too bad he could be such a jerk. I finally met Jake's gaze and his lips peeked with a smile. I went mushy inside.

"What are you staring at?"

"Oh, just a little raccoon." He brushed my matted, sticky hair away from my forehead.

"Oh, my God," I laughed. "I knew it! I thought the same thing when I got out of the pool." I futilely rubbed the towel under my eyes. The mascara was already dried, like black tar.

"Oh don't freak out," he chuckled, his eyes twinkling.

"You're the last person I expected to see here," I admitted.

"You told me to text, so I did. Then I remembered you said you'd be here, so I walked over." He took a step back from me, with his arms outstretched. "Everything ok?"

I watched the palms of his hands turn upwards. My head was swimming. I sighed deeply. "I just didn't expect you here, that's all."

"I just came over here to apologize about Rachel and to tell you I told her to cool it, that hooking up with her was a mistake." He huffed, backing away from me. "Maybe I shouldn't have come here, but I thought we had some sort of understanding. You know, no bullshit."

"I'm not bullshitting," I quickly affirmed.

"Aly, I'm not sure what's going on here, this thing with us." He shook his head, looking as confused as I felt.

"I know, I know…." I said, maybe a little too strongly. I put my face in my hands, speaking into them. "I just want to be alone with you, for a little while. This Rachel stuff is… she's super territorial, and I don't get it. And what do you mean by telling her it was a mistake?"

Jake stared back at me, blinking twice. He was silent for a long moment before speaking. "Ok, here's the deal with Rachel. She's been hanging around for years, literally." He sighed deeply, stumbling with his explanation. "She's best friends with Sienna. You know Dump, our drummer? She's his girlfriend."

"I know all this, Jake." I reminded him.

"Wait, just listen. I knew she'd always liked me, and one night, we were drinking after a show, doing things we shouldn't be doing, and we hooked up."

I swore the earth shook when I heard his admission.

"Ok," I said, trying to keep my cool. "So here we are. We admit we like each other, and now you're leaving on tour? I mean, when were you going to tell me?" I sighed, only able to stare down at my bare feet. I couldn't look at him. "I don't know what to think. I'm bummed to hear you're leaving for, like…weeks. The whole summer, that's all."

I finally lifted my head and met his eyes.

"Try not to think about it, then." He laughed and I gave him a tight stare. I didn't think it was funny. "Aly, I have shows here all over LA and OC, so I'll be home some of the time, and I'll be back one week before school starts."

Then I spotted more trouble bobbing and weaving in the distance.

"Great," I muttered. He turned to see what I was looking at. Matt and Grant were coming towards us on their skateboards.

Jake threw his hand up. "Ok, well, are you coming? I don't really want to hang out here, you know. Grant doesn't think the best of me since I didn't pick him to be in the band."

"Why didn't you?"

Jake shrugged. "Believe it or not, I actually do think he's better, but it's the age thing, with Grant being only 14. Notting, our manager, doesn't want to babysit."

"Really? Did you tell Grant that?"

"No, of course not," he guffawed. "We just picked Mike because he was the oldest. He fit pretty much what we were looking for. Look, are you coming?"

As soon as he spit out his last word, I heard the slapping of the skateboard against the cement curb.

"Hey," I greeted half-heartedly. Jake stepped away from me as Matt walked up. I felt as if I should have a sign on my head flashing *Awkward*. Matt still had no idea I'd had a change of heart. What if Jake had a change of heart about me while he was away? Then I'd be breaking Matt's heart for nothing. I was so confused, but every fiber in me wanted Jake, not Matt.

"Dude, Aly, what happened to you?" Matt chuckled. "You look like shit."

"Aww, did you get pushed into the pool?" Grant teased as he put his arm around my shoulders, giving me a squeeze. Grant stared at Jake, giving him a head nod. "Sup, Jake."

"Hey man," Jake said a bit uneasy. "Alright Aly, I'll talk to you later."

I was frozen. I wanted to say that I'd be right there, but nothing came out. I wasn't ready to tell Matt, but I knew he was about to find out. Everyone on the other side of the house now knew about Jake and I. I felt guilty. But Matt took his sweet time figuring out if he liked me, so I shouldn't feel bad, I told myself. I stood silent, watching Jake's God-like figure walk away down the street. I felt a hard nudge at my shoulder.

"What's he doing here?" Matt asked.

"Huh, what?" I responded, in a daze.

"I asked what Jake was doing here. Is everything ok?"

"Uh, yeah, everything's fine. I need to go home and change. Just look at me." I looked down at myself, holding my arms out to the side with a crooked smile. "Not my best look."

"Alright, you comin' back?"

"I don't know," I replied, distracted. "I need to go back inside for a sec."

Dashing back poolside, I quickly unloaded a plan and requested everyone not to let on about Jake to Matt. I wanted to do it myself.

They nodded back at me in understanding.

Chapter 17

ALYSSA

It was nearly dark and my stomach was in knots with the anticipation of the evening's unknown events. I said good-bye to my parents and walked out the door, hoping they wouldn't ask questions. I cut across our freshly mowed lawns, looking around to see if anyone was watching me. I felt like I was doing something wrong—which I was. If my dad knew what I was up to, he'd lock me in my room with a dead bolt. I knocked softly on the door and waited. I was hoping it would be his mom who answered the door, but it was Jake, in all of his bright-eyed perfectness. My knees buckled.

"Hey," he said, smiling, not too surprised to see me. As I walked past him, he leaned into me and sniffed my hair. "Strawberry girl."

"Hey." I giggled in return. "Where's your mom?"

"She's getting ready to go to Notting's."

"She's seeing your manager?" I asked, curious.

"Um, well, not sure really," he said, laughing. "I personally think so, but they keep it on the down-low, you know. They talk *band strategy*." He sniffed, gesturing with finger quotations. "I know Notting's in love with her, but she's still stuck on who knows what. She has issues."

"That must suck, for Notting I mean."

"Yeah, I'm sure it does." He turned, the hint of sadness gone, staring at me for a moment. "Let's go to my room. Unless you want to stay out here?" All I could do was shrug off the weirdness that filled me and follow him, wondering a bit more about his mom.

"Isn't it weird for you, knowing that your manager is into your mom?"

"There's so much to it, Aly," he said, almost contrite. "Notting's been around a long time. You don't remember him?"

"Not really," I admitted.

"Notting's been like a father to me, and not just managing the band. Him and my mom, they work together as a team."

"Oh, wow. That's awesome."

"Yeah, it's been cool. I guess." He shrugged. I felt as if he was trying to convince himself.

We settled into a conversation about his upcoming tour and the cities he was going to. This was a West Coast tour: California, Arizona, New Mexico, Oregon and Washington. Two dates were right here in the Hollywood and Orange County area. I was dying to be at each of them. I wondered if Rachel and Sienna normally traveled with them, and if they would this time, too.

"Jake," I asked, hesitant. "I have a question."

His eyes lit up cautiously. "Hmm?"

He cocked his head waiting for me to spit it out.

"Ok, well, I just want to know what you meant by *hooking up* with Rachel."

Jake's smile disappeared from his face and he squirmed, bending his neck from side to side.

"Aly, look…"

"Did you sleep with her?" I whispered, looking him straight in the eyes.

Jake leaned way back and rubbed his hands over his face.

"Aly, it doesn't matter what happened with Rachel." His shoulders slumped. He looked ill as he continued. "Ok, look, I'm not gonna to lie to you. Yes. I did. But it was…it was something that shouldn't have happened."

"So what you're saying is…you hook up with girls that you don't care about, and it means nothing for you to do so."

I knew that I was being unfair, but this is just what my sister warned me about. *"Guys like Jake."* I thought my insides would turn into gravel.

"Look, Aly, I don't want to make it more than it was, 'cause it was nothin'…and no, I didn't make it a point to hook up with her. It's just something that happened."

I didn't know what else to say. There was a sick and twisted part of me that wanted to know what it was like. I wanted him to give me a play-by-play. "Why did you do it, then?"

Jake looked at me blankly for a long moment, searching my eyes, and all the sound went from the room. All I could see was his beautiful face as I waited for him to give me details.

"Aly, what am I gonna do with you? Seriously, you make me crazy." He took a breath. "A good crazy."

He laughed nervously and moved closer to me. My heart pounded so hard I could feel the blood rushing through my veins.

"I thought I explained this," he said with a bit of edge. "We were all hanging out and one thing led to another. She came onto me and I just kinda went with it. Then it was over. Rachel obviously feels…"

"Feels what, Jake? If you were to sleep with me and blow me off, I would feel the same way," I interrupted, slightly hostile. I was angry at hearing the truth and more so that I felt a tinge of pity for her.

"Aly, wait a second," he said, beaten. He'd had enough of my verbal assault. "It's not like that with you. It sounds so cliché, but one day you'll understand." He sniffed. "The thing is, I don't really want you to understand."

"What's that supposed to mean?"

Jake cradled his head in his hands for a long moment. Finally, he turned to face me. "Aly, it's a physical thing with Rachel. That's what it was that night."

Vomit. Flashes of them together made my stomach lurch.

"And what does that have to do with you not wanting me to understand?"

He shook his head and closed his eyes, frustrated. When he returned my gaze, his eyes roamed my face. "I like you, Aly. I feel comfortable with you. I know you care about me for me for the right reasons, with us knowing each other forever, and all. That's what's so legit. And the fact that you feel free to question me without reservations…it's strong." He shifted, moving closer to me. "Not to mention I'm attracted to you, more than conversationally."

Every word echoed and etched itself into my brain.

"Who talks like this?" I marveled, blown away by his honesty.

Fidgety, I began to fluff the pillow next to me.

"What? You asked. I'm attracted to you." He pointed at his chest. "I felt it right away, but because you've been like family, it's made me think twice about the way I'm feeling. I know how your dad feels about you dating, considering what your sister went through." He took my hand into his and it sent chills up my arm. He noticed and rubbed my forearm softly. I couldn't feel any other part of my body, only the caress of his hand. He let out a huge sigh. "And this, this is what makes me want more, because I know you're for real."

"Do you just lay here at night thinking how to be clever with words?" I asked, enamored by his admission.

He laughed, embarrassed. "Sorry, I don't mean to sound lame." He put his arm around my neck and kissed my temple. I felt his chest rise. "I dig the way you smell."

Yeah, and I dig a million other things about you.

"Jake." My voice cracked. A big lump formed choking me. I gulped. Being so full of emotion, the tears came knocking without warning. I kept my head hung low. "Um, thank you."

He pulled me to him and our skin touched. My forehead dissolved against his neck. The scent of him was so overpowering that the lump in my throat liquefied like it'd never been there. Now I was fighting the urge to kiss him.

"Hey, you've been nothing but honest about your feelings. You deserve the same."

As much as I wanted to stay glued to him forever I was anxious to get going.

"So what's up with this party? I need to get over to Nicole's if we're going." I said softly.

"You're really coming?" he said, surprised. "Aren't you worried you'll run into your sister?"

Jolt.

"Oh my God, don't remind me. Do you think she'll be there?" Dread spread over me.

"Not sure, I don't see her around all that much anymore."

"Will you text me when you get there, let me know if she's there?"

"How you gettin' there? I can drive you guys," he offered, sweetly.

"That'd be cool, but I think because we have this thing going on with Nadine and Chris. He is supposedly driving us, so we'll meet you there."

"Chris who?"

"Chris Hamilton, Nicole's brother."

"Ah, yeah, that's right. Really? Those two?" he said in disbelief.

"Yeah. I guess I was worried about *us* for nothing. Apparently she's been really crushing on him forever and he's finally paying attention to her. Who knows," I said, laughing. "It gets a little weird with girls, Jake. We have these unspoken rules, you know."

"Ah. I see. Cool."

I stood up to leave. I wanted to kiss him, like really kiss him—but I was too chicken to be that bold. I had no idea what I was doing and I didn't want to embarrass myself.

"I'm gonna go. I'll see you later."

He grabbed me by the hips and my knees buckled. "You're awesome, you know that?" He paused, his impossibly perfect blue eyes looked intensely into my own. "Please, don't pay any attention to Rachel. This'll blow over. She'll get over it." he stood up and took my face into his hands. "I promise it'll all work out."

He gently kissed my lips and my eyes fell shut. I opened my eyes and his face remained close to mine. I didn't want the moment to end. His hands moved down my neck to my shoulders and he rested his forehead against mine.

"Aly, I care about what happens with you. I'm sorry if I've made some fucked up impression."

Jake pulled me close and held me snug. I ran my hands up his back, and for the first time, I really hugged him back. I pressed against him, wanting to smell like him when I left. I breathed him in so deeply. I felt him respond, holding me tighter.

"I've been hearing the vibration of your phone for the last half hour. I guess you'd better get goin'." He looked at me tenderly, like he wanted more. "I'm sure your girls are gonna want the low down."

"I'm not sharing *everything* with them," I said, curtly. "I don't need my sibs finding out anything. I mean Kyle would be cool about it, but Allison is so lame. You have no idea. Not sure what her deal is. You should have seen her face when I told her I'd hung out with you."

"Really?" His brows knitted together.

"Yeah…on the down low is all I gotta to say."

"Yeah, *my* mom would probably shit a bowling ball."

———

153

A Taylor Swift upbeat melodic tune was the dominant sound coursing through Nicole's house. I could also hear a TV battling for attention. It was loud and bright. I would have guessed every light was on in the house, another contrast to my darkened cave of a home. Nadine was already there. I could hear her singing along to the music, beyond badly.

Oh God.

I didn't know how Nicole's parents tuned it out. I hardly ever saw Nicole's father, Jerry. He owned some sort of building or Development Company, hence the robust lifestyle they were able to live. I envied Nicole and all of her stuff. She got everything she wanted and shopped at all the most exclusive boutiques. She was always loaning Nadine and me her clothes and shoes, which helped my pathetically unfortunate wardrobe. I barely had a sense for fashion.

I walked up the thickly padded stairs and Nadine's voice grew louder. She was so off-key that I wondered if she was tone deaf. *How embarrassing.* I laughed to myself as I cracked open Nicole's bedroom door. The music was so loud they didn't hear me. They were standing in front of a wall of mirrors, putting on their make-up, already dressed the part for our first high school party. I was giddy with excitement.

"Hello!" I said loudly. There was no way my parents would ever allow this much madness swirling around. Nicole's mom had to be either deaf or on meds to be so mellow. I walked over, turning down the music. "Hey, where are those black biker boots? I wanna borrow them."

"In my closet." Nicole pointed. "Boots, huh? That's a bit different."

"Good for you, Aly," Nadine said approvingly. "Let's see the outfit." She spun around, stuffing the mascara wand back in its hole.

"I had to raid Allison's clothes. If she finds out she'll kill me," I warned, pulling out my sister's shorts and the blousy black low-cut top. With my hand still in the bag, I paused for effect. The devil inside me cheered me on, and with theatrical flair, I pulled out the lace bra-vest.

"Shut up, hooker!" Nadine yelped, grabbing it out of my hands. She looked at me with animated fire. "Gahh, I wanna wear this! You're gonna look hot, and Rachel will have to step off!"

We all squealed in unified excitement. I begged for Nicole to do my hair. She was the one who subscribed to every fashion magazine and had every beauty product known to man. She'd know what to do.

"Sit there and put your makeup on," Nicole instructed, pointing to the Asian-inspired throw rug lying in front of her wall of mirrors. "You are gonna wear makeup, right?"

"Uh, duh, of course," I said sarcastically. "It's now or never."

I stared at myself for a long moment, wondering where to start.

Chapter 18

ALYSSA

We arrived at one of the many mini mansions that lined Circle Avenue. It had a waterfall pouring down the front of the house. The lights reflected off the water, shimmering like diamonds. There were lights all around lit up like a Hawaiian resort at night. The landscape was lush with tropical plants. The house was three stories tall, with windows everywhere. It was obvious during the daytime it would have an insane ocean view. We were only a few blocks away from the beach, perched on one of its small rolling hills in Hermosa Beach. You could hear the thumping of music as we parked the car. Chris turned to us, his tight stare bouncing back and forth between us.

"Ok, here's the deal. You guys stick together," he told us. "You'll need some cash to get in. It's not free, so I hope you have money. If the cops show up, leave and walk down to the Green Store on twenty-second street, and I'll pick you up there. If something happens, text."

"Why do we have to pay to get in?" I asked curiously, wondering why he'd failed to mention this until now.

"For the beer n'stuff," Chris explained. "Speaking of, Nadine, you don't need to pay me for the ride—just cover me getting in."

"Does that mean I don't have to do your laundry?" Nicole asked, hopeful.

"Uh, no. You still have to do my laundry," Chris said, laughing as he got out of the car.

"You bitch," Nicole whined to Nadine. "You're gonna help me do his effing laundry!"

"Dude, I'll do all of it." She smiled, shoving at Nicole to get out of the car.

My heart thudded so hard I could feel it in my fingertips. As soon as Nadine and Nicole got out, we were all shining like beacons. Chris came around the car to meet us, amusement painted his face.

"This'll be interesting. I feel kinda lucky. Hate to say it, but you three may make my game a little better with the ladies," Chris said, rubbing his hands together.

"Oh, get over yourself already," Nadine said, rolling her eyes. "Nobody wants you."

"Oh, shit, snap." Nicole laughed in Chris' face.

"Come on Nadine, you know you want me," Chris purred in her ear and practically draped his massive frame over her.

Nadine tried to shove him off and walk away, but he stayed attached to her, laughing. They actually made a cute couple. Chris may have met his match in Nadine—especially if he liked being slapped around.

We paid five bucks a head to get in. Chris knew every single person we passed as we made our way toward a crowd of people holding big red cups.

"I'll be right back, I'm gonna find me a cup," he said, and disappeared into the crowd.

"Hey, hello! Get me one!" Nadine shouted after him then turned to us. "He better get me one, or I'll kick his ass."

"Oh, my God, I'm so freaking nervous," I whispered loudly. "I don't wanna obviously be looking for Jake, but do you guys see him?"

"I'm looking," Nicole said. "I can't believe how many hot guys are here! It's like an Abercrombie candy store."

"I know!" I giggled, "Can you freaking believe we're here?"

I was wound up tight and totally trippin'.

"Ok—I see Jake," Nadine murmured into my ear. "He's way over on the other side of the pool. Ugh, Rachel is there too, along with a gang of other girls."

"Shit. I'm freaking out." I panicked and shook my hands violently, trying to distract myself.

"Calm down, Aly! You can do this. You look hot –stop slouching," Nicole ordered, slapping my shoulder.

Chris appeared through the crowd holding a stack of cups, and to my surprise he handed one to each of us. "One beer," he instructed, pointing his finger in our faces.

I looked at Nicole, pursing my lips. I didn't really want to drink beer, but I'd better fill my cup to fit in, I thought. Nadine and Chris were already in line, following the horde of other teens. Their arms extended forward in hopes that their cup would be filled next. Nicole and I followed the crowd. I hoped Jake would notice me. I glanced in his direction from time to time. He kept looking around, too. Looking for me? I couldn't believe how many girls were hanging around him and his band mates. The one standing the closest to him was Rachel.

Nicole finally joined us. "I see Jake way over there. And what a surprise! Not one girl is vying for his attention," she said sarcastically.

"Do you think I'll have trouble with those girls at school because of Jake?"

"No, they'll probably kiss your ass and wanna be your best friend," Nadine broke in.

"Beware of fake friends," Nicole warned, her eyes going wide. "Shit, Jake sees us...it's registering. Oh my God, you should see his face, Aly."

"Oh man, does Rachel see me?" I forced myself not to look in their direction in an attempt to play it cool.

"Does who see what?" Chris butted in, leaning in closer to us.

Nadine shook her head at Chris, ignoring his question.

"No, Jake's just standing there, staring. Let's go over there and get this over with," Nadine decided. "No chicken-shit shyness, Alyssa Montgomery. You're doing this for all of us! Chris, lead the way over to Jake," she ordered, shoving him forward.

I went numb. I couldn't feel myself move as I followed Chris, Nadine and Nicole. I focused only on Jake's face and anxiously waited for him to realize it was *me*. His eyes moved over each one of us and settled back on me. His mouth fell slightly open and a smile spread across his picture-perfect face. He squeezed past the crowd around him coming toward us. My heart was pounding harder than ever. He was dressed in all black, his hair was messy and sort of spiky; not the usual relaxed, fluffy way I'd seen over the past several days. He looked the part of everything a rock star should be. He didn't acknowledge any of the others and stopped close in front of me, placing his hand at the small of my back.

"Wow, I think I'm in a dream sequence," he whispered in my ear. I looked over at Nadine and she was smiling from ear to ear. She looked over in the other direction and I followed her glance. Rachel and the rest of the Envies were watching us. I looked back into Jake's eyes. "I'm speechless," he added. "You look amazing."

Jake's compliments made me woozy.

I giggled nervously. "Thanks. Um...everyone's staring at us."

"Yeah, so what? They're just wondering who you are, and to be honest, so am I."

"What?"

"What do you mean what? You look like a completely different person," he said. His eyes roamed over my new appearance. "Uh, you're owning it right now."

"So, you're not embarrassed to be seen with me? The super underclassman?"

"Aw, come on, shut it with that, most definitely not. You're amazing no matter what, but you just look tremendous all done up." He smiled. "What gives? I'm curious."

I hung my head, embarrassed. "Well, it's my first, you know, high school party, so I thought I'd dress the part." I leaned in closer to him, as if someone would hear me over the loud music. "You know, you're embarrassing me."

"Don't be. Lighten up, and please tell me you're not drinking that," he asked, pointing at my cup.

"Uh, you are, so why can't I?" I challenged.

"You're too young, that's why."

I didn't like that he always pointed out my age. I rebelled, bringing the cup to my lips and took the biggest gulp I could muster. I swallowed, staring defiantly at him with a smirk of triumph.

His eyes narrowed. "I don't think it's a good idea, but I'm not gonna preach."

"Good." I took another big swig, finishing it off. My first beer, and I immediately began to feel light-headed and less nervous. I hadn't had any dinner, so I knew it was the beer. "You know Jake, everyone here is doing the same thing. It's not like I'm any different."

"I still don't like it. I don't want you gettin' all sloppy drunk." He looked in the direction of Rachel and her friends. "See those girls? You don't wanna be them."

"Speaking of which," I said, eager to change the subject. "Has she said anything else about…the situation?"

"She's acting like nothing happened, but as you can see the others are catching on." He casually glanced over at them. "They're the fringe girls, the ones to the left. Do you want to come over and meet everyone?"

"You're not serious!" I choked.

"Hey, sorry to interrupt, but we wanna walk around," Nadine announced.

"Um," I couldn't spit any words out. I just wanted to be with Jake, and now I had to follow my stupid friends through this stupid party.

I jutted my chin towards Rachel. "You wanna walk with us, or are you gonna stay here with Almost Famous?"

I couldn't believe the words and the sassy tone that came up from my throat and out of my mouth. Jake's eyes widened and his eyebrows rose slightly. A crooked grin appeared on his face.

"Aly, you fascinate me," he said, looking at Nadine, Chris and Nicole. He proceeded to drape his arm around my shoulders. "Let's walk, screw them."

"You don't have to…"

He interrupted, "Aly, I don't give a shit about them. Bobby and Mike will manage fine on their own."

I wanted so badly to turn and see the look on Rachel's face as I walked away with Jake and my crew.

Chapter 19

ALYSSA

The house, if you wanted to call it that, was a set piece. It was something out of one of those decorator magazines, plantation style with dark hues and green leafy plants everywhere. The beamed ceilings were at least 14 feet high, and the floor plan was wide open. Jake led the way to a room that was as big as a 3-car garage. It had a pool table and a small movie theater-like sitting area with an actual movie screen. Growing up in this town, I'd seen my share of nice homes, but this home was definitely the most impressive of them all.

I leaned against the pool table and Jake stepped over, standing directly in front of me. He moved in closer, hips pressing against mine, and he wrapped his hands around my waist. "Let's walk to the beach."

His eyes were tender and penetrating, they made my blood rush. "Um, I'd feel weird leaving the girls here. So, who lives here?"

Jake nodded slowly at me, conscious of my detour. I was thankful he didn't call me out on it. "Alright, let's warm up this pool table then," he said kindly, slapping it. "And as for who lives here, Brandon and Sarah Miller do. Brandon's a senior volley guy and Sarah is in Nadine's class."

He moved away from me, running his hand along the emerald green felt of the pool table as he walked to the other side. He bent down, gathering the brightly colored balls. I decided to look for pool cues. At least I knew how to play pool and wouldn't embarrass myself. My eyes swept the room, spotting Rachel and Mike and the rest of their crew coming toward us. They looked like the cast of some TV show. Perfect, flawless and arrogant. *Shit, where are Nadine and Nicole?* I frantically looked around for them. Nadine was the only one I saw, and she was all the way on the other side of the room, enjoying her own spotlight. I turned looking in the other direction and my eyeballs slammed into Rachel, standing next to me.

"Hi. So, you're Aly, Jake's next door neighbor, right?" She asked in a totally callous tone, like she'd forgotten she'd met me earlier at Jake's house.

She held her hand out in some lame gesture, which prompted me to take it in mine. I looked her straight in the eyes, giving her limp, clammy hand a firm squeeze. "Yeah, nice to see you again."

I thought Rachel was pretty. It made me boil inside admitting it to myself. She had deep blue eyes and fair skin. She wore the same bright red lipstick that her friend, Sienna, wore. Rachel was drunk too, and hung all over Mike. Mike wore a perturbed expression and kept pushing her away—I didn't think she noticed. He gave me a crooked smile, shrugging his shoulders. Rachel looked back and forth between the two of us, giving him an unexpected firm push, shoving him away.

"What the fuck, man, are you making fun of me?" She swung at him and missed. She looked back at me swaying a bit, shaking her head. "The nerve. So where's Jakey? Oh there he is." She paused, giving him a long stare. I could see her brain churning. "So you play pool? We should play *teamsies*. Mike and I against you and Jake, come on. Whad'ya say?"

Did I really have a choice? She strode away toward Jake, weaving like the snake that she was. This had to be the most insane moment of my life. Mike moved in uncomfortably closer to me. "You look different," he said in a low voice, smiling approvingly. "I like it."

I was shocked at his compliment. The only thing I'd ever heard come out of his mouth was derogatory remarks about Jake wanting to do me because I was a virgin.

"Thanks," I said, looking up at him, checking out the scruff sprouting from his jawline. He was definitely good looking in his own scrappy-badass way.

"So, you and Jake official."

"What do you mean? Is that a question?"

"Not really. I guess it's more of a statement, but I want to hear it from you. You know a heart's been broken because of this," he informed quietly, not looking at me.

"What are you? The messenger?" I snapped.

"No, I just got my ear talked off. Rachel's been with Jake a long time," he stuttered—obviously shocked at my return.

"*With* Jake," I echoed, my tone sarcastic. "Is that right? He told me they were only friends, that they'd spent one night together."

"I guess that's how it went down." He paused and nodded. "So he told you that, huh? Anyway, she's still heartbroken."

"That's got nothing to do with me. I had no idea. That's between her and Jake." I was getting more uncomfortable. I felt like he was fishing in some faux friendly way.

"It has everything to do with you, in her eyes at least," Mike continued to explain.

"Look, did you come over here to give me a hard time? If you did, you can leave," I spat back.

"Wow, calm down. No, no, don't get me wrong. I'm sorry. Rachel just filled my head with a bunch of shit for the last hour. I just wanted to hear it from you." He tried to laugh off the ill tension between us. A moment passed as we watched Jake and Rachel mingle together, Jake clearly not having her attitude. "She's got you pegged all wrong. I did too. You're not some meek little pushover, are you?"

"Not when someone's giving me shit. Don't forget, I have two older sibs who think their shit doesn't stink either."

"Hmm, you just look innocent. Nice." He grinned, winking at me.

My stomach fluttered. Maybe I was being too rough on him. "I'm sorry, Mike, but she's crazy. I had no idea about her, and besides, why should I care?"

"You shouldn't. How long have you guys been seeing each other?" he asked, trying to be nonchalant.

I was getting sick of all the prying questions. I took notice of the full cup of beer in his hand.

"Can I have a drink?"

"Yeah, sure," he offered, handing me his cup. I took a big gulp, and as if Jake had an *Aly's drinking beer* radar imbedded in him, he was standing next to me taking it out of my hand, again.

"Dude what the fuck are you doing?" he spewed. Jake's eyes were on fire.

"Woah, bro, calm down. She's the one who asked, and besides, I saw her drinking with you outside."

"What did I tell you before? Don't fuckin' offer her anything," he spat, pointing his finger in Mike's face.

I stepped between him and Mike, placing my hands on Jake's chest. "Jake, calm down. I'm sorry. I asked him. It's not his fault," I explained, trying to defend Mike. I didn't want them to fight because of me.

Jake's clamped jaw relaxed slightly. "I don't need you going home drunk and stinking of beer, Aly. We'll talk about it later." He turned to Mike. "Hey bro, I'm sorry. I just don't need her parents finding out about this. Sending her home drunk is just something that'll set off a flare."

"Man, I get it, no worries." Mike took his cup back from Jake, taking a drink. "So, we gonna play teams or what?"

Jake glanced at Rachel, who was leaning against the pool table chatting with her friends. "I suppose, if she doesn't throw up or fall over first."

Jake took my hand leading me away. I looked back at Mike and mouthed *sorry,* and he waived his hand, signaling for me not to worry. He was the last person I wanted to piss off. I wanted him on my side.

"After this game I want to leave, ok?" he said firmly, as if there was no other option.

"Yeah, sure, but I'm supposed to be staying at Nadine's tonight, so I'm not sure how to handle leaving them."

"Oh, that's right." His eyes dulled. Clearly he'd forgotten whom I'd come with and my concocted arrangements. "I was just hoping you'd sneak back over tonight."

Would the girls understand if I said I wanted to go home? I searched the room for Nicole again. Where the hell was she? My eyes halted on Nadine and Chris, who were now making out in plain sight. Nadine was not the typical girl Chris went out with. His norm was the all-American cheerleader type. Nadine was a vampy sex kitten in the making. I envied her confidence and her *who gives a shit* attitude— I could never make-out in public like that.

"Let me talk to the girls and feel it out," I offered.

He nodded and gave me quick peck on the cheek. My eyes darted straight to Rachel as if I had no control over them. Besides her cool rise to grab a pool cue, there was no emotion or reaction registered on her face as she absorbed our every move.

"Ok, who wants to break?" she asked loudly, staring straight at me.

"I'll do it," I said with confidence, and smirked at her. Growing up with a pool table in my house, I knew I had to have this.

Our game went quickly. My elation over the win didn't last long when the thought of my sister popped in my head. I wondered where she was and if she was there. This was the first big party of the summer. She just had to be around.

"What's wrong?" Jake asked, concerned.

"I forgot about Allison. She's gotta be here. There's no way she'd miss this."

"Ok, calm down, we'll ask Chris and Nadine to take a look around," he said reassuringly.

"Hey Chris," Jake called out, walking over to him. "Will you do us a favor? Cruise around and look for Aly's sister. You know her, right?"

"Yeah, sure." Chris grabbed Nadine's hand and they whizzed off on their stealthy mission.

Jake measured me with his eyes, tracing my mood. "We'll just hang here until the coast is clear," he offered, rubbing my back.

He took my hand leading me over to the newly arrived Dump and Sienna. Sienna was amazing to look at. I loved everything about her style. She was like something off of a funky fashion runway. She was wearing a tight black low-cut shredded t-shirt with skin-tight, pinstriped knickers. The fishnets she wore underneath peeked out above her boots. Her signature red lipstick was flawless. I was speechless. I had no idea what to say to someone as cool as her.

"'Sup, man," Jake greeted Dump, exchanging a knuckle jab.

My confidence level was in the dirt standing there next to Sienna. I wondered what she saw in Dump. He was an oversized muscle-head with nearly translucent eyes. He was a few years older, twenty if I remembered correctly. He had a dragon tattoo on his bald head, and gnarly tattoo sleeves running up to his neck. Oddly enough, the both of them matched perfectly. She was china doll pretty, a gentle compliment to his harsh look and overpowering build.

She shocked me by introducing herself, extending her hand. "Hi Aly, I'm Sienna. I met you at Jake's last week." Her voice was sweet and sincere, taking me off guard.

"Hi, yeah, I remember. Nice to see you again." I had to look away from her, or I'd embarrass myself.

"You look quite different than the last time I saw you. I almost didn't recognize you." She nodded approvingly.

"Oh, yeah," I replied looking down at my outfit, afraid that *I* looked like I was the one trying too hard.

"It's a good look, I dig it." I couldn't believe my ears. She liked what I'd put together. I felt the heat starting to rise up my neck and it was about to hit my face at any second.

"I'll be right back." I forced a smile and took off to look for a bathroom. I couldn't believe my reaction to Sienna's compliment. I was nearly hyperventilating. I spotted a few girls who looked like they were in line for the bathroom. "Hey, is this the line for the bathroom?"

"Yeah," the cute hippy chick confirmed. She was clearly using the wall as a kickstand. I wasn't impressed with everyone sloshing around. I was thirsty and starving. My stomach grew sour, and it felt like it was eating itself. I took a few deep breaths and started to feel slightly better, realizing I actually did have to pee.

"Hey, so you're going out with Jake Masters? I saw him with his arm around you," Hippy Chick asked with a not-so-friendly smirk on her drunken face.

"Um, I'm his next door neighbor. We've been friends forever." I waved it off like it was no big deal, hoping they'd leave me alone.

"So what school do you go to? I've never seen you before," her friend with long black curly hair slurred.

Here we go. My stomach turned in annoyance.

"Oh, I'll actually be attending Seaside this next school year," I informed them, trying to steer clear of my freshman status.

"What's your year? Junior?" Hippy Chick prodded.

I gulped. I didn't see any way to avoid answering. I mean, I couldn't lie, could I? No! Then they'd find out and I'd be *that* girl. "Um, I'll be a freshman." I smiled, trying to feel good about myself.

"Really? That's, uh, news. You don't look like a freshman…I mean compared to my sister that is."

"Well, like I said, Jake's been my next-door neighbor my whole life, so, it's…" I jumped when I heard Jake's voice.

"Hey, hi, sorry for interrupting," he apologized, smiling with curious eyes.

The two girls choked out their next words. "Oh, no, it's ok. We were just getting to know…" Hippy Chick paused gesturing at me.

"Aly, my name's Aly."

Jake looked amused and turned his focus onto me.

"So you ok? You left so fast I thought you might be sick," he said warmly and placed his arm over my shoulders affectionately.

"No, I just have to pee," I laughed, reassuring him. "No worries. Did Nadine and Chris come back?"

"No, but I'll go look around. I'll meet you at the bottom of the stairs over there." He pointed.

"So, Jake," hippy chick hesitated. "Aly tells me she's gonna be a freshman next year."

The amused look disappeared from Jake's face and a forced smile replaced it. "Yes, yes she is." He turned to me, stiff. "Aly, there's a bathroom upstairs you can use." He led me away, and I didn't bother saying goodbye.

I wasn't sure what to think of those girls, but what I was sure of was Jake giving me an earful. He explained that I needed to censor myself; that not everyone was what he or she appeared to be. We arrived at a closed door, and Jake opened it without knocking. To my horror, we walked through the door and ran right into Rachel and Sienna. I'm sure they all heard my intake of breath. I felt like I had the wind kicked out of me.

"Oh man, sorry," Jake apologized, stammering, just as surprised as I was. "Uh, Aly needs to use the bathroom."

I was so on edge I began to dig my fingernails into the palms of my hands. I was surprised to see Rachel look like she'd been crying. She turned away quickly as Sienna chatted us up.

"Hey, yeah, the bathroom's over there." Sienna pointed and I quickly walked into the bathroom, locking the door, and pressed my ear against it trying to listen for any conversation. The murmur of their voices was too low, with the exception of Rachel's outburst. *"I don't fucking care, Jake, whatever!"* I turned looking in the mirror. I was holding up nicely. My makeup was still intact but my stomach was in a tight ball. I must have peed for five minutes straight when I finally managed to sit on the toilet.

I was a nervous wreck about walking back into the lion's den. When I opened the door, I saw Rachel and Jake sitting on the bed at the other side of the room. Sienna was looking at herself in a mirror. I'd concluded this must be a guest room, because it didn't look personalized. Jake immediately stood up. He said something inaudible and strode over to me with a weak smile. His eyes were wide with dismay. He must have felt bad about Rachel.

"Let's get out of here. I don't wanna stay here anymore," he said, grabbing my hand and opened the door. "Later, Sienna." He glanced back at her. Rachel never looked up from her hands, and I felt bad for her for the first time. She actually did have at least one sensitive human bone in her body. I tried to wipe it from my mind, feeling the warmth of Jake's hand in mine.

I spotted Nicole with some guy standing outside next to the pool. I tugged on Jake's hand and led us in a different direction, making a beeline for Nicole. I practically accosted her as soon as I reached her. "Dude, Nicole, where have you been? I've been worried about you," I demanded to know.

"Oh, I'm sorry. I was hanging with Mitch here. He's a friend of my brother's," she explained. "Mitch this is Aly and Jake."

Mitch appeared suddenly awestruck, staring at Jake, and didn't even glance my way. "Yeah man, Jake. I'm totally into your music, cool. I see you around campus, but you know how it is," he babbled on. I looked at Nicole trying not to laugh at Mitch's fan-girling. She snickered too.

"Yeah. You're varsity, with Chris, right?" Jake responded respectfully.

"Yeah, that's right," Mitch confirmed, beaming, satisfied that Jake knew who he was.

As if things could get any more dramatic, I suddenly I heard her shrill voice, my name being called out for the world to hear—*Alyssa Montgomery!* - I froze. It was my sister. My whole night was ruined in that instant. She was going to embarrass me in front of the entire school. I looked at

Jake with panic in my eyes and he knew instantly what is was. He glanced over my shoulder and then immediately left my side. I got tunnel vision and I thought I would pass out. Nicole grabbed my arm and steadied me. I could barely comprehend the words coming out of her mouth.

Everything moved in slow motion as I tried to focus on Nicole's lips. I took in a deep breath and closed my eyes, waiting for my sister to yank me out of there by my hair. The moments passed and she wasn't at my side. Finally, I was able to hear what Nicole was saying.

"Aly, calm down, Jake's talking to her." She rubbed my back. Mitch stared at us, looking around, confused.

"What's the problem?" he finally asked.

"She's not supposed to be here," Nicole explained, worry knitted across her forehead.

"Aw man, that sucks," he said, bringing a flask to his lips. He was obviously into the harder stuff.

"What's going on, what are they doing?" I asked fearfully, afraid to lock eyes with my sister. "This is killing me. I want to leave."

"They're coming over here," Nicole blurted.

Before I knew it, my sister was in my face, looking me up and down. Her new boyfriend, Owen Thompson, was standing next to her, looking confused by her angry outburst. He wore a Euro-inspired side-swept hairstyle and slim-fitting pants, probably because he *was* from England.

"Hey, Allison, calm down," he said, placing his hand on her shoulder.

Yeah, Allison, take his advice.

She shrugged it off, ignoring him.

"Hi," I managed to squeak out.

"Jake tells me he's gonna take you home," she said coldly and turned her ice-witch eyes onto Nicole. "And I'll bet if your parents found you here they wouldn't be so happy either." Whatever Jake said to my sister worked—sort of. I just wanted to find Nadine and get out of there. I walked away, tugging on Nicole's belt loop. Jake trailed behind, saying one last thing to my sister—I couldn't hear what it was. Nicole and I squeezed through the crowd, choosing an open path near the pool's edge. My sister and Jake followed way behind us.

We were slowly making our way out when I heard a voice near my ear. "*It was nice to see you again.*"

The next thing I knew, I was falling into the swimming pool.

Chapter 20
ALYSSA

No, this wasn't happening! I turned attempting desperately to grab onto someone, anyone. The person I tried to latch onto was Rachel, and with an evil glint in her eye, she yanked her arm away from me. I hit the water with a flailing theatrical plunge. As I was sinking to the bottom of the pool, I wanted to stay there, drowning in my humiliation. I gasped for air when my head bobbed to the surface, and the first thing I heard was my sister yelling. I treaded to the steps, trying not to cry. I climbed out, glaring at Rachel, wishing she'd burn into flames right then and there. I pictured myself tackling her into the swimming pool and holding her under, drowning her. My sister was going off like she had Tourette's, which meant she must have seen her push me in. Jake was immediately at my side, consoling me.

"That bitch did this on purpose," I growled. I sat, drenched, at the side of the pool, taking Nicole's boots off. Just then, another big splash erupted at the other end. Some guy cannonballed into the pool, thankfully taking the attention off of me.

"Damn, looks like you started a trend," Jake half-laughed, trying to make light of my soggy situation. Hoots and hollers came from all around. "Rachel said it was an accident and that she tried to grab ahold of you."

I interrupted, aghast at hearing him make excuses for her. "Are you serious, Jake?" I yelled. "I grabbed her arm and she yanked it away from me! She laughed in my face!" He was silent and switched his gaze from me to her in the distance. His face went blank, and disappointment replaced his concern.

I could still hear my sister going off, but couldn't decipher her words. The only thing I heard was *"fucking whore"* as she shoved people out of her way, making it to my side.

"Let's go! That stupid skank better watch her back," Allison hissed. I never knew that she'd have it in her to stick up for me.

"I'll take her home," Jake offered.

"Oh, you will? I bet you will, and what else, Jake?" she spat.

I interrupted. "Allison, let's go. Come on, all of us."

Jake held out his hand and helped me to my feet as he glared at Allison. We ran into Sienna and Dump on the way out. Sienna looked at me with empathetic eyes. She couldn't believe Rachel would do something so lame in such a public way, but in the same breath, she said she wasn't surprised, under the circumstances. That revelation took another gouge out of my already hollowed and ulcerated stomach. Some random girl came up, handing me a fluffy, oversized towel. Jake grabbed it away from me, wrapping me in it.

I thanked her.

"No problem. It was awesome watching Allison go off on her. I can't stand her." She laughed with joy. "Try and have a great rest of the night," she said, disappearing into the crowd.

Jake and I locked eyes. I squinted with rage. "I told you, she's freaking crazy, and nobody likes her."

"Let's go," Jake urged. He'd clearly had enough.

Chris stepped up and offered to take Nadine and Nicole. They wanted to stay at the party. I didn't blame them. Allison's silence was deafening. She would usually be going off for the world to hear, and it was killing me that she wasn't saying a word. I pulled on Jake's arm and we stopped to wait for Allison and Owen to catch up.

"Allison, please don't say anything to Mom and Dad," I begged, nearly in tears. I could feel my throat thickening and it made me want to scream.

"Aly, what the hell do you think you're doing? You're 14 years old. You haven't even officially started high school yet, and look at you." She held out both hands pointing out my appearance. "There are a number of reasons why I'm pissed, Aly. We'll talk when we get home."

"So, you're coming home now, with me?"

Allison stopped, looking down at the street. *Oh, here it comes*, I thought. She was about to erupt.

"Are you two seeing each other? I mean, I guess that's a stupid question. It's obvious you are." She paused with a perplexed look. I waited for Jake to say something but he just stood there, dumbfounded like me. Taking a deep breath, she continued. "I had one of my friends come up to me raving about how good you looked. How grown up you'd gotten, and everyone was talking about you and Jake."

She began pacing and glancing between Jake and me. "Aly, do you even know who he is? He's not just the cute guy who lives next door. Do you realize what you're getting yourself into?"

Jake's voice cracked the long silence and my heart almost came up out of my mouth. "Allison, we're just friends, hanging out."

"Just hanging out, are you a fucking idiot, Jake?" she barked at him, turning her fiery eyes onto me. "Aly, answer my question, do you realize what you're getting yourself into?"

"Allison," I paused, "he's just a guy, in a band, he…" I was interrupted by Allison's cynical guffaw and I was silenced.

"Aly, he is in a band that's on the brink of something. Why do you think everyone kisses his ass? Do you realize the life he's chosen? He's never going to be home. He's gonna be on the road, and you're going to be here, alone; heartbroken and hearing rumors about him hooking up with girls all over the country. That's what going to happen." She passionately explained with words I didn't want to hear. I looked over at Jake and he was glaring at her. I pictured her face melting off.

"Allison, come on, you're being ridiculous…" Jake cut in.

"Yeah, you're going out with Owen. He's in a band," I broke in. Daggers shot out of her eyes.

"Oh, I'm being silly, Jake? So what part did I get wrong?" she asked, ignoring me.

"I'm not going to be hooking up with girls all over the country," Jake answered.

"Why is it ok for you to hang with Owen and I can't hang with Jake?"

"Aly, Owen's deal is different," she paused, looking at Owen. "He isn't on the same path right now that Jake is." Her voice was softer, not wanting to offend Owen.

"Allison, why are you making a big deal out of this? It's not like I'm some random guy. Yes, I like Aly," he admitted. "We're hanging out, havin' fun. I'm not gonna hurt her, if that's what you're worried about."

"That's what you say now. I swear to God, Jake Masters, if you hurt her I will hunt you down," she said through clenched teeth. "Keep your dick in your pants. She's a kid, not some whore skank. If my dad finds out, your head's gonna roll. See you at home, Aly." She took one last moment to stare down Jake, as if everything she just said wasn't enough.

"I'm staying at Nadine's." I prayed she wouldn't make me go home when she realized Nadine wasn't with us. She stopped, looking back at me for a short moment.

"I'll see you in the morning, then." She hung her head as she walked away defeated, something I'd not seen in her before.

Relief washed over me like wave. A winning smile broke over Jake's face as we watched her and Owen vanish down the street. Finally aware of my surroundings, I noticed several people staring at us. I wondered how long they'd been standing there and what they'd heard. I was mortified. I reached up, feeling my hair. It was crusty. The hair product stuck to it like glue, and it was hardening like a helmet. In vain, I tried breaking it up with my fingers.

"Come on," Jake said in a breathy murmur.

We arrived home. There was no one out on the street. The moon lit up my house with a soft glow. I didn't have to worry about my parents. They were boringly predictable and already tucked away. Jake came around and opened the door for me. I didn't know what to do with myself. I had no clothes, and the key to my house was at Nicole's. We walked silently to his front door and into the house. He turned a few lights on, and I stood there with my palms sweating. He looked at me smiling, sympathetically.

"I don't have anything to sleep in," I piped, with a lop-sided grin.

"No worries. I'll give you something to wear." He walked past me towards his room, and I followed. "Why don't you take a shower?"

He went to the chest of drawers that stood nearly as tall as him and pulled out a t-shirt and boxers. My heart melted. I couldn't wait to put on his clothes. This was a dream come true. I'd always dreamt of being in my boyfriend's clothes. Was he my boyfriend? I wasn't sure. He hadn't asked me to be his girlfriend. Did older guys even ask? Or was it implied? Maybe it was just implied. That's why Rachel freaked out. What if I'm fooling myself, like Rachel. I shook my head as my mind reeled out of control. Jake took notice.

"What's wrong?"

"Oh, uh, nothing, I'm just trippin' out a little," I said, laughing off my mood. I grabbed the clothes from his hand and went into the bathroom. "I just wanna get cleaned up. I feel gross."

"You know, let me go get some shampoo from my mom's room. I don't think you'll like what's in there."

What he didn't realize was I wanted to smell like him. I paced in and out of the bathroom, waiting for him. I noticed that the snapshots that'd been displayed were no longer in their places. *Good*, I thought. I didn't want to see Rachel's face, ever. Jake returned quickly, handing me a few bottles.

"Thanks." I turned back into the bathroom and shut the door. I pinched myself hard on the forearm to make sure it wasn't a dream. I hurried to finish my shower, washing my hair with a cucumber-scented shampoo. I picked up the soap, smelling it, and my insides went gooey. I had to force myself to put down the soap. Finished with my shower, I stood dripping, realizing there wasn't a towel for me to dry off with. I looked under the sink, nope, no luck. *Shit*. I cracked the door open, and Jake was sitting at his computer.

"Jake, I don't have a towel," I muttered quietly, not sure if his mom had come home.

"Oh shit, sorry," he apologized, jumping up and moved quickly out of the room. I looked down at the small puddle of water pooling at my feet. He was back in no time. "Hey, here you go." He handed me an oversized sea foam green towel, looking away—I laughed when I noticed it was a beach towel.

How cute, I thought. My sister was wrong about him. My heart swelled. I looked in the mirror. Black mascara was still visible under my eyes, damn it! I put Jake's boxers on and rolled them up, which didn't help; they were nearly falling off of me. Pulling on his t-shirt, I stared at myself in the mirror. I was swimming in his clothes. I wrapped my head in a towel and opened the door, walking out with my wet clothes in hand.

"Hey, can I lay these outside to dry?"

I didn't want to look at him. I felt ugly.

"What's wrong with your eyes? Are you ok?"

"Yeah," I laughed, "I tried using the hair conditioner as eye make-up remover."

"Ah...do you need anything else?"

"Do you have lotion, or does Kate have any eye-makeup remover?"

"Yep." He dashed off once more, leaving me to wonder what to do with my clothes.

I opened the back door, and it was like an oasis. I could hear the water falling into the pool from the Jacuzzi. The back wall was covered with tropical-looking ivy, and it had little white flowers blooming all through it. A million white Christmas lights wove through it, illuminating the backyard. The air was warm and smelled sweet. It reminded me of Hawaii. I started to daydream that I lived there, that it was my backyard. I walked over to a lounge chair and laid out my clothes. I closed my eyes, inhaling deeply, and when I turned, he was standing next to me.

"I'm sorry. I didn't mean to startle you," he said, moving behind me, wrapping his arms around my waist. The side of his face pressed against my ear. He whispered, "I like the strawberry scent better."

"Me too," I whispered. I leaned my head back onto his chest and pictured being frozen in polar ice with his arms wrapped around me.

"Why are we whispering?" he said with a chuckle.

I giggled softly. "I guess I'm afraid they'll hear me. Their bedroom window is right there," I answered, pointing up to the right. "They have their windows open, you know.

Dad is too cheap to run the air-conditioning, so we suffer, sweltering like we're in Africa."

Jake laughed under his breath. "You have a way with words."

"You must be rubbing off on me," I replied.

We stood there for a long moment. Jake nuzzled my ear and it sent chills up and down my body. I wanted it now more than ever. I couldn't stand it anymore. I was going to ask him to kiss me. I wanted Jake to be my first real kiss.

"Jake, I want you to kiss me."

I could barely breathe. He didn't answer for a long moment. I could feel his chest rise as he took in a deep breath and held it. I turned my face up towards his so I could see his reaction. He stared at me for another short moment, and without saying a word, he touched my face and brought his lips gently to mine. I was paralyzed. He let go of my waist, moving away slightly. I opened my eyes. He was going to stop *No. Don't stop* went through my mind, then the words spilled out of my mouth before I realized it.

"Jake," I said, breathless, "Please don't stop."

He remained speechless. I could feel the warmth of his breath flash over my face and I closed my eyes hoping he'd continue. He brought his lips to mine, open, and I melted when I felt the warmth of his smooth moist tongue touch my lips. Without thinking, I mimicked his motions. He looked at me with dreamy eyes I hadn't seen before, and this time it was me who went in. I wrapped my hand around his neck and wove my fingers through his hair. I was lost in a dream I never wanted to end.

Chapter 21
ALYSSA

A pulsing sensation ran through me, from the top of my head to my fingers all the way to my toes. Suddenly, Jake spun me around, pushing me away. He forced me to sit on the lounge chair. He crouched down, and his hands remained on my hips. He hung his head.

"What's wrong?" I tried to catch my breath.

"Nothing," he said quickly, looking up at me. "Aly, this is, uh. I can't. We need to cool it." He hesitated and moved, sitting down next to me. His forehead rested in his hands.

"Did I do something wrong?" I started to babble. "I'm sorry, did I totally suck? Did I get it all wrong? I just couldn't control myself, I…"

He softly pressed his finger to my lips.

"Hey, hey, naw hardly. You, uh, you make me…you make me crazy, like…" he stammered nervously and sighed deeply. "Aw man, maybe someday I'll be able to explain to you."

"Then why did you stop?"

"Because I had to, Aly. Right now, it has to be this way."

"Do you want me to leave?" My mood went completely flat. My first make-out session went up in a puff of smoke.

"No, I don't," he answered, reaching over and taking my hand. "Aly, when I saw you tonight, it was like lighting hit me. I've never felt like I wanted to hang with anyone more than I want to hang with you."

His eyes burned into mine, making me look away. "I feel the same way, I think, I mean, yeah, I do." I confessed, "I'm mad about you. That's how I feel right now, at this moment and I don't want you to stop kissing me."

"Aly," he stalled and stood up. "Seriously, you have no idea what you do to me. Right now I think we need to just go in and put on a movie. I need to regroup."

Back in his room, I threw myself onto the bed while he tooled around with the TV. He chose an old school flick I'd never seen and said I'd be sure to like it. He turned off the lights and hopped in behind me. He pulled me close and all I could think about was our kiss. It took everything in me to not flip over and suck his face off. His smell, his taste; I was consumed by him. Thinking again of Allison's words, my stomach sunk—*"He's never going to be home, Aly…"* What was I going to do when he left? I would die like grass in a drought. What if he did meet someone else? Someone who would give him what he would eventually want from me? I knew he thought I didn't know too much about sex.

Jake didn't know about all of my late nights with Nadine and Nicole's sexually active teenage cousin, Stacey. She filled our heads with all sorts of firsthand information. She shared her encounters with her boyfriend in detail. I wanted Jake to know that I wasn't as naïve as he thought I was. I knew about *those* things, and those things weren't something I was ready to graduate to, no matter how heated it got. I just wanted to make out with him.

I thought of my sister. I wondered how far she'd gone with a guy. I knew Owen was in her room from time to time without my parent's knowledge. They kept the music blaring as a distraction, but I knew he was in there. I caught him sneaking into the bathroom late one night, and I was so freaked out I just shut my bedroom door. I used to think she was crazy, until now. Here I was, lying in some guy's bed, thinking about naughty things.

Jake's voice echoed in my head. "*I've never wanted to hang with anyone more than I want to hang with you…*" What did that really mean anyway? Like a sick heave, the question flew out of my mouth.

"Jake, how old were you when you had your first kiss, and did you have sex with the same person?" His eyes rolled back and he rubbed his forehead. Bewilderment plastered his face.

"Aly, why, why does stuff like this matter you?"

"I guess it doesn't really matter, but I wanna know, because what I feel is pretty intense. What happened back there wasn't lame or awkward for me at all."

"Ha, yeah, well, my first kiss was lame and awkward, and so was my first time having sex. I would rather not talk about it with you either." He shifted uncomfortably, moving away from me.

"Why not talk about it? You said you wanted to be the one, and now you are. Tell me." I pulled at his t-shirt. "Come on, Jake, share with me."

"Alright," he huffed, reluctant. "My first kiss was when I played truth or dare with a bunch of girls in the 7th grade.

I picked dare, and my dare was to French kiss a girl named Katie. She was in 8ᵗʰ grade. It was stupid and stiff."

"Ok, after that, when was it that you thought you knew what you were doing?"

"In ninth grade, I had a girlfriend, and that's when it felt more natural."

"Why did you break up?"

"Because she moved."

"Were you sad?"

"Nope. I mean, I was bummed, but I didn't give it too much thought."

"Ok, when was your first time doing it?"

I was riveted, waiting for his answer.

"Aly, why is it important for you to know this?"

"Because I know you think I don't know anything about it, but I do, and I know why you stopped kissing me. So I just want you to know that I get it. I understand how one thing leads to another."

"Now I'm curious as to how you know anything, if I'm the first guy you've really kissed."

"Well, we, Nadine, Nicole and I, have a friend who's a senior. She shares stories with us."

"Shares stories with you? Like what? Like Greg's brothers?"

"Yeah, I guess. Stories about her sex life."

"Really? I'm scared to ask."

"Are you asking?"

"I don't know. I feel strange talking about this with you," he admitted.

"Answer the other half of my question, Mister." I poked at his chest.

"Which was?" he smirked.

"Don't play stupid," I giggled, nudging him. My hand remained on his chest and I could feel his heart beating with every breath he took. I wanted to move closer, just those few more inches to feel his lips on mine.

"It was just last year, and it was with someone older than me," he admitted, and my heart stopped. This meant it wasn't something awkward like he said. How could having sex with an older girl be lame? She would know what she was doing, right?

"How much older?" I asked under my breath. I couldn't look at him.

"Aly, look," He lifted my chin and our eyes met. "This is why I didn't want to answer your questions. What I've been through doesn't affect how I feel about you."

"Tell me about it, Jake, I wanna know."

With a deep sigh, he proceeded. "Boy, you're relentless aren't you," he paused, "She was like 19 or 20 and we were playing in New York, and that's the first time I had actual sex."

"Ok, so you were 16."

"Yes. Last year, I was a junior."

"And before that, nothing with anyone else?"

"I wouldn't say nothing with anyone else. We're talking about sex, Aly, intercourse."

"Ok, ok. Tell me about it."

"Is this what you do to your friend?" A nervous smile peeked out. "I feel cornered."

"Actually, yes, we beg her to tell us stuff, and you wanna know why? It all started in sixth grade when we found dirty magazines in her parent's room. We brought them to her and asked her what the hell."

I laughed nervously at my admission.

"Shit, you're kidding." He laughed, too. "Aly, there's so much to sex than I can't explain, and to be honest with you, I don't really want to, because I don't know all that much either."

"Then why is it, from what I'm told, it's all guys think about? I mean, I hear my dad talking to my brother, and Nicole's brothers talking about this and that…"

Jake interrupted. "Thinking about it and knowing the nuances about sex are two totally different things." He hesitated and his eyes roamed the ceiling. "Okay look, think about how you felt when we were kissing. It's so much more intense than that."

I nodded in agreement. It did feel good, and it's all I could think about. "Um, I'm gonna bring up a sore subject. Rachel. You said you did it with Rachel…" He interrupted me again.

"Aly, I'm not gonna rehash that with you. It's done. It's over. It was a mistake. I don't wanna talk about her any more. As for you and I, I like how I feel when I'm with you, you make me feel…" He hedged, "You make me feel new, awake. I don't feel the urge to get fucked up anymore. I feel high just knowing you're there."

I gulped. The more he professed his affection for me, the more I was drawn in. We lay there for a long moment, silent, staring at each other. Every inch of me was wired. He reached up and touched my face, kissing me again, gentle and soft. I melted like wet sugar.

"You really have no idea what you do to me," he declared, rolling onto his back.

The fact was, I did, and I wasn't going to make any more of it. We fell asleep at some point, watching *Animal House*. Morning came too quickly, and I was awakened by a knock at Jake's bedroom door and his mother calling his name. I dashed into the bathroom and hid behind the door.

"Yeah," he shouted out.

I could hear Kate's muffled voice. "Love, I'm sorry for waking you, but there's a gal at the door for you. She says it's important."

I knew it was about me. If I went home wearing boy's clothes, I would never see the light of day or Jake ever again. My heart was pounding out of my chest. *Shit, this is what I get for sneaking around.* I was busted.

Jake jumped up, opening the door, and vanished. I leaned against the wall, sinking to the cool tiled floor. Next thing I heard was Nadine's voice. She was in his room. As soon as he shut the door, I walked out of the bathroom.

"You effing dogs, you," Nadine said, giving me a sly smile.

"Shut up," I whispered. "Jake, where's your mom?"

"She's in her room. She went back in before I got to the door. I think you woke her up, too," he said, looking at Nadine.

"I'm sorry," Nadine offered, looking over to me. "Aly, we called over to your house this morning when you weren't answering our texts, and your cell went straight to voice mail. Dude, your sister answered the phone, she said you weren't there, and we were like oh shit. And then she said she thought you were sleeping at Nicole's house." Nadine took a deep breath before continuing. "So then, of course

Nicole was sitting right next to me and we're like, oh shit, she must be with Jake—and damn—here you are. Your sister said you'd better be home soon."

"Oh my God, what the hell, you totally just gave me a heart attack. Oh, gahh! My phone is ruined because of the pool water. Shit, I didn't even think about that, it's in the shorts pocket I was wearing last night." I paced back and forth. "My clothes, my bag—it's at Nicole's still. I'm going to have to tell my mom the phone fell in the pool. She's gonna be pissed!"

"What do you want to do?" Nadine said, gesturing at me.

"Nadine, will you please go get my bag? I'm begging you." I held my hands in prayer under my chin.

Her face drooped. She was about to speak and Jake chimed in. "Nadine, that would be sweet if you could do that."

Her expression changed immediately when Jake asked her. *What an ass kiss*, I thought. I found it irritatingly humorous. Just like my sister said. *"Everyone kisses Jake's ass."*

Nadine was back in no time. Jake released his warm arms from around me when she threw herself through his bedroom door. Why couldn't she have taken just a little bit longer? She must have run there and back. Why couldn't my happy times drag by like I was in detention? No, only shitty times crawled by. I guess that's part of the punishment, like the fucking universe just knows or something.

With my bag slung over my shoulder, I stood unable to move. I didn't want to leave. Staring at the rumpled sheets on the bed made me ache inside. I wanted him next to me all the time, and it was getting more difficult to think of anything else but him. I pushed him from my head and got dressed, thinking about my impending volleyball practices, which would keep me away from him. I wanted and needed to spend as much time with him before he left. Volleyball would just have to wait.

"The party's over," I said, somberly.

"Oh come on, everything's chill. You'll see," he said, giving me a hug. "I would say text me later, but your phone is outta commission."

"I'll just see you later."

"I have an extended band practice today. We're going to a studio we've never been to later, and I have no idea when I'll be home. This week's gonna be tough. I'm not gonna really be around."

I knew this already. Thanks for reminding me.

"It's a bummer, and now I don't have a phone. Hopefully my mom or Kyle will take me to get a new one," I rambled. "All right, I'll see you later."

"I'll see you soon."

"This is kinda like ripping off a Band-Aid," I said, laughing.

"I'll be home late, so when you see my bedroom light on, come over."

A smile crept to my lips. "Ok, I'll see you later, then." I stood on my tiptoes giving him a quick peck and breezed out. I quickly ran across the cool damp grass of our front lawns, looking every which way to see if anyone was around. I took in a deep breath of relief when I arrived at my front door.

Chapter 22
RACHEL

Jake's voice echoed in my head. *"I'm sorry Rachel, I know it's a clichéd thing to say, but I never meant to hurt you…"* What the fuck? My mind spun outta control. This couldn't be the end. I replayed every moment from the first time I saw Aly all the way to my epic win at the swimming pool. I wouldn't let Jake slip away that easily. This was just a blip, a speed bump in our relationship. I couldn't allow myself to believe after all that's gone on these last two years and all the time spent together he would just throw it all away for some child. He would see soon enough, right? He'd have to.

I wouldn't be there helping him at the shows, cheering him on, supporting him. I wouldn't be there to work the merchandise table, or to make sure the shows got promoted. I wouldn't be there to get him whatever the fuck he wanted—beer, water, gum, earplugs or anything else. I started to hyperventilate, and sank deeper into the passenger seat of Sienna's car.

"As soon as I saw her lying on his bed that day…'

"Shit Rachel, I'm sorry, I really am. I don't know what to say," Sienna replied.

Of course, what could she say? The whole thing was just fucked.

"You could offer to take her out for me, or run her off the road, kick her ass or better yet, poison her?" I mumbled, through my tears.

"Rachel, *as if*...the best thing for you to do is act like it's no big deal, right? But then again maybe you're right. If you're not around to help him anymore, then he'll realize."

I kept replaying in my mind the way Jake stood close to her, torturing myself. I just knew he was into her.

"Sienna, what am I gonna do?"

"Rachel, there isn't anything you *can* do. One thing I'll tell you *not* to do is be lame and vindictive. That will only piss Jake off," she advised. "Just act like it's no big deal. You can't help what's going on anyway. You of all people know how it is. He's leaving on the road again, and I hate to say it, but he'll probably be hooking up with chicks all along the way."

"So, you're telling me that's what Dump does, and you're ok with it?" I replied dryly. "Besides, we're supposed to go with them this time."

"Don't be a bitch. What I do know is, whenever Dump's on the road he's calling me and texting me all the time, so what the fuck ever, Rachel." She spat back, "Don't be a bitch to me just because your shit isn't working out. Dump and I've been together for a long time. Now, if he was drinking and using, then I wouldn't be surprised if that shit was goin' down. But right now, I believe he's being faithful."

"Whatever," I hissed under my breath. I didn't want to hear how perfect her relationship was with Dump. They made me puke with their little happy house shit. "If I didn't tell the whole world about this party, I'd not have one."

"You're so full of shit Rachel. Who cares if you're seeing him or not?"

"Sienna, I'm in love with him," I squeaked out. The tears welled up in my eyes and ran down my cheeks.

By this time we were parked in front of Dump's apartment. I stared at Sienna through my tears and apologized. "I'm sorry for being a bitch, but you have no idea what I'm going through right now, or what I'm feeling."

Sienna reached out rubbing my arm. "Rach, look, I feel so bad for you and I know you want to hear that it's all gonna be ok with Jake. But I don't know. You've always just done what you do, no matter what I say. You ask for advice and you do the opposite. You live by your own set of rules. I just feel like no matter what I say to you, nothing ever matters."

"What *are* you trying to say?"

"I'm saying that it's hard for me to tell you how I see things. One, because I don't want to hurt your feelings and two, I just know my words will fall on deaf ears."

"Why are you being so brutal? Really, Sienna? You wanna kick me while I'm down?"

She huffed and slammed her fists on the steering wheel. "You see? You see what I mean? Do you hear yourself? I'm trying to be honest with you. You cry and pour your heart out, and expect me to tell you exactly what you want to hear? I can't do that. The fact is that you can't have everything your way. You can't make Jake feel something for you when he doesn't."

I sobbed. Deep down inside I knew she was right, but I wanted to prove her wrong.

Dump answered the door and saw my face. "What the hell's wrong with you?" he asked, unconcerned. I couldn't see how he had one caring bone, let alone enough affection in his body to show love to Sienna.

"Babe, she's all torn up about Jake. You know he told her it was a mistake him sleeping with her and all, and that it shouldn't have happened." Dump plopped down on a sofa that had seen better days. His place made my skin crawl. It stunk like garbage and dog. I stood there, not wanting to sit down. Sienna didn't either.

"Let's go, you know I can't stand it here, Dump, get up," Sienna begged.

"Shit man, let me finish watching this, like 10 more minutes."

"Dude, please tell me you haven't started staying over here," I whispered to Sienna.

"Yeah right, no, I never stay here." She frowned.

"How do you stand it?"

"Uh, hello, it's not him. It's his depressed alcoholic mother who doesn't give a shit." All of a sudden Sienna's eyes lit up. "Dump's been saving his money. I didn't tell you. He's moving out when they get back from tour."

"Thank god, because it's beyond super nasty in here, Sienna." I said, looking around like I was in pain.

"All right, bitches, let's scoot." Dump grabbed his backpack off the floor near the door.

I needed to know if he knew what was going on between Jake and this *Alyssa*. "Hey Dump, I have a question. You know that girl, Jake's next door neighbor? What's her story, anyway?"

"Aw man, yeah. I noticed a little. All I know is she's his next door neighbor and he's known her since she was three, so your guess is as good as mine."

"Dump, I hate to ask you this, but will you please find out what's up?" I begged. "You know how long I've been in love with Jake..."

Dump interrupted me by tossing his inked up arm in the air, a gesture for me to shut up.

"That's chick shit I don't wanna get into. It's not my fucking job."

Dump definitely had a short fuse, and I already knew I shouldn't have asked. I was hoping he'd feel a little sympathy for me, but no, the only one he cared about was Sienna. I seethed with jealously about their bond. I wiped it from my brain, and focused on the party later on. Jake would be there with the band, and she wouldn't be. At least I had that on my side.

——

I took my time getting ready and spoke to my reflection. *"This is where it's at, Jake Masters, you'll see."*

My parents arrived home while I was getting ready, and I was in no mood to see them. My mother irritated me. She was way too into her party planning—even though it was her job.

"Wow! Don't you look beautiful!" my mom complimented. "Where are you off to, going out with Jake?"

Her question stabbed at my heart. I hadn't mentioned anything to her. My mom and dad assumed Jake and I had been an item for a long time because he was all I ever talked about.

Sienna sent a text that she was waiting outside and I dashed out the door. Mike and Dump were already in the car. The temperature was finally cooling off. The warm breeze drifted over my bare shoulders like a blanket out of the dryer, soothing me only slightly.

"Wow, you look great," Mike complimented. "Trying to win your man back, I see."

My momentary bliss was stifled by Mike's bullshit comment. "You know what Mike, fuck you."

"Come on, I get it, you know," he yammered.

"So is it that obvious? That he's made his decision? Why didn't anyone tell me what was going on? You know I would have clued any of you in if you were in my shoes."

"Hey man, we had no idea. She was only over there for a little while each time and he made it sound like it was no big deal, you know—*It's my next door neighbor, we've been friends our whole lives*—shit like that."

"Tell me."

"It's like he's taken on the role of her protector or some shit. Jake told me after I'd made some comment, for me not to give her anything, like no booze, no drugs, shit like that."

"You shouldn't be doing drugs anyway, you fuck," Sienna chimed in.

"Yeah, whatever, you go on with your sober self," Mike teased.

"I will, and you'll end up in a ditch, dead someday," Sienna warned.

Mike ignored her, and I sat there stewing in my gloom. "So you think that it's nothing more? But what about how he acted with her, was I seeing things?"

"No, I saw it too, he wants some of that." Mike confirmed.

My stomach hardened like a rock.

"What can he possibly see?" I sulked, honestly perplexed.

"Well, she's hot, for one thing."

"I guess you like plain then," I said dryly.

"She's innocent in a teasing kind of way. There is definitely something there and he likes it."

"Yeah, and so do you, apparently."

"If Jake wasn't into her, I'd probably see what she's all about."

"Really," I said smartly, pulling my arms in tighter to my chest.

Mike's admission got my wheels turning. Maybe if Mike got Aly's attention. That's it. If Mike liked Aly enough to go after her...

My mood lightened. I felt better than I had in a long time.

Chapter 23

JAKE

I'd never been the type of person to openly and publically show affection for someone I liked, until now. Recalling everything that went down that night made my head spin. I found myself feeling something new: jealousy. Recalling how it yanked at me the first time I caught Mike staring at Aly, and how I blew it off. This time it was different, the anger more intense, rage brewing inside my gut. The more I became attached to her, the more prevalent the feelings became. I actually wanted to fight Mike as I watched him pour out sweet apologies. I'd never seen this side of him. He was trying to make some sort of impression on Aly. The way he looked at her intently, like he really cared about what she had to say, smiling. He kept whispering in her ear and touching her arm. What the hell was going on? Was Mike coming onto her, or was I totally outta my mind?

I looked over at Aly taking her hand. I wanted her to know not to pay any mind to what Allison had said.

"Aly, what Allison said back there, about me being on the road? What's seen or heard isn't always what's really goin' on," I explained.

"Jake, it's ok, really, I'm not stupid. I see how these girls look at you. The guys are as into you as the girls are." She returned my gaze, rubbing the top of my hand softly with her fingertips, sending chills up my arm. "It's just weird to see everyone all gaga over you. You're just Jake to me."

. "I don't think it's that way, Aly." I tried to shrug off her sentiment. It made me feel embarrassed. "I mean, I'm stoked to have everyone into the music, that's for sure, but I'm not sure about anything else." I tried to laugh it off.

My words didn't match my feelings. I was very aware. Things had changed since we appeared on local news segments and got our one and only music video aired on Fuel & Havoc TV. Getting on the Warped Tour schedule the prior summer for several dates was when it really changed. Our hard work was finally paying off, and getting on this other upcoming tour was huge.

I was living my dream, and I wanted Aly to share it with me.

"I'm sure it'll only get worse. Well, not worse…you know what I mean, more in your face," she said, grabbing me away from my thoughts.

"Right, I guess it's the price we pay, when and if we make it. But it doesn't have to be out of control. That type of celebrity is one in a billion." My stomach sank. "Think about how many bands there are trying to do what we're doing. The odds of that kind of attention, success and fame," I paused at the sobering thought. "Well, I don't wanna get depressed thinking about the odds."

That fact was true, but it never dissuaded me. I fully believed I would be there someday. "I just want to make a living playing music."

"It looks to me like you're on your way," She encouraged. Her little smirk and head tilt did it to me every time. I wanted to take her in my arms and protect her from all the bullshit and keep her from getting scuffed up by harsh realities.

I recalled the nervous excitement that gnawed at me as I watched Aly skip to my front door, disappearing into the shadows. Everything sped by too quickly and we were in my room and Aly was cleaning up from her pool incident. Another test was about to be dumped into my lap. I sat in front of my computer trying not to think of her naked, in the shower, only a few feet away from me. I laughed at myself, rubbing my hands over my face. What the hell was I thinking? Seriously, I was gonna get in some serious trouble if I couldn't keep it under control.

As much as I was sober, I felt buzzed from the adrenaline.

———

I found Aly standing out on the patio, and I drifted to her side. My actions weren't what my mind was telling me to do. Before I knew it, I was having my first real taste of her and a current ran through me like no other. My brain scrambled and I had to stop before I spun out of control. Her clean, sweet smell mixing with the warmth of her mouth—it was intoxicating. I pulled away from her and sat down on the nearby lounge, burying my face in my hands. She had absolutely no idea the power she had. I was so wound up I could have run to the bathroom to toss one off.

Aly wasn't as naïve as I thought. Feeling her warm skin pressed against mine, the warning bells were at an all-time high. I kicked myself for wanting her to stay the night again. I was in deep and sinking fast, way more quickly than I imagined possible.

I didn't give a shit if I drowned.

Chapter 24

JAKE

My dreams were so vivid. They had me feeling like I hadn't fallen back to sleep, and that Aly never left my side. I was inspired by all the new energy coursing through me. I decided I wanted to change things up a bit with the music. What would the guys say when I told them I wanted to write a couple of love songs? The thought made me laugh. They would think I was the gayest ever, that's what they'd think. Fuck'em, if they didn't like it, they could walk. It's not like I wanted to sing an R&B ballad. Getting up, I paced around. I picked up my phone, thinking about dialing Notting's number. I really needed someone to talk to, someone that wasn't my mother.

After four rings, Notting finally answered. "Hello, Son."

"Hey Not, um, do you have some time to talk?" I hedged, unsure if I should involve him, now wishing I hadn't called.

"Of course," he said. "Shoot."

"Are you gonna be at practice today?" I said, deciding not to say anything.

"Not unless you want me to be, why?"

"Oh, it's nothing, never mind. It isn't a big deal."

"Jake, when was the last time you've asked if I'd be there? And you want me to believe something important isn't on your mind?"

I sighed, Notting knew me too well.

"I wanna try something new with the music. I mean, not a huge departure, I suppose."

"What do your mates think?"

"I played the song for them and they liked it, for the most part," I offered.

"That's good news…and I suppose this has to do with the girl your mother told me has been coming over?"

Zing. I didn't realize my mom had been on to Aly and I. My heartbeat speed up. This must be what happens with lie-detector tests.

I couldn't lie to him. Why? Facts were the facts. "It has everything to do with her. Her name is Aly, by the way," I admitted, truthfully. "I've never been more inspired by anything, let alone by any one person."

My heart raced faster with this admission. I wished Notting were sitting in front of my face instead of on the phone.

"I see. We can meet before practice. See you soon."

I turned, facing my guitar and fragmented lyrics popped in my head. I grabbed my guitar and a note pad. The melody and words flowed from my mind out through my fingertips with ease. *Her innocence, she was like a blank canvas, just opened and new—dreams of you*—that's what I was doing, dreaming of that first moment. Those few words echoed back at me. *I'll wait for you*—I would have to. I had no choice. The human side of me wanted to just go for it, and Aly's willingness to allow me to have my way, made it that much harder to think of anything else. I sat writing one-liners and kept thinking back to the way she looked at the party. I wished she didn't have to leave.

I could hear my mother clinking around in the kitchen as I walked out of my room.

"Jake," my mother called out.

"Yeah," I responded, trying my best to look relaxed as I walked in.

She was cutting a cantaloupe, and the brewing coffee aroma wafting through the air caught my attention. I grabbed a large white mug out of the dish rack. I slowly poured the hot black liquid into my cup and locked in on the swirling steam as it rose in every direction. That's how I felt last night; hot and outta control.

"Are you feeling ok?"

"Yeah, why," I asked, irritated.

"You look flushed. Come here." She started to walk toward me.

I waved her off. "Naw, mom, stop, I'm fine. I just got out of the shower."

She looked at me sideways and pursed her lips. "Ok, if you say so." She resumed cutting her fruit, glancing up at me from time to time. "So, is there something you want to talk about?"

She caught me off guard, *again*. Were her motherly instincts kicking in? She was gonna crap when she found out Notting was on his way over to talk to me, alone, *without her*. My mother had always been a driving force of the band along with Notting, ever since my dad died. She knew everything, every single nuance about every person that had anything to do with the band or me. I'd never really spoken to Notting about anything other than music and guy stuff that *didn't* include girls I liked.

"Uh, Notting is coming over here to talk about the band stuff and whatever."

I delivered the news like it was no big deal, but just as I'd thought, the air sucked out of the room. She stopped cutting and slowly placed the fruit in a bowl. She then folded her hands on the counter. She looked up at me, and her stage-mother persona kicked into full gear.

"So, there *is* something you want to share with me?"

I really didn't want to deal with her. She was a control freak when she wasn't in the loop one hundred percent, but his situation was different.

"Mom, it's nothing. We're talking about music. Some things I'm workin' on. I just want his opinion. It's no big deal." I walked over, grabbed some fruit, tossed it into my mouth and kissed her on the cheek. "Really, if it was important, I would tell you."

"I'm just surprised to hear it," she said, tersely. "He didn't mention it."

"I *just* talked to him, Mom." I replied, agitated. I couldn't help but shake my head. "Speak of the devil."

We could hear the front door shut and Notting calling out for my mom—*"Hello Katie, love, surprise."*

"There you are," he said, making a beeline for my mom. "And you, too, I see." He looked over at me with his sly smile then focused back on my mother. "Good morning, my dear."

Notting greeted my mother with his refined English accent, planting a kiss on her forehead. He was a smooth operator, the textbook English gentleman—if you ignored all the tats etched up and down his arms. I felt sorry for him. He was madly in love with my mother, and I knew she loved him too; but for some reason she wouldn't take things to the next level. She wouldn't let him stay over, ever. I knew it had to do with me, her trying to set some sort of an example.

My mother's relationship with Notting was something that always gnawed at me, too. I always attempted to write a song about her, letting go of someone that was no longer there. She needed to let go of the past, but wouldn't. The guys would think that was lame too, I thought. Not rock or punk enough, or whatever they always thought. Mike was the one who always had a negative opinion. I was sick of him. I didn't want to sing about shit that was meaningless to me anymore. I didn't care if those songs got us to where we were. Bottom line, it was time to move forward. I wanted to broaden my range musically and lyrically…more melodic. I wanted to play around with more sounds. I wanted new pedals. I wanted our guitars to fill the space with more intricacy and texture.

"I'll be in the garage whenever you're ready, Notting," I said. Looking my mother in the eyes, I walked away without saying anything to her. She irritated me with her overbearing presence.

"What, I'm not invited?" Kate said, miffed.

"No, you're not," I paused, but kept walking. "I'll tell you everything later."

I let the door slam behind me. The garage door lifted with its familiar squeaking and gyrating. Walking out into the sunlight, I glanced over at Aly's house, wondering if she was inside.

"Alright, mate, let's get to it," Notting said loudly, coming out of the house and into the garage. He pulled over a nearby stool, slapping his knees.

My hands started to sweat as I walked back into the garage. I couldn't believe I was going to talk *girls* with my surrogate father. Basically, no matter how you sliced it, that's what it was about, not music.

"Ok, how do you suggest I approach telling the guys that I want to switch it up, like permanently?" I asked, trying to avoid the subject as long as I could.

"This new song, have you played it for them?"

"Yes."

"And? Did you ask for their feedback? It's not rocket science." He shrugged, chuckling.

"Yeah, well, they were actually pretty positive. But this is the first song I've written without their input," I said anxiously. "I've also been listening to a lot of 80's new wave tunes. I have to admit, you grew up in a pretty rad music decade. So many ass-kicking UK bands, it's crazy."

"Those were quite possibly the best years of my life. That's when I met your mother..." His voice trailed off in thought. I could tell he was reliving the moment. "Perhaps if you'd admit to why you want to make changes they would understand. Honesty goes a long way." Notting crossed his arms. "Do as I suggested and sit them down, like you have with me. They might possibly make what you've demo'd better, improving upon it. With Dump, he is in something with that Sienna. I'm sure he'll understand more than you think."

I took in a deep breath. "Yeah, I suppose."

216

"Now, on to this girl whose inspired you, your muse? Enlighten me, please."

"You remember Aly, right?"

"Vaguely. I do recall a young girl several years back with long brown hair and an infectious laugh. This is the same girl?"

"Yeah, that's her."

"Ok, so you're writing songs about her?" Notting said a bit surprised.

"Things have been pretty…intense. You know, with Rachel and everything." I paused, trying to figure out which way to take the conversation.

Notting took the pressure off.

"So Rachel is no longer in the picture, huh? I'm curious as to how she took that." He chuckled again. "She was pretty obsessive about taking care of you. Regardless of her motivations, she's been there for you and the band, Jake."

"Ugh, don't remind me, Notting. She's in love with me, apparently," I said, shrugging. "I don't feel the same way, and now it's totally effed things up, that's what I meant when I said intense."

Notting Frowned. "Jake, you make this right. I don't need to know the details, but Rachel's been around for a long time."

"What's that supposed to mean?" I asked, getting pissed. "I can't help it if I'm falling for someone else. For me, we were always just friends. I made the mistake of hooking up with her, man. I didn't realize it would be such a big deal. She thought because we hooked up, that meant we'd become official or something like that. I fucked up."

"I'll say you did," he affirmed. "Whoa. Well, son, you certainly have something to deal with."

We sat in silence. I didn't know what else to say. I felt relieved it was out in the open. *Now it just has to heal*, I thought, tapping a drumstick on the bench.

Notting's voice broke the silence.

"You must take care, do you hear me? I've kept quiet because you were younger, and I have to admit I was turning a blind eye to what may have been going on. However, now that we're on subject, and you've professed your feelings for this Aly, I just hope you use better judgment than you've used with Rachel. Aly is young and impressionable. I believe it would be more disastrous to enter into anything too serious with her."

My stomach dropped. It was too late to end anything.

"Don't worry. I know what needs to happen with Aly," I said in finality. I got up and headed toward the door, back into the house. "I need to take a piss."

I lied. No wonder kids didn't talk to their parents, it was a fucking downer, like they forgot what it was like to be young or in love. I stood still in the middle of my room. Did I just admit to being in love?

My hands tingled.

Chapter 25

ALYSSA

I was in the middle of the loveliest Jake dream when I was awakened by a door slamming and my sister's muffled rant about who knows what. It was 9:15 AM and the air was too warm and thick. I kicked off the covers and let the breeze of the ceiling fan roll over me. Lying there, I tried to make out my sisters words. She must be on the phone with either my mother or her boyfriend. My eyes were gooey. I glanced at my window and could see through the cracks in the window shade that it was sunny, no marine layer to deflect the heat. It would be another day lounging by the pool, and I was getting sick of it. I was sick of watching Nadine and Chris play kissy face and Nicole and Grant disappearing to be alone. Matt seemingly fell off the face of the earth when he found out about Jake, and I still felt terrible about how it all went down.

Lying there thinking of the dreams I'd been having of Jake embarrassed me. I never knew I could dream such dreams. He consumed me all night long, and it all seemed so real. Waking up dripping with emotion was driving me crazy. Jake had been in the studio until two every morning, and we hadn't seen each other in days.

I closed my eyes and let my mind wander. I could picture Jake sprawled out on his bed, lying on his stomach with one arm under the pillow and one leg bent out to the side. I wondered if his back door was unlocked, and what he would think if snuck over and woke him up. It gave me chills just thinking about it. He'd called me his muse in the last text he sent at 12:30 AM. I would never delete any of the messages for the rest of my life. I even took screen shots, emailing them to myself.

I reached for my phone, reading them over again to remind myself they were real.

———

My brother was chilling in front of the TV, watching old episodes of *Entourage* in the adjacent family room. I shuffled over to the fridge, taking out the strawberries and rinsed them off in the sink. The cool water ran over my hands and felt refreshing. It was already way too warm in our house. I stared out at the back fence in a daze, watching the leaves on the bushes rustle in the breeze. The swimming pool shimmered, catching my eye and I daydreamed I was wrapped around Jake in the cool water.

My daydream screeched to a halt when Kyle's voice broke in. "Hey!" I jumped when he shouted at me. "Hello, turn off the water, we're in a drought."

"Oh, shut up!" I stuffed a strawberry in my mouth, glaring at him for scaring me.

I hadn't seen him in days. "Where have you been lately?"

I noticed he was a little tanner than he normally was.

He picked up the remote, pausing his pre-recorded show, and stared at me blankly. "Now what do you want?"

"What have you been doing this week? You look tan, Mr. Non-beach-goer."

"If you must know, yes, I have been going to the beach."

"Really? Who paid you, and how much?"

"I don't mind going to the beach."

"Alright, who is she? It has to be because of a girl." I snickered.

He ignored me. "Want some strawberries?" I obnoxiously held the bowl right in front of his face.

"Yes…thank you," he said, grabbing the bowl out of my hand.

I contemplated telling Kyle about Jake. I wanted him to go to the party with me on Saturday. If I were with him, my sister would have to suck on it. I watched my loving, yet annoying big brother eat my strawberries. He was kind and thoughtful. A nerd, but whatever, I knew I could trust him.

"Kyle, there's something I wanna tell you," I paused. "But you have to swear on your life you won't tell mom or dad."

He stopped chewing mid-mouthful, looking over at me. "Uh oh."

"Well, um, I guess there's no other way to say it. I've been seeing Jake," I admitted. Just like in the movies, Kyle started choking.

"What!" he exclaimed. "Aly, please tell me you're kidding!" He continued coughing, trying to clear his throat.

"Why?" I whispered loudly putting my hand over his mouth.

Kyle collected himself as I waited for his reply.

"Aly, you gotta know what he's all about, right?"

"Yes!" I said loudly, "I'm not an effing idiot!" I got up and grabbed the bowl out of his hand and huffed into the kitchen. His response wasn't what I expected.

"Woah, Aly, come on, I'm just looking out for you…"

"Yeah, whatever, that's what Allison said, too. I don't need to hear it from you either!"

"Hey, calm down," he said, walking into the kitchen. "So, Allison knows and you're worried about me telling mom and dad?"

"She's not going to say anything. I got dirt on her. She doesn't know I know though. I prolly should make sure she does, though, before she screws me."

"What dirt? I got dirt too." He raised his eyebrows, humming a silly dooms-day tune.

"It's probably the same dirt," I said smiling. "Is it those late-night rendezvous with Owen?"

"Yep." We both laughed. "She's an idiot to think that none of us wouldn't notice him creeping around in the middle of night. It's a matter of time before Mom or Dad catch them."

"Whatever, I don't care. I just don't need her threatening me."

Kyle cocked his head and his eyes narrowed in on me. "Tell me what you mean that you're seeing Jake."

"We've been hanging out the last couple of weeks, and we both really like each other."

"Isn't he seeing Rachel what's-her-face?"

"No, and he never was. They're just friends."

"He told you he likes you? Or are you just assuming he likes you because he's nice to you?"

I sighed. "Kyle, he's told me way more than that. We were at a party together last weekend…"

"What?" he cried out. "You went to a party?"

"Yeah, that's when Allison found out. She caught me there with Jake. A whole bunch of drama with this Rachel chick went down and it was crazy," I confessed. "That hoe-bag pushed me into the pool."

"Wait, you were at a party with Jake?" he asked again, stuck on the impossibility of it all. "And he was with you? In front of everyone else?"

"Yes. He held me, kissed me and introduced me to people." I shrugged, trying not to come off too excited, even though I could have shot to the moon.

"Wow." He leaned against the counter in complete shock.

"That seems to be everyone's reaction," I said. "Which is kind of a bummer, like I'm not worthy or something."

"Hey, that's not it. It's just, well, you're always in a bubble with your little clique of friends, and I just want you to be careful… 'cause I don't wanna have to try and kick his ass or anything," Kyle teased. "Jake's an alright guy. I guess he just gets a bad rap because he's in a band…you know, chicks, drugs…rock and roll. You know they go together like mint and chip."

I couldn't have loved my brother more than at that moment.

"So have you heard anything bad?" I wanted more of his perspective.

"Actually no, no I haven't, that's what I mean by a bad rap. I've seen him hanging with chicks at parties, but at school, he's totally low profile. Rachel was always around though."

"Huh, sounds like you know a lot for being the quiet one," I jabbed playfully.

Kyle winked at me. I was relieved with the way our conversation went. Now I had to ask him to take me to the party. Ugh, the way he dressed would laugh us out the front door. He so needed a makeover, desperately. The only problem was he didn't have anyone to borrow cool clothes from. Did guys even do that?

"I have an idea, Kyle. What do you say about taking this girl you won't tell me about to a party this Saturday?"

I batted my eyes at him with a crafty grin and he looked at me sideways.

"Would this be a party that Jake's gonna be at? Just give it to me straight, Aly." He crossed his arms to his chest.

"Yes, it is, and it's at Rachel's, and he's playing. This is the first time I'll see the band play live, and if I'm not there I'll just die. You just have to take me."

I stood there with my hands clasped underneath my chin, looking as pathetic as I could.

"Please," I begged, whimpering.

Kyle contemplated, rubbing his chin. "On one condition. If I want to leave, you'll have to leave, too," he said, "no matter what. I don't care if Jake says he'll take you home."

"Ahhh!" I screamed and launched at myself him, hugging him. "You are the most awesome brother ever!"

"Stop!" He pushed me off. "I'll look pretty cool taking Chelsea," he said. "Plus, with my little sis seeing the most popular guy in school, this may just seal the deal."

God he was *such* a dork.

"Oh, so you're using me?" I playfully accused.

"Uh, I think you were using me first."

I laughed. "I love you!"

I ran up the stairs and into my room and frantically searched my bed covers for my phone. I was electrified by excitement and couldn't wait to tell Nicole and Nadine.

- *KYLE SAYS HE'LL TAKE US TO THE PARTY ON SATURDAY –*

I waited anxiously for what seemed like 15 minutes, finally Nicole replied.

- *AWESOME, CHRIS SAYS HE WAS PLANNING ON TAKING US THOUGH, HE'S STILL SEEING NADINE. CAN U BELIVE IT?—*

I wanted her to dish!

- *SPEAKING OF, WE NEED TO TALK, R U ALONE? CAN I COME OVER?*
- *YEP, COME OVER— CALL NADINE, TELL HER TOO, I WANT THE SCOOP –*
- *NO, I'LL GIVE YOU THE SCOOP, JUST COME NOW, GRANT MIGHT BE HERE SOON –*

I rushed to get ready. Running down the stairs, I screamed out to Kyle to text me when mom got home, and that he and I were going shopping.

"What do you mean, you and I are going shopping?"

"Your polo's aren't making an appearance, Kyle!" I hollered, stepping out the door. "And we need to do something about your hair!"

I rushed down the street as quickly as I could toward Nicole's. I spotted my friend Marshall in his driveway, looking way too fashionable to be washing his brother's car. I hadn't spoken to him since Grant chased him away with his immature teasing two weeks prior. As I approached, a smile spread across his beautiful, flawless face. His funky, usually coifed hair was pulled back in a silver headband.

"Hey Alyssa, what's up," he said as he walked around to the front of the car.

"Hi Marshall," I said cheerily. "How are you?"

"Pretty good, just trying to finish up Jon's car before he kicks my ass." He laughed.

"Right, what scares me is he probably would try," I remarked, concerned.

"I know, right!" He agreed, animated. "Naw, not really, he'd just give me shit."

"Why are you washing his car anyway?"

"Well," he paused. "Good question. I guess because he told me to, and I just don't need him being a dick any more than he already is. Plus, he gave me five bucks."

I smiled sadly and reached out, grabbing his elbow. A silent understanding passed between us.

"Hey, what are you doing Saturday? You wanna come to a party with the girls and me?" It made me happy to include him.

His eyes lit up and my heart instantly soared. With Marshall being a different kind of guy, with a truly feminine side, I knew he would appreciate hanging out with us.

He smiled, embarrassed. "Yeah, sure I'd love to go with you. Are you sure? I mean I don't wanna put you out or anything."

"Marshall, I wouldn't have asked you if I wasn't sure, silly," I responded, smiling.

"Cool, that's cool. Thanks for asking." He beamed.

"Ok, cool. I'll come back by on my way from Nicole's. I gotta get over there, they're waiting."

"Ok, see ya later!" he shouted as I trotted away.

My heart was full. I remembered when we were in fifth grade and the boys were teasing him because he liked to hang out with the girls and do dance routines. They called him *fag* and *gay boy*, making him cry. I just stood there staring, wanting to cry with him. I felt like such a loser for not saying anything. I decided right then I would never let anything like that happen again. We were all going into high school in a couple of months and we would do it together, as equals.

Chapter 26

ALYSSA

Nicole sat at the edge of her bed and tucked her legs up underneath her. She looked like she'd just woken up. She turned taking her nearby laptop into her lap and tapped away. "Gah, I don't know where to start. Grant is so amazing. I totally love him."

She didn't look at me while she talked…and typed.

Tap, tap, and tap…

"So you've told each other *I love you*." I lurched forward, shaking her knee so she would look at me. "Shut the front door! Who said it first?"

"Dude, I'm totally and completely head over heels for him. He said it to me first, in so many words, not actually—*I love you*…but then he came over late one night and spilled his guts," Nicole explained.

"Wow. You guys have been hanging out *forever!* I'm so happy for you!" Nicole smiled. Her eyes sparkled for only a second. Something else was on her mind. She kept looking down, playing with her bracelet. "What's wrong?"

She shrugged. "Besides Grant, it's just this thing with Nadine and my brother. It's kinda weird now that Nadine is actually *seeing* him. It's bummin' me out. I feel in the middle, then left out, not knowing if she's here to hang with me or Chris."

"If it makes you feel better, this entire thing is killing me, you with Grant, Nadine and Chris…and Jake and me. It's crazy how fast things changed."

"So what about you and Jake, what's he up to?"

"I won't see him until Friday, unless I see him late tonight when he gets back from the studio. How am I going to live without seeing him for weeks when I feel like it's already been a lifetime?" I wondered out loud, looking at Nicole for enlightenment. She reached out and squeezed my hand.

"It'll be fine. Time will go by fast and then you'll be together again. We'll keep you busy," she assured, smiling. "So, Friday, that's when you'll see him huh? Dude, tell me what it's like with him—has he tried to get in your pants?" Nicole asked eagerly.

"Ha, sadly no, he hasn't, he's been awfully, how should I say it…gentlemanly about it. He hasn't felt me up or any-thing. Really, we *just* kissed, like serious tongue action mind you, for the first time the other night," I said. I sighed deeply and grabbed my chest, collapsing on the bed. "You have no idea how I just want to crawl all over him. I had no idea how revved up you could get. It's all I think about."

"You're telling me!" Nicole agreed, lying back next to me.

We laid there in silence, staring at the ceiling, and I relived my first kiss for the millionth time.

"If he wanted to do it with you, would you do it?" Nicole whispered.

"Oh my God, I would just die if he asked me or tried anything. I don't think I'm ready for that. I'm scared to death it would hurt and that I'd get pregnant."

I rolled over to face her.

"Yeah, me too." She looked at me with a serious expression. "Dude, it's different for me though. Grant hasn't done it with anyone else, he's still a virgin," she said pausing. "I'd be nervous if I were you, too. I mean can you imagine how many girls he's been with?"

"I know of two. He's never said anything else about more," I divulged.

"He told you that?" she asked surprised.

"Only after I asked."

"Ok, you have to fill me in! Stop being a holdout!" she exclaimed, sitting up. She brushed the blonde hair from her face. "Spill the beans, bitch."

Nicole just about died when I gave her the Jake play-by-play, especially when I admitted to staying the night with him more than once. She admitted some things of her own. Sure, she and Grant may not have done *it*, but they might as well have.

Grant showed up with Greg and Matt. My heart ended up in my throat and I was shaking. Matt immediately stopped walking towards us when he noticed me. His reaction made my stomach drop. I wanted so badly for things to be carefree like they were just a few short weeks ago.

"Go talk to him," Nicole urged, pushing me toward him.

I slowly walked toward him, imagining him gunning me down like in one of those gangster movies. He seemed taller than he did a few weeks ago. His green eyes stood out against his tanned face.

"Hey," I said sheepishly.

"What's up," he replied coldly.

"Matt, I don't want this weird thing between us. I hate it," I whispered softly.

His face drooped.

"Well, you should've thought of that before you decided to ignore me. Oh wait, you totally blew me off for your rock star boyfriend, that's it," he berated me, looking down at his feet.

"Matt, come on, how long have we been friends?" I asked. He looked up at me, not saying a word. "I know it's not...look can we go outside? I really want to talk to you."

I walked toward the door and was relieved to see him following me. Stepping outside, the warm air filled my lungs. We walked out to the street and stopped under a tree.

"All right, what?" He said sharply, still not looking at me.

"I'm sorry. I don't know what to say. It's not like I planned this."

"Whatever Aly, it's over. I've moved on."

"But I don't want any weirdness. You say it's over, but then you stiffen up when you see me, and I'm pretty sure you would have ignored me if I hadn't come up to you."

His posture loosened up and he looked me up and down. "Aly, I've liked you for a long time, and I thought you liked me, too. I'm pretty sure you did, and then bam. Right when I get the balls to ask you out, you disappear and stop taking my calls."

I was embarrassed. He was right. I was a jerk.

"What happened?" he asked, shaking his head. "Jake Masters, fuck, of all people, Aly? Come on, he's just using you."

Nuclear bomb detonation.

"You know, Matt, shut the fuck up, you and everyone else for that matter," I growled, pointing my finger at him.

"Whatever, Aly, you'll see. Just don't get caught up in all the bullshit and forget your friends. We may not be here for you when it comes crashing down."

"You're an asshole, Matt. I just wanted to say I was sorry for hurting you, and you're just being a dick. It's not like I planned it. It just happened!"

He rubbed his forehead with his hand and started pacing. "Aly, whatever. I'll get over it. I hope for your sake he doesn't screw you over."

Just as more face-slapping words came out of Matt's mouth, Jake pulled up a few feet away from us in his truck. I almost passed out when our eyes met. I looked back at Matt and his mouth gaped open. His eyes went tight and his mouth pursed shut. Then he smiled, falsely amused.

"What are the odds? You probably planned this to show off." He abruptly walked away back into the house.

Matt slammed the door so hard it echoed off the neighboring houses.

I stood there with tears welling up in my eyes. I didn't want to turn around, for Jake would see me crying. I took in a deep breath, looking up at the blue cloudless sky. I blinked and let the tears spill down my cheeks, wiping them away as quickly as I could.

"Aly, hey!" Jake shouted out the passenger's side window.

"Hey." I turned to face him and his smiled faded from his face.

"Are you ok?"

"Yeah," I said, leaning against the car door.

"Why are you crying?"

"It's nothing, no big deal," I said, trying to blow it off. "What are you doing here? I'm surprised to see you."

"I'm just getting back from the studio and wanted to see you." I zoned in on that brilliant smile that made my knees go weak. "I need to catch some Z's for a few hours before heading back at 6. Wanna come over?"

I lit up. "Yeah, sure."

"You need to tell someone you're leaving?"

"No, I'll text Nicole."

"What about Matt? That *was* Matt, wasn't it?" He leaned back in his seat as I crawled in the cab.

"Yes, it was." I shut the door and the cold air-conditioning blasted me in the face. It felt good, and dried the perspiration that had accumulated on my forehead. I wiped my eyes again. The last thing I wanted was for him to think I was being a baby.

"Now that I have you held captive, why were you crying?" he asked, glancing over at me. Jake grabbed my thigh, squeezing it.

"Ouch," I yelped and laughed. It was short drive and I sighed, looking out the window as we turned into Jake's driveway. As I got out of his truck, my sister happened to pull into our driveway. *Just great*, I thought. Jake came up next to me and we both stared at Allison. We were all frozen there, silently mad-dogging each other, as if waiting for the other to say something. She just glared at us and walked on, disappearing into the courtyard.

"She fucking hates me, doesn't she?" he said, resigned. "Man, I really can't cut a break with you, can I?" He placed his hands on my shoulders, looking down at me. "I don't care what anyone thinks or says, just so you know. I love being with you, I love how I feel when I'm with you, and I love how inspired I've been since you've come back into my life."

"Ditto," I agreed, smiling. "So you wanted to know why I was crying? Matt said you would screw me over, and he reminded me not to forget who my friends are." A lump in my throat started to build with the sting of impending tears. What the hell? Taking a deep breath for the millionth time, I walked away.

"As much as it pisses me off to hear that, you should be stoked you have so many people who care about you," he said, "to my detriment, unfortunately."

He grabbed my hand, giving it a comforting squeeze, and led me into the house. I heard Kate's voice in the distance, and then another voice I'd never heard before: a male voice, with a British accent. I loved British accents. The smell of food wafted through the air making my mouth water.

"Oh, hey," I said, pulling him to a stop. "Before I forget, I invited Marshall Lawrence to come to Rachel's party with me. I hope you don't mind."

Jake looked stunned. "The little flamer that lives down the street? Why?" he asked, half-laughing.

I huffed, appalled at his reaction and comment. "What?" I asked loudly. My face must have said it all. Jake immediately backpedaled, stammering.

"Well, come on, he's not exactly trying to hide the fact that he's gay."

"And, that's a problem?" I asked, miffed and offended.

"I've never given him any thought, Aly, but I see him around town and it's...I don't think he'll have very much fun, that's all I'm saying."

"I think he's the sweetest ever, so there. I'm bringing him. I hope you'll give him a chance," I blurted out passionately, taken aback by his ignorant comments.

Jake gave me a mild grin. "You're right. Fair enough, now come on. I'm starving."

We came around the corner into the kitchen and a tall man with dark hair and tattoos all over his arms flashed us a huge smile. I began to wonder if and when Jake would begin his permanent etchings, as it seemed a requisite to being in or dealing with a rock band.

"Aw, hey Notting, I didn't expect to see you," Jake said, slapping the man's back. Kate placed a clear glass bowl on the counter and Jake grabbed a handful of chips.

"Jake, we mustn't be rude. Aren't you going to introduce me to this beautiful young lady?".

"Oh, yeah, I'm sorry. Notting, this is Aly, Alyssa Montgomery. She lives next door."

Notting and I shook hands. I admired his rough, handsome features.

"It's lovely to finally meet you, Alyssa. Jake has had nothing but wonderful things to say about you."

I felt the heat rising higher in my face with each kind word. I shot a look in Jake's direction, but he either ignored Notting or didn't hear him as he placed a mound of what looked like hot pastrami on his piece of rye bread. My mouth watered even more. I was so hungry.

"Honey, would like to join us for lunch?" Kate said, looking at me all sweet and motherly.

"I'd love to, thank you."

"Help yourself," she said, sweeping her arms in the direction of the food.

I was a little self-conscious.

As we ate, I learned Jake had the potential for a huge tour a couple months after school started, and that he may have to do home schooling for his senior year. This made me anxious and excited all at the same time.

"Would home schooling be only when he's on tour?" I asked.

"Well, that's what we'll have to figure out," Kate explained.

"Mom, you know I'd rather stay enrolled here and just work it out with my teachers," Jake broke in. Obviously, this had been a topic of past discussions.

"We'll do what's be best for everyone in the band, Jake. It's not only you we have to worry about," Notting added. "We've much to discuss. Where are we at with the studio schedule? You boys are to finish by today, if I remember correctly."

"One more night in the studio, we'll be finished tonight. I'm stoked on the new tunes. The only one givin' me shit is Mike," Jake admitted coldly, stabbing a fork in the leftover pastrami on his plate.

One more night. Then what?

Chapter 27

ALYSSA

Kyle was such a girl. He could never get out of the house like any normal guy. Sitting there for what seemed like fifteen minutes, I got fed up and went back into the house, shouting his name.

"Are you ready?"

"Yeah, you talk to mom?"

"Yep, she's cool."

On my way back out, my sister appeared at the top of the stairs.

"Where you guys going?" Allison asked drily.

"Shopping, *like it's any of your business*," I snapped.

"I would watch it with the smartass remarks," she warned.

"Oh, really, what, what are you gonna do? Tell mom and dad about Jake? Well, go ahead. Then I'll just have to share how you've been having Owen stay the night right under their nose!" Kyle stood next to me, listening in horror.

Her eyes flashed with concern for a brief second. "Oh please, Aly, like they'd believe that desperate attempt." She laughed nervously, looking down at Kyle. "You have no proof. You're just making it up."

"Yeah, well," I paused, I didn't want to blurt it out, but it came out anyway. "Well, they'd believe Kyle, he knows, too!"

"Damnit, Aly, don't drag me into this," Kyle begged, backing away from my contaminated dialog.

"Don't be such a puss, Kyle. She's always pushing you around, like she knows everything. She's just jealous because Jake's hanging out with me, and she's stuck with some second-rate wannabe musician who only wishes he was Jake!" I spat cruelly.

Allison came flying down the stairs with fire in her eyes and I ducked behind Kyle.

"You little bitch!" she shouted, reaching out to strangle me. They stumbled around as Kyle tried to hold her off.

"Allison calm down!" he said shoving her away. I dashed towards the kitchen.

"You think your all that? You'll be broken all over the floor when he uses you, or better yet, when you don't cave into him and he dumps you!"

That was it. The dam broke and the tears were flowing down my face. Allison turned, making her way into the kitchen with Kyle right on her tail.

There was a long silence.

"Oh, come on, you talk like you're all big shit and now this?" said Allison. She laughed in my face. "You're such a baby, Alyssa."

"Shut up! Just shut the fuck up already! I hate you and all the bullshit you stand for!" I shrieked. "Do what you want, Allison. I don't care. Come on, Kyle, let's go."

Kyle and I didn't say a word all the way to the mall. All I could do was sit there sniveling, doing that hiccup-air-snort thing from crying too hard.

Our shopping spree was fast and resolute. Kyle didn't argue with my suggestions and demands, ending up with a pair of black Levis and a black, subtly printed short-sleeve button-up. We arrive at the hair salon an hour later. I gave Kyle's name for the wait list and waited patiently for one the hairdressers. The girls in this salon were the edgy, tattooed kind, like the girls who worked at the MAC makeup counter at the department store.

A petite ghost-white girl with tattoos up and down both of her arms walked behind the counter. She opened her mouth and called out Kyle's name, and a glint of shiny silver metal caught my eye. She had her tongue pierced. Kyle looked at me to make a move, nudging me. I think he was scared of her.

"Hi," I said standing. "My brother, Kyle, needs something a little bit…not so nerdy."

Kyle shot me a cross look and punker girl laughed sweetly.

"Hmm, I can see that," she said, smiling and winked at him. "I think I can help. Follow me. I'm Tracy, by the way."

"Thanks, Tracy!" I chirped. Hopeful Kyle would come back looking cool.

Kyle leered at me and reluctantly walked away with her. An hour later, he was back with a stylish choppy cut, a bit like Jake's, but shorter.

Spending the afternoon with my brother was a rarity. Fighting with my sister wasn't. We arrived back home, and I stood at our front door hoping I could make it to my bedroom without seeing her. I wasn't that lucky. Allison stood at the top of the stairs. She didn't look mad. She looked sad.

What now? I wondered.

"What's wrong with you? Did you tell on me to mom or something? Where's your happy smile?"

"You're so lame, Aly. Yeah, I want to tell mom, so she can try and save you from yourself and yeah, I admit, at first I was a little jealous about Jake. But that's not the reason why I'm concerned."

She was uncommonly *calm*.

"Why are you such a bitch about everything? Ever since you found out, you've been ten times worse," I pointed out. "You and everyone else think he's someone he's not. I've spent a lot of time with him, Allison, like late nights, and he's never once tried to get in my pants."

She stared at me with an amazed look. "Well, I'm glad to hear that. I don't know what to think about it." She shook her head slowly. "Owen…he's a great guy and he really cares about me. So don't be lame saying those shitty things, calling him a wannabe. You don't know him."

I knew I deserved *that* scolding. The remorse filled me like floodwater.

"I'm sorry. I didn't mean to call him a wannabe."

"Aly, just watch your back. Don't be naïve. I don't want you to get hurt or pregnant or anything else."

"I know. I get it, I promise." I huffed. "And for your information, he's even said it himself, that I'm not ready."

"You talked about it?" she asked, surprised.

"Yeah, we talk about a lot, Allison." I paused, taking in her sincere disposition, which was taking me completely off guard. "It's been easy with Jake, never lame or awkward for either of us. I feel comfortable with him. I'm just me, like I am with you, and it's no big deal."

She stood staring at me, looking intently upon me. I got the impression she wanted to say something, so I waited.

"I can see why he likes you. You're probably the only normal thing in his life right now," she said, trailing off.

I could tell she had some sort of an issue with it.

"Aly, I want to tell you something, because I think it's time." She walked to the sofa, sitting down. "Come here." She pointed to the chair our father always sat in. "I never thought I'd ever say anything to anyone. You know, until you started seeing Jake, that is. Now it's something that keeps popping in my head, like I see the same thing happening to you. Not that it would happen to you, but I don't want it to happen to you. You know, like history repeating itself."

I was riveted. I had absolutely no idea what she was talking about. My imagination went wild while she was contemplating her next words. My heart sank when I thought she was about to tell me Jake and her hooked up and he dumped her. I bet that's what it was! They hooked up, and they promised never to say anything to anyone. That's why she was acting like a super bitch about Jake.

My stomach went sick.

"There's only one other person who knows about this, and it's mom." Huh? What? "You can ask her if you want, but if you ask her, you'll have to tell her why I told you. You have to be the one to tell her about Jake." she whispered. "Dad has no idea."

As soon as Allison and I became old enough to have our own friends, we barely ever spoke. I never knew her to be so serious with me. She never seemed to care much for me, other than bitching out Rachel, and that was a first.

"Do you remember Justin?"

"Yeah and you cried all the time."

"Do you realize when that was going on I was the age you are now? And that he was older than me, he was 19."

"I didn't realize the age thing. I just recall he had a car."

"Aly, I got pregnant by Justin when I was fifteen, and I had an abortion." She spoke softly, her words barely audible.

My heart sank. I couldn't believe my mother, of all people, would keep something like that from my father. Allison looked at me, waiting for my reply, but I was speechless.

She continued. "It was a really fucked up time for me, Aly. I was really in love with him, and when I told him I was pregnant, he started being a jerk and he said he didn't believe me. When I took one of those pee stick tests at his house, proving it, he immediately talked abortion. He left it on me to figure out. He blamed me because I wasn't on the pill. He said that once I took care of it, we could see each other again."

"Allison, I'm sorry. I can't believe it," I choked out, subdued.

Tears began to form as I watched my sister fight her own from falling down her cheeks. She buried her face in her hands. "Yeah, it was really messed up. The worst part is, I tried to take care of it myself, going to one of those free clinics, and they didn't get it all. I got really sick and passed out in the kitchen, right in front of Mom. When I came to, I was in the ambulance. I had to tell them and her what happened, obviously." She looked back up at me, mortified by her confession. "Dude, they didn't get it all out." She repeated herself, making sure I understood, and my shock lurched.

"What?" I asked, horrified. "What's that supposed to mean?"

"They didn't get all of the fetus out. Parts of it were still left inside me," she explained. "I felt so dirty and so, like, damaged. I still do. I haven't had sex with anyone since. Owen's a great guy. He's the first one in a long time not to pressure me."

We sat in silence for a long moment. I felt sorry for my sister. I took her hand in mine, rubbing the top, and then hugged her tight. When I pulled back, she was tear streaked and that made me start crying, too.

"Stop it. We don't need to get all emo about this. I didn't tell you to gross you out, or make a statement or anything like that. I just don't want you to have to go through anything remotely like what I had to go through, not even having to make the choice of having an abortion or not. I mean, you can catch diseases and shit, Aly."

"What did mom say?" I asked timidly.

"By the time I realized what was really going on because I was so out of it, I was out of surgery. They had to go back in and clean everything out they should have gotten the first time. Mom was pretty scared. She cried a lot, beating herself up pretty bad, wondering what she'd done wrong for me to feel that I couldn't go to her. That's when our relationship changed for the better. I could have died, Aly. The doctor said it was like getting poisoned. If I would have passed out in my room, alone, who knows what would have happened."

"Wow. This is insane news." I grappled with its hard-core meaning.

"And that bastard had the balls to try and go out with me again, can you believe that?"

"What did you say to him?"

"I told him off, what do you think I said?" She laughed scornfully. "If a guy ever treats you badly, you better get the hell out of there and fast. It won't ever get better. An asshole will always be an asshole."

"Thanks for telling me. I love you," I said, giving her another hug.

I couldn't remember the last time I told my sister I loved her.

Chapter 28

JAKE

I don't think I ever recalled being bummed about leaving to go on tour, but I was. I was already missing Aly and it wasn't even the beginning. Sitting in my truck, I thought about what we'd do the next time we were together. I wanted it to be memorable since I'd be gone for so long. The hot tub popped in my head or maybe Malibu or The Getty Museum.

I was seriously tired of everyone but Aly. Mike was turning into a total tool, and every day that went by I regretted choosing him to be in the band. Not only was he not agreeing with the creative direction I wanted to go in, he was constantly asking about or referring to Aly, but in ways that I couldn't accuse him of coveting. He had the nerve to give me shit about how I was letting her influence me, as well as the band's direction.

I thought Mike would fit in. He had me sold in the beginning. In fact, I had to convince Bobby and Dump to let Mike in. Now Dump was in the "*I told you so*" mode. Dump warned me that Mike was a total liability with his drug and alcohol use, but who was I to judge? I liked to drink and smoke weed now and then. I chalked up Dump's doubts to his recovery, not wanting to have those things near him. Now, looking back, I had blinders on, only seeing Mike's ability to play the guitar.

The silver lining in the whole increasingly toxic mess was Jeff Arnault, our new producer. He had an impressive roster of A-list solo artists and bands with hit singles notched in his belt. Jeff and Notting agreed with the new music; that's all that really mattered. I couldn't do it without the guys, but the push back and negative energy from Mike was not something that was conducive to creative flourish.

A bang at the tail end of my truck shocked me out of my daze. It was Dump and Sienna. "What's up man, why ya sittin' out here?" Dump asked, poking his head in through the passenger door. Cigarette smoke gusted in with the breeze.

"Dude, get that cancer-stick outta here," I said, rolling down the window farther and fanning my hand in front of my face.

"Aw man, sorry," he apologized, holding his cig back behind him. I guess being a recovering addict, Dump needed to keep his two-pack-a-day vice.

Rolling up the windows, I reluctantly got out of my car, not wanting to deal with anyone, especially my mother after seeing her demeanor. I spotted Rachel pulling up and my stomach sank. Great, she was the last person I wanted to see. The guilt swelled inside me. I hadn't seen nor talked to Rachel since the whole Aly encounter. I wondered what she was doing there. She certainly couldn't have been driving by. I looked over at Sienna, who gave me a shoulder shrug.

Rachel stayed in her car at the front of the studio, waiting for someone to acknowledge her. I approached Dump and Sienna, and before I could mutter a word, Sienna came clean.

"Jake, don't look at me that way. She just wants to talk to you before the party tomorrow. I think she's pretty much over everything."

"Yeah, well," I mumbled, looking over my shoulder at Rachel's car, surprised to see Mike bent down, talking to her at the driver's side window. "What? She hooking up with Mike now?"

"That guy? I'll lose what little respect I have for her if that's the case," Dump piped, flicking his cigarette butt in their direction. "Sorry bro, but Mike is on my last nerve, *and* Rachel for that matter. Oops, sorry," he said, covering his mouth. "I guess I can't go there." He gave Sienna a wry smile, throwing his arm around her shoulder, and pulled her in for a quick peck.

"Don't be an asshole." Rachel tried to untie herself from his grip.

"Aw, come on, babe, you know she's a nutcase," Dump said, laughing.

"Don't forget that this isn't all her fault," Sienna replied, looking in my direction.

"Ok, that's enough. We don't need to rehash this stinkin' shit," I said, walking in Rachel and Mike's direction.

Sienna and Dump followed.

My nerves frayed with every step. I put my sunglasses on to shield my eyes, hoping it would hide my discontent. Mike looked extra scruffy. I'd become too familiar with his many faces. He was hung over.

"'Sup, man." Mike nodded. I glanced down at Rachel. She made no attempt to get out of her car or even look at me. "She wants to talk to you."

Mike took a cigarette out of its pack and lit it up. White smoked puffed up around his face. He walked away, giving the silent treatment to Dump and Sienna. I wanted to reach out and knock that cig out of his mouth. *What a dick*, I thought. Something's gotta give with his shitty attitude. I'd never been so on edge in my life. It was making me ill.

"Bro, not sure how long this'll last. I can't stand the vibe," Dump said in a low growl. He reached out for Sienna's hand and dragged her towards the studio doors.

The sun beat down on my black t-shirt and I began to sweat. I turned, walking up to Rachel's car. The air-conditioning was blowing her hair around her face, and pieces stuck to her red lipstick. She turned, looking up at me. I stood waiting for her to say something.

"You're just gonna stand there? Aren't you gonna say hi?" she asked sarcastically. "Wipe the sweat from your upper lip, Jake. God, how can you not feel that?"

I was relieved to hear her candor. "What's up, Rachel?" I asked sincerely, patting my upper lip. "Mike says you need a word."

"Uh, yeah," she said pausing, her face pained. "I've been wondering if you were still planning to play at my party, that you're not going to bail at the last minute." She finally looked at me.

"Yeah, of course we're playing. I wouldn't bail like that. I'd like to think you'd know me better than that by now."

"Our last face to face was pretty dramatic. I'm sorry, Jake, it's just tough."

Rachel being sincere tugged at me. This, combined with the last time I was with her, painted a more human side to her than I'd known all these years. She was always tough as nails, an ironclad fortress of no-nonsense, too confident and too cocky.

"Rachel, can we just move forward, please?" I asked, nearly pleading. "I admit it's been weird not having you around."

I had to be honest. Being the one dealing with the promoting and everything else was daunting. I was so used to Rachel and Sienna dealing with it all. Rachel had led the charge; now I was left giving direction to Sienna.

"Yeah right, you and your new girlfriend would just *love* having me around."

Her perfectly manicured hands wrapped tightly around the steering wheel like she was ready to run me down. "Come on Rachel, come inside," I ordered, standing upright. "I'm sweating my balls off."

"Jake, I really don't have anything else to say. I just wanted to tell you I'm sorry… and I miss you," she said, staring straight out her windshield.

"Come on Rachel, come inside, hang out for a while," I asked once more.

"Park your car." I slapped the side of her car in finality.

As I walked away, I thought about how she pushed Aly in the pool. I didn't want to believe she could be so vindictive, but now I kinda understood being pushed to the edge. My gut was telling me that Mike had some weird, secret obsession with Aly. I was never a fighter, but it made me wanna kick his ass.

This was our last day at La Brea Recording Studio. Anxiety gnawed at me knowing Rachel would be walking through the door. I decided to move myself into studio three and wait there.

As I grabbed my guitars, Mike and Rachel walked through the door.

"Glad you decided to join us," I said with a wry smile.

"Why not, I miss everyone," she said softly. Her eyes shimmered like she was holding back tears.

Great.

Mike passed us with his guitar cases, and I could smell pot and alcohol on him. Since I'd stopped smoking and drinking, I was hyper aware of when others were using. I looked back at Rachel, realizing the glint in her eye was instead the glazed-over look from ripping the ganja.

I took the phone from my pocket to text Aly.

- *HEY ALYCAT—THINKING OF YOU, WISH U WERE HERE.*

I waited, hoping she'd hit me back right away, and she didn't let me down.

- *HI, WISH I WAS THERE TOO. I MISS YOU. ALYCAT, HUH? I THINK I'M LIKIN' MY NEW NICKNAME.*
- *YOU LIKE THAT, EH? I THOUGHT IT APPROPRIATE, CONSIDERING.*
- *HA! CONSIDERING WHAT?*
- *AH, HAHA, I'LL TELL YOU TO YOUR FACE, AMOUNGST OTHER THINGS I'D LIKE TO DO WITH YOUR FACE.*
- *HMM? REALLY AND WHAT IS THAT?*

I smiled. Was she egging me on? Or was she innocently wondering? The more candid and open she was with me, the more I fell for her. She took me to a place of feeling. I didn't want to be numb with her. I was jacked up on the way she made me feel.

- *I CAN'T WAIT TO TASTE YOUR LIPS.*

I hit send, and I waited, and waited. She didn't come back right away, and it killed me that I couldn't see her face. Then the ping came, one word.

- *DITTO*
- *I'LL TEXT ON MY WAY HOME—KEY TO MY BACK DOOR IS UNDER*
- *THE RED POT. HOPE YOU'LL BE THERE*
- *I WILL.*

The familiar ache ran through my body. I was electrified with what was yet to come. I threw my head back and rubbed my eyes, telling myself to focus on the music.

"That good, huh?" Mike startled me with his insinuation.

I ignored him and laughed, *if he only knew*. I took my guitar out of its coffin and plugged in. As I tuned it, he persisted.

"You know, man, Rachel's smokin'. You really done with her and hangin' with that Aly chick?"

A rage ignited, but I quickly caught myself, giving pause. I chuckled. I couldn't believe what I was hearing.

"Mike, first of all, it's none of your business, and second, if you think Rachel's so fuckin' hot, go for it. I have no ties. She's a friend, and whatever happened between us once, shouldn't have. All free and clear, bro, you have my best wishes."

"Yeah, Rachel's hot and all, but she's not my type."

"What is your type, Mike? The last time I saw, you were running with some sleaze. Rachel'd be an upgrade."

Fuck him, I thought, he deserved my insults.

He laughed contemptuously with a malevolent grin, studying me with his blood-shot, glazed eyes. The wicked smile faded from his face.

"You think you're a badass motherfucker, don't you?" he said, placing his guitar in the rack. The perspiration on his brow and upper lip shimmered in the light. For a moment I wondered if he was on something other than weed. I hadn't seen a violent streak in Mike since I'd known him, but I readied myself for a fight.

"Dude, what the fuck is wrong with you? Why are you all over my shit about Rachel and Aly?"

Just then, the entire tribe arrived. My mother, Dump, Sienna, Jeff and Notting rolled through the door, with Bobby leading the way. Bobby stopped dead in his tracks and everyone piled up his rear.

Mike continued with his verbal attack. "You know, one of these days everyone is gonna get sick of your my-way-or-the-highway bullshit, Jake. This music, this new shit, we sound like a bunch of pussy-whipped faggots. It's not what I signed up for."

Rachel came through the door just as I struck back.

"So fuckin' quit then!" I shouted at Mike, then looked at everyone else. "Does anyone else have a problem? I know Notting and Jeff like what they hear! You think a platinum record producer is gonna get tied up in some shit that'll reflect on him?"

I could have killed Mike right then and there with my bare hands.

"Does anyone give a shit what I think?" Mike asked looking around.

"All right, children!" Notting shouted. "Calm down! Everyone not in the band please leave! The chaps and I need to have a little pow-wow."

"Naw, Notting, I've had enough of Jake and his love-sick bullshit," he said, looking around. "Come on, you think Dump's gonna have my back? He's just as whipped as Jake is."

Mike pointed directly at Sienna.

"Wait a sec, don't drag me and Sienna into your baby bullshit," Dump growled.

"Whatever, I'm outta here," Mike said under his breath. He stormed past everyone, grabbing his guitar and its case.

Rachel grabbed his arm in an attempt to stop him, unsuccessfully. Everyone stood in silence for a long moment glancing between each other.

"We don't need him to record," I growled. "I can do it myself."

"We need him for the tour! We need him, period!" Notting roared.

I buried my face in my hands, grabbing my hair in frustration.

"All right, Jake, go shake it off," Jeff ordered. "Dump, man your drums, we'll do you first. We gotta get this shit started. Time is eating away."

———

I could see Rachel and Mike through the glass doors, smoking cigs. Rachel paced back and forth. It looked like she was bitching him out as he sat on the black wrought-iron bench, with his head hung low. *Interesting*, I thought. I tried to imagine what she was saying to him. As much as I wanted him out, Notting was right, we needed him. We'd all worked too hard.

I sat staring at the same Beatles and John Lennon artwork for a half hour, wondering what it would have been like to be them. If it could happen for them, it could happen for us, right? I thought about his murder and what a waste it all was. I wondered if he would have said it was all worth it.

I decided to go get Aly.

Taking the phone out of my pocket I dialed Aly's number. After a couple of rings, her sweet voice touched my ear.

"Hey Alycat, um, I was thinking since it looks like we're gonna be here for a while, and instead of waiting until later," I paused, "you think you could sneak out and come to the studio? I'll come and get you right now."

"My mom and dad are home now. I mean, I guess I could lie, but aren't you like in Hollywood?"

"Yeah, but it'll only take me a half hour or so to get there."

"Huh, ok, well, you can't come here to get me," she warned, laughing slightly.

"Duh, I know that. Can you go to Nicole's?"

"Yeah, call me when you're around the corner and I'll walk over, but I don't want to go in…so just meet me down the street from her house."

"Cool, see you soon."

"Ok."

I was hopped up as I walked out the front doors of the studio. Rachel straightened her posture and Mike stood up, approaching me. "Hey man, I'm sorry. I didn't mean to go off on you like that. I just got all this pent-up shit inside me."

Mike looked and sounded sincere. It was tough for him to look me in the eyes when he spoke. He played with the pack of Marlboro red box cigarettes held in his hand. Rachel silently coaxed me to respond.

"Man, Mike, it's just tough, you know your moodiness. It's like we're oil and water," I offered, totally meaning it, trying to be fair.

"Yeah, I know. This whole direction, man, it's just different."

"Look, I didn't mean what I said about you quitting. I don't want you to quit, if that helps any."

He finally looked at me, nodding his head. His blood-shot, glossed-over eyes were unreadable.

"Cool. I'm in."

"Cool…I'm going to get Aly."

A gust of warm air whipped up the fallen, dried leaves, swirling them around my feet. My eyes first went to Mike. His expression lit up ever so slightly, then faded back into his hooded eyes. I was afraid to look at Rachel when her voice broke the silence.

"I guess that means I should leave," Rachel offered, disappointment rising in her voice.

"You're more than welcome to stay, but it's up to you," I replied.

I glanced back and forth between them. Neither attempted to say another word.

The excitement I was feeling was intense. I couldn't wait for Aly to sit in the sound room, for her to hear one of the songs inspired by her, to see the look on her face. I wondered if she would get it. Driving down La Cienega Boulevard, I was agonized by the traffic—and also knowing that once my mother found out I had left the studio, she would rip me a new one.

I felt drunk. *Drunk love*, was that what I was high on? Was I in love? Was this what being in love felt like? I was almost certain it was.

Chapter 29

JAKE

I spotted Aly as I drove up our street and signaled to her that I'd turn around. Driving slowly back down, I didn't see her on either side. I slowed, looking around. She was standing in Marshall's driveway. *What the hell is wrong with him?* I thought. I pulled up, checking out his patterned t-shirt and tight white skinny jeans. He had his hair flared out a la 80's band *Flock of Seagulls*, accentuated with a hot pink leopard fabric headband. He was definitely wearing make-up. It took everything inside me not to ask him if he looked in the mirror before going out in public. I thought better of it because of Aly, but I seriously didn't get it.

I waited patiently while they talked a more few minutes, but I couldn't keep waiting. "Hey Aly, I gotta get going," I shouted and waved at Marshall.

Aly thoughtfully stared at Marshall a moment longer and the breeze whipped her hair around her face. Everything slowed down as I focused on her plump, naturally pink lips. I loved that she didn't wear lipstick. *Loved it*. Her tan legs carried her towards me. Her strut flowed with an ease of a feline…*Alycat*. The thought of the nickname I gave her made me smile. I wondered if she thought it was corny.

She opened the passenger side door and tossed her shiny silver metallic bag onto my not-so-clean floor mat. The bluster of wind stirred a new, unfamiliar fragrance into the cab, a clean citrus scent. Aly slammed the door shut and a smile spread across her face. I wanted to kiss her. A bit of self-consciousness came over me.

Why does that keep happening?

Marshall stared at us in earnest, smiling. I smiled back and waved goodbye. Poor kid, maybe he didn't have a choice whether to be gay or not. *And,* he seemed not to mind it, being perfectly aware of who he was. Huh, I couldn't say I knew who I was any more, that was for sure.

Driving down the road, I couldn't stop glancing at her. It had been days since we were near each other. I felt that rush of energy Aly always spoke of – a live, invisible wire. I couldn't take it anymore, and pulled over before we reached the light going out to the main road.

"What's up? Why are you pulling over?" she asked as we came to a stop.

Without answering her, I leaned over, bringing her face closer to mine. She didn't fight me, and she moved in quicker than I expected. She grabbed both sides of my face. Taking her lips to mine, I felt a frenzy overcome me. The way she smelled, the way she tasted, the softness of her lips, her tongue and her skin were spinning me out of control. She was equally aggressive, completely inebriating me. I backed my seat up and pulled her over onto my lap. She felt my excitement and a gasp escaped her.

"Am I hurting you?" she whispered, heavily.

"No," I couldn't help but moan.

Her black eye liner had started to smudge under her eyes from the heat we were generating. Our chests heaved in unison, and her warm sweet breath flashed over my face.

"Aly, this is what you do to me," I admitted, brushing her hair away from her cheek. She started to kiss me again.

A car horn startled us.

"Shit, who is it?" she said, burying her head into my neck.

Hoots and hollers followed, and the honking persisted from an unfamiliar beat-up Jeep Cherokee. We realized it was Chris and Nadine.

"Get a room, you two!" Nadine shouted over Chris, who was in the driver's seat.

Aly shouted back. "You scared the shit out of me!"

"Ha, that's what you get for sucking face right where your parents could drive by!"

"Later," Chris hollered and sped away.

"Aly, call me first chance!" Nadine shouted, her voice faded away with every word.

I didn't want to go back to the studio. I wrapped my arms around her, burying my face in her hair again, and filling my lungs with her breath.

The heat of the day didn't have anything on what we were conducting in my truck. I wondered how long it would be until we were satisfied. The pressure was building at a dizzying pace when another disturbance knocked me to my senses.

My mother's name flashed on the screen of my phone.

"Shit, it's my mom. We need to go." I planted one last kiss on her swollen lips and she moved back to her seat, buckling herself in.

"Are you in trouble?" Her brow furrowed with worry.

"Yeah, you could say that." I laughed it off. "We should have been back by now."

I reached over blasting the air-conditioning as high as it would go to cool us off. I grabbed my groin, hoping the sticky wetness wouldn't show through my pants when I got out of the car. That's just what I needed, was for my mom to see a nice jizz stain on my pants walking through the door with Aly. Thank god for black denim.

I was too afraid to answer my phone. I just wanted to get back there, take care of my shit and leave.

We finally arrived, and thankfully Rachel and Mike weren't outside. My eyes darted to where Rachel's car was parked and it was still there, unfortunately.

"I have to tell you something and I don't want you freaking out, ok?" I looked at Aly picking up her hand. "Rachel is kinda back in the picture."

"What? What does that mean?" She snatched her hand away from mine. "What the hell, Jake? That bitch pushed me in the pool and totally has it out for me!"

"Wait, look, whatever happened between you two, I'm sure she feels bad. You know she apologized to me."

"So the fuck what, Jake? She's just kissing your ass." She pouted, looking out the window. "Whatever, Jake. I guess I'll just have to deal with it."

"She's here, that's why I'm telling you. I didn't want you to walk in and be surprised. I was actually hoping she'd leave while I was gone. I told her I was going to get you."

"Are you kidding me?" she shouted. "I'm not going in there, then. You're out of your mind, you know that?"

"Aly, please, come on. Don't do this. She's been hanging out with Mike. Let's just see where it goes. I have no problem telling her to scram if she starts acting lame."

"Put yourself in my shoes," she said, unbuckling her seatbelt. "Change places with me. Say I had some guy I just fucked once, who totally had it out for you, hanging out at my house? *After* he completely humiliated you in front of the entire school. How would you feel?"

"I get it, Aly, but she's Sienna's best friend. Is she supposed to make new friends because we decided not to hang out anymore? We have to move on and just get over it, Aly. Let's just see how it goes."

"I'll walk home from here, Jake, if I feel uncomfortable."

Now she was being unreasonable. "We'll both leave if it gets weird, I promise."

Walking into the studio, the first person I saw was my mother pacing back and forth, her cell phone pressed to her head. Great. I tried not to make eye contact. I held Aly's hand, dragging her along as quickly as possible toward the sound room. I could see Mike in the booth.

"Jake Michael Masters!" my mother shouted. My hair stood up and my heart came out of my throat.

"Brace yourself," I warned Aly.

My mother came tearing around the corner. "Where have you been?"

"Mom, aren't you going to say hello to Aly," I said dryly.

Aly stepped back behind me, afraid of my mom's wrath.

"Aly, I'm sorry you have to witness this ass chewing. But since Jake has made the decision to include you in his bands happenings, this is part of it. And since Jake seems to be completely blind as to the impact his choices are having on our bottom line, well, I need to be the one to point them out."

I thought the veins in her forehead would explode. Notting walked out of the sound booth, saying goodbye to Rachel, and I felt Aly stiffen beside me. Rachel's face said it all, too. Neither of them was ready to be in the same room with each other. They were like two cats ready to pounce on each other. Rachel turned to Notting, hugging him, and quickly said goodbye to me without making eye contact or acknowledging Aly.

My mother picked up on this like a metal detector would a gold watch buried in the sand. She shot me a look of contempt, and I wanted to crawl under the chair sitting next to me. Why was everything getting so complicated? All I wanted was to be with Aly and play music with my bros, and everything seemed as if it were falling apart.

As soon as Rachel left, my mother glared at Notting and me, demanding an explanation. "What the hell is going on?" she wailed. "Aly I'm sorry, but Jake and Notting have some explaining to do."

"Darling, calm down, there is nothing going on," Notting reassured.

"Don't patronize me, Notting." She crossed her arms to her chest and turned to me. "As for you Mr. Masters, I know I'm your mother and there are things, personal things," she said, pausing to look at Aly. "That you'd rather not have me know too much about, but when these things start to have an impact on others and important decisions, I think you'd better make sound choices."

Now it was my turn to have an aneurism. She had no idea how important Aly was to me.

"I'm outta here. I can't do this with you here, mom. This is bullshit." These were the only words I could find without completely going off and regretting it.

"Jake you'd better watch it," Notting growled.

"Jake, don't talk to your mother that way," Aly whispered under her breath, pleading and clung to my arm.

My mother was seething, with alarm in her eyes. I was too afraid to look at Notting. I'd never spoken to my mother like that.

"I'll see you at home in no less than an hour," she said through clenched teeth, blowing past us.

"Well, mate, looks like you've got some 'fessing up to do. I didn't realize you'd hadn't spoken to her about Miss Aly here."

"Notting, it's bad enough she runs every other aspect of my life. I don't need her running this too. Let's go, Aly."

Aly hesitated, sheepishly mouthing "*Sorry*" to Notting. I wasn't sorry. This whole thing was getting blown way out of proportion.

———

Aly and I drove most of the way in silence with the stereo blaring. She sang along to a compilation of old school Aerosmith, Nirvana, Rolling Stones and the new breed of independent artists. She had a sweet voice—slightly pitchy, but solid enough that if she had some training, she could really sing well.

I didn't want to go home. I wanted to be with Aly.

"I'm not going home. I'm either going to get a hotel, or stay at Dump's," I affirmed, bouncing her slender fingers around in my hand.

"What? Why?" Aly gripped my hand, stopping my nervous fidgeting.

I didn't want to give her an inkling that my mother probably wanted to tell me to stop seeing her, because A) that would not happen, and B) it would only hurt her feelings and make her self-conscious about coming over. I had to figure out how to convince my mom that Aly wasn't going to be an issue.

"Uh, hello, aren't you gonna answer me? Kate will worry, and you can't *not* go home, Jake. That's totally irresponsible. It's the exact reason she went off on you in the first place."

"What are you now, my conscience?" I snapped, and as soon as I did, I felt bad. She sat there staring at me through narrowed eyes, speechless. "I'm sorry." I clinched the steering wheel. I was pissed at my mother for being such a miserable bitch, always poking her nose in every little thing.

"Aly, it's complicated. If I were to go back to my place, she and I would have it out, and I wouldn't see you tonight. I wanna be with you as much as I can before I leave."

She had no idea how bad I wanted to be with her.

"Don't remind me about you leaving. I've been trying not to think about it," she said softly. Her head dipped down, her hair now covered her face.

"Hey, we have this weekend, and then I'll have two shows here in L.A. The time will blow by. I'll be home before you know it."

"Yeah, for you it will. I'll be stuck here dealing with my sister telling me *I told you so*. But whatevs," she grumbled, shrugging her shoulders. "I'll stay with you. I'll tell my parents I'm staying somewhere else."

I thought about where to stay. I didn't want to be in Dump's scumbag apartment. I shuddered just thinking about it. No, it had to be a hotel. Hermosa Beach had a few to choose from, but then that was too close to home. Someone might see us. Venice or Santa Monica would be better.

"Are you sure?"

"Yeah." She smiled, grabbing my hand. "I've never been so sure. It's been easy so far doin' it." She laughed. "I'll call my mom now and tell her I'll be at Nicole's."

I was uneasy.

Chapter 30

ALYSSA

I was stoked to finally be alone with Jake, with parents far, far away. I wondered if he would try to do it with me, and if I could if he did. My heart started thumping hard just thinking about it, and about how bad I wanted to earlier, feeling him firm against me. I couldn't believe I turned a guy on. The thought of it made my insides tingle. If we did it, would it make us totally official? I reasoned with myself, like I was making some sort of a deal. I really wanted this to be more, to give him what he wanted, so he'd know what would be waiting for him when he returned. I didn't want to be the immature, innocent little girl that he perceived me to be. He was always babying me, being my protector. I wanted to move past that. I wanted to prove that I was worthy of someone like him and that I could hold my own.

"What's wrong?" he asked, shaking my hand.

"Nothing, why?"

"I don't know." He shrugged. "You got all quiet. If you're having second thoughts, we don't have to do this. We can go home."

"No, no, I want to be with you. I don't want to go home," I reassured him. I sighed deeply and like a ruptured water pipe without warning, words just spilled out of my mouth. "Well, there is one thing. You know, since it's obviously changed between us."

I couldn't spit the rest out. I froze.

"What do you mean?" he asked smiling at me, tugging on my fingers.

He glanced back and forth at me, and the road ahead.

"It just seems so..." I hesitated. "Intense now."

He waited and turned down the radio.

"And?" Coaxing me along which was one thing I loved about him. He always made me relax.

I laughed nervously. "Jake, I feel, like, self-conscious now, it's weird. I find myself thinking about every little thing. I want this weirdness I feel to go away."

"If it makes you feel any better, I feel the same way," he admitted. "I have to be honest, right? Going with what feels good and right. I trust you."

Untangling our fingers his warm hand rubbed my bare thigh, sending butterflies right up my spine.

"Ditto."

"We're gonna live it up tonight, since this may be the last time we see each other for a while."

"Why's that?" I asked uneasily.

"Kate's gonna kick my ass up and down the street when I come home tomorrow."

"What about the party tomorrow night?"

"Ha, the party's no problem, since we're playing. But she'll demand I come straight home and lecture me about bullshit I'm not doing right. She won't let me live this down for a while, but whatever." He shrugged off the thought. "So, on to our epic eve, Alycat. Where would you like to stay? In a fabulous high rise overlooking the city or on the beach?"

My stupid, juvenile reaction was to giggle. "I don't know. You pick, since this is your idea."

"Ok, we'll stay on the beach. I've been to this swanky hotel called *Shutters*, and it's pretty rad. The rooms are pretty snazzy."

"Really and when was the last time you were at this *snazzy* hotel?" I questioned warily.

"We went to meet up with some people hanging out at the pool, partied there one afternoon. This was last year. I'm sure not much has changed." He smiled, turning the music up louder.

I'd only been away from our beach town and into the city two other times, to shop on Melrose Avenue. This was a different life. There were bums everywhere. Come to think of it, we didn't have any bums. Well, we had our one local bum. Our bum looked better off than these bums. I felt sorry for them with their ill-fitting shoes—or no shoes at all—their filthy clothes, grimy, greasy, unkempt hair, and toothless grins. I noticed many of them talked to themselves.

"Hey." Jake shook my leg. "Why the silence? I'm beginning to think this may be a bad idea."

"Oh, no, I was just thinking about all these homeless people around. Why are there so many here? It's really sad, I'm sad for them, like wondering if they ever had families."

"Yeah, it's pretty crazy that you've got million dollar homes and swanky hotels juxtaposed with the homeless. Santa Monica is pro-homeless. They feed them over near the civic center, by where the court buildings are," he explained, shrugging. "I fed the homeless one Thanksgiving there."

"Really? That's really sweet of you."

"At first I didn't want to, but when I got there, there were like, regular people there, with their kids. People who looked like you and I, people down on their luck. It's eye-opening to think how your life can change in a heartbeat."

All I could do was nod sadly.

Lost in my melancholy, I hadn't realized we arrived at our destination and he was right, it was over the top. There were those valet guys with black suits, rushing around taking and retrieving vehicles for their obviously wealthy customers. I felt ill at ease, waiting for our turn at having our car doors opened by one of these crisply pressed worker-bees. I looked at those stepping out and retrieving their Range Rovers and Mercedes-Benz, the Lexus and BMWs. Ours was the only regular ride in view. Even the hipsters, who looked like rock stars and movie stars, were driving super nice cars. At least when Jake was away from his truck, he would fit in with these L.A. types. Glancing at him, with his disheveled black hair, his perfect skin, and his stubbly jaw line, I went weak.

His brilliant, impossibly blue eyes shot a look at me, catching me off guard.

"This is why I love being with you, Alycat, because it's all too real with you. You see things through different eyes." He smiled broadly at me with his brilliant white teeth.

"I'm sorry?"

"Your concern about the bums," he reminded me.

Just then, one of the hottest valet guys I'd ever seen opened my door. He couldn't have been much older than Jake, and had blonde beach-boy hair, tanned skin and a thousand-watt smile. I was sure I blushed, because I felt the heat rise instantly.

"Checking in?"

"Um, yeah," I answered awkwardly.

His eyes twinkled, not leaving mine, and I couldn't help but smile back at him.

He glanced around quickly, as if he was looking for someone in particular. "Parents already checked in?"

Did he really just ask me that?

Before I could squeak out one syllable, Jake was at my side, with his glasses on and looking beyond the part. I could have passed out. Abruptly, he put his arm around my shoulders and pulled me close. My heart stopped. Valet Hottie stood taller, and a cool smile appeared on his face as he and Jake stood eye-to-eye. I held my breath, not knowing what to expect.

"They're no parents here," Jake responded brusquely. "Thanks."

Jake pulled me away towards the hotel entrance, and all I could do was smile a quirky grin at Valet Hottie as he wished us a nice stay. I was a little embarrassed, and I wasn't sure why. I felt totally out of place, like everyone just knew was a virgin, about to have my cherry popped by my obviously older boyfriend. My only savior, my one slight relief was my attempt to look the part, with my new duds and my new polished face. I looked like I could, potentially, be an acceptable match for someone like Jake.

Hiding behind my bed-head hairdo and my mask of black eye make-up, we entered into the sleekest lobby I'd ever seen. It was quite a contrast from the Motel 6's my family stayed at in the past. *Pictures don't do a place like this justice.* I'd seen pictures of top-rate hotels on those travel shows, but until you actually see one of them first hand, you'll never fully understand.

"I guess that's a little taste of what I'll have to worry about when I leave," he whispered, pressing his lips to my temple. Was that a question? I wasn't sure, so I didn't make a peep. There were no peeps to be had.

I was snapped out of my love haze when he asked me to—"*wait over there.*" He pointed to a group of tan fabric couches surrounded by lush green banana trees.

"By myself?" I asked, confused. "Where are you going?"

"I need to get a room."

"Why can't I go with you?"

"Calm down. It's just easier, ya know," he explained, holding me close, casually looking around. "Trust me."

I let go of him and walked unenthusiastically towards the suggested target. *Stand straight*, I told myself. *Don't be such a baby. Hold your head high. No immaturity allowed. No mistakes.* I talked myself up as I plopped myself down onto an over-sized, stiff-cushioned chair. I purposely sat with my back facing the vast expanse of the lobby so I wouldn't catch leering eyes probing me (as if, but just in case).

The voices and music collided together, echoing against the stamped concrete floors and the immense vast ceiling. I tried to make out what was being said by those nearby, but it was impossible. I was obsessing that we were being talked about, that they suspected us to be doing something wrong and call our parents and I would never see Jake again. Just the thought made me light-headed. I breathed in deeply through my nose, catching the sweet scent of the nearby freesias. I loved flowers, and the scent slowly calmed me down.

"Ok, let's go check it out." He smiled, flashing the plastic room key.

Jake held out his hand, helping me up from my petrified state, and we slowly walked toward the bank of elevators in the distance. I loved how I fit right under his arm, how he draped himself over me when we walked. I firmly held his hand as it dangled from my shoulder.

"My mom's gonna be calling any time now, wondering where I'm at. Not sure if I'm gonna answer it." He looked at our reflections in the shiny elevator door, which stared back at us. I'd never seen what we looked like together, and I could have stood there all day. "Ha, we look pretty good, don't we?" He laughed softly.

"Ehh," I squeaked, shrugging my shoulders.

He laughed again, pulling my head to his lips as the elevator door opened and a gang of people poured out. The elevator carried us to the fifth floor. Jake shifted a duffle bag over to his other shoulder. I hadn't noticed it before. Why would he have a duffle bag? Did he plan this? If this was planned, it changed the game as far as I was concerned. I wasn't about sneaky shit, and my sister's warning screamed loudly in my head.

The doors opened and the elevator informed us, in a soft female voice that we'd arrived at the *Fifth Floor*.

"Aly, you're killing me with how quiet you're being," he said, stopping at room 513. "Seriously, we don't have to stay here. We can turn around, just go hang for a while some-where else, and go home later."

"Jake," I hesitated. "Never mind. It's silly. We'll just stick to the plan." I smiled bravely back at him.

"Okay, whatever you say." He smiled, sliding the key card into its place. The little green light flashed, unlocking the door.

Jake held the door open for me, and I walked in to find the most amazing hotel room I'd ever seen. I could see the ocean through the sliding glass doors at the other end of the room. The place was huge, and it had a sunken living room that led out to a balcony facing the water. The bed was gigantic. I skipped with laughter, diving onto it. I sank into the pile of fluffy white pillows and flipped over on to my back. I watched Jake dive right down next to me. I shim-mied to prop myself up. He lay on his back, with both arms tucked under his head. His blue eyes gleamed.

"Jake, did you plan this? I mean, what's up with the duffle bag?"

"No, I didn't." He answered in a slow deliberate tone and stared straight up at ceiling.

I waited for him to say something else, and just as I was about to speak he continued.

"My mother is going to kill me. She's gonna freak out if she sees the charge on my credit card for this." He rolled over onto his side, propping his head to face me. "But I don't care. I'm sick of everyone giving me shit about every fucking thing I do."

He reached out, placing his hand on my stomach and slid it over to my hipbone. My insides went berserk. I took his hand in mine, hoping it would stall him from feeling me up. I started getting light-headed thinking about it.

"What's in the duffle bag if you didn't plan this then?" I asked, smiling.

"I always carry extra shirts and stuff because of sweating during gigs. You know, deodorant and shit like that."

Yeah, I could see that, and was immediately relieved to know he didn't have some grand scheme to deflower me.

"Aly, don't worry. I'm not planning on making you do anything you don't wanna do. I don't wanna go home. I wanna be with you and not at some fleabag hotel or worse, Dump's place. It's that simple."

"So you had to go to the other end of the spectrum, which will cause you to get your ass handed to you, and make her have another reason for you not to see me," I said sarcastically.

"Yeah, basically." He laughed. "By the time we're done here, it's gonna cost about $600 dollars."

I choked on my spit, sitting upright clearing my throat. "What! Dude, that's insane! How are you gonna pay for that? Your mom already complained about the extra cost for the studio time, and then you go and do this?"

Lying back flat, he covered his face with both hands, then looked as if he'd rip his hair out. "Yeah, well, don't let her fool you with dramatics. When my dad died…let's just put it this way, we were taken care of," he explained. "And besides, I have my own money, that *I've* made. Not a lot, but it works, and when I turn 18, she can suck on it." He sighed, his hands still covering his eyes. "I'll dig ditches if I have to, to pay for this."

"Has it always been this complicated?" I asked. "Dealing with your mother? And what about Notting? He's been around a long, long time, Jake."

"Yeah, it's always difficult dealing with her." He huffed lightly. "This is just the first time I've ever stood up to her or done anything like this."

"I got the impression she doesn't want you seeing me," I murmured.

"That's not gonna happen. She can't stop me from seeing you. I mean, fuck, I haven't seen you all week. She's got no idea what the hell's going on. It just pissed her off that I left to get you, and then the whole thing with Rachel. I haven't been keeping her apprised, and that burns her up. She's a control freak."

"Why do you think she's all over you? Do you give her a reason to be?"

Jake stared at the ceiling.

"No. I've just been so accustomed to it. Not wanting to upset her. She's been through a lot with not having my dad around, you know. It's part guilt, I guess, and me allowing it to happen for so long."

"What about Notting? You said he's been in love with her."

Jake squirmed, uneasy.

"I'm sorry. We don't have to talk about it." I offered. But I really wanted to know.

"It's not something I like to talk about, Aly. Their whole relationship, I'm not sure what to think of it. I know my dad loved my mother, and he treated her really lovingly in front of me. We were very happy. He adored her, so I thought."

"What's that supposed to mean? We're talking about Notting?"

"No, my father." Jake sighed and finally looked at me. "Check this out. My ex-girlfriend Renee, who wasn't my girlfriend yet, and her older brother witnessed something that I've never shared with anyone else."

"What?" I was fixed.

"The night my dad died in that crash, he was with another woman. Not in the car, but he was probably on his way home or something."

"What? No! Why do you say that?"

"Renee was driving with her brother and *saw* him on the road, *with* this woman. She was kissing him, leaning over kissing him. There was no mistake, they said."

I gulped.

"So what does this mean? Did your mom find out?"

"Aly, it was such a hectic time. I didn't find out about it until months later. But Renee and her brother were at the funeral, and they said they saw the same woman there, and that she was crying like she lost *her* husband. My dad worked with her, apparently. After the shock of everything, I started wondering, you know, and rehashed it with Renee after we started dating. I recalled the day a woman called the house. My mom wasn't home. A woman asked for my dad, and she wouldn't give me her name. She said, "*I'm just a friend and I'm trying to reach him.*" I recalled how suspicious I was, for no reason, like something was telling me it wasn't right. I told her she was no friend if she couldn't give me her name and I hung up the phone."

"Wow. So you've been holding on to this?"

"What am I supposed to do? My mom was a wreck. If it weren't for Notting, who knows what would have happened? Notting is a whole other story, too."

"But your mom and him are together now?"

"Not officially. They've never told me they are together. I've never seen them kiss. But I feel it. They think I'm stupid."

I felt very grown up and safe. All of my absurd thoughts of earlier flew out the window. I felt I could tell him anything, like it'd been all those weeks ago when we were just friends.

"Yeah, I guess I'm gonna text Notting. Tell him what's up and not to worry."

"Why don't you just text your mom."

"Because she'll start in on me, and Notting won't. He understands, trust me."

Sitting close to Jake, I watched the letters quickly appear on the screen of his phone:

- *NOT, I'LL BE HOME IN THE MORNING. I JUST DON'T WANT TO DEAL WITH MOM AND I NEED TIME TO THINK.*

"My mom will probably take my phone away, once she realizes it's me, if she's with Notting." He laughed.

- *WE'LL SEE YOU IN THE MORNING.*

"See," Jake said, giving me a closer view of the text message. "I told you it was that simple. I love Notting. If it wasn't for him, I probably would have quit by now, or have asked for emancipation."

"What's that?"

"It's when a minor petitions the court to be on their own before 18."

"Really, you can really do that? I thought that was a myth."

"Nope, you can do it," he answered, throwing his legs over the side of the bed.

"Let's go for a walk on the beach."

"Okay, but don't you think we need to get your money's worth and hang out here as long as possible?" I said, kissing his cheek.

He rose quickly, wrapping his arms under my legs to give me a piggyback ride out to the balcony.

"So, you're telling me you want to stay in here and not go out there?"

It was breathtakingly beautiful, especially the hotel grounds. The ocean was masterpiece backdrop. The pool was off to the left, and our balcony had a panoramic view. The black striped cabana's outlined the entire perimeter of the pool. Fabulous men and women, young and old, lay out on teak lounge chairs. These people were the ultimate Envies.

"I suppose we can go explore." I smiled. "This is so amazing, Jake. I'm not going to want to leave tomorrow."

Jake came closer, wrapping his arms around me from behind. "I'm not gonna wanna leave either, trust me, for long list of reasons."

Chapter 31

ALYSSA

I admired the general finery of the lobby, with its polished dark wood furnishings, artwork and lush potted greenery, as we made our way out toward the swimming pool. Jake grabbed my hand as we approached a large gazebo, which held the fluffy striped beach towels I'd seen from our balcony.

"Two towels please." Jake requested from the hip blond attendant with a pageboy haircut.

"Room key?" she asked. She didn't look at or acknowledge me. Jake flashed our plastic access card at her. "Room number and last name?" she purred.

"Masters, room 513," he answered with a crooked grin, glancing at me.

"Great, let me know if you need anything else," Gazebo Girl replied, batting her eyes.

Jake thanked her and put his arm around me as we walked away.

"I guess we both have our own fan clubs here," I teased.

He was quiet. No good-humored retort. Maybe he didn't like the jab.

He pointed to a sign posted with "Beach Access" written in bold black letters at the other end of the swimming pool. It took us past the rows of lounging people soaking up every last minute of sun. We made our way to the shoreline, walking hand-in-hand. Our feet sank into the wet sand. I glanced back, wanting to see our footprints side by side. These moments were imbedding themselves into my memory, binding me ever more tightly. I was wholly fixed to him, and I would remain, unaltered.

Soaked in my Jake stupor, the cool water shocked me from my daydream as large waves came barreling towards us, soaking our legs. Jake laughed, cursing humorously under his breath.

"Oh, I see, you think this is funny?" he teased. He grabbed the towel from my hands. Tossing our things away from the water, he charged at me.

Jake scooped me up in his arms and I begged him not to throw me in. He quickly sloshed us out into deeper water, and without much of a fight, I gave in. The water was cool against my heated skin, giving me chills and I clung to his warm, well-built frame. He let my legs loose to float freely under water.

I tried to find the bottom.

"Are you standing?" I asked, holding tight to his arm around me.

"Yep."

"At least I know the bottom's just right there." I smirked. "It's creepy not to be able to see the bottom. You're lucky you're a head taller."

"Yes I am." He smiled and moved me directly in front of him. He held me under my arms and picked me up out of the water, above him. "You're a perfect fit."

I melted into him as my legs cut through the water and wrapped around his waist. The water lapped at our chins as we moved deeper. We were both mute, staring at each other for a long moment. I was filled with so much elation I felt like I could explode, and my words gushed out of my mouth.

"Will it always be this way?" I asked softly. Water splashed up into my mouth, forcing me to pause to spit it out. Jake remained hushed. "You know, this feeling?"

"I don't know about you, Aly, but what I feel grows stronger every day," he admitted, holding me tighter.

The water pushed and pulled at our bodies. My heart raced, and I felt breathless. He kissed me hard on the lips and turned, taking us back to shore.

"I think you'll be able to stand now."

"Ha, oh no! You carried me out here, you're carrying me in," I laughed mischievously.

"Oh, you think so?"

"Uh, yeah?"

He gallantly carried me all the way out of the water, my weight barely fazing him. He let my legs free and my feet hit the sand. We sauntered along for what seemed like a mile. Finally, we stopped, laying our towels out. Jake looked as flawless as ever, even with the sandy salt water lines dried over his toned chest and arms. I'm pretty sure I didn't look as wonderful, with my hair crispy and matted to my head. I hastily played with my hair in an anxious attempt not to look warped.

"What up?" he asked, shaking me. "Talk to me, Alycat, tell me what's on your mind."

His cheeriness under his own circumstances was inspiring.

I sighed, stuttering, "Um, my mind just starts racing with all these thoughts and what if's."

"For example?"

"Please don't embarrass me…"

"I'm not," he laughed softly. "I wanna know, Aly, c'mon."

"Ok. I just think, like, what's gonna happen tonight?" I admitted, "And what's it gonna be like when you're gone, and what's it gonna be like when school starts? Stuff like that."

"Yeah," he whispered. "I think of those same things, too."

"Yeah," I replied quietly.

"But you know what? As long as we're ok, right?" he said lightly, gesturing between us. "The rest'll fall into place." I felt his hand move from my shoulder as he gently wove his fingers through my hair to the roots. I felt his cool fingers against my warm scalp. He pressed my head into his neck, holding me tight.

The Santa Monica pier looked tiny in my view, and I marveled at the pink and orange hue of the sky. The sun's last bit of rays reached out over the vastness of the atmosphere. Scattered as far as I could see were wisps of clouds and a trail, as if a bunny hopped around leaving its footprints.

We began to walk back and Jake was an open book. I walked and listened. His avalanche of resentments toward his mother surprised me. He shared a bit more about his father's death, and how he wanted to pretend he never learned of his affair. What went on gnawed at him. He was torn by guilt and love for his mother, and other things I didn't understand.

Her involvement in the band was at its breaking point.

"I get it, she wants us out there meeting fans," he huffed, bringing his free hand to rub his eyes. "But fuck, she never gives us time to decompress—me especially, I'm the buffer for the guys. We're exhausted after a show. We're sweaty and thirsty and she's back in the dressing room, rushing us along. Like the world's gonna end if we take one more second."

"Have you tried talking to her?"

"Are you kidding?" he said, whipping his hand way from his face. "Yeah, but she doesn't give a shit. I'd like to see her get up on stage and pull off a forty-minute-plus set."

"I'm sorry," I said, nuzzling into him a bit more, trying to imagine what it must be like. The only image I could conjure up of my own mother was when my friends and I didn't wipe up the trailed-in pool water. She'd act as if her hard wood floors would bend and buckle right there on the spot. "Yeah, my mom can be a freak about stuff, too."

"Aly," he said and shook his head. "There's no comparison."

"What do the other guys think? Like Mike, what does he think?"

Jake grew rigid at the mention of Mike's name, and I was unsure what to make of his reaction.

He sighed. "Mike, he's another chink in the chain."

"What's that supposed to mean?"

We were now at a standstill near the ocean's edge. He was silent for another moment, turning his gaze toward the distant pier. The air seemed to grow dry as it filled my lungs.

I gulped. "Um, hello?"

He sniffed and chuckled. "Aly," he paused, glancing at me. "You know when you have a hunch about something, like, when it's in your gut?"

"Yeah."

"Well," he said and bent down, scooping sand into his hands letting it run through his fingers. "I don't think Mike was the right choice. That's just between you and me."

I sat down next to him. "Why? I don't know too much about guitar playing, but he seems to be pretty good."

"That's not why. His ability isn't what's in question," he said. "He's just a fucking mess, ya know. The drugs and drinking are more than I thought. Or maybe because I'm not in it with him anymore, it's just more apparent."

"And that's it?"

Finally he looked at me. "There's how he treats Bobby. He practically ignores him. He used to tease him in front of fans. The only time he talks to him is to bum a cig. It's just weird. I seriously don't understand that guy," he said, hesitating. "And then there's you."

"Me?" I said. My insides contracted.

"Yep," he said. "Since the beginning, the way he talks about you or questions what's going on, it's irritating."

I shifted uncomfortably, not knowing how to react to this revelation.

"Jake, I'm sure it's just small talk."

Dusting the sand from his hands, he moved to get up. "Yeah, my guts tell me different," he said, holding his hand out to help me up. "We don't need to talk about this anymore."

I sprung up from sitting cross-legged in the sand. "Ok, but don't let it get you down. I'm sure it'll work itself out, right?"

"Yeah, I hope so," he said skeptically.

"I'm thinking this is like the third or fourth time since we've been…" I said, pausing. Been what? What were we actually? A couple? Boyfriend and girlfriend, what exactly? Shit. "Um, whatever you wanna call us…you know." I wiggled, feeling strange for bringing it up. "That I've looked like a drowned rat more times than I can count," I said, hanging my head, embarrassed. "I mean I really am starting to lose track."

Throwing his head back, he laughed loudly. "You're right. What is it with you?"

"I'm blaming you." I smiled.

He chased me all the way back to the hotel and we made a ruckus walking through the pool area. I could only imagine what we looked like.

We stood at the elevator and Jake moved from my side, bear hugging me from behind. I felt his warm breath on my ear, and it sent chills running over every inch of my skin. I wanted to squeal, but the growing crowd of people waiting for the elevators challenged me to keep quiet. Jake seemed not to notice and acted as if no one was around.

"We're gonna order room service, watch movies, and act like there's no tomorrow," he whispered.

"Technically, there isn't gonna be a tomorrow," I said, "well, maybe a tomorrow, but after that, it'll be weeks." I grabbed his arms.

"It'll go by fast, you'll see."

Yeah right, for you, maybe.

I irrationally worried (or maybe it wasn't irrational) about getting caught by my parents sitting in a towel, in a hotel room, far from home. Jake's theatrical—"*Oh yeah, baby*", rattled me from my worry. He came out of the bathroom holding two plush white bathrobes. They had the hotel insignia embroidered in black thread on the breast.

"Take a look at these, darlin'," he said, walking past me and laying one of them on the bed. He slid one on over his broad shoulders. His eyes bore into mine with a devilish grin. "We're gonna play it like Jay'z and Beyonce tonight." He walked over close to me. "Come here."

All my angst nearly disappeared, hearing those words flip from his mouth.

Chapter 32

JAKE

The drone of the TV was no distraction from the buzz of energy I felt between us. That same energy Aly spoke of all those weeks ago, something I'd never understood or was too intoxicated to feel with anyone else. Holding her cool, thin hand in mine, I decided this was something I'd never felt before and I wanted to define it. A melody flew through my head and I began to hum.

"Wha'cha singing' about?" Aly said, squeezing my hand.

Opening my eyes, I was a little embarrassed. "Oh, somethin' that's been simmering a little while, but guess what? I think I wanna make it a duet."

"Can't wait to hear it."

"Have you ever wanted to sing?"

"No!" She laughed and shook her head like it was the most insane thing she'd ever heard.

"You've never thought about it? For real?"

"Nope. Never."

"You have a really sweet voice, Aly. Like, it's really nice."

"What?" She looked at me, stunned.

"Yeah, I hear you singing all the time, and on the way here I really paid attention." I paused, wondering if I should say what I'd been thinking since then. "I think it'd be cool if we recorded one together. You know, just for us."

Her eyes opened wide with surprise and her brow furrowed. Then she smiled broadly, clenching her hands under her chin.

"Wow, really? You think my voice is good enough for that?"

"Yeah, I do. We could record it before I leave, simply, in my garage. I do demos there all the time."

"Oh my god, sure. I mean that would be so cool. Are you sure? Really?"

"Yeah, of course. I've been thinking about it since we got here," I said.

"Ok. Let's do it!" She shrieked with excitement and jumped on me. "Oh my god, I'm so nervous about it."

We sat tangled together, kissing, and I wondered if I should suggest us moving to the bed.

"You getting tired?"

"Ehh, not really, but I'm lazy." She giggled, emphasizing with a huge stretch. "What time is it anyway?"

I laughed when I glanced at the bedside clock in the corner of the room. "It's not even nine o'clock."

"You're kidding," she said. She sat upright, licking her lips and looking back at the TV. "This movie blows. Let's pick another one."

She slid to the edge of her seat and her mouth fell open. I wanted to lick her lips.

She stared at me for a long moment, searching my eyes as if looking for an answer. "I don't want this to end."

I scooped her up, cradling her in my arms as she squealed with laughter.

"This is only the beginning," I said. She yelped as I tossed her on the bed.

The longer we kissed, the more open she became. My excitement began to build as I ran my hand over her silky smooth skin. She was eager and aggressive, unquestionably willing to go further, but how far? I wondered through my haze of licks. I held back from going to second base. The thought of asking permission ran fleetingly through my mind until she wrapped one of her legs around me. Then *bam*, my hand was filled with her bare breast. This only made Aly press into me harder. I continued to obsess over her hipbone and caught myself as I nearly took advantage of her bare-openness. I quickly retracted, lying flat on my back.

"Fuck," I whispered loudly.

Her chest heaved and a surprised look splashed across her face. "What, what's the matter?"

I laughed, embarrassed. "Aly, trust me, there is nothing the matter, *ever*," I said, reassuringly.

With her hair all messy and robe falling off her shoulder, the temptation was nearly too much for me. She went to kiss me again, and I held her firmly away by her shoulders. "Aly, I can't do this," I said, feeling her warm breath flash across my face. "Not right now. I can't believe I just said that."

She backed away, sitting up, correcting her disheveled appearance. "I can't believe you said it either." She crossed her legs up underneath her. "I thought this is what you wanted."

She didn't look at me. Her voice was barely audible, and she hunched away from me. "Aly," I said, stuttering. I reached out rubbing her back, but she didn't budge. "Is that seriously what you thought?"

I caught myself holding my breath.

"Um, I just figured, that's all, so I just…" her voice faded.

"You just what?"

"I just went for it," she said burying her face in her hands. "Like you said, let's just go with it. That is what you said." She raised her head. "So, now I feel stupid, like I'm not good enough for you…but Rachel is."

I felt bad, guilty, confused and mad all at the same time. The TV rambled loudly, and I looked for the remote, turning it off.

There was complete silence.

"Aly, you have no idea how bad I want you," I admitted, wriggling with embarrassment. "And, it takes everything in me to hold back."

"What if I don't… want you to stop?" she said slowly.

Scooting over more closely to her, my mind raced. If it were anyone else, I would have probably thrown her down as soon as those words hit my ears. I was torn with wanting to go for it and doing the right thing.

"Do you really mean that?" I coerced her to lean back and hovered over her, feeling the rise of her chest on mine. I moved my hand under her robe, embracing her tiny waist, and pulled her closer to me. Her expression changed and hesitation spread over her.

She turned away. "Now that you're asking, and we're not, like, making out." She struggled. "I don't know."

"Aly, look at me," I said, bringing her face toward mine. "I can't tell the future. All I know is, I'm alive when I'm with you."

This time I was the one who turned away, self-conscious. "And when I'm not with you, you're all I think about. And it's not because I want to have sex with you." The pent-up words made their debut. "You're like a constant melody streaming through my mind, and all I do now is write songs in an attempt to define what this all even means." There was a long moment of silence, as we both ruminated on my admission. I felt like a total pussy for wearing my heart on my sleeve.

"I believe you won't use me." Her words prickled at me.

"Where are you getting the word *use* from?"

She stared off, her eyes darting the thoughts in her head. I waited. "It's all anyone talks about, you know," she muttered. "The guys talk about who's gonna tap who, who hooked up with who. Like it's a game. I believe you're not playing a game with me." She shook her head, convinced.

I wasn't sure how late we stayed up, but the last time I looked at the clock it was 2:30 AM. Now the clock read 8:16 AM. I groggily sat up and noticed Aly wasn't in the bed. Looking around the room, I didn't see her. *Thank God*, I thought, having the biggest pee boner. I jumped up and headed toward the bathroom.

"Jake?" Her voice rang out.

"Yeah, in here," I said loudly, adjusting myself, making sure I was fit to be seen just as Aly poked her head into the bathroom. "Hey, where were you?"

"On the balcony. It's so warm outside already," she said pulling her hair back away from her face. "My phone is going off right now." Shaking her head, she started texting. "I need to get home. I'm a little worried."

"Yeah, I feel the same way. Def not looking forward to walking through my front door."

———

I was not looking forward to this day, and wanted so badly to rewind back to yesterday and being on the beach with Aly. The mid-morning sun shone too brightly for me, and I attempted to shield myself from it by slapping down the sun visor. The morning joggers, cyclists and weekend worriers were getting their exercise on and making their way to the boardwalk. It reminded me that we had to take the trailer in for inspection, and the appointment time was 8:30 AM. Great, just one more thing for my mom to rag on me about—I could hear her now. Today was ramping up to be another winner.

Aly sat silently next to me, texting away. I was curious to whom Aly was communicating with and what she was sharing. I needed to know that what happened between us would stay between us. As we pulled up to another red light, I reached over, gently putting my hand on her thigh. Her fingers stopped moving across the phone's keypad and she looked at me.

"Who ya texting?"

"Nicole and Marshall."

"About?"

"Seeing if they were awake yet."

"Aly," I said apprehensively. "Will you make sure to keep what happens between us, between us?"

"Yeah, of course," she replied. "Why?"

Why did she have to ask why? I leaned my head back against the headrest, looking out through the rear view mirror as if the right words would appear, helping me out.

"Because it's no one's business what happens between us when we're alone." I said firmly. "No matter what you say, people will assume what they want, and if you say something to one person…you know how it goes. Shit gets taken out of context as it travels down the wire, spinning out of control to where what really happened is lost."

"Yeah, I understand."

"I'm just trying to protect you."

Chapter 33

JAKE

I'd become numb to arguing with my mother. I usually knew exactly what to say to her because she was usually so predictable, but now I wasn't so sure. She laid into me harder than ever.

"You just disappear and think it's okay to waltz right back in here?" My mother's brow furrowed in anger. "Enough is enough already, Jake."

"I didn't disappear," I said, raising my voice. "I told you already. I texted Notting that'd I'd be home in the morning and here I am."

She blinked, taking in my words and her eyes narrowed. "If you think you can come and go as you please, without any accountability, you're sorely mistaken."

"Mom! Why can't you just leave me alone?"

She glared at me. "Because I need to know what you're doing and where you're at when so much is going on with the band, Jake. I've invested too much to let you just run things into the ground. What's wrong with you? What's going on with Alyssa?"

"No, no you don't need to know everything about me, mom! I need privacy! This, this right here." I gestured between us. "You're making it really easy for me *not* to want to talk to you. You act like I'm freaking ten years old! I'm not an idiot…"

"Well, you're certainly acting like one!" she shouted in my face, cutting me off. "You're going to ruin everything if you don't stop acting like you've lost your mind! Now, what the hell is going on with Alyssa?"

"Nothing's going on with Alyssa. We hang out sometimes, and she asked if she could come to the studio. I didn't think it would be such a big deal. Her friend Nadine likes me or something." I tried to throw her off by slipping in another girl's name. At least it wasn't an outright lie, I told myself.

———

My mother's warnings echoed around in my head as I sat in my truck, deflated. I started feeling bad about arguing with her. I knew I was wrong, but she was too, that I was certain. I stared at the cracks in my house's tan--colored stucco, wondering how long it would take for them to get bigger and how much it would cost to fix them. Just like the dents in my truck. Ugh, I bet that's how my mom felt about me. I'd been cracking, denting and ruining everything in her eyes.

As I drove to Rachel's I wondered were Bobby was. It was strange I hadn't heard from him yet. I dialed his number.

It sounded like I'd woken him up. "Hello," he said in a raspy, tired voice.

"Dude, where are you? Did you forget that we're playing at Rachel's soon?"

"Aw, man, yeah I did."

"So?" My voice grew anxiously louder. "You're comin', right?"

"Yeah man, I'll be there," he replied reassuringly.

"A late one, I'm guessing," I probed.

"Hollywood, yeah."

"Who'd you go with? Anyone I know?"

"No one you know."

"We ever gonna meet these new friends of yours?" I asked with a half-laugh. "You should invite them to a show."

Another deep sigh came. "Yeah, well, our music isn't really what they're into," he explained, grunting. "They like that club shit, ya know."

"So you're going dancing?" I laughed. "Man, she better be throwin' down for that one!"

"Yeah, something like that," he said dryly.

"There was silence on the other end. "Hello?" I said, thinking we'd been disconnected.

"Uh, yeah," he replied. "Man, I'll see ya there in a bit."

He hung up on me, completely unlike him, but whatever. I knew what it was like to be horribly hung over. I had to admit, the vibe was strange and my curiosity piqued, thinking back to the group of girls from Hollywood who always came to our shows and flirted with Bobby. I wondered if the person he'd spent the night with was one of them.

I arrived at Rachel's and we had another tense moment—it was always some bullshit conversation with her. I rolled my eyes, looking over her shoulder, watching everyone arrive. I walked away when I spotted Kyle, Aly and Marshall. I could hear her complaining to Sienna behind my back. I smiled when I heard Dump tell her to shut the hell up. Thank God the music blared so loudly; no one appeared to hear us. Sure enough, everyone quickly noticed Marshall and the whispers started. He was the most fashionable of any chick there. I had to actually give him props, thinking vintage *David Bowie* or *Culture Club* all the way, Glam Rock. Yeah, he had style.

"What's up, man," I said, giving Kyle a slap on the back. I gave Aly and Marshall a nod of acknowledgement. "How's it look out front?"

I was curious to see if there were people still trying to get in.

"Dude, there's a line." Kyle nodded happily.

I felt awkward standing there with them. "We go on in about a half hour."

Marshall leaned in, whispering something to Aly, and her eyes roamed around the vicinity.

"Is there beer?" Aly asked, to my surprise. She knew how I felt about her drinking.

"Um yeah, over there," I said pointing. "Uh…"

"Come on," she interrupted. "Marshall wants to, how do you say it? Take the edge off."

She took Marshall's hand and walked in the direction of the growing crowd surrounding the keg. I felt like I had the Scarlett Letter emblazoned on my back. Everywhere I looked, people were watching. They pointed at Aly and Marshal and looked back at me. I felt increasingly defiant. I kept reminding myself not to be intimidated by the force of peer pressure. As I followed them up to the keg, I noticed

Mike and Bobby standing next to it, filling their plastic cups. Marshall was certainly making a first impression. I couldn't figure out if it was good or bad.

Aly decided to grab a cup and I worried what Kyle would do. I didn't want him to think I condoned her drinking.

"Hey, you think that's a good idea," I whispered loudly in Aly's ear. "Don't wanna make a bad impression."

"Kyle doesn't give a rat's ass, trust me, he's just stoked to be here," she replied, pinching my chin.

I bent in closer and kissed her, lingering at her lips. As I glanced to the side, I noticed Cara Walters was sucking all over Mike, and he couldn't care less. He just leered at Aly and me. He wore an arrogant grin. Handing the keg nozzle to Bobby and he dragged Cara away with him.

I caved and decided to grab a beer too, since Aly had to be bold and drink in front of her brother.

"Hey, Kyle," I said loudly. "I told her not to."

"Dude, no worries. I suppose she's gonna start sooner or later," he said, laughing. "At least she's here with us."

I was annoyed at his liberal thinking. If it were my little sister, I wouldn't even want her there. We stood waiting for Marshall to have his cup filled by Bobby, who seemed particularly talkative. I noticed Bobby's hair matched Marshall's pants. I laughed, partially amused.

"Dude, check it out," I said to Aly, pointing. "The color of his hair is the same."

"Aw, yeah, I noticed that right away," Aly giggled. "It's like they planned it or something…um, thanks for putting up with this."

I put my arm around her waist and squeezed tight. "It's different, I'll give you that," I concluded, whispering in her ear, taking in the strawberry scent that I hadn't smelled in a while. "Both of you certainly have everyone's attention."

Aly began to speak, abruptly going silent upon Mike and Cara's approach. Cara Walters was your typical beach party girl, with long blonde hair and nothing else interesting about her, except for her rockin' body. The type of girl that, once she opened her mouth, you knew right away there was nothing really there.

Her smug attitude towards Aly disgusted me.

"What is this," Cara slurred out in a nasty tone, eyeing Aly up and down. "Since when do poo butts get invited?"

I frowned at Cara, appalled. "You're kidding, right?" I glanced over at Mike. "Get rid of her." I wasn't kidding.

My attitude only added fuel to Cara's inane tirade. "What, Jake," she seethed, "You losin' your mojo? You have to hang out with toddlers?"

I wanted to punch her in the face. "Yeah, Cara, that's it," I laughed. "It's better than being hit on by a used skank like you," I growled. "Scram."

"You're a fucking asshole, Jake," she hissed, leaning into Mike.

To my shock, Mike began to back away from her, pushing her away as she tried to hold on to him. "Cara, chill out," He demanded. "Aly, Cara's a little fucked up, you'll have to excuse her."

I thought I was hearing things. Mike making excuses and apologizing for Cara's foolish behavior?

Cara's face looked like it would melt off as it twisted into a frown. Her mouth hung open before she spoke. "Oh, I see," she said, trying to steady herself on her own. "You're an ass kisser now."

"Come on, let's go get you some Redbull," he said, wrapping his arm around Cara's waist. He gave me a hard stare and focused back on Aly. "Sorry."

It was like Cara developed immediate amnesia, forgetting her discontent with all of us as she wrapped her arms around Mike's neck. She purred happily in his ear, like we'd never had an altercation. "You know what I want, and it's not Redbull."

Bobby grabbed me by the shoulder, shaking me from my haze of confusion. "What just happened?" he asked, perplexed.

I turned to Aly, who looked like she wanted to cry. "Aly, screw her, she's a fucking cling-on."

"I can't believe you hang out with people like that," Aly said, shaking her head.

Marshall was the center of attention, explaining to everyone what happened, and Bobby was hanging on his every word.

"Come on man, let's do this," Dump said, taking a long drag on his cigarette.

———

Standing, ready to play, I watched Aly from a distance. She was a true, legit beauty. She was light years away from average and she had no idea. The way she moved like a gazelle, long and fluid. Her smile literally radiated beyond anyone's I'd ever seen. I started to feel unsure of myself, nervous about the new songs. What would she think?

"Dude, I gotta redo the set list," I barked to Dump. "Now."

"What the fuck, dude. We gotta do this thing before the cops show up!"

Bobby stepped over, hearing my plight.

"Aw man," Bobby moaned. "You're kidding, right?"

"Guys, I just can't do'em here." Firmly shaking my head *no*, looking each one of them in the eye. "I'm not ready, I'm sorry."

Mike began to laugh. "Yeah, you may start a cat fight again." Suddenly a serious, callous expression melted over his face. "Or you're just a pussy, or pussy-whipped."

I wanted to punch his teeth out. Dump chimed in, putting him in his place.

"Dude, shut the fuck up, you're just bent 'cause the only pussy you get is from the coke whores who use you for drugs." He chuckled, flicking his cigarette at Mike's feet.

Mike never dared to spar with Dump; he just sneered at him. Dump took his seat behind his drum kit and I slung my guitar strap over my head. I turned, looking out over the crowd, and the click of Dump's sticks took over my consciousness.

I closed my eyes.

As soon as I started to play, my foul mood died out. I was impassioned as soon as my fingers felt my guitar strings and Dump's galloping beats filled the air. I spotted Aly as she made her way to the front, and I don't think I'd ever been more stoked in my life. Bobby's dense base kicks retreated, and the wall of guitar riffs Mike and I built up crumbled down on everyone. I began to sing our newest radio song—*Ever After*. As the lyrics parted my lips and my voice carried over to Aly, I stared at her in the eyes as I sang. The lyrics began to have new meaning—*"I see you watching, how does it feel? The little drops take you away to something real…"*

Bobby seemed extra pumped, bouncing around as we ended our set, and I wondered if his chick was around.

"Bobby, man, sick energy," I said, grinning and slapping his back. "What gives, your chick here?"

A strange look fell across his face, though he remained smiling looking out at the crowd. There was a shift in his eyes that caught my attention. Following his gaze out over the crowd, I searched for someone, anyone that looked like she could be the reason. I only spotted Aly and Marshall. I waived for them to come over.

"So?" I asked, wanting to know what she thought.

"I'm speechless," she said demurely.

"Thanks." It meant more to me to have her approval than anyone else's.

"I thought you guys rocked," Marshall complimented. "I never really paid attention to this kind of music." He bounced on his heels. "But I'm all over it now."

"Thanks, bro," I said, feeling like a dick for thinking asshole things about Marshall.

I felt hands grasp my shoulders and I turned. "Oh, hey," I said, surprised to see Rachel behind me. I backed away, putting some distance between us.

Her eyes widened. "Don't run." She laughed, playfully.

"You're unpredictable, Rachel," I said, grinning cautiously.

The smile faded from her face. "Why do you say that?" she said, folding her arms loosely at her waist.

"You scare me sometimes." I smiled and laughed, hoping she would find humor in my remark.

I was relieved when she laughed. She threw her head back, almost losing her balance. Rachel grabbed a hold of my arm to steady herself. I used to find her attractive, but seeing her high, drunk, and looking used, made me feel sorry for her. Her hands were cold and clammy as I took them in mine.

"Hey, look," I said. "Not sure what your deal is, you know, like how you're feeling with all this. But I just wanted to thank you for, like, not freaking out or anything."

I was floating in an ocean of emotional girl stuff, and I wasn't sure how to navigate the highs and lows of Rachel's tides. She seemed fine at that moment.

"Aw, come on, Jakey," she purred. Her eyes drooped nearly shut. She moved in closer to me and grabbed hold of my shirt collar. "I'll always be here for you. When all this," she said, waving in Aly's direction, "whatever this is, that you're going through, is over, I'll be here." Rachel's eyes burned into mine as she kissed her fingertips and placed them on my lips. "Oh look." She backed away, pointing behind me. "Mike is breaking in your little girlfriend and her freaks and geeks." She laughed out loud. "I think I'll join them."

She stumbled off in their direction. I squinted my eyes, trying to see clearly through the dim light, wondering what she was talking about. Like a bomb, my insides exploded when I saw Aly bring a shot glass to her lips. She tipped her head backwards, clearly knocking back a shot of who-knows-what. I bolted to her side, trying to keep my cool. Rachel grabbed the bottle and shot glass out of Mike's hand, pouring one for herself.

"Cheers, everyone!" Rachel shouted, holding the shot glass up over her head. Drops of the Jagermeister's black liquid dripped down her arm.

Shouts of enthusiasm rang out over the pumping music.

"What are you doing? You're gonna get sick," I warned grimly in Aly's ear. "Let's get outta here."

Aly swayed into me. She was drunk. "Aw, no, no, let's stay!" she said joyfully. "I'm fine."

I was fuming. "I'm gonna get my shit together, and we're leaving."

Aly gave me a sad, pouty expression. I turned to Bobby to tell him, but he was engrossed in a conversation with Marshall, and Kyle was hanging all over some girl I'd never seen before. As the night wore on, I felt more and more like I was in a parallel universe. Here I was, tagged as the ultimate partier, and I was dead sober, watching all these fucks and the girl I was falling for, get hammered. I gathered my stuff and kept glancing in Aly's direction. Mike was too close to her, whispering something in her ear, as she nodded her head in agreement. Mike looked directly at me. Obviously they were talking about me. I seethed inwardly. What the hell could he saying be saying to her?

I walked over to them. "Let's go," I said to Aly, ignoring Mike.

"Jake, I'm fine," Aly slurred, hanging on my arm. "We don't have to leave."

I dragged her away toward the exit.

"Yes, we do," I said tensely, stopping. "This," I continued, waving my hands up and down at her. "This isn't gonna work for me. Sorry to say."

As soon as the words came out, I regretted the way they sounded. Her face went pale.

"Jake, I'm sorry, I…"

I sighed. "I didn't mean it the way it sounded. Let's just go."

As the night grew later, the ocean air finally cooled everything so much that waves of fog floated by us as we walked toward my truck. Aly sulked, walking next to me.

"Aly, I'm sorry, I just feel responsible for you. You know, when you're with me," I said, trying to explain. "Hey, Marshall, sorry to kill the fun, man, I'm just not into watching her get fucked up."

"Aw, that's so sweet." Marshall cooed.

Just what I suspected would happen, did. Aly started to feel sick to her stomach. She began to complain as she clung onto Marshall's arm.

"Oh my God," she gasped, leaning forward. "I feel sick, like really sick. I need to lie down."

"Oh shit, oh shit, oh shit," Marshall buzzed, spazzing out and dragged her to the curb. "Come on, I've got you."

Aly collapsed on the patch of grass next to my truck. She laid on her side, panting in an effort to thwart her urge to hurl.

"Ugh, every time I close my eyes, my head spins." She winced. "I can't believe I did this to myself."

With those words, she bolted upright, puking into the gutter. Marshall held her hair back. I hurried to load my guitar and gear into the back of my truck.

"Oh my God. I'm so sorry, honey," Marshall consoled. "You should have only done one."

"What?" I cried, aghast.

"Uh, yeah," He said, his eyes wide as saucers. "That guy, Mike, poured all of us one, and then dared her to do another one with him."

I saw red.

Chapter 34
Alyssa

I hated myself.

We sat in his driveway for a long time. He rolled down the windows and turned the radio on really low. The Foo Fighter's *'Never Wanna Die'* was playing. I couldn't help but think that one day Jake would be as big as them. He would be like Dave Grohl. I wondered what it would be like, if we really stayed together. I knew it was probably impossible. We were too young, I thought somberly.

"Hey," he said, putting a halt to my churning mind. "Wha'cha thinking' about?"

"You," I said honestly.

"And?"

"About last night."

"Yeah, go on. Stop torturing me," he said, laughing, pulling on my arm for me to come closer to him.

"Just that how it's all happened so fast, and now you're gonna be gone, like it never happened at all."

"Aly, that's not true," he said, burying his face in my hair.

"Eww, don't do that," I said, pulling away. "I really want to brush my teeth."

———

I entered Jake's bathroom and took the mouthwash out from under the sink, rinsing the rancid taste from mouth. Opening the vanity drawer, I remembered the toothbrush he'd given me a while back—it sat right next to his. Moving into the shower, I heard my phone vibrating on the bathroom counter. I worried it was my mother, and hoped it was my brother or the girls. I quickly rinsed off and hurried to dry myself. I reached over to check my phone and my stomach sank. The text was from *Mike*. I'd forgotten we'd exchanged numbers earlier.

-    *HEY, SORRY ABOUT TONIGHT. HOPE IT DIDN'T CAUSE TOO MUCH TROUBLE W JAKE. P.S. DON'T TELL HIM I TXT U. HE'LL BLOW IT OUT OF PROP.M.*

My heart raced. I looked behind me, like Jake would be standing there looking over my shoulder. *As if.* Only the towels hanging from a hook on the door stared back at me. Stupid Mike. *You know he'd be upset. So why are you texting me?* I thought, wishing I could say it to his face. *Jake was right about that shit you made me drink.*

At least Mike was sorry for putting me in an awkward situation. I thought about Jake's deal with Mike, and didn't agree with Jake's assessment of it all. Jake was being a hypocrite, but I wasn't going to point that out, at least not yet. Mike joined the band thinking he was getting a party buddy as part of the package. Whatever. It wasn't my problem. I just needed to be careful, like I was told.

I stood still for a long moment and closed my eyes. The spins were finally gone. Thank goodness for a shower and water and *barfing*. I made a promise to myself that I'd never drink like *that* again.

Jake was already lying in his bed and he looked super comfy under the covers. The back door was open and I worried that his mother or Notting would come out to the backyard and see us. I walked over, shutting it.

"No, leave it open," he said, startling me.

I jumped. "Jake," I whispered. "I thought you were asleep. I won't be able to relax let alone, sleep, if this is open and your Mom's home."

"Alright, turn the fan on, then?" he asked, pointing at a switch at the far wall.

No matter how many times we'd kissed, the thought of doing it again with him made me weak in the knees. He looked perfectly rumpled as I rushed over, crawling up next to him.

"Nothing's ever going to match this, ever in my life," I purred. I didn't give a shit if I sounded like a lovesick teen. I was, so whatever.

He inched over closer, lying on his side, caressing my leg. I didn't care if I got grounded for the rest of the summer. I didn't care if my parents found out in the morning. I was too tired to cover my tracks, too tired to text Nicole, Nadine or my brother. This was the last night of my life, as far as I was concerned.

Jake moved, his forearm grazing my boobs, and my heart stopped. Was he going to try to have sex with me tonight? My hands began to sweat. His hand cupped around my face. Our lips touched, sending a surge through every inch of my body. All the ill feelings evaporated. We made out for I don't know how long, but every time he moved his hands or shifted around, I worried he would try to remove my clothes or touch me *down there*. I would just die, because things were going on down there, and I was embarrassed. Every time he felt my thigh and lifted my leg to wrap it around his hips, I moved it back.

"Aly." His voice was husky. "I'm not gonna try going any further than this," he reassured, kissing me more firmly. "I just wanna be as close to you as I can."

A knock at the door sent my heart running across the floor. I gasped so loud Jake grabbed my head, stuffing it into his chest.

"Fuck, you gotta be kidding me," he murmured.

I lay unmoving with my ear pressed against his heaving chest. His heart was racing.

The muffled voice of Notting wedged through the door. "Jake, you awake?"

"Uh, kinda."

"Can we talk?"

I looked up at Jake, shaking my head *no*, frantically. He scrambled up, pushing me, motioning for me to get in his closet. I still shook my head no. I held my hands out, gesturing at his obvious arousal, and he grabbed his junk in response. I slapped my hands to my mouth, smiling, trying not to laugh.

"Yeah, hold on, the door's locked," he said, moving toward the door, still holding himself and waving for me to disappear.

I shut the door, holding my breath and listened to their conversation. I was silently dying inside, hysterical with laughter and embarrassment.

"*Hey,*" Jake said.

"*Hello, I didn't wake you, did I?*"

"*I was almost out.*"

"*Sorry, mate. Just dropping Kate off. We went to a late dinner and met up with a promoter at the Viper Room.*"

I could hear Notting had moved all the way into the room. My heart started to beat louder and faster. I was barely breathing, exhaling as quietly as I could. I prayed I wouldn't feel sick again when the wooziness returned. Then he spoke.

"*Really quick,*" he paused. "*Your mum is really concerned about this friend of yours and I, uh, just want to see where your head is at.*"

I wanted to pass out when I heard his words. Kate didn't like me. I was instantaneously crushed. How was this supposed to work between Jake and I if she didn't approve of me? My mind spun out of control.

"*Nott, look, man, she's pissing me off. She's making this a bigger deal than it is. I'm sure Aly wouldn't be too happy to know she was feeling this way.*"

"*No big deal, eh? You're writing love songs about her, and it's no big deal?*"

There was silence. I was for sure about to shit a basketball. I couldn't believe it. Hee really was writing about *me*. Oh my God, Jake was probably dying, knowing I could hear their conversation.

Jake laughed nervously. "*Yeah, well, she inspires me like that,*" he said flatly.

"*I'm not going to pry. I'm not going to lecture. I'll be here if you want to talk,*" Notting said in his refined English accent.

God, I loved his accent. He sounded like Jude Law. *I wish Jake sounded like that,* I thought. I sat quietly with my knees pulled to my chest.

Finally, Jake spoke. "*Nott, ok, here it is. What's going on with Aly is unexpected. She's not all fucked up like the other girls who follow us around, you know.*"

"*I see.*"

"*I mean I don't know what the big deal is.*"

I could hear Notting sigh deeply. "*The big deal, son, is she's too young for you.*"

Now, I really could have shit a basketball, strike four. Now that's four people who didn't want me in Jake's life: Rachel, Cara (whoever she was), Kate, and Notting. Not to mention my sister, who would have a fucking field day if she could hear this. I was sick and defeated.

"*I thought you weren't going to lecture,*" he said, cynically. "*Don't you think that's my choice?*"

"*You're right, I'm sorry.*" He paused. "*Yes, ultimately, it is your choice.*"

"*Notting, haven't you ever liked anyone younger than you, when you were my age? Seriously, man, I don't get it. I know plenty of guys that have younger girlfriends.*"

"*Yes, I have gone out with younger women,*" he admitted. "*However, my situation was quite different than yours.*"

"*No, no it wasn't.*" Jake's voice grew louder. "*You were in a band, just like me at my age, so you're telling me you never liked or hooked up with girls younger than you? Tell me the truth, Notting. Geez, I'm not even eighteen yet.*"

"*Jake, that's beside the point. These are different times. Please tell me that this is still an innocent diversion.*"

"*Yes, it is.*"

"*So, you have no intention of taking this girl's virginity, assuming she still is one.*"

I almost choked on my spit. *No, he didn't just ask that! Oh, my God! Wait until I tell the girls. They're gonna die.*

"*No.*"

"*The longer this relationship continues, the harder it will be for me to believe that,*" Notting replied.

"*Why does it matter?*" Jake asked defiantly. "*I mean come on, Notting. Since we're being what you'd call 'frank', everyone loses their virginity at some point as a teen.*"

"*That is very clear to the both of us. Your mum is mental about what the deal is with you.*"

"*Come on…*"

Notting interrupted Jake. "*We're old enough to read between the lines.*" Notting chuckled. "*We both know you've had relations with girls. Of course, your mother refuses to think about it, but here we are.*"

"*Ok, I get it. I'm not shagging her. I have no intention either,*" Jake responded.

"*Ah, well, I hope that's the case.*"

"*Are we done?*" Jakes voice was faint.

"*Sure. I'm heading home now, too. Good night.*"

I sat waiting. I heard the door shut and it seemed like forever before I heard anything else. I wondered if Jake walked out with him, but I didn't dare move. I couldn't believe what I'd just overheard. I peeked out. Jake stood near the door, looking at me sheepishly.

Chapter 35

JAKE

If Aly didn't realize what she'd meant to me...sitting in that closet gave her an indication, if not affirmation. I was both euphoric and terrified all at once. She crept out with her shirt pulled tight and wadded at her chest, nervous, and looked at the door. I turned, locking it. I couldn't formulate my next words. What else could I say? She stood next to my guitar, looking ever more demure, and I wondered what she must be thinking. I was too afraid to ask. How ironic. At that moment both she and my guitar were *staring* at me. I'd always expressed myself through my music; now my words were raw. I was completely exposed.

"You know that song I'd mentioned to you earlier?" I said as I walked over next to her and grabbed my guitar. I lingered a bit, taking in her eyes, trying to read her.

"Yeah," she said softly.

I brushed past her and the energy coursed through me.

I reached into my bag, taking out my leather-bound notebook. I thumbed through the pages, finding what I was looking for. "Here, these are the lyrics." I handed her the notebook and readied myself with a highlighter pen.

I glanced over my shoulder to check her reaction. I could see her eyes roam over the words. Her slender fingers came up, covering her mouth.

"Oh, Jake…"

I cleared my throat. "See, these words here." I said, taking back the notebook, sitting down on the bed. "These are the ones that you'd sing."

I ran the pen over my writing. The black script lit up under the transparent bright yellow ink and my heart raced with each stroke.

"Jake, is this how you feel?" she whispered, taken with emotion.

"Yeah. It is." I smiled and shrugged. "I'm kinda assuming a lot here."

I tapped down hard on the highlighted lyrics, the ones that spoke of love.

"Those are mine, huh?" Aly sat closely to me and put her head on my shoulder dreamily. "Yeah, I think I'm there. I feel like I'm there, but I don't know. When do you really know?"

I rested my head against hers. "I don't know. I guess it's just how you feel inside. This is how I feel inside." I reached over for my guitar. "Whad'ya say that we give this a spin?"

Aly giggled and motioned for me to go for it. I began to play the tune.

"I'll sing it through first, and then we'll sing the whole thing together, and then we'll do separate parts."

<u>I SWEAR</u>

Open your eyes
I won't see them for a while
With all that space left in between

First Kiss

Now close your eyes
Let me hold you for a while
And feel me sweetly as I sing

I swear, I swear
That I won't let you go
If you're fallin', I'm fallin' too
You know, I swear

When I close my eyes
And I hold you into me
All I feel is everything
And all want, is all I got
all I need is your love

So baby won't you sing
sing with me

I swear, I swear
That I won't let you go
If you're fallin', I'm fallin' to
I swear

This is my heart
Can you feel it beating
It has it scars, but it isn't bleeding

I know you're leaving
There's one last thing
I wanna say before you go
Cause I need you to know

I swear, I swear

I swear, I swear
That I won't let you go
If you're falling, I'm falling too
You know, I swear

We never did sleep. We played and sang that song over and over again, until Aly was satisfied she sounded good enough and had it memorized. Once her voice was warmed up and the more she felt confident, she sounded as sweet as could be. I couldn't wait to have her voice recorded. At 6 AM, I went out to see if my mom was home. She'd already left for the gym. Perfect.

"So what do you wanna do?" I said, coming back through my bedroom door quietly. Aly was snuggled under the covers. "Kate's not home. I'd like to record this. You up for it?"

"You're too used to being up all night. I'm so tired. Listen to how horse my voice is."

She was right. Her voice sounded way tired, and her eyes were glossed over, hanging half-open.

"Ok. We just have to do it before noon. That's when everyone will be here to pack to leave."

My stomach dropped, thinking that I'd soon be away from Aly for more weeks than I wanted to be. Damn, I was really gonna miss her.

I climbed in bed with her and brushed the hair out of her face. She was nearly asleep. I don't think she realized I was next to her. I lay there, staring at her, taking in every nuance of her features. I wanted to remember every curve and every bend. I thought about taking pictures of her. I hadn't taken any pictures since my photography class had ended. It'd been more than six months. I wondered if Aly would be into it. We could shoot *and* record.

At 7 AM, I groggily went out into my studio and tracked my acoustic guitar and my vocals for our song. I'd set the alarm for 9 AM. to remind me to wake Aly, and it was tough getting her up. Her eyes were even redder than before, and her voice sounded worse.

"Hey," she said and her hand quickly came up rubbing at her throat. "Oh no. I don't think I'll be able to sing."

"Sure you will. It used to happen to me all the time when I first started singing. I'll make you some tea. Get up. We only have a couple of hours, and I wanna do something else, too, before Notting and my mom get back."

She rustled up. "What? What else?" she asked curiously, rubbing her eyes. She looked as cute as I think she'd ever looked, natural and beautiful.

"Stay just like that. Don't move one inch." I rushed to my closet. "I wanna take some pictures of you just like that."

"Oh *no*, you are not!" she protested. "Are you kidding? I look like shit!"

"No, no you don't. I promise," I begged. I threw shoes out of my way looking for my camera bag, finally finding it.

"Jake, you can't be serious."

"I'm very serious. These will be black and white. I promise they'll look good, if they don't we'll delete them, together." I held up my camera. "It's digital."

She slumped, resigned.

"Oh come on, Alycat. Give me a smile?" I said, taking off the lens cap and pointing the camera at her. I began clicking away.

She smiled warily and threw a pillow at me, but I just kept clicking away.

"Ok, ok calm down. Sit there, please. Please do this for me?"

She sighed. "Ok. If you promise to show me every single one."

"I'll just take a few. Get back in bed and pull the covers up around you, like peek out over the covers, playful-like." I directed. "There you, go."

Aly got into it, and I took more than just a few. Now I wanted her to take her shirt off, to get her bare back.

"Ok, now don't freak out when I ask you this, but I want you to take your shirt off."

She froze. My stomach sank and we just stared at each other. I watched her gulp.

"Um."

"Aly, I don't wanna see your tits. I mean I'd like to see your tits, but I don't need to see 'em now. I mean you know what I mean." I stammered and I felt myself get hot. "Fuck." I laughed.

She laughed, too.

"Turn around," she said softly.

"Wait, get up outta the bed and stand with your back toward me and wait until I tell you to pull the shirt over your head."

Catching a glimpse here and there of her side boob, she was the most innocent yet sensual thing I'd ever seen. I cleared my throat. "You can put your shirt back on," I said, turning around, clicking through the images on my tiny camera screen. "These are gonna be so good. You look great."

"Really, you swear?"

"I swear," I said, winking at her. "Take a look, and I promise I'll delete every single one that I don't use. I'll have something put together soon."

Aly turned and grabbed her shirt. I looked at the camera screen and back at her as she was pulling my white Hanes V-neck over her head. She caught me staring at her bare breasts as the shirt draped down, covering them. The heat flashed through me.

"You're beautiful."

She smiled softly. "You make me feel beautiful," she said, hugging my arm. "Let me see."

These last few days have been the best days ever, I thought. I'd never felt more close to anyone in my life than I did at that moment.

"Come on. Let's get to it. I really wanna finish the song before I leave. I packed all my gear, and I'm ready to go too, so all I'll need to do is mix the song while the guys are packing the trailer."

"You're so business like," she said, mocking me. "Ok, lead the way."

In my garage studio, Aly sat on the stool as I handed her the headphones. "Ok, you know the lyrics, right?"

"Yes."

"Ok, the music's gonna start playing. You'll hear my voice and then you'll know where to fall in. Just sing into the mic and we'll go back and fix the parts that aren't right during playback."

"You mean you can pick up right in the middle?"

"Yep, even if it's just a blip."

"Cool." She beamed, excited.

The hoarseness in her voice was gone, and she sounded amazing.

Chapter 36

ALYSSA

I sat on Nicole's bed with a smile a mile wide. Nadine and Nicole were in rapture with my story, but I didn't include our recording session. It was just too much. It was enough that I was sharing everything else.

"I just can't believe I sat there listening in on Jake and Notting talk about me. It was like, surreal, to say the least." I swooned onto the bed. "Jake admitted to writing love songs about me and I had to hold my breath. You could have probably heard a pin drop."

"No freaking way!" Nicole gasped. "I woulda passed out for sure."

"I woulda shit myself." Nadine laughed.

I looked at Nadine, wondering what it was like for her and Chris. She just had to be doing it with him by now.

"Nadine. What's it like?" I asked flat out.

"What?"

"Don't act stupid. You've gotta be doin' it with him. He's all over you."

"We only make out. You know, heavily, over and under the clothes touching." She admitted. "But don't get me wrong, if I wasn't so scared of getting pregnant, I would. He's to die for."

"La la la la la!" Nicole sang out, stuffing her fingers in her ears. "I really don't wanna hear how you'd like to do the dirty with my brother."

We all laughed out loud.

"I full-on touched his junk. It's crazy how big it gets," I admitted, stuffing my head in a pillow.

The girls squealed.

I sat there, wondering if I should share every other little detail.

"Oh look at her. She's day-dreaming about Jake and his snake," Nicole teased.

I gasped and grabbed the pillow, hitting her with it. I felt the heat rise in my face. I shouldn't have shared that bit of info with them.

"Aw, come on, we're just teasing you," Nadine jabbed.

"Whatever," I said, staring defiantly at Nicole. "So, what's your story? Nadine and I always spill the beans about our encounters. You never share about Grant."

"It's the same," she said simply and shrugged, trying to avoid sharing too much. "Obviously he's not as advanced in the sex arena as Jake and Chris. I mean, come on, he *is* only 15, and I like it that way."

I actually agreed with her remark. It must be nice and way less intimidating to be on the same playing field.

"What's Matt been up to?" I asked. I couldn't help it. Every time Grant's name was mentioned, I thought of Matt. They went hand in hand.

Nicole shrugged. "He's been hangin' with Greg, you know, since we all kinda have boyfriends. He hates to hear about it," she said, looking straight at me. "You know, you really crushed him."

My mouth hung open. "What, it's not like I wanted to hurt him," I replied. "I mean I didn't have a choice. I can't help how I feel inside."

"He doesn't see it that way. He thinks it's cause you wanna be popular."

I was shocked and hurt. What was I supposed to say to that? Of course Matt thought that, and I'm sure lots of other jerk-offs did, too.

"So, what did you say to him when he said that?" I was curious.

Nicole gave a worried look. "Well, I don't really say anything at all. Don't be mad at me, please. I just don't wanna argue with him, because it makes Grant edgy, and then we'll fight."

"Oh, ok. Real nice," I huffed, folding my arms to my chest. "So basically you *not* saying anything just makes him think you're on his side."

I was pissed and hurt. Of all people, I thought Nicole would have my back. Nadine sat with her mouth clamped tight, glancing back and forth at us.

"It's not like he's so far off base…"

"What!" I screamed. "I can't believe you just said that! What's going through your head? I mean really, Nicole."

"Well, you did say in the beginning how cool it would be for us to walk on campus the first day of school…."

I stood up, staring down at her. I was so shocked at the bullshit that was spilling from her mouth. "You told him, didn't you?" I said, interrupting her.

"I, I didn't mean to make it sound like that. We were just talking about relationships and I mentioned how cool it was that you…how popular you think you'll be…" she stammered on.

I started shaking. "Those are the words you used? *How popular I think I'll be?* You're a freaking idiot, Nicole!"

"You know what, Aly, screw you!" Nicole spat. "I've always supported you, giving you a new look, helping you with your clothes, letting you borrow stuff that helped you get Jake! How dare you!"

I was more than livid. My mind raced looking at her, with her long blond hair and stupid preppy-girl outfit. She was the epitome of a dumb blonde. No wonder she didn't get it.

"It doesn't surprise me. You're probably jealous or something…or just too dim." I fumed. "Some friend you are."

I grabbed my bag and stormed off toward the door.

"You know, they're right about you. You do think your shit doesn't stink, now," Nicole yelled. "Matt's too good for you anyway! He deserves someone better than you. You're nothing but a user."

I couldn't believe my ears. Nicole must have been beside herself listening to my stories about Jake. She just had to find a way to burn me because she was jealous. I bet they sat around talking shit about me while I wasn't there. I just knew it. I felt it in my bones. I couldn't believe Nadine just sat there staring at me like an idiot. She obviously felt the same way. She was probably the most jealous, since she had her eye on him first. Now it all became clear. No wonder Nicole and Grant disappeared last night.

I felt totally and utterly betrayed. I didn't know if I should scream or cry. Jake was leaving me for what felt like forever, and my two best friends were choosing Matt over *me*.

Approaching my house, I spotted Mike in front of Jake's house. A big huge trailer was hitched to the back of a big white van. Notting was there, too. They were loading gear into it. My heart started to race, thinking of the text message he'd sent me last night. I never replied. I hurried up my driveway, but I wasn't quick enough. He spotted me.

"Hey, Aly," Mike called out, waving.

He was actually smiling a real smile, not that *I think I'm the shit* grin he always wore.

I waved back at Mike. He looked over toward the garage and waved for me to come over. My heart sped. I walked over slowly and worried Notting would come back out.

"Hey," I said with a crooked smile.

"You mad at me?" he asked with a somber look in his eyes.

"Where's Jake?" I looked around uncomfortably.

"What, you don't know where your boy's at?"

I gave him a tight stare and ignored him. What game was he trying to play with me? Our eyes danced with each other, for a long moment and it made me uneasy. I looked away.

"Just wanted to say sorry again," he said thoughtfully. "Jake seems to think I've got some hidden agenda."

Uh, yeah he does. My curiosity got the best of me. "About what?"

Mike hung his head, laughing softly. "He thinks I want to corrupt you or something."

"And he said that to you?" I asked. I was stunned by his honesty.

"Not in those words, but pretty much that's what he said." He nodded. "So, really, I'm sorry, if that's the idea I gave you."

I most definitely looked at him in a new light now. I didn't like to judge people based on other people's ideas. Sure, he was a party boy, but who wasn't, really? My brother locked in the drunk zone last night and didn't even come home. It couldn't be all that bad.

"Thanks. I think Jake's just trying to protect me from myself." I sniffed.

"Yeah, but we're all young. Being serious will come soon enough when we graduate." He smiled. "You need to live your life how you want to. I'm gonna have a good time as long as I can."

"Yeah."

"Don't let him control you, Aly. If you wanna have a good time and experience life, do it." He smiled, his eyes crinkling at the corners. "We're only young once."

Notting came out through the garage door, calling out Mike's name. Mike became rigid, standing taller. I backed away, saying good-bye and waved to Notting in hopes of a kind response. His demeanor was cool, but he waved.

I walked back to my house and sent Marshall a text, begging for him to get back to me.

- *MARSH, WHERE R U! I NEED U, U'LL JUST DIE! I'M GONNA GO 2 THE BEACH AND FEEL SORRY 4 MYSELF.*

I threw myself onto my bed. I wanted to sink into the blankets and never feel anything again. I felt a void I'd never felt before, ever in my life. My best friend turned into a jealous back stabber, and my boyfriend was gone, hanging out with skeezies all over half the country.

My brain ran in high gear, and my stomach sank when I thought of the last two volleyball practices I'd missed. I was surprised neither of my parents had said anything, and surprised the coach hadn't called yet. I would miss practice again next weekend, too, if I was going to attend the shows. I schemed to figure out a way. The *ping* of my phone brought me to the present; I prayed it was Marshall—it was Mike.

- *FOR BOTH OUR SAKES, DON'T SHARE TOO MUCH WITH JAKE ABOUT OUR TALK. I DON'T NEED THE DRAMA, AND NEITHER DO YOU. M.*

I felt guilty, like I was doing something wrong, but I wasn't. I was only being friendly. And Mike was right; we're only young once. I smiled reading his text. I liked that he liked me, that he treated me like I wasn't a freshy. I was who I was, and he was cool with that. He gave me the courage to be rebellious. I decided to text back.

- *I AGREE. HAVE FUN ON TOUR. HOPEFULLY I'LL SEE YOU GUYS NEXT WEEKEND.*

Mike text right back:

- *HOPE TO SEE YOU THERE. TEXT ANYTIME IF YOU HAVE A HARD TIME GETTING AHOLD OF JAKE. IT CAN GET IFFY AND PRETTY BUSY. M.*

I smiled. See, he wasn't so bad after all, I thought.

- *THX.*

———

I couldn't remember the last time I walked down to the beach alone. I felt disconnected, like I was floating down the street. I looked around to see if I might know someone on one of the volleyball courts, but I didn't. It would have been nice to grab a game.

I stepped into the warm sand and flashed back to my time with Jake at the beach. I remembered how our wet bodies rubbed together, smooth and cool; the way his body glistened and his electric blue eyes smiled at me. I began to cry, sniveling as I treaded through the sand. I laid out my towel as far away from anyone as I could find and threw myself face first into it, sobbing like someone had died.

Marshall finally replied to my earlier text message and made his way down to my side.

"Aww, Aly, sweetie." He smiled warmly. "Your nose is as red as a tomato," he said, pinching the tip of it.

I couldn't help but laugh. "I'm sure."

I spilled my guts to Marshall, feeling weird at first, because we were really never that close. I hoped I wouldn't scare him away with all the drama. He hung on every word, consoling me every chance he could.

No matter what, Marshall always looked way fashionable; other than Sienna, he had it down. I admired his cutoff jeans that frayed right above the knee with layered tanks and a really sheer collared shirt. His hair was loose and tied back with a signature bandana, and he had these thick, tiny hoop earrings in each ear. He was masculine and feminine all at the same time.

"Dude, I like your outfit," I complimented, reaching out to touch the shirt. "Where do you find your clothes? I envy your style."

He giggled. "I shop at thrift stores, these little boutiques when there are sales, and I go to the outlets. I couldn't stand the clothes my mom wanted me to wear," he explained. "She still has a hard time dealing with my *way of being*."

"How's your dad with it?" I was curious. "You don't have to talk about it if it's uncomfortable."

I watched his delicate features toss between wretchedness and resignation. "No, He's ok. I am who I am, I can't help it." He smiled thoughtfully at me. "I knew I wasn't like the other boys as far back as I can remember." He shrugged.

"I'm sorry if asking was too bold," I said, crossing my legs underneath me and flicking sand off my knees.

"So, you wanna hear a theory I have?" he asked. A tight smile spread across his face, like he had a secret.

"What?" I whispered, like someone was gonna hear me.

"I think Bobby's gay," he said with confidence.

I looked at him with wide-eyes and a laugh popped out. Marshall was crazy. It must be because he was crushing on Bobby or something.

"Come on, Marsh," I said, bewildered. "I don't mean to laugh, I'm sorry."

The look Marshall's face told me he was embarrassed. He looked away from me, and now I felt like a jerk.

"I get it. He doesn't come off like I do," he said, making his case. "But why else would he ask for my number?"

My heart stopped. No freaking way. I wondered if Jake knew.

Chapter 37
ALYSSA

My life slid into boring nothingness.

It was only my third day at beach volleyball practice. This whole volleyball thing, I had to admit, I loved. It had become a welcomed distraction from all things Jake. Thinking of my fair-weather friend Nadine, who was *"caught in the middle"*—those were her words. I seethed with jealousy that she was always with Nicole. Nadine told me the only reason she hung with Nicole so much was because she's Chris' sister. *Whatever*, I told her. I felt slighted. I still couldn't believe Nicole hadn't apologized. She totally barfed all over my reputation by making me out to be some Envy wannabe. The truth was if those bitches did a play back, we were all scheming together the night they helped me transform. We were all Envy wannabes.

I stretched in the sand as other girls started to arrive. A new girl showed up, along with another girl named Stephanie. Stephanie stood out because she had the most amazingly fierce reflexes. I yearned to be that good someday. She introduced the new girl as Renee. She was beautiful, Envy status in a sporty way, with long limbs. I smiled, waving hello. Renee stood eyeballing me and it made me uncomfortable.

What the heck is she staring at?

"Are you the girl who's with Jake Masters?" Renee asked in a tone I couldn't quite place.

"Uh, yeah, maybe," I replied, trying to play it down. "I'm Aly."

"Hi, yeah, I recognize your face," she said, nodding her head. "I mean, you look different, but yeah, it's you."

"It's nice to meet you."

Renee smiled thoughtfully at me and it finally clicked. This is the Renee that was Jake's ex-girlfriend. This seriously wasn't happening. She glanced up in the direction of The Strand, where the pedestrians walked. There were a few guys standing about, waving. She waved back, smiling. I wondered if one of them was her boyfriend. I also wondered what happened between her and Jake, and why she never said hello to him at either of the parties I now recalled seeing her at.

We rallied for about fifteen minutes and then started a game. It was exhilarating for me to be playing with others who were at an entirely different skill level. It made me play harder and learn faster. I was teamed with a girl named Sarah, and watching Renee from the other side of the court made me long for her ability. I took in everything about her. I glanced up at The Strand and the guys were still there, now sitting and watching. I now wanted to be like Renee; a little of Renee and Sienna. I was totally girl crushing on the both of them now.

This was the first full game of two-man beach volleyball I'd ever played with girls my age. I'd always played with grown-up leisure players. I didn't think I would be able to hang, but I did it. I dug fiercely served balls, made nearly impossible recoveries getting the ball up, blocked and hit at the net on the five-foot line, straight down. I set the ball with precision, and my control couldn't have been more spot-on. We won. I was covered from head to toe with sand like a sugar cookie. Sweat was pouring down my face, and the girls had nothing but accolades for me. I kept looking over at Renee, waiting for her to say something too, but she was quiet. Her expression was cheerful, though, as she wiped herself with a towel.

The boys still perched on The Strand distracted her.

"Is one of them your boyfriend?" I asked curiously.

"Yeah, the taller one, Ethan," she replied.

"Does he go to your school?"

Renee didn't answer me right away. She took her time stuffing her towel into her bag and taking drinks from her red water bottle. I began to feel awkward standing there watching her. Maybe I shouldn't be so nosey, but I couldn't help myself. The other girls took off toward the coach, so I decided to follow.

"Uh, it was nice meeting you," I said quietly. I slowly turned to walk away. I felt like an idiot.

"Um, Aly, you played a really good game. You've got a lot of skill," she complimented. "Ethan goes to USC. He plays volleyball, too." I looked up, trying to get a better look at him. I wondered how her parents felt about her going out with an older college boy.

I walked the 10 blocks into downtown Manhattan Beach and sat on a pier bench, waiting for Marshall. He was always down for anything. It seemed we were each other's only friend at the moment. Watching the familiar faces of other kids from school ride by on their bikes made me wonder how Nadine and Nicole were doing. I still couldn't believe Nicole hadn't called to apologize for making me look like an asshole. She must really believe the things she said about me. I was crushed.

"Hey, you!" I turned, hearing Marshall's familiar voice.

I jumped up. "Oh my God, I'm so happy you came!"

"So, what's up?"

I took in a deep breath. "Jake wants me to send him a picture of me in my bikini," I blurted out, slapping my hands to my face. "And I really wanted it to be in the sand, candid, you know. Not some cheesy pose."

Marshall laughed, bowing. "Mr. Shutterbug at your service." He reached out opened handed. "Hand me your phone."

———

It was boiling hot. The skin on my shoulders sizzled as I admired the few photo's Marshall took of me.

"Which one should I send?" I asked, handing him my phone, rubbing my shoulders. "You pick. I can't do it."

"Geez, Aly, any one of them would be great." He smiled with a glint in his eye. "I like this one. You look like Teen Vogue."

"Stop it," I said, shoving him. "Don't be cheesy." I laughed, fanning my face.

"Aww." He reached over, giving me a shoulder squeeze. "Don't be, you look good. Now send it."

Selecting Jake's phone number, my heart began to race. I couldn't believe I was sending a freakin' bikini girl pic to him. Glancing up at Marshall, I hit *send*. "Oh, my God, I did it!"

My hands shook with anticipation of his response.

"Let's go get some pizza," Marshall suggested, grabbing my hand and pulling me up. "He's gonna take that one to bed."

My eyes bugged out at the thought. "I don't wanna know that," I shrieked, running up the hill towards the pizza place.

The ringtone, only assigned to Jake, blared out loudly as I dug the phone out of my bag.

"Hello," I said, breathless.

"You're delectable," Jake said in a low, raspy voice.

My heart lurched as my veins exploded throughout my body. I melted into the ground. I wished so badly that I could see his face.

"Why, thank you very much, sir," I said in a playful Texas drawl. My eyes darted around. I felt like the whole world was watching me.

"I gotta go, just wanted to tell you that. We're heading out."

"It's your turn to lay birdseed," I flirted.

"Birdseed, hmm, I like that. What were you thinkin'?"

A burst of loud sound came through the earpiece of my phone, forcing me to hold it away from my ear. I could hear Mike's loud mouth, shouting out something I couldn't comprehend, and female laughter. My stomach curled into a knot. Jake screamed out, "*Dude, shut the fuck up! Get out, I'm on the phone!"* A commotion, more laughter and then nothing, silence.

"Hello?" I said, wondering if the call got dropped.

"Yeah, sorry," Jake said, "Mike's gettin' on my last nerve. The regrets are slapping me in the face."

"That sucks…"

"I'll call or text soon. Everyone's waiting on me," Jake said, interrupting me, his edge evident.

"Hey, don't forget the birdseed. Send me a picture of you, too." I reminded.

"Most definitely, I'll do that as soon as I can. Later."

I sat at a table watching Marshall order our food and then stared at my phone. I tried to talk myself out of sending a text to Nadine, but my curiosity and hurt feelings got the best of me.

- *HEY. LONG TIME NO TALK. I'M NOT GONNA PRETEND LIKE NOTHING HAPPENED. WHY HAVEN'T YOU CALLED OR TEXT? AFTER ALL WE'VE BEEN THROUGH? YOU ACTUALLY PICKED A SIDE? REALLY? ANYWAY, WHATEVS. I HOPE YOU AND CHRIS ARE GOOD.*

I hit *send,* and now I couldn't take it back. It was forever out there in the texting universe. I sat picking at my nails and cuticles, worrying that Nadine would ignore me, when Marshall dropped down a tray full of pizza slices.

A ping rang out. It was Nadine's response.

- *DUDE, DON'T BE LAME! I'M NOT THE ONE. YOU GUYS NEED TO GET OVER THIS. YOU PLAYIN BALL? TEXT ME WHEN YOU GET HOME, WANNA COME OVER.*

I ruminated over Nadine's text—I was pissed. Bottom line, she coulda reached out. Dishing out the slices, Marshall's words pulled me to attention.

"So, I have news," he said. "And you have to swear on your life and the life of everyone you care about, that you won't repeat a word of it."

My mouth fell open. "Oh shit!" I said, grabbing the pitcher of soda and pouring a glass full. "Spill it." I was beyond eager to hear his news.

Marshall straightened his back and smoothed out the napkin he'd placed in front of him, perfectly. He paused for effect. His eyes finally met mine. "Bobby *is* gay…and he likes me."

It took a second for it to sink in. I heard the words, but it was like I couldn't process the meaning. I thought of Jake and wondered if he knew all along Bobby was gay. Not that it mattered, but now Bobby was professing feelings for my new BFF. I wondered if boys talked like girls did.

"Wow," I said, finally smiling, my shock apparent. "Sorry for the delayed response, but that's huge news." I reached out, squeezing Marshall's hand. "This is really exciting!"

"I'm so happy," he said, swooning. "This is the first time someone's told me they like me. You know, without wanting to hook up. So it's a huge deal, and my stomach's been in tangles! I wasn't supposed to say anything to you."

"Did he ask you not to tell me?"

"Yeah, he did." Marshall admitted with hesitation. "But, it's only because Jake doesn't know he's gay."

"What!" I felt like I had a thousand-pound elephant sitting on my chest. I gulped. "That's a big secret, Marshall. What else did he say? I mean, when did this all happen? It's only been a few weeks since you met him."

345

"I know," he said through a mouthful of pizza. "You know what they say. When it happens, it happens."

He sat nodding his head slowly, picking pieces of charred pepperoni off his pizza and stuffing them into his mouth.

"We talk and text non-stop. It's been a whirlwind, Aly. I just hope it works out," He said with hopeful eyes. "You can't imagine what it's like for me. You think you guys have it tough, straight teenagers looking for love. Try being a gay teenager, who everyone knows is gay and makes fun of. I can only hope for the best."

"I hope it works out for you," I said quietly, my mind reeled from his news. "Um, so, have you guys kissed?"

"No, but we've talked about it. I can't wait to see him again."

Marshall beamed with excitement. I was beyond stoked for him, but my concern quickly sprouted.

———

Marshall and I sat in my bedroom, perusing the band's social media accounts. We clicked on the pictures attached to the newest posts and my stomach instantly sank seeing Jake entwined in another girl's arms and much more. My head swam, uneasy and I thought I'd be sick. We scrolled through each one silently. Marshall rubbed my hand to console my undeniable sadness. As we reached the end of the picture diary, our eyes locked and a mask of sympathy etched across his face. This blazing tribute to a warning I chose to ignore tore through my mind, as I fought to figure out how I would handle this revelation.

"That last picture was taken last night." Marshall pointed out achingly. "I'm sorry to say it, but it looks as if he was making out with her or…something."

I swear I thought I would pass out. Tunnel vision closed in. "What should I do, Marshall?" I got up, throwing myself onto my bed, and the tears began to fall.

"Maybe it's not what it looks like. I mean, he's been calling and texting you. It's not like he's ignoring you."

"Whatever…he was touching her…like he liked it! I wonder who took that picture."

The afternoon whittled away, with me obsessively scouring the Internet for anything about the band and Jake. Marshall planted himself on my bed, watching YouTube videos and texting Bobby. I hated everyone: my sister for being right, Nadine and Nicole for abandoning me, and my entire life. Staring at Marshall with a soft smile painted on his face, it was hard for me not to be jealous. I believed Jake when he told me he cared about me. I also thought that meant he cared enough not to flirt and hang all over other girls. Apparently, that wasn't the case.

I stared at my phone, with my palms sweating, confused and fuming with malicious thoughts, day-dreaming about ripping that girl's hair out. Marshall's voice rang out, grabbing my attention.

"Bobby says they're heading to Arizona now, then home for their shows here. Then up north and to Washington." His fingers punched away at his phone screen.

"Great," I said, dryly. "Freakin' asshole. I'm so upset I don't know what to do."

"Call him and just ask him what the eff, man." Marshall sat up, egging me on. "I would. Screw it, Aly."

My phone pinged with a text message and we both whipped our heads around, staring at it. I sat frozen. Scared it was Jake, and how I would respond to him.

"You check. I can't do it," I said, burying my head in my hands.

As Marshall picked up my phone, I heard the doorbell ring. I wondered who it was. Normally I would be the one bounding down the stairs, but I would let Allison deal with it.

Marshall held out the phone to me. "It's Mike."

I gulped, sinking two levels. "I'm gonna ask him. He's been cool about stuff. I bet he knows what's going on."

"Aly, don't fool yourself," he said, looking at me as if I had two heads. "Friends cover for friends. Look what you've been doing. You think they aren't doing the same?"

Ignoring his painfully truthful words, I read Mike's text and a new emotion took over me.

- *HEY ALY. WHATCHA DOIN'? I'M BORED. JAKE'S ASLEEP. WE HAVE A LONG DRIVE AHEAD. TALK TO ME J*

My heart raced. I felt uplifted to receive his text, deceitfully happy now that I'd been doing it behind Jake's back.

"You know what?" Marshall said, closing the laptop lid. "I betcha Mike likes you? Why else would he be talking to you?"

I huffed. "Thanks a lot," I said, shoving his shoulder. My breathing sped up thinking of that possibility.

"Seriously, why else would he?" he reiterated.

"I didn't want to think that, but you're right. Why else?" I said, trying not to smile.

I wasn't going to pretend I wasn't happy. *This was what Jake gets*, I thought. What girl wouldn't want guys to like her?

I ignored the fact that the Mike thing may have been true for some time. Thinking back, he was always attentive, in his scumbag way. No wonder Jake said he didn't trust him. His guts told him right.

"I refuse to feel guilty," I said, punching my fists into the bed, trying to convince myself. "Jake's off doing whatever, and the only reason I'm talking to Mike is because he offered to keep me in the loop. I didn't ask him."

"I'm dying to hear what Mike has to say. Text him back." Marshall pointed at my phone.

- *HEY MIKE, YEAH LONG DRIVES SUCK THE BIG ONE. I SAW PICTURES FROM LAST NIGHT. DO YOU KNOW WHO THE GIRL WAS SITTING ON JAKE'S LAP?*

Marshall and I sat frozen, barely breathing in anticipation of his response, finally a ping.

- *NO, I DON'T KNOW HER. I JUST TOOK PICTURES LIKE I ALWAYS DO AND POST THEM FOR THE FANS TO SEE WHAT WE'RE UP TO.*

I replied:

- *DON'T TELL JAKE I ASKED. I'M JUST BUMMED AS YOU CAN IMAGINE. TYPICAL I SUPPOSE.*
- *ALY, THERE'S A LOT OF THINGS THAT GO DOWN WHILE ON THE ROAD. IT'S PART OF THE JOB DESCRIPTION. WHY DO YOU THINK I DON'T HAVE A GIRLFRIEND? JUST SAYIN'. SORRY, BUT I DON'T KNOW WHAT WENT DOWN.*

Chapter 38

JAKE

The thing I hated most about being on the road were the long drives between states in the West and Midwest. I shook my head while giving the evilest of eyes to the dry, barren Arizona desert. As if this God-forsaken land was staring back at me, I flipped it the bird through the window, for good measure. Now there were two things: the long drives between venues and being away from Aly; and being away from her blew harder than anything I'd ever known before.

Moving uncomfortably in my seat, I stared at her digital image on my phone. Each minute that crawled by meant I'd be home sooner. Waves of nausea washed over me, thinking about last night's antics. I kicked myself for drinking too much and acting like an ass. Regret consumed me for allowing myself to be coerced by Mike and Rachel into doing shots and playing Flip Cup. *I should've stuck with Flip Cup and stayed away from that fucking devil juice*, I thought, holding my stomach. I should've just not drunk at all. Now I had some random girl who I couldn't really remember texting me.

Running my hands through my hair, I wanted to rip it out by the roots. *Fuck. Every time, without fail, it happens.* It's like I lose my mind or something. If I could punch myself in the face real good, I would. I worried I'd be like my father. How many other women had he been seeing? Or was she the only one? I swore to myself I wouldn't be like my dad.

Sitting up, I stretched my arms high above my head, taking in a deep breath. I could smell the faint, boozy aroma that was seeping out of half the occupants riding in the van. I wanted to puke. The aftermath of the night we had wasn't my gig anymore. The regret ran too deep. Getting up, I moved to the front passenger seat next to Notting. I wondered what he thought. *Why do I care?* I'd never given a shit about what he thought, whether he knew or not about our carrying on. I wondered if he could smell what I smelled, or if I was just being sensitive and hung over. I was anxious inside, and really wanted to pick Notting's brain.

"How much longer?" I looked back over my shoulder. I was startled to lock eyes with Mike, sitting a few rows back. My blood began to simmer. Something still gnawed at me about him, and I couldn't put my finger on it.

Notting's voice pulled me back. "Six or seven hours, depending on any stops." He reached over, grabbing my shoulder. "Might as well get some shut eye. You look like you need it."

"Yeah," I agreed softly, glancing down at Aly's image. "How long did you wait?"

"Wait for what?"

"For Mom."

Notting stiffened at the question. I slouched lower into my seat in an attempt to muffle my voice.

"Notting, I'm pretty sure I'm in love with Aly," I whispered, not believing what I was hearing myself say. "When did you know you were in love with Mom? I know you guys think I'm not aware of what's going on, but I am."

He stared out the window and I wondered if he would open up.

"I've always been in love with her, Jake," he admitted, his voice barely audible, "for as long as I can remember." He nodded pensively.

I admired Notting's honesty. With his hardened good looks and everything else he stood for, he really was one cool package. It didn't bother me hearing his admission. I assumed he meant he loved her even when she was married to my father. I wondered if he knew of my dad's affair. I was too chicken to ask him outright.

Notting always doted on Mom. Even when he was in other relationships, they always had a special bond. Maybe he did know about my dad's infidelity and felt sorry for her. But thinking back to one particular moment in time when I spied them in an intimate conversation, he had brushed the hair away from her face and looked lovingly at her. I thought it was brotherly back then. Now I knew it was much more than that. He looked at my mother the way I looked at Aly.

"I can't explain it," I said in a hushed tone, hoping no one could hear me. Dump and Sienna were nearest, and appeared to be asleep. Rachel was at the back, asleep next to Mike, and Bobby had his earphones over his ears.

"Jake, you can't choose who you fall in love with. You just have to hope that person loves you back, enough that it's worth it."

I contemplated his words, wondering if Aly felt the same way, or if I was just an infatuation. I fully believed in our connection, the invisible energy that pulled us together in the beginning, the same binding sensation that kept me wanting more. I thought of my father, and an unfamiliar ball instantly formed in my throat. I loved him and missed him, even though he wasn't the man I thought he was. Who was I to ruin his memory for everyone else? No, I'd keep the secret and bury it, as I'd been doing.

Notting let out a big sigh and it startled me to attention. My heart started to race. His mouth hung open like he was about to say something.

"I've had a lot of guilt about loving your mother, Jake." He gripped the steering wheel tightly, forcing the muscles to shift underneath his tattooed forearms. "Love, for me, has been a complicated matter, I'm not sure I'm the best person to be having these discussions with. I've broken cardinal rules, son. I coveted another man's wife for years longer than I care to admit. I almost walked away from the both of you when you needed me most because of the thorny, convoluted situation."

"You don't have to go there, man," I suggested. "I didn't ask the question to pry. I asked because I don't know how I'm gonna get through this."

"You'll figure it out." He breathed heavily and reached over, grabbing my shoulder again. "I knew one day this moment would come."

We sat in silence for a long time, and all these questions filled my head.

"When did you and Mom get serious?"

"We weren't for a long time after your father's death and we're still not that serious, Jake."

"Really?" I said quietly. "Is it her? Or you?"

"She can't let go. She's told me she feels guilty about how her feelings for me may have affected their marriage and she needs time. After so long, I just let her be. I figure it will happen when it happens, or something else will happen."

"How many years does it take, geez?" I stated dryly. "Anyway, I'm just looking for my own answers, Notting. Thanks for sharing. I know it's gotta be weird talking to me about it."

"I don't have the answers, Jake." He breathed in deeply. "Just do the best you can; make no promises you can't keep. Be honest, and if it's meant to be, it'll be. I must say one more time, though, you're messing with fire with her being so young."

I began to relax, mulling over my thoughts and his advice. I didn't realize I'd drifted off to sleep until Mike's loud mouth woke me up. We pulled into an inconspicuous strip mall in some Podunk town. The van doors swung open, and the heat slapped me in the face.

"Shit, it must be 120 degrees out here!" Bobby said as he stepped out. "I need to piss."

One by one, they got out, scuffling away from the van.

"I could fill a fucking five-gallon water bottle," Dump said as he stretched tall. "Guess there, huh?" he said to Sienna, pointing to the building. He grabbed Sienna's hand, taking long strides toward the local drug store. I shut the passenger door and followed everyone in.

Half the store appeared to be for personal care, everything from make-up to hair products. All of it was targeted toward girls. While Notting searched for pain meds, I wandered the aisles, looking for nothing in particular, until I noticed the shampoo bottles. Smiling, I made a beeline toward them, looking around to see if anyone else was near. I was the only one in the aisle, and I quickly picked out a strawberry-scented shampoo. I hoped it would be the same scent as Aly. *Strike one*, I thought. I quickly placed it back on the shelf and moved to the next one.

I went from brand to brand until I found what I was looking for. *Suave Naturals* was the name. I closed my eyes, holding it under my nose, picturing her wet hair, smooth legs, and lying next to me. I wanted to go home. No more hanging out with fan girls. If I'd only picked up the phone when I wanted to last night, I would have spent the night talking to Aly and not acting like a total dick.

A sudden hard shove at my back knocked the bottle free from my hand, and the gel-like contents squirted out all over the place.

"You fucking homo!" Mike's voice rang out and his laughter filled the air.

"Shut the fuck up, Mike, why's everything gotta be gay and homo with you?" Bobby chimed in angrily, as he came up the other side of the aisle.

I wanted to rip Mike's head off his shoulders for pushing me, and for a million other reasons. I bent down and picked up the bottle with its cracked lid. "I'm gonna have to buy this now, you asshole."

"What the hell you sniffin' fruity shampoo for anyway?" Mike shrugged, shaking his head. "I'm sorry, but you gotta admit that's gay."

"What the fuck is so gay about it?" Bobby growled, moving past me so fast I didn't realize he was attacking Mike.

Bobby flew at Mike with a rage I'd never seen. His momentum carried them into the shelves of neatly lined products. Like an explosion, the bottles went flying and tipped over in a domino effect. I stood there in shock, watching Bobby wail on Mike's face. Mike quickly regained his footing and sent Bobby tumbling to the other side of the aisle, continuing the path of destruction. Mike got one good punch to Bobby's face.

Finally I found myself trying to break them apart.

"Stop, stop it! Fuck, you're gonna get us thrown in jail!" I shouted, pulling Bobby away.

"You little piece of shit, I'll fucking kill you!" Mike fumed. "Don't you ever fucking touch me again, I swear I'll fucking kill you!"

"Fuck you!" Bobby spat back. His chest heaved. The side of his cheek was split open about an inch, and blood trickled down his face.

"Dude, your face is bleeding." I pointed at Bobby. He took his shirt off and used it to cover the cut.

"You need to check yourself, dude," I barked, shaking my head at Mike. He bent down, picking a phone up off the ground. "Are you retarded or something?" I asked, as if he'd admit it.

"Me, I'm retarded?" he shouted. "He's the one who started it." He pointed at Bobby, his face twisted with rage.

Bobby turned and began to walk away when he saw two store employees coming toward us. Mike held out the phone that was in his hand. "Dude, this is yours. Nice screen saver." He sniggered, staring at Aly's bikini clad image. "Aly's lookin' good."

Mike took a closer look at the screen. The picture of Aly posed in a bikini stared back at him. It was the straw that broke the camel's back. His out of character kindness toward Aly, his indifference toward Bobby, his shitty attitude toward the new music and me in general, along with the look on his face as he admired Aly's picture, made me snap.

The next thing I knew, Notting was pulling me off of Mike as blood gushed out of his nose. The commotion stirred an epic mess involving the cops. The three of us sat lined up outside the drug store, staring at three cop cars and a paramedic truck. Mike was getting his face looked at, and my hand was swollen up like a balloon. I'd never broken anything, but I was pretty sure my hand was broken. None of us said one word to each other. I stared at Notting as he tried to work out some deal with the store manager and the cops. I prayed we all wouldn't go to jail. Mike was moved over to the bumper of the paramedic truck, and they informed him that his nose was broken. He needed to go the hospital.

It was about a fifteen-minute drive to the nearest hospital. Dump was the only one who wasn't involved and he wore a smirk stitched across his face. I could tell he wanted to say something so badly.

"What, what are you looking at?" I decided to break the silence.

"Are you fucking kidding me?" He shook his head grinning. "You assholes really had to go and duke it up? Bobby, I didn't think you had it in ya." He chuckled.

"I guess this means the tour is over?" I was startled to hear Rachel's voice crack. "I mean if Jake's hand is broken, how's he gonna play?"

"That's just fucking great." Mike broke in, sounding like he had a head cold.

"You shut the hell up," I said, pointing at Mike with my good hand. "You just can't keep your mouth shut. I don't blame Bobby. I blame you."

"I blame all of you! I can't take one moment to go to the loo before you act like you're in primary school? What the hell is going on?" Notting shouted. "Everyone one of you is responsible! Cut the shit! Like little fucking girls you are, little fucking girls!"

Not one gasp or breath could be heard. I don't think any of us had ever seen Notting lose it this bad. A swear word coming out of his mouth was a rarity, and never in anger. We arrived at the hospital, and it must have taken over 4 hours for Mike and me to get looked at, put back together, and sent on our way. Mike definitely had a broken nose, and I had a broken hand. We were issued citations of some sort. I was too afraid to bring it up with Notting, so I sat there barely moving, waiting for him to bring it up. I fucked up royally, and all I cared about was locking myself in my hotel room and calling Aly. We had another three hours to go. This would be the longest drive of my life.

No one said one word the entire rest of the way. Only the faint sounds of music and movies streaming through earbuds could be heard. The whirring of tires spinning and the sound of book and magazine pages being turned broke in softly from time to time. We finally passed into the city limits of Phoenix, Arizona. I viewed the small green highway sign with population info as it flashed by in an instant. I perked up, hoping I had reception, and sent Aly a text with my good hand.

- *SUP ALYCAT—TRIED TO TXT DURING DESERT DRIVE. NO RECEPT. GOING TO CALL U SOON AS I GET TO HOTEL. IN PHX NOW. ONLY A 6 HR DRIVE FROM HERE TO HOME. UR NEVER GONNA BELIEVE WHAT HAPND.*

I wanted to turn around to see what everyone else was doing. I could hear movement and the quiet voices of Sienna and Rachel. I halted my breath, trying to hear what they were saying.

"I don't know, probably not, it's over," Sienna whispered.

What is she referring to? I wondered.

"This totally effing sucks. It can't end like this." "Rachel said. *"But, this could be the most perfect thing though, right?"*

Right, what?

"Rach, I don't know. I don't wanna know anymore. This whole thing is messy and I'm out."

"Oh come on. It's just a matter of time. The band first, you know that."

"You're totally delusional. You're not seeing what I'm seeing." Sienna's whispers grew louder. *"Just stop."*

"Rachel, shut the fuck up already," Dump's gravely deep voice stomped.

Silence commenced. Everyone struggled to pull themselves together as our hotel came into view. Thankfully, I was in the front seat. I swung the door open while the van wasn't even stopped and hugged my backpack to my chest, jumping out. I hightailed it through the hotel lobby and up to the front desk. An older lady with perfectly coifed chin-length blond hair and orange lipstick smiled at me as

I approached. The hue of her fake tan matched her lipstick and her long fake coral-colored fingernails.

"Hello, I'm checking in. Jake Masters."

"Hello, Mr. Masters." She smiled at me with bright white-capped teeth. "How is your day going?"

"Been better. Broke my hand." I smiled crookedly, holding up my cast.

"Oh my," she gasped. "I hope it doesn't hurt too much."

"Nope," I smiled. I bent in closer, giving her a wink. "They gave me the good drugs."

She blushed. "Well, that's good." Her eyes crinkled with her smile. She glanced back down at her computer screen.

I took note of her nametag. "So, Suzanne, you got that room?" I was antsy. I wanted to get the hell outta there before Notting came through the door, but luck wasn't on my side.

"We need to talk, young man," Notting's smooth voice rang out, echoing through the lobby.

"Oh my." Suzanne jumped as she brought her hand to her mouth. I gave her another wink and closed both eyes. Taking a deep breath I spun around, leaning back against the counter.

"About?" I said calmly.

"Oh, let's see," he said and looked up at the ceiling with forced calm. "Jumping out of a moving vehicle, breaking your mate's face and your hand, basically screwing up the last dates of this tour sponsored by a label I was hoping would sign you one day…"

"Stop, just stop," I said firmly, holding my hand up as the others made their way into the lobby. "Can we talk about this later?"

I turned to face Suzanne again. "Please get me outta here?"

"We will talk as soon as you drop your bags into your room," Notting barked at the back of my head.

I didn't want to turn around. I knew what I was about to do would send him over the edge when he found out, but I didn't care. We didn't have a show now, and there was no reason why I had to stay around.

Arriving at my room, I pushed the room key into its slot. I pretended I didn't hear Rachel call out my name. Opening the door, I let it slam shut behind me, hoping she'd get the hint.

I took my phone out, dialing Aly's number. It went straight to voicemail. *"Alycat, uh, call me back a. s. a. p. I wanna come home and get you. We're done with the tour early. I'll explain later. So yeah, call me back."*

I could hear Rachel's muffled voice calling my name through the door. Opening the door, I stood there staring at her disheveled appearance. Her face was drawn and tired.

"I just wanted to check on you. Make sure you're ok," she said with a soft smile. "Do you need anything?"

"Rachel, I need you not to care," I begged with a heart-felt expression.

Notting stopped directly behind Rachel, looking at me over her shoulder. "I'll be back in five minutes."

Rachel watched and waited for Notting's door to shut. She looked back at me with a wrinkled forehead. "What's going on with you?" she asked, shaking her head. "Jake, whatever's going on, we're friends, right?"

"Yeah, of course, but this," I said gesturing between us. "This has to stop. I can't have this. It's never gonna be the same." I had to say it, recalling what I'd heard between Sienna and her.

"But why, why does it have to be different? Why can't we move on?"

"Rachel, I know you and Sienna are best friends, and you and Mike are gettin' close. But ultimately, it makes it weird for me, and I can't have it. I'm sorry."

She remained still, staring at me with her mouth open, searching my face. I wasn't going to budge and I hoped she wouldn't start crying.

"Look, Rachel, I'm sorry. I gotta go, Not's gonna be here any minute," I said, looking down at the tan and black patterned carpet.

"Fine," Rachel said, forcing me to look up. The softness I'd admired on her face was gone, and the evil glint she was known for emerged in her eyes. She turned briskly, walking away. I didn't try to stop her. I was tired of feeling bad. I stepped back and let the doors weight slam itself shut.

I tried calling Aly again. Finally she picked up. "Hey," I said, relieved. "What up? Did you get my message?"

"Hey you, yeah," her voice trailed off. This was not the reaction I was expecting. There was silence, and instantly my hands began to sweat.

"So?"

"Who was that girl you were with last night?" Her words clubbed me over the head. My mind raced, wondering how she found out. I wasn't going to try and lie to her.

"Aly, it's not what you think it is," I stammered.

I closed my eyes tightly, waiting. There was silence, no crying or screaming. Not your typical girl reaction. I paced the room, waiting for her to say something. I noticed the sun hung low, and I needed to get on the road if I was going to see her tonight.

"Aly, please don't do this, say something."

"Do what, Jake?" she said bitterly. "I'm minding my own business, trying to feel close to you. So I get online, looking around, and I see you practically sucking face with some hoe-bag." She paused and my heart raced. "Just be honest with me, please."

My heart cracked.

"I wanna come and get you, Aly," I said, breathless. "If you think you can pull it off. We'll be back tomorrow afternoon."

"So that's it, no more explanation? I'm just supposed to believe you?" Her voice strained.

"Yes, you are. It was nothing, and it never is. Come on, I wanna come and get you," I begged. I could hear her breathing rapidly and I kept begging. I admitted to behaving badly, and promised it would never happen again. She finally agreed to meet me later that night.

As soon as the call disconnected, there was a rap at my door and my stomach churned. It was Notting, ready to unleash his fury. I glanced at the clock, and it was nearly five o'clock. I hoped this wouldn't last long.

Chapter 39

JAKE

A stone-faced man stared back at me from across the room. I sat down on the bed quietly waiting, watching the clock's bright numbers glare back at me.

"What is going on with you?" He paced angrily. "Do you have any idea the mess you've caused?"

Now I was getting pissed. Was he really blaming me for this entire thing? "Oh really," I said condescendingly. "You have no idea the shit I put up with. Mike, he's a piece of shit, and I don't wanna be around him. I can't put up with it anymore."

Notting pointed his finger at me. "You two are in some serious trouble. This is going to cost us money, money we don't have." Notting's voice raged. "I don't give one shit about the little issues you have with Mike. He was your choice to be in the band. This is a business we're running here. He's an important part of the equation, my friend. So whatever your problems are, you'd better work them out."

Notting stood at the foot of the bed glaring at me. If he had fangs, they'd be showing.

"What if I said I don't want him in the band anymore?" I closed my eyes quickly, waiting for another eruption. Instead, the bed moved. I opened my eyes to see Notting sitting at the edge of the bed, with his back facing me.

"Why?" His voice was raspy and tired.

"For one, I don't like how he treats Bobby…and the drinking and drugs are more than I thought." I wavered, not sure if I should mention Aly's name, but who was I kidding? "I don't like how he is with Aly. There's something' goin' on there."

I continued my explanation of what led me to this place, and Notting just kept pinching the bridge of his nose and squinting his eyes. He looked overwhelmed. Periodically I glanced over at the clock sitting on the table next to the bed. I felt evermore anxious as the red digital numbers clicked closer to 5:30 PM.

He didn't say a word about Aly and her obvious part in my decision.

"It takes two to tango, my friend." Notting got up, pacing again. "It takes two or more in any spectacle. I'm done here. You are the one who needs to make this whole. School is beginning. Next tour may or may not happen now. When you're ready to make a decision, let me know." He laughed quietly at my audacity. "Call your mother. I'll let you tell her. You better do it now."

He walked out the door and the sound of it slamming shut absorbed into the walls. I ran to the door. "Notting, I need the keys to the van," I yelled out. I wasn't going to say a word of my plans. By the time I returned, he would be asleep and none the wiser until morning, and I'd be gone anyway.

———

Walking out to the van, I explained and apologized to Bobby for dragging him into my mission. We hadn't said one word to each other since the incident.

"Naw, man, no biggie," Bobby said, slouching along. "He deserves that broken nose. Maybe he'll learn to shut the hell up. So, are you serious about getting rid of him?"

"Yep, I just need to figure out how to do it."

"Just fucking say *you're fired!*" Bobby laughed hysterically, flipping a dual middle finger to an imaginary Mike.

The heat index was still intense. Invisible waves rose up in a blurred haze off in the distance everywhere I looked. Driving the van and trailer to the backside of the hotel, we unhitched the trailer and were on the road before six. I prayed that no one would screw with it. Notting would definitely cut me off if anything happened with our gear. I'd be dead. I had to let him know.

I handed Bobby my phone and I instructed him to text Notting.

- *NOT—BOBBY AND I BORROWED THE VAN. FIGURED YOU GUYS WOULDN'T NEED IT SINCE EVERYTHING'S WALKING DISTANCE. TRAILER'S IN BACK OF HOTEL. BE BACK LATER. TRYING TO SORT THINGS OUT.*

"Shit. Dude, I'm scared," Bobby said with jumpy chuckles. "He was pissed earlier. What's he gonna say to this?"

The ping of a new text message rang out and we shot each other a quick glance. "What's he sayin'?" I held my breath.

Looking down at the phone, Bobby smiled, holding it up to my face so I could read it myself.

- *CALL YOUR MOTHER.*

"I bet he wants to talk to her, and doesn't want to be the bearer of bad news," I said, rolling my eyes.

The first two hours of the drive went by in a blur. I finally got the courage to call my mother, and she handed me my ass. She sounded like a loud jet engine. I promised to sit down with her when I got home, to make a plan of action, because that's how she always liked to handle things. It was her way of controlling the situation. She didn't stop hammering her disappointment at me for a long time. Even though I understood, I didn't really care. I kept glancing over at Bobby to check his reaction to anything I was saying, but he was occupied by texting and it continued on well after my call ended.

I drove on, into the nothingness of the darkened desert, thinking how to approach Mike. My attention changed back to Bobby when he snickered. I was curious as to who the hell held his attention lately. I'd never noticed him so attached to his phone, ever. It must be a new girlfriend of his.

"When we gonna meet this girlfriend of yours?" I piped. "You've been texting like a chick for weeks now."

I kept giving Bobby quick glances to assess his demeanor and what I saw surprised me. Instead of a smile on his face, a serious expression dominated his exterior and my stomach sank.

"Dude, don't tell me you wanna quit the band because of some chick," I blurted out.

What else could it be? *It has to be that*, I thought to myself. He was in love and didn't want to be away from her.

368

It happened all the time and I knew it. I would be a fool not to admit I hadn't thought about it at least once.

"Come on, man, spit it out," I said, putting the pressure on.

Bobby kept taking in deep breaths and sighing loudly. Finally he glanced at me. "No, I don't wanna leave the band."

"Don't jerk me around, Bobby," I said seriously. "Just say it."

"I'm not gonna leave the band, unless you kick me out."

"Why would I kick you out?" I laughed, relieved. "Don't be a dick." I began to fidget with the radio.

"Dude, you might wanna pull over. I think I'm gonna be sick."

As soon as I pulled over on the side of the highway, Bobby launched himself out the door, puking as soon as his feet hit the dirt. Dry heaving for a bit, he finally calmed. I sat with my hands glued to the steering wheel.

"Are you ok? What do you need, man?" I didn't know what else to say. It was obvious he wasn't ok.

"Naw, man, I'll be alright," he said weakly, getting back into the van. He fiddled with the air vents, making them blow on his face. Beads of sweat trickled down his forehead and gathered on his upper lip. He finally looked at me. "I'm sorry."

"Dude, don't worry about it. You think you have the flu? You wanna keep going? Shit, we're half way there. I could just take you home when we get there," I said, worried about him and worried I'd catch whatever he had. "Man, I hope I don't get sick, too. They won't have a way back."

"Jake, there's something I've been meaning to tell you for a long, long time, and there was really no reason to, until now."

"Ohhh kayyyy," I said slowly. Looking in my side view mirror, I started pulling away.

"No, don't go yet," he said, grabbing at my forearm. "Just wait 'til I'm finished."

"Dude, fucking spit it out already, you're killing me," I said, slamming on the breaks.

"I'm gay."

In one breath, his two words came out clear, concise and fast, yet my brain processed them in slow motion. I felt like my jaw had been hanging there for a while, and Bobby buried his head in his hands as he began to cry.

The last time I saw Bobby cry was when he got beat up in the third grade. Even back then I had his back; I went after that dick-wad, Cameron, and kicked his ass. Moments of our childhood flashed through my brain. I realized that it'd been subtle, but I guess the signs were always there.

"Man, come on," I said, wanting to give him shit, hoping he was fucking with me, though he clearly wasn't. He was emotional and I couldn't ignore it. "Does anyone else know?"

He shook his head *no* and wiped the few tears that spilt from his eyes. "Dude, when my dad finds out he's gonna kick me out. He's gonna hate me." That's when he really began to sob.

I felt a million different emotions. Telling Aly was the first thing I wanted to do. She would know how I should handle this, with her having Marshall as a friend and all. Maybe he could give me some advice. I immediately pulled onto the highway again, getting up to 80 mph. We didn't talk for at least an hour as Bobby continued his texting mission. Probably telling his lover or whoever, that he dropped the bomb on me. He remained emotional for a little bit longer. I was still at a loss for words and thought about his hard-ass man's man father.

I floated through the motions and pulled off the freeway to fill the gas tank. I couldn't quite wrap my hands around what was going on. *Bobby and Aly*, I thought, *two of the most important people in my life, have me turned inside out*. I thought about Bobby being afraid to tell his dad and I felt worse. All these words filled my head and burned themselves into my brain. All the things, the emotions and feelings we hid from each other for acceptance. That's what it came down to, acceptance, by our friends, our parent's and our peers. It was all fucked. Getting back into the van, I quickly searched for my note pad, writing down what was floating around in my head:

<u>NEVER ENOUGH</u>
It's all contrived,
My state of being through these lies
Life looks so different through these eyes
And it won't survive like this
It's a compromise
That keeps on giving hell

Raping all my feelings
it's just never enough
Letting go from indecision
and the people you trust
From the cry of every person who has felt this lost
It leaves me feeling empty
It's never enough

371

I'm never enough

And all these feelings that we hide
To reveal is social suicide
we're given rules we must abide
When do we decide what's right?
There's no compromise
I don't care what you say,
Cause this whole thing ends tonight

Raping all my feelings
it's just never enough
Letting go from indecision
and the people you trust
From the cry of every person who has felt this lost
It leaves me feeling empty
It's never enough

Bobby was lost again in text messaging, unaware of how long we'd been sitting parked at the gas pump. As weirded out as I was, I actually wanted to give him a hug; instead, I opted for a shoulder grab.

"Bobby, if your dad kicks you out, you can live with us," I offered. I meant it too. I sat there, letting his words resonate with me. It didn't matter to me if he was gay, really. He was like a brother to me.

"This changes things now, doesn't it?"

"Not really," I assured him, trying to believe my own words. "But you gotta know this is a freakin' whopper." I decided to lighten the mood and hoped he wouldn't get offended. "So, who's the lucky dude?" I asked playfully.

Bobby remained subdued. "Was that not something I should ask?" I wondered out loud. "Man, you gotta let me know somethin'. I don't want to be on eggshells with you now. I wanna treat you like I normally would, right?"

"Yeah, man, just because I'm gay doesn't mean I got no sense of humor." His voice was gruff. Just another reason this was a shocker. Bobby was a good-looking dude. He sounded and looked like any typical guy, and girls loved him. I thought he was just shy with the ladies.

My best friend was gay. My mind reeled processing this.

"Well, then, it's final. Mike really has to go now. When he finds out, he's gonna have a field day." I laughed. "Shit man, no wonder you freaked out at the store."

"Dude, I'm so sick of that guy. Gay or not, he's a dick." Bobby took out his cigs, lit one, and rolled down the window.

The night desert air was warm and it felt good as it wrapped around my exposed skin. I wondered more. "Do you plan on telling anyone else? Or is this just between you and I?"

He kept rubbing his eyes in deep thought. "I'd been seeing someone in Hollywood, but that ain't happening anymore." He took a long drag on his cig. He exhaled the smoke, and I held my breath as it whipped around my face. Normally I would give him shit and make him put it out, but considering what just happened, I kept my mouth shut. "I met someone else, though, and this time it's more, more emotional, more feelings or whatever." He continued, "He's my age, a little younger." He paused. "The other person was older, way older."

My insides rolled around picturing my friend hooking up with another dude. I just couldn't go there. "This is almost too much, man." I sighed. "You gotta know I'm a little weirded out. I love you like a brother, so I'm not gonna judge."

"Yeah. So anyway, he's Aly's friend, Marshall."

"What!" I was more shocked that Aly didn't say anything to me. I knew she just had to know. I stepped harder on the gas pedal, looking at the clock. We'd been driving for five hours and were on the outskirts of San Bernardino; almost home.

"I knew you'd react this way," he said, flicking his cig out the window. "But I had to tell you, because I don't wanna hide anymore and I'm with you more than anyone else."

I took in a deep breath. "You wanna be the one to tell Dump?" I thought about what Dump's reaction would be. He'd just laugh his ass off and not say anything else. Dump was the last person to judge someone, with what he'd been through in his life.

"You think he'll freak?"

"No, he may laugh in your face," I said flatly.

"Yeah." He sniffed. We both shook our heads slowly in agreement.

Passing Downtown Los Angeles, the tall buildings stared down at us menacingly, lit up like they were filled with people. It was just past 11:30 PM. I dialed Aly's number, confirming the pickup.

"Hello," she said whispering.

"Hey, we'll be there in about half hour."

"Ok, we're at Nadine's," she confirmed. "Why didn't you call earlier?"

Glancing at Bobby, I was bummed. I felt like Aly had been lying to me or setting me up. *No games*, I told myself.

"Aly, I know Marshall's with you, you know why I didn't call you."

She was quiet. "Jake, this wasn't my secret to tell. This is between Marshall and Bobby. Bobby's the one that needed to tell you. So get over yourself," she said cynically.

"Ok, you're right. I'm sorry. It's just been a fucked-up day, and I'm sure by now you know why."

"Yes, I do," she admitted. "You think you're the only one having an effed up day? Jake, just because you said nothing went on with that chick doesn't mean my hurt feelings are just gonna go away, *or* that I'm just gonna let it go. That whole thing was just screwed."

Boom, there it was. She wasn't gonna let that go easily, and I really didn't blame her. I was just hoping. "I know. I don't expect you to get over it. We'll talk about it when I get there."

"How's your hand?" Her tone softened.

"It hurts."

"I can't wait to see you." Her voice cracked and my mood instantly lightened, her voice sweet like sugar. I could practically taste her.

"I'll be there before you know it."

I drove like a madman, and made it to Nadine's house in fifteen minutes.

Chapter 40

JAKE

She was like white light when I pulled around the corner. Aly waited in the darkness, shielded from the streetlights by massive hovering tree limbs. She stood in a white sweater, with three others, glowing like an angel. I couldn't get out fast enough and left the van running. Rounding the backside, I ran into her as she threw herself at me. She wrapped her arms around me tightly. I held her face with my good hand and kissed her hard. Her soft lips and sweet smell made me weak. I'd never been so excited to be with another person in my entire life. I pulled away, taking in her beautiful, flawless features.

"Man, you're a sight," I said, breathless. I looked around to see if anyone could see us, and grabbed her hand, walking toward the others.

"Sup, man," Chris said smiling broadly, extending his hand.

"Ha, not sure how smart I am trying to pull this off," I said, taking his hand and squeezing it firmly.

"Shit dude, what happened?" Chris said surprised, pointing at my other hand.

Aly gasped. "Oh, no," she whispered loudly. "I forgot, I didn't notice. Does it hurt?"

"Yep, it's throbbing," I said holding it up for everyone else to see. "And the story is too long to go into. Let's just say there're changes on the horizon."

Everyone uncomfortably looked around at each other, waiting for someone to say something.

"Thanks so much, guys, for covering for us." Aly moved toward Nadine, hugging her. "I'll text when we're on our way back." She bounced with excitement.

———

I held Aly's hand while I planned out our next move. I most definitely couldn't take the pain meds. It would have to be a handful of Advil's. I instructed Bobby to leave when he saw my truck pass by. Was I crazy? Yeah, I was, but it was worth it.

"Alright, let's do this," I said eagerly.

Swiftly walking our way down the block to my house, Aly brought up the pictures she'd seen. "What were you thinking, Jake? When you were with that girl?"

"Aly, I wasn't thinking. I never meant for that to happen. It was a quick moment, and I never saw or spoke to her again." I said remorsefully. "I promise nothing like that will happen again. I'm done drinking like that. I promise." We stood at the foot of my truck. Holding her tight against me, she was the only one I wanted.

"Jake," Aly whispered. "Your mom will think someone stole your truck when she sees that's it's gone."

"Don't worry. I'll text her that someone needed to borrow it and I forgot to tell her. I've loaned my truck out before. She won't think twice about it."

My mother's car was parked right next to my truck, and my heart started to race faster, knowing she was just yards away. Her bedroom window was at the front of the house, and I prayed she wouldn't hear us.

"Oh my God," Aly whispered loudly. "I would die if Kyle or Allison pulled up."

"Don't worry, get in." I clicked the remote, and the head and taillights lit up the night with a flash.

Aly got in, shutting the door gently. Every sound we made echoed through the still night. I held my breath as I got in.

"Ok, we have a 6-hour drive back. I have to stop to get Advil and fill up the tank…"

"Oh my God," Aly gasped, interrupting me. An alarming look spread over her face and my heart jumped to my throat. "Your mom," she croaked out.

Time stopped. My mom was standing on the darkened front porch, staring at us.

"Fuck." I closed my eyes. "We're screwed."

I grudgingly got out of the truck without looking at Aly. My heart was beating so fast I couldn't think clearly. I knew as soon as Kate saw my wrapped-up hand, she'd really freak out.

"Get Aly out of the truck." She walked inside.

"I'll tell her to go home," I gulped, trying to sound level.

"No," she said, turning back. "We're all gonna have a little talk."

Aly had her head buried in her hands. I tapped on the window and signaled for her to get out. She looked like she wanted to cry, and I didn't blame her. I felt a knot growing in my throat too, but I swallowed it back down.

"She wants us both to go in," I said miserably.

"Shit, you think she's gonna tell my parents?"

"I hope not." I pulled Aly close as she stepped out of the truck, kissing her forehead. As we turned, my mom was standing there watching us. She shook her head in dismay.

Standing in the kitchen, paralyzed with anxiety and dread, Aly and I stood close to each other. We waited, staring at Kate, ready for the explosion. Instead, she paced back and forth, looking down at the floor. I looked at Aly, and we both shrugged at the same time. I almost burst out laughing. I really was losing it.

"You think this is funny." Her words buzzed in my ear, electrocuting me to attention. "What's going on?" she asked, making eye contact with both of us, back and forth.

"Mom, look…"

"You broke your hand fighting with your band mate. You irresponsibly drive back home to see…" she paused, motioning toward Aly, "leaving your other mates and Notting." Aghast, she shook her head in disbelief. "Please explain to me what could possibly be worth all the damage you've done."

"Mrs. Masters…" Aly tried to cut in.

"Alyssa, please tell me…" she said, turning her attention full force onto Aly.

"No," I shouted out, interrupting them both. "No, you're not gonna do this." I moved toward my mother, pointing at her, separating them. "Aly," I said firmly, never taking my eyes off my mom, "go home. I'll see you later."

"Jake, please." She said and her domineering stance diminished.

I turned, looking at Aly. Her eyes began to pool with tears. "Please, just go," I ordered firmly. She shook her head in agreement and the tears spilled down her cheeks.

"Alyssa, please…" Kate interjected again.

It was more than I could handle, and I lost it. "Stop it, just shut up!" I shouted at the top of my lungs. Finally, there was silence as my mother stood there looking at me, horrified. Hearing the front door slam shut, I continued. "Leave her out of this, period. This is all *me*."

"What am I doing wrong?" My mother's lips trembled and she began to cry, too. She collapsed back into a kitchen chair, staring at me, bewildered, the tears dotting her cheeks.

"Don't make this about you, mom," I barked. "There's so much more going on here. Didn't you believe me when I said I'm kicking Mike out of the band?"

"I was hoping it would work out," she replied coldly.

"He's just not a good fit. There're too many other things I have to think about now. No one likes him," I explained, sitting down next to her. "Mom, come on. I love you. Don't make a huge deal out of this."

"You have so much potential," she said, wiping her face with her hands. "I need to know what's going on with Alyssa, Jake. Seeing her in your car this late at night is something that I don't approve of. We're friends with her family, and I highly doubt she's been allowed out like this."

I didn't want to lie to her anymore. "She's means a lot to me, mom."

A big sigh rushed out as her chest heaved. "I don't want to repeat myself."

"Then don't," I said firmly. I stood, staring down at her. "Nothing you say is gonna change my mind. I like being with her. She makes me happy. I don't care how old she is, and no, I'm not screwing around with her. So drop it."

She looked back at me with sad, disappointed eyes. "Okay, then, I hope you know what you're getting yourself into. The decisions you make now will be with you for the rest of your life."

"Stop being so melodramatic," I begged. "You're outta control, always making a big deal outta stuff! Stop it."

I knew I took a risk by leaving Arizona, but sitting there seeing my mother in a heap of disappointment made me realize it was totally a terrible idea, regardless of everything else going on with Mike. I apologized for not thinking clearly. I never mentioned Aly's name until she brought her up again. We were both calm, and I admitted a little more of how I felt.

"I'm in love with her," I confessed. "But I'm not gonna say anything to her. I'm not gonna go there yet." I was beyond shocked that my mother said nothing of it.

Back outside, I approached the van. I could see Bobby and Marshall were already out waiting for me.

Bobby took a long drag off his cigarette and shook his head. He knew I'd been caught. "Dude, is your mom raging mad at us?"

"Where's Aly?" Marshall asked, concerned.

"Dude, sorry, game's over." I shrugged. "Kate caught us in the driveway and yeah, pretty much." Feeling strange, I rambled on. "Uh, so yeah, I guess you can take the van and I'll get it tomorrow."

"My shit's still at the hotel," Bobby said. He dropped his cig on the ground, stepping on it.

"I'm sure they'll grab your things," Marshall reassured him.

I stared, bewildered, at my lifelong friend and his new *boyfriend*.

———

As I shut my front door quietly, my mom called out my name from her bedroom. The flicker of the TV was the only thing lighting the way. Walking in, I was hit by the scent of her and clean sheets, the comfortable smell of home. It brought me back to when I was younger and would lay in bed with her to feel safe. A wave of guilt and remorse washed over me. I pushed the feelings down.

"I'm gonna go get my pain meds. Be right back," I announced as my mom got under the covers, pulling them up to her chin.

Drained and anxious, I popped the lid off the bottle and shook out one lone pill into my hand. I wondered how long it would take to work. I popped it into my mouth and swallowed it without water. I wanted to see Aly again as soon as possible, and sent a text:

- *HEY, THINGS R GONNA BE FINE. GONNA TALK TO KATE A BIT MORE. I'LL TEXT WHEN I'M DONE. WANT YOU NEXT TO ME.*

She pinged back right away:

- *OK, SEE YOU SOON.*

It was nearly one in the morning. I felt like the life had been kicked out of me. The only constant was the pain in my hand. I stood in the doorway of my mother's room, wondering if she'd fallen asleep. I walked in, sitting on the bed next to her, kicking off my shoes. I didn't want her to be mad at me. I wanted this whole thing to settle down, but it seemed to only get worse. What the fuck was gonna happen with my band? Now that Bobby had professed his gayness, and Mike was out? Would I have to look for two replacements? Bobby said unequivocally he didn't want to leave the band. Did that mean he would continue living a secret life? As much as I wanted to talk to my mother, I didn't want to hear it from her, either. I just wanted her happy and *quiet*.

I rested back on the pillow. An immediate relief to the constant pain I'd been feeling took hold. I was now floating, painless and relaxed.

"Man, those meds worked just like that," I slurred out, surprised at the looseness of my tongue. "Geez, I'm so tired."

"You need to sleep," my mother said, patting and rubbing my arm. "We have much to work through, Jake. We're still not done talking about what's happened." Hearing her sigh loudly, it echoed in waves through my brain. I felt paralyzed, like I couldn't move even if I wanted to, as if I was encased in a plaster body cast. I felt so heavy. My eyelids felt like they had sand bags holding them shut.

Tomorrow would be a new day, a new attitude. *I should get up and go to my room*, I thought. I began wondering through the dark house toward my room. The hallway looked super long and distorted, like a funhouse. The lights were on in my room, and shone brightly through the crack between the floor and the door. Did I leave my light on? I didn't recall even going into my room. I squinted my eyes as I opened the door, expecting it to be shining brightly. Instead, the only thing on was the TV and *Aly* was sitting at the head of the bed, wearing only her bra and panties, looking at me seductively.

My heart jumped. Without a word, I went for her, crawling up next to her, kissing her neck. She sighed ardently, wrapping her arms around me, pulling me onto her. I could barely breathe. She smelled and tasted like sugar. She was so eager, without any hesitation, and I couldn't control myself. If she wanted me, I wouldn't stop. She would belong to me one hundred percent. Rolling her on top of me, I removed her bra. The softness of her was nearly too much. She pressed into me, holding my face in her hands, kissing me hard and deep. This was unlike any other make-out session we'd had. This was gonna be it.

I heard my phone ringing, the musical ringtone blaring loudly. Who the hell could be calling at this hour, I wondered? My eyes sprung open, and it was daylight. *Shit*. Lifting my head, I realized I was in my mom's room, in her bed, and thankfully, fully clothed. I quickly got up. What the hell? How long was I dreaming? Did my mom notice? I was mortified, and I jumped out of the bed looking around the corner into the bathroom. She wasn't there. Walking into the living room, I saw her in the kitchen, on the phone, as usual. I quickly went to my room and looked around. It hadn't been disturbed since I left on tour. Clean clothes were piled in nice neat stacks on my bed. I walked over opening the back door and padded out to the patio, looking up at Aly's house. Taking my phone out of my back pocket, I clumsily dialed her number with my good hand.

"Hey," she said groggily. "What happened? I fell asleep waiting for you."

"I'm sorry," I said in a low voice. "I took those meds and passed out talking to Kate."

"Aw, how's your hand?" she asked, concerned.

"It aches." I paused, holding back asking her what I really wanted to ask her. "Um, think you can come over?"

"Is your mom home?"

"Yeah, but come the back way, so she won't know."

"Um, I'll try, give me five minutes."

Chapter 41

JAKE

I stared at my neatly made bed, picturing rumpled sheets and Aly as she was in my dream. It was the most sexed-out dream I'd ever had. All the pent-up desire was getting to me. Distracted by the piles staring at me, I began putting my clothes away. It was just after 10 AM. I wondered what had happened to Bobby, but didn't want to call him. Checking my other text messages, there were several from Dump and one from Rachel. I didn't begin to read them, not wanting to feel bad, or mad, or any bullshit for that matter. It was all over for now. I had to search for a new rhythm guitarist. I decided to put the word out.

Aly arrived, still in her PJ's. She stuck her head in and leaned against the door, looking like the girl next door that she was.

"Hey, you," she beamed. "Where's your mom?"

I turned holding a finger to my lips. "Shhh...just in case."

I jumped up, going to her, and we hugged and kissed for a long moment.

Wiping my lips dry with the back of my hand, I needed relief. "Will you please type for me? I need to finish this email about a new guitarist," I said and walked away, sitting on my bed. I was still exhausted.

"I can't believe you're gonna get rid of Mike. Are you sure there's no way to work it out?" she said, sitting in front of the brightly lit computer screen.

"No. End of," I said, going into the bathroom.

"Aly?" *My mother, fuck.*

"Hi. Um, Jake's in the bathroom," Aly stammered.

"Hey, mom, I'll be out in a minute," I said loudly, frantically finishing up.

"I didn't hear you come in," Kate said in a questionable tone to Aly.

She was gonna start in on her. I flushed the toilet and zipped my pants.

"Oh, yeah, I called Jake...." Aly attempted to explain, but I couldn't have that.

"What's up?" I cut in, breezing through the door swiftly, startling the both of them.

Kate looked at me sideways, tripping over her words. "I was going to water the plants and I saw your door open. I went to shut it and..." she said, motioning to Aly.

"She's helping me with emails for Mike's replacement," I said, stepping in between them, wanting to protect Aly from her impending verbal bullets.

Kate's eyes narrowed and an incredulous smirk sprouted at the corners of her mouth. "Ok," she replied heading toward the door. "Notting is on the road already. You know, had to rent a truck to get the trailer home." A heavy sigh sounded from her. "You'll need to be available at around three o'clock. This has to stop."

"Fine," I said coldly. We stared each other down for a long moment. Finally, she turned and left without another word.

"Oh my God, she hates me." Aly looked at me, bowled over.

I wondered that myself. "I don't want her asking questions, backing you into a corner," I offered. "I can't handle her anymore. She needs to find something else to obsess about."

"And that means?" Aly probed.

"It means that if I keep letting her in, she won't ever leave, she'll just keep asking questions. I just want to have something that's mine alone."

"I feel weird being here now. Should I go?" she wondered.

"No," I said, looking at her perfect, clean face. "I like when you don't wear make-up."

Aly bopped up from my desk chair and sat next to me taking my hand. "Ok, no changing the subject," she scolded playfully. "You know, why don't you just tell her how you feel?"

I couldn't help but smile at her simple way of thinking. "I told her last night how I felt about you, Aly, and she kinda ignored the fact. Besides, let's be real, how simple is it with your parents?"

"My life is incomparable to yours. Besides, my parents don't know about you like *that*."

She lifted my broken hand to her mouth and kissed the soft wrapping of my temporary cast, the swelling had to go down before a hard one would replace it. "As long as I get good grades and don't get complaints…" Her voice trailed off. "In other words, as long as it's quiet, they pretty much ignore all of us."

"What I wouldn't give for Kate to ignore me." I sniffed, wishful.

"That's what you say now," she said, placing my hand gently down on her thigh. "What I wouldn't give to have my dad cheer me on."

"One extreme to another," I said ironically.

"Yep. He hooks up the best training, the best tutors or whatever it is we need, but then he's never around to see how well we're doing. I used to look out over the crowd at a game or school performance, searching for him or my Mom. Mom would show up now and then, but Dad, *never.*" She shrugged, sighing deeply. "At least he cares enough to make sure we have the best coaches and stuff, I guess."

"I'll be there to watch you, Aly. Every chance I get," I said, wrapping my arm tight around her shoulders. "We'll cheer each other on…"

———

Waiting for Notting and the others to arrive was nerve-wracking. I paced back and forth over the worn and tattered area rug beneath my feet. *The rug is what my nerves probably looked like*, I thought, as I banged drumsticks against my thighs. Taking in the mess and the clutter surrounding me in my makeshift studio, I felt overwhelmed even more. I had no motivation to clean. I tossed the drumsticks over my shoulder, walking back into the house. During his fuel stop, Notting called to inform me I had to tell Mike today that he was out, in person; no other way would do. I wanted so badly to just send him a text message or email; however, it wasn't going to go down that way. Instead, I sent him a text asking him to come over to get his stuff out of the trailer when it arrived.

- *DUDE—WE'RE GOING TO HAVE TO TALK WHEN YOU GET BACK. YOU'LL NEED TO COME AND GET YOUR SHIT WHEN THE TRAILER GETS HERE.*

I stood unmoving in the middle of my living room, waiting for him to reply with some smartass comment, but he never did. I sat and listened to the birds and the wind chimes blending together. They moved me to a place I longed to be more often. I closed my eyes and sunk deeper into the sofa. The coolness of the leather against my skin gave me chills. I reached out grabbing the nearby blanket and pressed deeper into its softness. I pictured a bird perched near the wind chime. It was as if we were writing a song together...

Tell me it's not for nothing
Tell me it'll be all right
Tell me you'll be there after the fight
Broken made new
I hate to admit it's all you

Loud voices startled me awake. I sent a text to Bobby asking him to come over, pronto; I needed him there, too.

"*Wait here.*" I heard Notting's voice, firm and loud.

Untangling myself from the blanket, I turned and Notting was staring at me.

"Uh, hey," I said, smiling weakly.

"Hello," he replied flatly. "How are you feeling, your hand?"

"It still hurts."

"Mike called looking for his things. He's outside. You ready to do this? I don't want to drag this out. I'm tired and not pleased, as you can imagine."

I gulped. "I wanted Bobby to be here for this, you know, since this whole thing involved him, too."

Notting sighed loudly. "Dump wants to talk to you. I'll send him in. I want this shit over with," he repeated as he headed back outside. "I won't be surprised if Mike quits on his own. He may have already left."

Dump stomped in like a grizzly bear, and before I could speak, he laid into me. "What the fuck is going on, man?" I could tell he was trying to control himself. "This better be good."

"You have no idea, Dump, don't fucking start with me," I said defensively.

"Start with you? You fucking left us stranded there, with no way to get our shit back! What? You swallow a self-ish pill or somethin'? So fucking what, you and douchebag got in a fight, shit happens. You don't leave your band, your friends…" he said, pausing for emphasis, "stranded in another state." He paced back and forth, taking his cigarettes out of his pocket. "I need a smoke."

We walked through the kitchen into the backyard, Dump with his lighter at the ready. Puffs of smoke surrounded his head by the time I turned around.

"Look, man, Bobby's gonna be here soon. Mike's gotta go, you know that."

"Yeah, and?"

"And there's more to this whole shit mess than just me leaving you guys in Arizona, but it didn't start out that way."

"You're not making any sense." Puffs of smoke trailed behind his every word.

"It's because I have to talk to Bobby first, you know. I'm a little caught off-guard."

"About what?"

"Just, everything!" I shouted in frustration.

"Does all this have to do with Aly?"

Overwhelmed, I tip-toed with my words. "You'll probably think it *all* has to do with her."

"You're probably right, and you're confusing me. Stop being evasive. It's pissing me off."

"Dude, I'll fill you in soon enough. Let me just get rid of Mike."

By the time I walked out to the front of my house, Mike was leaning against Cara Walter's car. He'd already loaded all his stuff in. Bobby was in the garage sitting quietly on a stool, brooding, ready to spring into action if needed.

Taking in a deep breath, I let unplanned words fall from my mouth. "Hey man, you wanna step in?"

"Actually, no, I don't," he said cynically.

Without mincing words, I let it out. "Dude, I don't think this is gonna work out…"

"Yeah, well considering you fucking broke my nose, I figured as much," he said, interrupting me. "Whatever, Jake. It's your band, your plan, and no one else has any stake in what's going on anyway. You all like to pretend this is a band," he said loudly, gesturing to everyone standing there. "But it's not. It's some fucked up excuse for you to use people to get you to where you wanna go." He sniffed, opening the car door, "Whatever. Good luck finding a replacement."

"Mike, come on," I said, surprised I was feeling bad for him. "Dude, you gotta admit it's been jacked. We're just not going the same speed."

"Same speed? You're kidding, right? Dude, the problem here is you actually think I give a shit." He laughed. "This is hysterical. You know, I caught on when your chick decided not to trust you."

Mike slammed the car door, hanging his arm out, and stared at me with a disturbing smirk. I wondered if my jaw actually dropped to the ground as I watched Cara speed away. Mike flipped me off as they vanished around the corner. Everyone stood around sweating with their mouths open. The heat was as intense as the moment. I took my t-shirt off, wiping my face. I didn't notice Dump had joined Bobby in the garage. They stood there quietly staring at me, waiting for me to say something.

"What? You feel the same way he does?" I yelled, holding my arms out to the side, waiting for them to agree. "What the hell is he talking about? My girlfriend, what?" I asked looking everyone in the eyes.

I felt like everyone knew something I didn't.

"I have no idea," Bobby motioned with his hands.

"Man, dude's just tryin' to save face," Dump assured.

"Alrighty, then, now that that's taken care of," Notting announced. "Enough of this bullshit. What's next?"

My mind reeled. What the hell did Mike mean about Aly? "I'll be right back," I said, pointing toward the door. "What ever happened to the girls?" I wondered out loud.

"Dropped them off on the way here," Notting mumbled.

"Thanks." I couldn't think of anything else to say, and I knew Notting didn't want to hear any more of my excuses. I was just glad it was all over with.

———

It was incomprehensible to the parental units, or to Dump, that I could become *"So disconnected from reality to not care about how my actions affected everyone around me."* Those words poked at me throughout the finals days of summer. It wasn't that I didn't care. It was that I cared too much. I cared too much about Aly and wanted so badly to prove to her that I was *more* than what people perceived me to be. I wanted to prove to myself that I wasn't anything like my father. I was paralyzed by fear of making another wrong decision, about not making my dream happen. I was fearful of failing in so many ways, for the band and for my mother and Notting, on top of not being able to decide on a guitarist.

Fear made me angry.

I kept tossing around the idea of being a 3-piece, but I couldn't commit. My hand was still in a cast; any other show dates had to be cancelled. My days were spent writing new songs and obsessing about how the recordings had come out from our last studio session. The only people that had heard them were the band and the label I was hoping to sign with. We hadn't heard back, good, bad, or otherwise. It was slowly killing me.

I still wasn't committed to homeschooling. Bottom line, I wanted to go to school with Aly. Experiencing normalcy and sobriety was a nice change, and a girlfriend without an agenda and a summer filled without travel...I was happy I'd broken my hand.

Chapter 42

ALYSSA

A new text message flashed in front of my eyes. It was from Mike. My heart thumped from the shock, hitting my fingertips, tingling. It had been a couple of weeks since I'd last heard from him, and I was relieved he had left me alone. At the same time, I was stoked that he still wanted to be my friend. One more senior to know in high school made it that much better. Seeing he was popular and hot made it even better:

- *HEY ALY, THINKIN'BOUT U. READY FOR TOMORROW?*
- *HI J YEAH, EXCITED & NERVY. HOW R U? WHAT HAVE U BEEN UP 2?*
- *DON'T B, IT'S NO BIG. IF ANY1 GIVES U SHIT, SEND'EM MY WAY. LOL. JOINED A NEW BAND AND IT'S MORE MY SPEED. THINGS GOOD W/ U & J?*
- *OH, COOL ON THE NEW BAND! CAN'T WAIT TO HEAR ABOUT IT. J & I R FINE.*
- *COOL. C U TOMORROW THEN.*
- *KK. BYE.*

I looked up to see my reflection in the mirror, and it had a stupid smile plastered across it. It surprised me. Ok, I had to admit, I was happy Mike reached out. I could be friends with him even if Jake wasn't, right? He was always nice to me, and I hated people who took sides. I refused to be a jerk to Mike just because Jake hated him.

I hopped off my bed to find something to wear. Thankfully, the heat wave we'd had all summer was going away, and it was cool. I looked at the time. Nadine was supposed to be here by now. It was already 11 AM. I sent her a quick text.

-   *WHERE R U?*

Just as I hit *send*, there was a soft knock at my door.

Nadine's face was tear-streaked. I was choked for words and stammered. "Oh my God. What happened?"

She sat at the edge of my bed with her head hanging between her knees, hyperventilating, and handed me her phone. It was lit up with a message from Chris, telling her he had an awesome summer and that with school starting, he wouldn't be able to hang anymore. Not believing it could be true, I read the text over and over again.

I was speechless.

I didn't know what to say to her, so I just sat there bewildered, rubbing her back. My own paranoia crept in. School was starting the next day, and today was supposed to be the raddest day prepping for our first day of high school.

"Nadine," I said, taking in a deep breath. "You didn't, like, you know?" I hoped she would get what I was trying to ask, and by the looks of it, she did. With a snivel, she choked out a word that surprised me. "No," she answered as she ran the palm of her hand up her runny nose. "I need a tissue."

Her phone pinged with a new text message, and she looked at the screen. Nadine cleared her throat as she placed her phone on my bed, pointing at it. "That was Nicole. She's coming over here. I hope you don't mind."

"Really, she's coming here?" I said dryly. "Huh, that's a shocker."

"Well, I text her what happened. I obviously couldn't go over there. I told her I was coming here. Come on, Aly. She's been hurt, too, by this whole thing. We've both been kinda bummin'," she explained. "And I think it's really shitty that neither of you tried to call each other."

"Are you kidding?" I said, miffed. "You guys are the ones talking shit on me, gossiping to each other about stuff that included all of us. We all want the same thing, Nadine."

Nadine sat with her mouth slightly open, considering my words. "Yeah, well, it just seemed you got full of yourself and…"

"Can't you be happy for me?" I interrupted loudly. "Let's go back a day or a week, before you read the break up text from Chris." My voice pitched higher, strained. "I was so super stoked for you, Nadine. Happy that you had a guy that you wanted and he was into you, but what do I get? I get a bunch of shit just because my guy isn't part of our group. And you guys think the worst of me just because I'm not around. That's so lame."

A tap came at the door and stifled my rant. "Come in," I barked.

It was Nicole, and my nerves were instantly on edge. This was the first time I'd seen her since our fight. I stood there, frozen. Her hair had grown out longer in the front, and the layers that had framed her face were now united with the rest of her golden highlights. Her tan was deeper, leaving her light eyes to stand out even more. In an instant, I felt like I wanted to bawl my eyes out. All of the angry emotion I kept bottled inside me turned to mush, and a lump grew larger and larger in my throat. Still, no words came out of my mouth. Nicole shook her head and her arms extended out toward me. Her lips trembled, and she too began to cry as she hugged me.

"Aly, I'm really sorry. I never meant to hurt you," she sniffled, tears pooled in her eyes.

I returned her gesture, holding her tight. We both babbled like idiots, yammering apologies on top of each other.

"Nadine, I'm so sorry. If I'd known my brother was such an asshole, like a real one, I would have told you. I never saw this coming," Nicole said, remorseful.

"Yeah, I know." Nadine said, shaking her head. "I wanted to believe in it, you know."

I grabbed a handful of tissues, wiping my face, giggling. I was stuck on Nicole's dialog. "A real one!" I laughed harder. "What's the difference? You're either an asshole or you're not."

We all laughed together, feeding off of the energy that'd been bottled up. I was beyond happy that we were all together again. There was so much I wanted to share with them, and so much I wanted to find out.

Nadine sat quietly, staring down at her tattered wad of mascara-laden tissues. "You guys, why do you suppose it's different for me than for you?" She started to tear up again. "Is it that big a deal to go all the way? Is that really what'll keep a guy around?" Her tears were again full throttle. "I really thought he liked me enough to just be ok with the way things were, for now. It's not like I wouldn't have gone all the way with him, eventually."

"Nadine. You knew Chris was a player to begin with," Nicole said softly, rubbing her back. "I really thought it was different with you. I'd never seen him go after someone so convincingly."

I was stalled at her last comment. "What do you mean different for us than for you?"

She squirmed before she spoke. "You've obviously done something to keep Jake around, Aly. That's what I mean. Look at Nicole and Grant…"

"Hey, my situation is completely different that you guys," Nicole interrupted. "Grant and I, you know, we've never been with anyone else. For the record, we haven't done it."

"You guys," I huffed. "I don't know what you're thinking, or who's saying what but Jake and I have never gotten past whatever the bases are after kissing. I've never touched his junk like *that*, and he hasn't tried anything other than boob squeezing."

They both looked surprised. "Well, girl, that's not what people are saying."

"What do you mean?" I choked on my spit, clearing my throat. "Who's saying what?"

"I don't know how it got brought up, but one night hanging by the fire pit, Chris brought up that he never thought you had it in you."

"What the fuck?" My mouth went dry. "And, what else?"

"That people are saying you're sleeping with Jake."

I looked at Nadine in horror. "I can't believe you didn't tell me."

"I didn't think it was a big deal. I mean, so what, he's into you. I just hoped he wouldn't use you and drop you like he did Rachel, and by the looks of it, that's not gonna happen…so whatever."

"I can't believe I'm hearing all this just now. You guys don't know anything!" I shouted, storming out of my room and down the stairs. My sister called out my name as I rushed out the front door. Pacing around the courtyard, I couldn't see straight. My mind was spinning. Did I already have a bad reputation before I even set foot onto campus?

"Aly," My sister's voice startled me. "You ok?"

"Uh, yeah," I smiled, trying to fake her out, but by the smirk on her face, she saw right through me. "You still fighting with Nicole?"

"No. Well, we made up, but…"

"Aly come on," Nicole said, swiftly coming outside. A look of alarm dotted her face when she saw my sister. "Oh, hey, Allison." Nadine came up behind Nicole, not saying a word.

"What's going on?" My sister's eyes narrowed as she glanced back and forth between all of us.

My heart raced. I didn't want her to know what I was upset about. "Nothing, we're still talking through stuff," I blurted out.

Allison was on a need-to-know basis as far as Jake was concerned.

She sniffed, shrugging her shoulders. "Ok then, just checking," she said, giving Nadine and Nicole the cold shoulder as she passed.

As Allison turned walking back into the house, she gave me a soft smile. I still wasn't used to her being nice to me.

"What's up with that?" Nicole whispered. "Why'd she look at us like that?"

"I never said anything to her, but she probably heard me complaining," I admitted honestly.

"Ok, see, there you go. You talked about us too, behind our backs," Nicole pointed out with an exasperated expression.

"That was only after you talked shit about me," I huffed.

"I didn't mean to, Aly. Don't forget, Matt's got a pretty bruised ego. He took what I said and ran with it. I feel bad, and I'm sorry." She stepped forward, holding her arms out to hug me, and I caved. "I mean you go from being perpetually single to being some *older* guy's girlfriend. Of course he thinks you're messin' around like that." She backed away, holding my shoulders. "We all kinda did."

"Jake says just because a guy wants to have sex with you, doesn't mean he cares about you." Saying these words empowered me. I turned to Nadine. "So, yeah, for me it is different. Be happy you didn't give it up to him."

My words cut deep into Nadine, but she wanted to know. So I was brutally honest and I hoped she wouldn't hate me. She stood there with a trembling lip, trying to hold back her tears. She shook her head bravely in agreement and wiped away newly spilt tears with the palm of her hand.

Nicole and I moved quickly to Nadine's side, hugging her. We babbled supportive words and apologies for being lame to each other, but all I could really think about was Jake.

Chapter 43

ALYSSA

The breeze, cool against my sun-heated skin, reminded me I had an end of summer volleyball session at two at the beach.

"I have to leave for volleyball soon," I said, bending over picking a flower from the pot that sat next to me. "I'll be back by five. You guys wanna come over for dinner?"

"Yeah," Nadine said quickly. "I don't wanna be alone. You know, need to keep my mind off of shit."

"I can't, Grant's coming over," Nicole informed us. "So, does this mean you're not gonna come over anymore?"

"No, but I'm not ready to act like this is no big deal," Nadine admitted. "The guy *just* dumped me via text message. He's an asshole, Nicole. I don't wanna see his face. I'd prolly punch him in the nose."

———

Nicole bailed, and we sat on the edge of my bed, staring at each other in my closet mirrors. The redness in her eyes had faded, and all that remained was glossed-over puffiness.

"You remind me of a bunny rabbit." I pointed to her nose, smiling. "Chris will regret dumping you, you'll see. Screw him. Hold your head high, like it was you who did the dumping. You know, that's what he liked about you, your fearless attitude. He may even realize he effed up." I was serious when I spoke. I didn't want to give her false hope, but I'd seen it with my sister and her boyfriend. He'd broken up with her, and then came back kissing her ass when she acted like she didn't give shit.

Nadine picked up my phone, giving me a sly smile. "So what's up with you and Mike?" She handed me my phone. "I saw a text from him flash up after you stormed out of the house earlier."

I sighed loudly. "Jake doesn't know I talk to Mike."

Nadine's eyes widened. "You little weasel." She looked surprised. "What's up with that?"

I laughed, a bit uncomfortable. "Nice choice of words," I laughed, shoving her away. "It's Mike. He's the one that reaches out. I don't wanna offend him. He's nice to me, so why should I be a bitch just because Jake hates him?"

"Are you retarded?"

"No." I huffed.

"He likes you, Aly. Duh!" She threw herself back on my bed, slapping her forehead. "And here I thought I might have had a chance."

"No he doesn't." I really wanted to believe what I was saying, but I had to face the possibility.

"Uh, *yes* he does." She hesitated. "He was always staring at you and shit." Her arms fell hard to her sides and bounced on the mattress. "I can't wait to go to school tomorrow and start fresh. Fuck these pricks."

"Nadine!"

"Aly, you can't deny it," she moaned, propping herself up by her elbows.

"I really think he's just being cool, you know, like the other guys." I fidgeted with my ring. "He acted as if he was doing me a favor by staying in touch while they were on tour."

"Um, dumb-dumb, the other guys aren't texting you asking how you're doing behind your boyfriend's back." She sat up. "Are you seriously that dim?"

"No." I folded my arms to my chest. "I didn't want to think that way, I guess."

"Be careful, Aly. If Jake finds out, he might not have it," she said ruefully.

I grew panicky. "Do you think I should tell Jake? Shit, you know, I knew it wasn't right. But I didn't want to offend Mike, and have him be a dick to me," I whined.

I slumped, sitting back down, and went limp.

"Just tell him to leave you alone. He's sneaky," she said, nodding her head slowly. "I'm sneaky, so I know sneaky." She wagged her finger at me. "Be careful with him."

"Ok," I agreed. My mind spun, wondering how it would go down. "Ugh!" I groaned loudly. "Now I'm all freaked out! I gotta get ready and get outta here."

"If you don't mind, can I come down and hang with you?"

"Yeah, of course," I said, pausing. I took in her pathetic expression. "Come down whenever you want. Jake's meeting me down there. I was hoping Marshall would, too. I wanna catch up with him. You know." She returned my glance with knowing eyes, but still no questions or comments on the gay boyfriend matter.

———

I stopped at the top of the hill before making my way down to the sand, letting the light breeze dry my moist skin. I took this time to catch up with Marshall via text messages. He was full-blown into Bobby, and I was excited for him. Bobby was semi-Abercrombie status. He was totally unlike Marshall, and I wondered how their whole deal would go down at school tomorrow.

I was tugged to reality when I heard a familiar voice. "Hola," the deep tone greeted. "Look what I picked up along the way."

With a knot the size of a bolder churning in my stomach, I faced Mike and Nadine. I smiled awkwardly, struggling to get up. Mike reached out grabbing my arm, helping me to stand. The warmth and strength of him took me off guard. His hair was loose, and his expression lacked the hardened air he normally wore.

"Hey guys, this is a surprise," I said cheerfully, playing it cool.

"Aly!"

My teammates called out, waving for me to come down, they were starting a game. I looked around one last time for Jake. Finally, I faced Mike and smiled half-heartedly. I wanted to ask him what he was doing there. My heart raced as I passed on the side of Nadine and turned away from him. My eyes locked onto hers and I mouthed "*What the hell?*"

I hoped now that Jake wouldn't show up until after Mike left.

"I'll be about an hour or so, Nadine," I said loudly. "Later, Mike."

"I'll be here," he snickered. What the hell was he laughing about? Why the hell was this happening? I looked to the sky as if there would be a written explanation.

I waved my hand, not looking back. Down on the sand, I was distracted beyond belief, and things rapidly went downhill. I was being shouted at by my teammates for my lack of ball control, and while I was staring up at Mike and Nadine, a ball gave me a full-on facial. My head flew back and my body followed in slow motion. I slammed down onto the sand. Next thing I realized, I was laying flat on my back, with my teammate Renee hovering over me.

"Holy shit, Aly, you ok?" Renee said, breathless and wide-eyed. I held the side of my face. My ear burned with a high-pitched ring. My vision cleared to focus on Mike and Nadine. Watching her hang all over him, playing with his hair made me…*mad?* Why was I mad? Was she really playing with his hair? "Dude, Aly, can you hear me?"

Renee shook me.

Rubbing my face, I finally looked at her. "I'm ok." Rolling onto my side, I pushed myself up. "I'm sorry. I'm not feeling good."

"You're def not feeling good now, that's for sure. That was an epic facial, the ball wrapped around your head," she said, trying not to laugh.

Renee helped me to stand. "I'll see you guys tomorrow. I need to go home," I explained weakly.

"Ok, feel better." Renee nodded. "And put some ice on your face when you get home."

Walking across the sand toward the stairs, both Nadine and Mike were watching me. I was so utterly embarrassed they'd witnessed me get my face splatted off.

I anxiously looked around for Jake.

"Man, Aly, that didn't look good." Mike scraped Nadine's hands off his arm and stepped over to meet me as I came up the stairs. "Shit, your face is really red." He reached out, grabbing my chin, and turned my face to the side to get a better view. My stomach flipped when his fingers made contact.

I stepped back. "Yeah, I need to get ice on it, this sucks." I tried to laugh it off.

"I can cruise home with you...guys." Mike offered. His eyes searched my face and my bikini-clad body. I became uncomfortable. He glanced at Nadine. Her eyes tightened and her demeanor shifted. She was wise to his game.

I was confused. Mike was complicating things for me, and I didn't want to be a bitch to him. I actually liked him. I stepped away, dialing Jake's number. Mike continued to look at me thoughtfully and Nadine stepped in front of him, grabbing his attention.

The call rang to voicemail.

Chapter 44

JAKE

My mother silently paced back and forth in front of me. It made my hands tingle. Ignoring Aly's calls made it worse. I knew there was a possibility Kate would find out about the hotel charges, but I was hoping it would have been one of those things that slipped by, seeing as she only audited from time to time. There were plenty of times I would charge high-priced items, like gear for the band, and she never said a word. I was about to get a shellacking.

"So that's it, you stayed at this five start hotel, *alone*? Is that what you're telling me, Jake?"

Her nostril flare indicated she was forcing herself to stay calm, but her rage was clear in her flushed cheeks. Her white sleeveless blouse was halfway un-tucked as she swung a thin black belt from side to side, as if waiting for the perfect moment to lash out and snap me with it.

Finally, I spoke. "I had some friends come by," I stammered. "Mom, it was an effed-up day for me. I needed to just get away from the band."

She stood with her arms folded tight against her chest, and her French manicured nails disappeared into her flesh. "I'm giving you a chance to tell me the truth, Jake. I know there was more than one person who stayed in that room."

I gulped as my temperature rose and heat seeped out of my skin. She had me backed into a corner. I needed to make a choice, and fast. Lie to her and lose all trust for the foreseeable future if she found out, or tell her the truth and dive into the unknown abyss of repercussions.

"Mom, just friends, all the usual suspects and yes, Aly was there." I danced carefully with my explanation, praying she would let it be.

With another deep breath loaded into her lungs, she was about to unleash it on me again. I closed my eyes. Before she spoke another word, a knock came at the door. *There is a God*, I thought as I sprang up from my seat. I was quickly pushed back by her bark.

"No! You sit there, I'll answer it." She pointed angrily at me before she sped off to see who was bothering us. Looking at the clock, Aly had another half hour of volley-ball practice. Maybe I could make it.

I tiptoed over to see who could possibly be at the door, and my heart sprung up into my throat when I saw Aly standing next to my mom in the foyer. Kate was holding Aly's head, looking at the side of her face.

God, this isn't really happening, is it? I thought to myself. I quickly turned, stepping back to my original position. Maybe my mom would turn Aly away after her inspection and Aly would leave. *Please God, let me off this one time and I promise I'll do whatever my mom wants without being a dick.*

I'm never praying again.

"Hey, Aly," I said, as I continued to curse God in my head.

My mom saw right through me and rolled her eyes, looking back at Aly. "Jake, please go get an ice pack for Aly. Apparently she got a ball to the face, real good by the looks of it."

"Shit, what happened?" I said, quickly moving to her side. "Aw man, your eye's already bruised." I reached out, gently touching the injured area.

"Ah, ouch, it really hurts." She coiled back.

"Hold on." Dashing into the kitchen, I rummaged through the freezer, looking for the blue icepack beneath the frozen chicken and fish. I couldn't find it. The seconds ticked away as I pictured Aly spilling her guts about our hotel romp. Tossing packs of frozen peas and green beans, it finally dawned on me to use one of them.

"Here you go," I called out, attempting to stifle their imagined conversation. "I have a bag of frozen veggies, they'll do the trick."

My mom huffed. "Jake, if you would have taken another second, it's in there. I just saw it this morning."

As she disappeared into the kitchen, I unloaded, breathless and low. "Mom found out about the hotel. Don't say anything. I'll take care of it." A petrified expression spread across Aly's face. I held the cold bag to her eye and her hand covered my own, pressing tighter. Our foreheads rested against each other. "Trust me, I'll take care of it," I whispered. "What are you doing here, anyway?" I said, wrapping my good hand around her neck. My fingers weaved gently through her hair. I was lost in her scent of sunscreen and fruit. Shock waves went through us upon hearing my mother's voice, propelling us three feet apart.

"Ok, this thing with you two…we need to talk," Kate said, waving her hand at us. She walked over, taking away the frozen veggie bag and replacing it with the blue ice pack I'd failed to find. "Aly, seeing that Jake can't play straight with me, I need to ask you…"

I jumped in front of Aly in an instant, interrupting her. "No, no, don't drag her into this! I told you what went down."

Kate's eyes flashed wide as she stepped back from me. "Jake, don't you dare do this again." She pointed angrily at me. "I have a right to know what the hell's going on." She walked over to the coffee table, grabbing a small pile of papers. "This bill is over six hundred dollars! Bad choice, my dear, not to mention the possibility of inappropriate behavior going on," she said, pointing directly at Aly. "Aly, did you stay the night with Jake at Shutters?"

"Don't!" I yelled, my heart pounding so hard I could feel it in my ears. "Don't answer her," I said facing Aly. "I need you to go home, please."

My eyes pleaded with her.

"Aly," my mother tried to regain her attention and I wedged in once more.

"This is none of your business!" I yelled louder, moving closer to her face.

Daggers flew out of my mother's eyes. "This is my business." She said waving the papers in my face. "How dare you!"

Slap.

I was shocked into submission. We all stood there, silent. I tried to grapple with the fact that my mom just hit me. She'd never laid one hand on me in my entire life.

"Aly, please, go home," I said calmly. My eyes were locked to my mother's. She was as angry as I'd ever seen. Her chest rose and fell rapidly as her eyes darted between Aly and me.

"Aly, I need you…"

"No, you don't need anything from her," I said once again, more firmly.

We were at a standoff. The air was so thick with tension we all stood paralyzed by it. My mind scattered in a million different directions. I quickly moved to Aly and grabbed her hand, dragging her through the foyer and out the front door. I was surprised Kate didn't shout out or come after us.

"Oh my God, Jake." Aly sighed, desperate. "What's gonna happen?"

"Don't worry about it," I reassured her, taking her face in my hands and planting a hard kiss on her lips. "I don't know when I'm going to call you. She'll probably turn my phone off."

I watched Aly run across the lawn, and I wanted to take off after her and keep running. Turning to walk back into the house, I caught my mother's image in the window. There was no doubt she saw our whole exchange. Sure enough, as soon as I closed the door, she was standing right there, following me back into the living room.

"You leave me no choice, Jake." She stood shaking her head and her shoulders slumped.

"No choice for what, mom?" I said smartly. "All you do is poke your nose in shit that has nothing to do with you. I'll pay for the goddamn bill, all right? Now just drop it."

She took a step back and her stature hardened.

"If you ever," she paused and her voice trembled, "*ever* raise your voice at me like that again and blatantly show disrespect, you can move out of this house and forget any further support. I've had it with you." She pointed angrily at me.

The weight of her words sat heavy on my shoulders. She was right. I knew I was out of line. I shouldn't have reacted that way, but I couldn't help myself.

"I'm sorry. You're right. Look, I know I have some things to work on and I'll sell something to pay for the bill…"

"Something that I paid for!" she yelled. "You don't get it, do you?"

"No, I don't get it!" I raise my voice again, but caught myself. "What? You think what I'm doing here isn't work? That I don't deserve what you've given me? All I do all day long is work for my future. And by the way, I *am* making money, if you've forgotten. My music, *my* money." I was so angry I had to remind myself to breathe and to try and remain calm. "You know, I never asked for you to turn this into a business. If I knew one day you'd throw this shit in my face…" I stopped mid-sentence, not wanting to say anything worse than I already had. I buried my head in my hand while my broken one ached. "Look, I'll pay for the bill," I said, defeated. "Please, can you just drop it?"

She searched my face and sadness painted hers. "Jake, you asked if I believed in you after your father passed away. You asked me if I would keep supporting you in your music. This isn't just about the money." She lingered in front of me, finally sitting down on the sofa.

I sighed deeply. "I don't know what to say. I'm sorry. I really am."

She looked bewildered. I fought the guilt that crept in, reminding myself that while she was right about a few things, she had no business butting in my relationship with Aly.

She must have read my mind.

"I thought the whole thing with Aly was cute in the beginning. I thought she just had a little crush on you. Then all the antics started, and bad choices. You telling me you're *in love* with her?" she spoke slowly and pulled at the corners of the pillow that sat in her lap. "The unrest with the band...now Mike's gone...and now staying in hotels with Aly, it's just too much. She's too young for you."

"Mom, she didn't stay with me at the hotel." I lied before I realized it. Without another word, she rose walking toward the front door. "Where are you going?" My heart raced. *Fuck*, I thought. "Alright, stop!" I shouted, but she didn't stop. "Mom, alright, she stayed with me." I admitted, quickly running toward the door.

She slammed the door shut.

I was frozen for a moment, picturing her telling Aly's parents everything. I ran out the front door and she was already half way across the front lawn.

"What are you doing?" I said running in front of her stopping her in her tracks. She attempted to move around me.

"Jake, I want to talk to Aly..."

I grabbed her arm tightly, desperate to stop her. "No, you're not gonna to talk to her," I said firmly.

She gasped. "Let go of me, Jake." Jerking her arm away, she pushed past me. "We're all gonna have a little talk."

"No," I said loudly, "Stop!"

Never in my wildest dreams would I have thought I would have done what I did. Grabbing my mother, I clumsily picked up her small frame, with my hand now throbbing beneath my cast, and threw her over my shoulder. She yelped, kicked and screamed, pounding at my back for me to put her down.

I was completely blind with emotion. "Mom, you have to listen to me!" I pleaded, huffing with each step. "Don't do this, please. This has nothing to do with her."

"It most definitely does if you're acting this way! Put me down!" she insisted, breathless.

Just as I released her onto the front porch, a hard yank pulled at my shoulder and I went flying and rolled down the steps.

"What the hell do you think you're doing?" Notting yelled. Rage painted his face, "Have you lost your mind?"

Stunned, I moved slowly. "Notting..."

"Not another word! Get in the house." He growled as he picked me up by my shirt neck, throwing me through the front door. "I've had enough of this bullshit, Jake."

Feeling a tickle at my elbow, I rubbed at it. It was bleeding from my fall. "My elbow's cut," I huffed, looking cross at Notting.

"You deserve more than you got, boy, handling your mother like that!" He growled, pointing in my face. "Do you care to explain yourself?"

My normally attentive and talkative mother just stood there glaring at me, her arms wrapped tightly around her.

She obviously wasn't going to get anything for my lacerated elbow, so I gently dabbed at it with the bottom of my faded black t-shirt. Notting hovered over me, pacing slowly. I sat there, numb, staring at his scuffed leather boots as they stepped back and forth in front of me.

"Does it really matter what I have to say? No matter what it is, it's not gonna matter," I stated calmly, staring directly at my mother, then to Notting. "She doesn't *hear* what I'm saying. That out there? Picking her up? It was because she wouldn't take one moment to stop and listen. She doesn't care that I want to have certain things private in my life…and…Aly isn't allowed to officially date anyone right now…"

"Well, there we go! It seems to us that you've thrown all caution to the wind and you don't care about rules," Notting cut in sharply, raising his voice with each word.

"Just because I do things that don't make sense to you, doesn't necessarily mean they're wrong. Aly and I are friends, and we care about each other more than you know…well, maybe you do know." I shook my head and glanced between the both of them, thinking about their relationship. My blood simmered. "Look at you two, you have your own stuff you wanna hide," I said condescendingly, unable to look them in the eyes after I said it. I knew I was pushing it. "She needs to leave Aly out of this, period."

"It's apparent that you're very serious about her if you're risking so much." Kate's voice cracked, making me look up at her. She shook her head like it was a bad thing. "I had no idea it's gone this far. Jake, how far has this gone?"

Notting held up his hand. "Kate, darling, I don't believe it's gone that far, at least that's *my* understanding."

Notting's emphasis made my mother become more rigid. She hated being an outsider. My stomach grew tighter, watching her glare at me with her mouth half open.

"Mom, come on. I'm not some perv without self-control." I half-laughed, trying to cut through the tension, but she didn't find any humor in it.

Instead, she began to explain my inexcusable behavior with the hotel and Aly. Her words pressed into Notting's brain, and his face grew somber as she spoke to the heavens and then to me—'*I can't believe I didn't see it and I can't believe you thought you couldn't talk to me.*' I fought off the remorse. She always did this shit. She always pushed her way in, guilt trippin' me.

"Why do you always turn everything into being all about you?" I finally snapped. My mind was full of explanations, yet I couldn't spit them out. I decided to be honest. "I wanted to talk to a guy, mom. There are things I'm just not comfortable talking about with you anymore; this whole thing is a perfect example as to why." I held out my arms for emphasis. My voice grew louder. "You just had to go and talk to Aly, after I kept begging you not to. I'm sorry if hurt you, but you wouldn't listen to me. You *never* listen. You *never* hear what I'm saying."

I couldn't help but repeat myself over and over again, thinking maybe one time she would hear how important it was for me to have my privacy.

"Jake, relax with that tone," Notting rumbled. "Have some respect. I think we've both tolerated your choices; but now, spending the night with her? When she's not supposed to be dating anyone at all? I'm certain this isn't the first time you've stayed together."

My world came to a screeching halt when the conversation drifted to the suggestion that I not see Aly anymore. In fact, they agreed they couldn't and wouldn't condone me seeing her, knowing she wasn't allowed to have a boyfriend.

"Ok, Jake. I'm hearing you now. I've listened and I'm going to give you a chance to make this right. I won't talk to Aly or her parents. I will trust that you will take care of this by putting this relationship on hold for a while." My mother and Notting shook their head in agreement at each other, like they'd concurred world hunger or something. I was beyond any feelings I could describe. I just wanted to run to Aly.

Sitting alone, wading through my thoughts, I'd finally realized it was nearly dark. I couldn't remember the last words that were spoken to me. The room took on a grey haze that matched my mood.

Fuck them, like they could keep us apart.

Chapter 45

JAKE

The only sound in the house was a faint murmur from a TV far off in my mother's room. I didn't even know if Notting was around anymore. How was I going to explain to Aly what the hell had gone down? All I could picture was her beautiful, pathetic face splashed with worry as my mother tried to lay into her, and it made my blood boil. Pulling my phone from my pocket, I called her.

"Hey." I whispered.

"Oh my God, I'm dying. What happened?"

"Not good, Aly. Can you sneak over?" I paused. Bad idea. "You know, never mind."

"Why? I wanna see you."

I wanted her, and I wanted my mom and Notting to fuck off. "There's no easy way to say this. But they think we need to stop seeing each other."

After the initial tears on her part and long silences on both ends, we agreed it was ridiculous how they thought it was so easy for them to make that decision for us. I felt calm for the first time in hours.

"I'd better go, it's almost midnight." She sighed deeply. "It's hard to be excited about my first day of high school."

I wanted to tell her I loved her and that everything was going to be fine. "Aly, I, um," I hesitated and chickened out telling her that I loved her. "This whole thing'll blow over. Tomorrow's gonna be fine. I'll pick you up at Nicole's instead. No one's gonna find out. I'm just not gonna say another word about you to them."

I tossed and turned the entire night, lying there wondering how long my hand would be outta commission once I got the cast off. Finally I got up, worrying, it would never be the same and I would never be able to play again. Would that be such a bad thing? Was all of this even worth it? What was so bad being normal? *Ordinary.* As these thoughts swirled through my head, I didn't realize I was awkwardly typing away at the keyboard. I was stoked that even with the throbbing in my hand, I was able to type a bit.

Tapping out lyrics to yet another song I had floating around in my head. Staring at my acoustic guitar, I longed to play it. It had been weeks. The longest I'd ever gone without touching it. Before I knew it, it was 7:30 AM and I had the entire song written. The melody filled my head, and I sent Bobby a text letting him know I needed him. I wanted to sing it to him and for him to play the music for me. I didn't want to wait until I could bring it to life:

- *DUDE. I'LL NEED YOU AFTER SCHOOL. I WANT YOU TO BANG OUT SOME TUNES FOR ME. SO MAKE NO PLANS. PLZ.*

This was the first time I'd asked anyone else to help me with anything and it felt good. Bobby would be stoked. He'd always tried to put his two cents in and I wouldn't allow it. Today, I would listen and consider it.

- *HELLZYEAH!*
- *AWSOME! STOKED UR INTO IT. MOST DEF DIF. I'M SURE YOU'LL*
- *DIG. DUMP'LL SHIT HIMSELF THO. HA.*
- *FUCK HIM.*

I laughed out loud at the irony of it all. Dump would most definitely die when he heard this new song and if he didn't…he'd kill himself when he found out Bobby was gay. Shaking my head, I wondered, *who have I become?* Getting into the shower, I felt relieved. Holding my cast up over my head to avoid getting it wet, I sang out the new song, feeling more alive and normal than I had in 12 hours.

ORDINARY

I taught myself to abide
I learned enough to get by
But I've been tried
And I just got to get away
I thought that I was alive
I pinched myself when you arrived
And I got high
Off what had just come my way

Now the hardest part for me
Is deciding what this means
Could everything just come undone

Is everybody meant to be this sad and lonely
What have I done

Who have I become
Is everybody chasing down stars and dreams too far to
hold me
What have you done
You made me become
Ordinary

I found the road for my life
I drove so fast, could've passed you by
But you caught me
The picture still is in my mind
Now I'm walking down the street
Instead of running down my knees
Could everything just come undone

Is everybody meant to be this sad and lonely
What have I done
Who have I become
Is everybody
Chasing down stars and dreams too far to hold me
What have you done
You made me become
Ordinary

Ordinary's good to me
Ordinary let's me be
More than enough is you and me
Ordinary lets me be free

———

Rolling into the school parking lot, it was full throttle crazy. It was also apparent who a few of the Freshies were, with their new shoes and un-faded-freshly-pressed clothing; the ones with their parents dropping them off and causing a cluster-fuck in the lot. Thank god there was a senior parking area. One by one, I noticed the familiar faces as they looked into my cab, staring at Aly in the front seat. Then I spotted Rachel and Sienna, and my hands got moist. Rachel was the last person I wanted to see. I looked over at Aly for any sort of reaction. She didn't seem to notice her, yet.

"You ready?" I asked, grabbing her hand, squeezing it.

"As ready as I'll ever be," she said flatly.

"Come on, biotch!" Nadine piped happily from the back seat. "Stick with me and you'll be just fine."

Making our way through the throngs of stares onto campus, I didn't know whether to put my arm around Aly or to just let her be. I never got the chance to make a decision before friends I hadn't seen all summer barraged me. I'd lost sight of her for a moment, and when we locked eyes she smiled and waved, giving me a reassuring nod before she disappeared into the crowd. Aly would be ok with Nadine.

I stood in line with all the other slackers who didn't take the time to get their schedules before school, and of course, I had to have the line that Mike was standing in and the one Rachel was working—she probably picked the "M" line on purpose. Her first period must be working in the admin office. *Shit, just my luck*, I thought. If I moved now it would be obvious. Mike had already noticed me, leering in my direction. He kept glancing round, as if he was looking for someone. I knew that someone was Aly. Rachel was doing the same thing. They were so obvious. It was all so apparent to me now. This whole thing with Aly really rocked the boat, and they fell out.

As I approached Rachel, she had my schedule out, ready to pass it off to me. She smiled without saying a word.

"What? You're not gonna say hello?" I said smartly. I was over her.

"You're capable of saying hello, too, ya know," she said under her breath, looking around to see if anyone could hear our exchange.

"Whatever."

Turning to leave, I saw some of her fringe friends staring at me, whispering.

What a bunch of bitches. "Didn't your parents teach you that whispering and staring at someone is rude?" I said loudly, stopping in front of them. "You better be sure which team you wanna cheer for."

Their twisted faces gave me a good laugh as I walked away toward my first class. It seemed like a floodlight had been turned on. The longer I was sober, the more aware I became of all bullshit behavior that went down. Everything I'd never noticed before was so horribly evident.

I couldn't believe I'd associated with some of these people.

Chapter 46

JAKE

I was awakened by my mom, shaking me violently by the shoulder as she shouted in my face for me to wake up. I'd slept past my alarm and was late for school. I'd picked up Aly after her volleyball practice, and we went and hung out in a Torrance Starbuck's, doing our homework. I was supposed to meet the guys for band practice, but I'd blown them off *again*. Instead, Aly and I went to the movies. I knew I needed to be playing, seeing I'd just gotten my cast off a couple of weeks prior, but I just wasn't feelin' it.

I hurried to get ready, and could hear my mother talking loudly in the other room. "What is it?" I rushed into the kitchen. "Sorry I slept late. I took a pill because I couldn't fall asleep."

"Jake, you can't be taking pills to sleep. You need to exercise and eat right."

"Mom, get off my case already."

"You're leaving again in two weeks, Jake. Working out will help your hand. You need to take care of your body."

I grabbed my keys off the kitchen counter. "Mom, running on the treadmill won't help my hand," I mocked, flatly.

"No, but lifting weights will. Its movement and weight bearing."

"Mom, stop," I said dryly.

I whisked around her, grabbing a breakfast bar, and bolted out the door. I barely made it to school before they locked the gate, but I still had to go into the office to get marked off as tardy. Great. Rachel would be there. I hadn't really had to deal with her since the first day of school and that had been weeks prior. We didn't have any classes together, thankfully. Maybe she would be busy with some filing project or something, and I would avoid having to talk to her.

I pulled on the cool metal handle of the bright blue door and it swung open with ease. I scanned the area for Rachel and spotted her behind the counter near the attendance office. I walked steadfast toward her, like I had somewhere important that I needed to be, and school wasn't it.

"Hey Rach." She turned around, surprised.

"Oh, hey."

"I'm…um, late." I shrugged.

Rachel pulled out a little yellow card from under the counter and began writing on it. "Why are you late? Do you have a note?"

"No note. Missed my alarm."

"Late practice?" she asked as she scribbled my name down.

"Somethin' like that."

She stopped writing and stared at me, her eyes narrowed.

I slumped. "I'm not trying to be a dick, Rachel."

"Mhmm." She nodded and looked back down and checked the *unexcused* box.

I huffed, whispering. "Oh come on, Rach."

"No note, no excused tardy. Sorry, rules are rules. I'm not putting my neck on the line for you anymore, Jake."

"That's fine. I understand" I took the white piece of paper she'd ripped off the top of the yellow card.

We stood staring at each other for a few long, awkward seconds. I wanted to say something else, but what? I wanted to ask how she'd been doing, and if she was happy with her classes, but she probably didn't want to hear any more from me.

"Sorry, Jake." Her hands disappeared from the counter in finality.

"No worries. I get it," I said and turned to leave. "Talk to ya later."

"See ya." She smiled. "Oh, I'm planning another party. Not sure when, but maybe you guys can play?"

"We'll see. We're leaving again in two weeks."

Her face fell. "Oh, ok. Well…"

"Rachel?" Mrs. Ogelvy piped up from her desk, interrupting us. "Jake, move along, please."

"Yes ma'am." I respectfully waved goodbye.

The bell rang out, echoing over the campus, bouncing off the cinder block walls. In a matter of seconds, students swarmed like bees, making their way to their next class. I never did make it to my first period. I didn't finish my homework anyway; while Aly sat doing hers, I wrote songs. I'd been getting pressure from Notting about home schooling, and I knew it was only a matter of time, so what did homework matter anyway?

The snack bell rang at 9:45 AM, and with that, it was basically the end of my school day, with only one more class. Normally I would have headed out to the quad to say goodbye to Aly, but instead I decided to meet her as she was leaving her class. I don't think you're ever prepared to see another guy hanging on your chick or him making her laugh, but that's what I'd witnessed. I seriously blacked out for a second when I realized the guy with his arm draped over her shoulder was none other than *Mike*. He'd dyed his hair. His bleached-out look now a natural brown. I slowed my pace in disbelief. I looked around to see if anyone else noticed what was going on.

Aly was smiling and staring up at him. She finally pushed him away, playfully. My heart raced and I shouted her name before I realized it. She turned, and her face went white. Not a good sign. I glanced at Mike and a cool smile sprung to his lips. Was he laughing at me? What the hell was going on? As I approached, Mike nudged Aly, ignoring me.

"Later, Aly." He paused, stared me down, and walked away. "Hey, don't let Ms. Taylor get to you."

Aly came up, taking my hand and I snatched it back.

"What was that?"

"Jake, he came up behind me, just saying hello."

"You know I can't stand that guy," I reminded her. "Why do you let him in?"

"Because he's been nothing but nice to me, Jake. I'm not gonna be a jerk to him just because you don't like him."

"I don't wanna see it, Aly."

"I don't like that you're still friends with Rachel, either. I watch you be friendly with her and I have to suck on it. She still has it out for me, you know."

I hated when she was right.

"Aly, she's over it."

"Whatever. Mike and I are friends, but barely talk. It's not a big deal."

I glanced around and people were staring at us now, walking by slowly and whispering to each other. *Great*, I thought, *witnesses to our first public fight*. I thought about what Mike had said all those months back, about Aly not trusting me. How long had she really been *a friend* with him?

"How long have you been *'friends'* with him, Aly?" She didn't like that.

She huffed. "Does it matter?"

"I'm not sure if it matters. Maybe it will."

She leered at me and stomped away. What the hell? I followed her, embarrassed, because now more people were staring at us.

I grabbed her elbow and she yanked away from me. "Aly, hold up."

"No, Jake," she said loudly. "You hold up. How dare you, how dare you!"

She spun around and walked faster, away from me.

"What, this is my fault now?" I yelled back, going after her. I grabbed her hand and walked faster, taking longer strides, dragging her behind me. "You, need to calm down. How would you feel?"

"Stop, Jake!" she insisted and tried pulling away from my hold. I held tighter. "I know how you feel! All the time I feel it, watching girls throw themselves at you! And you just lap it up. So screw you for making me out to be the bad guy! You're such a hypocrite!"

By this time we were outside the gates of the school. Mr. Langley, our burly and balding Head of School Safety, stood watching us cautiously. Her words burned with every lash; she was right, beyond right.

"Look. I'm sorry. It was just a shock to watch that go down, considering what's happened."

"I know," she said, stalling. "I just try to ignore it when *I* see it and focus on how it is between you and me when we're together. Otherwise I'd be irate all the time."

She stared at me, puzzled, like I was an idiot. I felt like one that was for sure.

"Aly, I'm sorry."

Mr. Langley had had enough of our little show. "You two lovebirds made up?"

"It's all good." I waved half-heartedly.

"Good, now move along, Masters." He pointed toward the parking lot. "You, Little Miss, you're running outta time to eat."

"Yes, Mr. Langley," Aly replied indifferently.

"I can pick you up...but I gotta go to practice tonight or the guys will kill me."

"I know...I gotta figure out what I'm gonna say to my coach. I got practice right after school. I'll just see you tonight, maybe."

I gave her a quick peck on the cheek as Mr. Langley barked out at us to scram. I felt like a dick.

Sitting at my kitchen table, I tried to work on a report that was due, but the whole Mike-and-Aly thing ate at me. I didn't like how I'd left it with Aly. I decided to take a ride to catch her at volleyball practice. When the coach's whistle blew, I stepped inside the door as the girls gathered around for last minute instruction. Aly had her back toward me in the distance as she yanked, pulled and replaced her hair into a ponytail. Soon enough, the other girls began whispering and she turned to see me. Her eyes lit up and she smiled and waved discreetly at me.

Aly trotted up to me, smiling tenderly. "I'm glad to see you. I'm really sorry about what happened…"

"No," I interrupted. "I'm sorry. I'm the one that has to get over it."

I bent down and kissed her on the lips.

"I thought you had practice, too," she probed.

"I do, I'll just be late. I wanted to see you. I can't stand that I'm gonna be gone soon."

"Me either."

We sat in my truck until every last car associated with her volleyball team pulled away. Reaching over, I pulled her face toward mine. We fogged up the windows for who knows how long, and I wanted to go back to my house.

"Let's go home. Sneak over."

"I have so much homework," she said breathily. "And it's already six-thirty."

"I hate homework," I said, taking her lips again. My hand slipped up under her t-shirt, and her normally perky breasts were bound tight against her chest. "What the hell is this?"

I slipped my fingers underneath the thick elastic that wrapped around her.

"It's a sports bra, silly." She giggled.

"I had no idea these things suffocate your tits!" I laughed. "It's like an ace bandage. That thing has got to be uncomfortable."

"It's actually not."

"I bet they'd like to breathe." I teased playfully, pulling at it.

She giggled. I loved her laugh.

———

I could hear our familiar tune thumping and trilling down the hall the closer I got to our studio door. I stopped and popped another pill in my mouth before I stepped through the door, just so my hand or mood wouldn't bother me. Immediate silence greeted me as soon as I stepped in.

"Dude." Bobby looked at me, bewildered, and pointed at his watch. "Come on, an hour and a half? Really?"

Dump looked at me like he could kill me. "What the fuck, man! We've been calling you. Where the hell were you? Oh wait, I know, you were with Aly. Right? Please tell me I'm wrong, Jake?" he shouted.

"I lost track of time, man, I'm sorry," I said, looking each one of them in the face.

"We're tired of your sorrys, man!" Dump roared. "We don't have time for your love-sick shit anymore. There's too much going on!"

"I'm here now. Let's do this…"

Dump stood from behind his drums so quickly his stool toppled over. "We're done, man. What'd you think? You can just cruise in here whenever *you're* done with *your* little girlfriend and we're just gonna wait around for *you*?"

"Dude, you know what, I don't need this shit…"

"Need this shit?" Dump repeated my words, louder.

Dump charged me so rapidly I didn't have time to react. Or maybe I was just shocked with disbelief that he could move that fast. The weight of him forced me to stumble backward, and the full strength of him wrapped around my neck. He was choking me. I could hear Bobby shouting for him to stop, and Devon Weir, our fill-in guitarist, yanked desperately at him to release me. I gasped for hair as Dump released my neck and pressed me against the wall by my chest.

"You little fucking shit. We put up with this long enough. I'm done. Have your chick play drums for you."

He released me and I crumbled down, leaning on my knees. Dump apologized to the guys, grabbed his shit and left. I was beyond shaken by what occurred. I staggered going after him, slamming into Bobby and he steadied me.

"Jake, what's going on with you?" Bobby asked. I didn't know how to answer him.

"Dump!" I shouted. "Dude, please, I'm sorry!"

I stood at the door watching him walk away. I was in deep shit and didn't know what to do.

Chapter 47

JAKE

I really thought things with Dump would've blown over. Two days had gone by, and I'd sent him a million apologies and a really long heartfelt email explaining myself, promising I'd get my shit together. I'd really meant it. I knew I'd been slacking. I knew I'd been taking way too many of those pills, too. I swore to myself that I'd stop, and took a stab at it the night before. I'd tossed and turned something fierce, finally giving in to snapping one in half. It didn't really do anything.

I woke up to an empty house and late for school, again. I rushed onto campus just as the bell rang for break. I'd go to the office later, after I met up with Aly.

I felt sick to my stomach.

"Are you ok?" she asked as she walked up to me.

"Not really. This thing with Dump and the band is making me ill, I guess."

"You're perspiring, and it's not hot. Are you sure you're not getting sick?" She tried to place her hand on my cheek.

"No," I snapped, and moved her hand away. "I'm fine. I'm just stressed out, and I didn't sleep good."

"Fine," Aly replied, holding her arms in mock surrender. "But you don't look ok."

"I have a headache."

"Here, I have Advil and a RedBull. These will work." She smiled and dug in her bag taking out a little white bottle and the silver, red and blue can. "Here."

I reached out and tugged her neck toward me, kissing her on the forehead. "Thanks," I said, taking the can of RedBull. "But I think I'll need something a little stronger than Advil."

I reached into my backpack and took out my own bottle of pain pills, popping one in my mouth and washed it down with the insanely sweet energy drink. "There, that should do it."

"What are those?"

"Vicodin."

"From what?"

"From when I broke my hand."

"Shouldn't you've been done with those by now?" she asked, and more concern painted her face. "I mean, you've had your cast off for forever now."

"They help me sleep and take the edge off, you know."

Aly looked at me like I'd lost my mind. "You take them every day? Like every day since you broke your hand?"

"No, not really…look, it's no big deal."

She didn't look convinced.

During my last class, I didn't pay any attention to the text from my mother asking me to come straight home after school. She could wait. I had to pick up a new amp, and I wanted to grab Aly when she got out of school. I'd barely made it to the school lot before the bell rang, and I waited in my usual spot. I'd sent Aly a text, but she didn't reply. It wouldn't have been the first time. I spotted Nadine a short while later and she came straight to my truck.

"Hey, have you seen Aly?"

"No, I thought she'd come out with you…"

———

I bolted home, and as soon as I came through the door, my heart stopped. Everybody I didn't want to see was gathered in my living room, waiting for me. I looked straight at Dump. "Really?"

"Jake…" Notting said, and stepped forward.

"What the hell is this?" I broke in, looking at my mother. "This is all you, isn't it?"

"Stop it." My mother stood up. "This isn't about just you anymore, Jake."

"Where's Aly?" I said, looking at my mom and Notting, then at Mr. and Mrs. Montgomery, who I couldn't believe were sitting in front of me. "This is really out of control. Nothing is going on with Aly and I, if that's what this is about." I looked straight at Aly's parents.

"Jake, take a seat…" Mr. Montgomery said firmly. Those were the last words I wanted to hear, and he cleared his throat. He stood up and stretched taller to make a point. That irritated me more, making my heart race faster. I felt like my blood would pour out of my ears any second. "I want to know what's been going on here," he said, and stepped behind his wife, placing his hands on her shoulders. Mrs. Montgomery stared at me like I'd hurt someone, with her eyes sad and her brows twisted with concern. *Really?*

"Frank. Let me explain," my mother said. With that, our whole perceived relationship spilled out all over the floor.

"You're making this sound like it's a bad thing!" I countered, raising my voice. "Ok, look, I know the whole Arizona thing was not the best idea. I'm sorry, we were just excited to see each other and I didn't think it was *that* big of a deal, seeing we'd be home basically the same day, but the rest of it? It shouldn't be a bad thing. We wouldn't have to sneak around if you'd see that we're not getting into trouble," I stated desperately looking at each of them in the eye. "Why is hanging out with Aly such a big deal? I don't get it! And no matter what you say, I'll never understand it. It's ridiculous!"

"Jake. It's one thing to come over to the house," Mrs. Montgomery chimed in, "It's another thing to be taking her all over Los Angeles without us knowing where she's at, and staying the night together? This is just not good news, not good news at all. Now, I know that's not entirely your fault. She's to blame for lying about where she's been and whom she's been with, but you *knew* she wasn't allowed to do those things."

"I'm sorry. I'm sorry for everything you guys think is wrong." I slumped deeper into my seat. "I don't know what else to say. I love her and I know she feels the same way."

My words didn't mean anything to them. They all just stared at me with bobbling heads. My future was laid out in front of me as my mother paced back and forth behind Aly's parents. "Jake, you'll no longer be going to Seaside. You'll be enrolled into home schooling immediately," she said firmly, looking at Aly's parents. "We've been discussing this for a long time because of the band, but seeing our new circumstances here, it's definitely time."

I swear I could have been dreaming.

Finally, to my surprise, Aly came through the door. She'd been crying, her eyes were puffy and her nose was red. As soon as she saw me, she began to sob. I didn't care who was in the room. I got up and went to her.

That was the last time I touched Aly.

I'd completely lost it and went off on my mom for the whole world to hear. She was the one who went knocking on The Montgomery's door. I was conflicted about my outburst. I'd cracked open the door to so many unanswered questions, but it was too late. The longer I thought about what I'd revealed to everyone, the more I regretted my explosion—"*...you need to stop butting into my business and worry about Notting! Before he leaves your sorry, stuck in the past ass! Dad wasn't the man you thought he was! So get over yourself and me and Aly!...*"—Shit. What did I do? The whole house erupted like a Wall Street sell-off.

I lay on my bed, hearing every word Mr. Montgomery had spoken, like he was sitting next to me in an easy chair. It was as if the God's were against Aly and I. At every turn, someone was there to keep us apart. Not only did Aly's parents get a rap on the door by my mom, they got a call from Aly's volleyball coach about her being placed on probation for missing too many practices. That very same day, Dump and Bobby met with Notting about the band and gave him an ultimatum, and boom, it all rained down shit balls. I remained in my fossilized state, thinking about how and when I'd be able to see Aly again.

This has to blow over, I told myself.

School was no more. I was full-on enrolled in online homeschooling.

Aly was ultimately off limits. We were officially broken up.

I received a text from Nadine, but it was Aly, and my heart sprung to my throat.

- *HEY, IT'S ME, ALY*
- *WOW, I WAS WONDERING WHEN & IF I'D HEAR FROM U*
- *I'M DYING W/O U*

I started tapping out *I love you* and stopped. I'd never told her I loved her.

I did love her. It was now or never, right?

- *DITTO—ALY, I LUV U & WE'LL MAKE IT THROUGH THIS*

I hit send and waited for her reply. I didn't get one for about 5 minutes.

- *UR MY EVERYTHING, JAKE. <3*
- *WHEN WILL I SEE U?*
- *I'M WORKING ON KYLE*

Kyle made it happen for us a week later. I met them off the beaten path, at a burger joint about five miles outside of our town proper. The same spot that I'd been meeting a guy to refill my pill supply. I'd cut way down, but with all the stress, I needed to keep my mood smooth, and I used this opportunity to replenish my stash.

No one we really knew, or who would have known of our situation, should have been there. This was the perfect place. As soon as they pulled in the lot, I got out of my truck. Kyle was with his girlfriend, Chelsea, the same girl from all those months ago. She was hot, in a librarian sorta way, with her hair tied back and she sported cute little blue-rimmed specs. Aly finally climbed out of the back seat and I strolled over.

She launched herself at me.

"Oh my God. I swear I thought I'd never see you again," she whispered in my ear. She backed away, looking me up and down. "You look tired…and you look like you've lost weight."

"Yeah, this whole thing's zapped my appetite, and sleeping's been tough. But I'm here," I said, taking her against me tightly.

"You guys hungry?" Kyle shouted. "Let's do this."

I wasn't hungry. I just wanted to stand there, running my hands through her silky hair, holding her forever.

I barely took a bite of my food. As soon as my burger arrived, my stomach went sour. I kept looking at the clock as time ticked away. I had to go to practice and I couldn't be late. We were going back on the road in two days, and I'd made a deal with the guys and Notting to pull my head out of my ass.

"I gotta get outta here in a minute, guys." I looked around the table. "I've got practice."

Aly buried her face in my neck. "This wasn't long enough."

"It's never long enough." I moved her away from me. "Walk me out."

I threw a twenty-dollar bill on the table and said goodbye to Kyle and his chick. Aly and I walked hand-in-hand out the door. "Come sit with me for a minute. Someone's dropping something off to me."

"Who?" she asked innocently and I didn't want to tell her.

"Just something for the trip. It was either hanging with you, or driving out to meet him. I chose you and begged him."

I laughed it off, even though I was on edge.

We sat in my truck and I played with her fingers. I thought about the text message I'd sent her, telling her that I loved her. "Aly, I meant what I wrote, in that text."

She squeezed my hand tight and looked at me. "You know, we talk about this stuff all the time, the girls and I. I feel it so strongly, Jake. Whatever it is, if it's love, I feel it…"

We both jumped sky high when a dark figure came at my window, tapping.

"Shit, man!" I laughed, grabbing my chest. "Hold up," I said to Aly and got out shutting my door.

I handed the guy named Felix two hundred dollars for the pills and grabbed the brown paper sack from his hand. "Thanks, man."

"No problem." Felix was a man of few words. Make the deal and leave.

I turned and flipped open the side compartment at the back of my truck bed and tucked the bag deep beneath some towels. Getting back in my truck, Aly was texting away, innocently unaware of what just went down. For the first time, I felt like a scumbag. I would never do this again with her near me.

"Aly, I gotta get outta here," I said, rubbing her thigh. I leaned over, kissing her. She dropped her phone in her lap and wrapped her arms around me. Her hands and fingers touched lightly at my face and her sweetness wet my lips.

I glanced in my rearview mirror. There were flashing blue and red lights. *Shit.* My heart sprung into my throat. *Fuck.* Then a tap came at my window. My heart froze.

"What's going on?" Aly turned, looking out the back window. "Why are the cops blocking your car?"

"Shit," I said and leaned my head against the window.

"Sir, please step out of the vehicle," the police officer demanded, his hand on his gun holster.

I slowly opened the door, and a few cars down, Felix also had the cops on him. They had him spread out on the hood of a cop car, and a few brown paper bags were perched on the roof of his tricked-up El Camino. I wanted to die. Before I knew it, the same thing was happening to me. Then I was handcuffed, and Kyle was yelling, '*What the fuck*' and who knows what else, and Aly was hysterically crying.

Mr. Montgomery arrived shortly thereafter. It was all a nightmare.

The last words I recalled were Mr. Montgomery's… "*You won't be able to come within fifty yards of her, Jake…*"

Chapter 48

ALYSSA

I watched the secondhand slowly move by each number - 1, 2, and 3…over and over again. Mr. Chin was way too enthusiastic about biology, as far as I was concerned. I just wanted to pass, but I was failing miserably. I was also failing miserably with getting over Jake. I watched my pen write his name with little hearts around it for the millionth time. It was nearly unbearable being at school without him. I was so sick of explaining what happened to everyone, and even though I told them exactly what went down, I still heard through the rumor mill that Jake broke up with me because I was causing too many problems for him and his band. In theory, I guess it was true. The drug bust was another sprout of rumors.

The bell finally rang inching me closer to the edge of true failure. Even a D was failing in my parent's book. I was moved from attendance probation to academic probation on my school volleyball team, first because of missing too many practices to hang out with Jake, and now because of nearly failing Biology. I needed to get my grade point average up to a 3.0, and fast.

I waited for almost everyone to leave the class before I got up to beg Mr. Chin for extra credit, anything that would get me to a 3.0. "Um, Mr. Chin. I was wondering if there's anything I can do, like extra credit or something...I..."

"Miss Montgomery, studying for your tests is the only way to pass this class. Paying attention is the only way to pass this class. I do not offer extra credit. What I will offer you is the chance to turn in your missed classwork due to your recent absences. I will also offer you to retake the anatomy exam you've just missed," he offered.

"Thank you, Mr. Chin! You're a life saver, thanks for giving me another chance."

He looked at me blankly, with barely any emotion. He was completely disinterested with my theatrics, but I was so happy that I didn't care to contain myself.

"I'll have the test criteria to you tomorrow. You'll need a partner, and we'll schedule it right after school next Friday. You'll have a week to turn in your missed assignments and prepare for testing."

"Thank you, thank you, thank you!" I bowed at him like he was a king, with my books clasped tight to my chest. "Can anyone be my partner?"

"I'm not grading them. They'll be there to assist you. Just make sure they know what they're doing." He waved me off without looking at me.

I turned and nearly floated through the classroom, I was so happy. I was beyond relieved and made a mental checklist. I turned out the door and was startled by Mike leaning against the wall. He was waiting for me. Every single school day for the past three months, Mike strolled by and met up with me after Biology. We'd walk to break together and stand in line to pick out crappy snack food, and every-day I'd see Rachel in the distance. Once she'd even come up and taken our picture. *"Say cheese, guys!"* She said it was for the yearbook. Great. Mike and I never hung out for long, splitting off as soon as we left the snack line, until I had a crazy idea.

Mike smiled, pointing toward the door I'd just exited. "What gives? I poked my head in and Chin was lecturing you."

I shrugged and sighed. "I'm on volley probation because of my D average and I begged him to give me something to bring up my grade…" I paused. *Don't go there*, I told myself, but I kept going. "Hey, how'd you do in Bio?"

"I dunno. I guess I did ok. I gotta B."

"Do you still remember all that anatomy stuff, like cutting into creepy dead creatures?"

"Yeah, I suppose. Why?" He looked at me suspiciously.

Oh my god, here it comes… Jake, please don't hate me if you find out.

"Because I need a partner and it doesn't matter who it is. It'll be next Friday, right after school. It's no big deal, Nadine will probably do it."

I rambled on like an idiot as we made our way through the snack line. I tried to act normal, but I felt like everyone knew what I just did. I kept looking around, and I swear everyone I looked at made eye contact with me. Kari from History, wearing her stupid rainbow beanie, and Gil from English with his ridiculously overstuffed backpack that took people out whenever he'd maneuver around. Then, of course, at the end of the line, bobbing back and forth to get a glimpse of us, was Nadine.

"Yeah, I guess I could do that," Mike said, jolting me to attention.

"Really?" I asked, shocked

"Yeah, why not?" He cracked open the bright blue bottle of Gatorade and took a gulp.

"You're supposed to pay for that before you open it, Mike." The pimply, round-faced cashier scolded.

"Bite me, Eric."

I looked sideways at Mike, whispering. "He's greasy-looking, like he hasn't showered. He shouldn't be working around food looking like that."

"Hear that, Eric?" Mike said at the top of his voice. "Maybe you should take a shower before you come to work. You're scaring the girls."

I gasped and pushed past Mike. "Um, he's paying for my stuff," I said, without making eye contact with *Eric*.

Nadine was laughing, and chewed her apple opened-mouthed. "That guy's seen better days."

"Stop it!" I pleaded. "Oh my god." I was mortified, poor guy. Now I felt terrible for saying anything at all. "Let's go."

"Nice move, Monty." Mike laughed harder. "You owe me $3.50."

I kept looking back at Greasy Eric. He didn't pay us any attention. "I don't owe you anything. That's your price for being mean!"

Mike smirked. "We'll be talking Bio. Later."

Mike walked away, all swagger. I realized I had a stupid smile on my face, and Nadine was smirking at me. She wasn't chewing her food anymore. I looked over to the nearby cement benches, and my friends were all staring at me, too.

"What?" I said to Nadine, walking toward the gang. She followed right on my tail.

"What do you mean, what?—The *what* is, Mike gotta nickname for you now? Monty?"

I exhaled heavily, rolling my eyes. "I have no idea what that's about."

"Dude, he's totally into you," Nicole announced. "I think you like him, too."

"Oh my God, shut up! I do not! We're just friends."

"Man, that guy's been following you around ever since Jake left school," Grant poked in.

My heart froze at the mention of Jake's name.

There I was, about to keep secrets again.

———

Ever since the Jake Drug Bust, the tension in my house was at an all-time high. My father had used his connections and got a restraining order against Jake. He would go to jail if he came near me. How did my dad do it? I don't know, but he did. I guess being a lawyer had its perks. He basically ruined my entire life and my mom was totally on his side. The closeness between my sister and me stalled because my father forbade her from inviting her boyfriend, Owen, over any more. Kyle didn't give a crap because he never brought his girlfriend around anyway.

Every night, my dad made a lame attempt at getting us to talk, and this night was no different. I didn't know why my parents insisted we eat as a family. None of us ever had anything to say to each other. "Anyone have anything they want to share? Kyle, how are those college applications coming along?"

"They're coming along," he replied flatly.

My dad pushed his food around on his plate and his jaw clenched. *Uh oh.*

"You kids need to realize that everything I do, I do for you…"

Snap.

"Cut the crap, Dad!" Kyle said, snidely. "I'm so sick of hearing how you do this and that for us. Yeah, we know. We know, we know, we know! But you know what? I've got an announcement. I'm moving out. How you like them apples? I can't take living here anymore." Kyle pushed his seat away from the table and began to leave the room.

I never saw that coming.

My mother gasped. "Kyle, you come back here right now…"

"Ha!" Kyle turned and pointed, mockingly at my mother. "See, this is a perfect example. Mom, this isn't the 1950s! Stop with the dramatics."

Kyle disappeared into the kitchen. My father didn't know what to do with himself. He raked his hand through his hair.

"Kyle Montgomery! Get your ass back here right now!" he roared.

My mom was in tears, dabbing her eyes with a napkin. My heart sank, seeing my mom so disturbed. I wanted to go to her, but was paralyzed watching the train wreck in front of me.

Allison and I sat holding our breath. My brother walked back in and calmly but firmly told my father everything he was feeling and what brought him to his decision. Then he brought up me. "You are a great provider, Dad. There's no question. I just can't watch this anymore." Kyle pointed at me. "This whole thing with Jake and Aly, that whole thing that happened…a restraining order? Was that really necessary? Instead of turning your back and pointing fingers, maybe we should be there supporting him. Drug addiction is a disease, Dad! And we don't even know the half of it with him. You just judge like you're the end-all."

"Kyle," my dad shook his head and rubbed his face. "You have no idea what you're talking about."

"Dad, isn't that what growing up is all about? Learning on our own, making mistakes? *Getting* the idea along the way? Being controlled by you certainly isn't helping us. It's alienated us from you, Dad." Kyle swept the room with his arms and stood on his tiptoes.

"Kyle, if you move out, we won't let you move back."

Kyle snorted and shook his head. "One more last threat? Dad, you won't have to worry about that."

Chapter 49

ALYSSA

My mother quietly cleared away the plates from the table. I tried to hold back tears, and surprisingly, my sister kept rubbing my back. My dad's hair was messy from running his hand through it. He always had it combed neatly, like Superman's Clark Kent.

"Can we be excused?" Allison asked timidly.

My mom paused. "Girls, you can go."

"No. I have more to say," My dad said, looking at both Allison and I.

"No, Frank. You've said enough." My mother never took center stage, but it was her turn. "I've let you be the leader, knowing you do what you do out of love for our children," she said turning her gaze on us. "I can't stand being lied to anymore, girls. Your father does the best with what he has. He provides for us and there are rules, regardless if you agree with them or not. We need to take a step back. You two think that we don't know what's going on, but we do. We see the bigger picture because we've been there. You may think we're too conservative or not cool, but the fact is, we've been through our share of heartbreak."

Allison sat, shaking her head. Finally brave enough to speak. "Mom, it's just tough to listen to you guys. Just because Aly got trapped up into something doesn't mean I should be punished too. Not allowing Owen to come over is so lame. It's not gonna keep me away from him. It's not gonna change my past either." My heart sank when I heard her last words. I looked at my dad for any kind of reaction. My mother's lips went tight, and my dad looked sadly at my mom. What kind of look was that? Did he know about Allison and her past?

Allison pushed her chair away from the table and its legs made a deep screeching sound against the hardwood floor. I held my breath. "Jake isn't a bad guy. He's taken care of Aly. Maybe in ways you don't approve of, but he has. We're all just experiencing what it's like to be teenagers, and you guys act like it's a crime. I didn't know that Jake had a drug problem. I don't think anyone did. I think you're being way harsh on everything, Dad."

My dad looked like he aged ten years right in front of me as he hung his head. Allison disappeared without another word and I sat like stone, as if I'd stared into Medusa's eyes.

"Alyssa, you think I don't know about what goes on under my roof or outside of these walls? I know I may not know everything, but I know how it feels to love and lose. I know what it feels like to be alone. I know what it feels like to be lied to by people who say they love you. I know what battles to fight. Your mother and I tell each other everything, whether you all think we don't. Under the circumstances of Jake, I thought it was better not to have Allison's boyfriend hanging out. I thought of you when I made that decision. I didn't want him flaunted in your face. Maybe I should have said that."

"Why don't you tell her now?" I choked out, holding back tears.

"I will when the opportunity presents itself."

"Dad, I'm sorry," I said, trying to gulp down the golf ball-sized lump in my throat. "I still don't understand what the big deal is."

"Alyssa, I don't think you will until you have your own children. Jake just turned eighteen. You're fourteen."

"I'm gonna be fifteen soon," I piped.

My dad just rolled his eyes at me and went on. "He's not your typical teenage boy, Alyssa. He never was. I thought he'd end up more like Kyle, the studious type, but he took to music and the road. However, in light of his drug addiction, I think he needs to know what rock bottom is. If not having access to you is hitting rock bottom, then hopefully it'll help him to realize what he's lost because of it. I'm going to say this one more time, for the last time. I will not sit here and allow you to have an intimate relationship with an 18-year-old, drug-addicted rock star. I don't care how long we've known him."

———

My mother and I sat on my bed and barely said a word to each other. She kept getting up, milling around and putting my clothes away. "Mom, can I please go to Nicole's? I just wanna get out of here for an hour. Please?"

She looked long at me. "Where's Jake?"

"He's on tour."

"How long has he been gone?"

"I think three weeks."

"You still keep track of him?"

I sank inside. "Not too much lately."

She gave me a sympathetic smile. "Sure. One hour. It's late already."

Instead of going to Nicole's, I ended up on Marshall's overly plant-laden doorstep. I sent him a text to come out. "Hey," he said as he opened the door. "You look awful, what happened?"

Marshall pulled the bright blue scarf off his head and retied it as he waited for me to reply. "Do you know that sometimes I wish I was you?"

"Aw honey, you shouldn't. It's a shit show being me." He laughed. "Be careful what you wish for."

"Seriously. You and Bobby, no one cares. They let you be who you are, you know. I mean I know your brothers give you a hard time. But your parents, they leave you alone. You still get good grades, you have a job, you have an older boyfriend and they just let you be." I began to cry, the tears spilling down my cheeks. "I wish I were you."

I sobbed, leaning into him. "Oh Aly, I'm sorry. But time will go by faster than you think."

"No, it won't. I haven't talked to him in eight weeks. He told me when he got out of rehab that he needed to focus on the band because he was going on tour again and that we'd talk when he got back. I don't think it'll ever be the same."

"Girlfriend, it can't be the same. Maybe it'll be better. Think positive."

"You make it sound so easy. By the way, my brother went off on my dad and told him he was moving out after graduation. Dude, you shoulda been there, you woulda shit yourself."

"No way!" His eyes flashed wide in disbelief. "What'd your dad do?"

"He just made threats. Everything at home is a big, huge downer. You can actually feel it in the air. Everything's changed." I sniffled the snot back up my nose. "I feel like it's all my fault, like if I'd just done what I was told, my dad would be happy." I began to sob again. It was uncontrollable. I felt overwhelming guilt. "And Kyle wouldn't be moving out." I wept harder and Marshall held me.

"Oh Aly…" Marshall rested his head on my shoulder and grabbed my hand.

"And Jake wouldn't have gotten addicted to those pills!" I couldn't control my crying. I began to hyperventilate, hiccupping and snorting with each breath.

"Aly, you can't blame yourself for all that, seriously."

I sighed out loudly. I knew he was right. "You're right, but I still feel so bad, you know. Marshall, I'm gonna call him."

"Really? Isn't he still in rehab? Like no phones allowed?"

"I have to hear his voice, Marshall." I stared at my phone. "He got out of rehab three weeks ago and is on tour again."

"Why do you have to talk to him?" Marshall looked at me warily. "I don't think that's a good idea."

"Yeah, well, nothing I do is a good idea."

Marshall and I took a short walk to the nearby park down the street. It was a park that was in an odd spot, as if a house should have been built there. It was a square lot between two huge houses, like someone donated the lot space or something, but there was no plaque stating such a thing, just a wooden sign with painted blue trim—"Jefferson Park". We walked up and sat on the swings.

"Ok, here it goes."

My hands shook slightly and my palms grew wet. When I heard his voice, I melted into a puddle. I could tell by the sound of his voice he was surprised and happy to hear from me.

"Hey you," I said, my voice shaky.

He breathed heavily into the phone. "Hey, Alycat."

My heartbeat jumped. "How are you?"

"I feel pretty good, I guess."

"Where are you?"

"In Nebraska." He laughed softly.

I felt the tension pulling through the phone line. "Um, Kyle told my dad he's moving out after he graduates. It was a shit show at the house earlier."

"Aw man. How did your dad react?"

"In the same fashion as he always does. I can't worry about Kyle. I just want this all to go away. Like, I wanna move on with my life without my dad pushing me down, you know."

"Sounds like you're moving on just fine," he said flatly.

My stomach dropped. "What's that supposed to mean?"

"Nothing, Aly. I just want you to be happy. It's just tough though, you know. Hearing things. I miss you every single day like this shit just happened yesterday and when I hear that you're hanging out with Mike it makes me wanna vomit."

I thought my brain would bleed out when I heard his words. "What are you talking about?"

"It doesn't matter. Don't try to spare me," he said cynically, the sweet tone disappearing from his voice.

"Jake, I'm not hanging out with him."

"Whatever you wanna call it, Aly."

"Jake I miss you like you've died. I listen to our song a million times every day, all day long. I read your text messages over and over again, and I draw little stupid hearts around your name every time I have a pen in my hand. It's not going away. There's this huge emptiness, always."

The whoosh of cars passing by was all I could hear. I moved the phone away from my face to check if the call had been disconnected. The seconds remained, ticking away. He was silent, and the tears welled up in my eyes. Marshall was right. I should have never called. Just because he said he missed me, didn't mean anything would change. I sat rocking back and forth on the swing, trying to kick the sand beneath my feet farther and farther away. I'd dug a huge hole before I realized it. Marshall sat staring at me, viciously chewing at his dark purple nails.

"Jake?"

"I'm here, Aly, I'll always be here." I barely made out his words, and I cried harder when I realized their meaning.

"Really? You don't hate me?"

"Aly, I love you. Everything I do, I think of you. How could I hate you? I'm where I'm at now, because of you. Everything I create is about you."

The world stopped.

I sat staring at the phone in my hands, my sad tears now replaced by happy ones. "Marshall, I wish I could speed up time, like in the movies."

"What did he say?"

"All the things I wanted to hear." I smiled, wiping the tears away. "I gotta get back home. I told my mom I would only be gone an hour."

We strolled past Nicole's house, and I could hear laughter coming over the wall from their backyard. I thought how I missed hanging out with her and how so much had changed. Her and Grant were still going strong, just another couple that was no big deal.

"Is it bad that I'm jealous of Nicole and Grant?"

"No. We all get jealous. I'm jealous of you," he said, giving me a goofy grin.

"I'm jealous of you, too." I nudged. "I guess we all have our shit, right?"

Marshall grabbed my hand, squeezing it tight. I didn't let go, and he didn't either.

"Aly, you're an angel. I prayed so hard that going into high school would be easy. I prayed to make new friends and for them to accept me for who I am. Then you came along and my life changed. You're the angel that God sent to me."

"Why are you gonna make me cry more?" I laughed through more tears and wrapped my arm around him. "Marshy, I couldn't have gotten through so much without you."

Chapter 50

JAKE

Being home from tour made it that much harder for me not to think of Mike and Aly being friends. I wondered if he'd tried to make a move on her yet. The thought of him touching her soft, clean skin with his smelly cigarette hands made my ears ring. The sad fact was I had to get over it. He wasn't going anywhere. He was near her, and I wasn't. I could only hope that if he did come on to her, that she'd kick him in the nuts. I had no room to complain, because Rachel was hangin' around too.

I didn't tell anyone I'd been talking to Aly again. My feelings for her were stronger than ever, but it didn't mean anything either. We couldn't be together. She was bound to get over me at some point and find another boyfriend. The thought of someone else being with her made my ulcers burn. The ulcers were the lovely side effect from all my pill popping. I had no idea how bad the physical toll that they'd taken on me. I'd lost nearly ten pounds by the end. I was a disheveled mess, and looked like shit. The good thing was the ulcers were slowly healing. Each day was a struggle, and the only outlets I had were my music and calling my sponsor, Amy James, in addition to Narcotics Anonymous meetings.

I was determined not to be a druggie like those people in the meetings. Some of them were successful, and some of them had lost it all. Lost their families, husbands, wives, and their babies were born addicted. My situation came on so fast I didn't want to admit I was stuck.

Dump was my supportive load-bearing wall. I didn't know what I'd do without him. He knew exactly what I was going through. The depression and withdrawal effect were the most agonizing things I'd ever gone through, sweating and reeking with weakness. I think if Dump hadn't gone through the same thing, he'd beaten my ass and left the band for good. Thinking how everything unfolded after my drug bust made me cringe. I'd attacked Dump when he tried to block my exit from the rehab facility, ripping and tearing at his favorite vintage Sid and Nancy t-shirt. I'd destroyed it. He'd bear-hugged me until I could barely breathe, and the sobs that followed came deep from within me. I still couldn't believe I behaved that way.

Once again, Aly and I made plans to see each other with Kyle's help. It was just after dark, and I sat wringing my hands and running them through my hair in nervous antici-pation of her arrival. *My hair*, I thought. Aly didn't know I'd let the black dye grow out and fade away. It wasn't as blond as it was before I dyed it, but it was certainly blonde enough, much like my mother's. Would she recognize me?

I'd developed a new, acceptable habit of drinking cof-fee. Coffee was my new vice. I knew exactly where every Starbuck's location was on any well-traveled route I took. I was painfully eager and watched every car pull into the parking lot through the dusty, water spotted window. When I recognized Kyle's black Toyota Land Cruiser, my hands tingled. Kyle's girlfriend sat in the front seat. Aly was in the back. I rubbed my damp palms on my jeans and stood up from the stool, then sat back down. I laughed to myself and looked around to see if anyone noticed my indecisiveness. All the people around were in the midst of their own preoccupied coffee-loving antics, putting cream in their cups and slurping away, their faces lit up by their computer screens.

I stepped outside and Aly approached me, apprehensively. The closer she got, the more I felt that familiar verve that brought me to life. Her doe-like eyes searched mine cautiously. "Hey, you," she said tenderly, as if I would break if she spoke any louder. "Look at your hair. You look so different and so much better. I was so worried about you."

I was such a pussy now. I felt like I could cry. Instead, I bit down on the inside of my mouth, hard. "Time and lockdown does wonders," I said, trying to be humorous. I was afraid to touch her.

She reached out, wrapping her arms around me, and held me snug. My arms floated, taking her tighter against me. I felt my eyelids droop as I dropped five levels into temporary paradise. I rested my cheek on her head and breathed her in, burying my face into her hair. I took her face into my hands. She was crying, tears wetting her face. I kissed her eyes and her cheeks, tasting their saltiness.

"Aly, don't cry." I whispered, my voice cracking, trying to choke back my own tears. "Hey, listen. This is all gonna pass."

"It's just hard, you know. Trying to move on without you." She sniffed, wiping under her eyes.

"Let's sit down." I suggested. "How long do you have?"

"Kyle's going to the movies down the street, so however long that is. He said to call him if you needed to go."

I held her hand tightly, as if it would be the last time. I didn't let it go as I pulled two silver chairs next to each other at the farthest end of the patio.

"How've you been?"

"Ok, I guess." She paused, looking down. "That's a lie. I can't believe you're here."

She laughed half-heartedly, pinching the tips of my fingers between her own. I felt like we were being watched. I glanced around, but it was hard for me to make anything out in the distance. Was there anyone watching us? No. I was just paranoid.

"I'm sorry, Alycat."

"What's there to be sorry about?"

"The pills. Lying to you about them. At the time I didn't really think I had a problem."

"The most important thing is that you're okay now, and things with your band are great. Our chances were slim before that. I still believe...in us." She sniffed, pulling her hand away from me.

My heart ached. "I believe, too. It just blows that it can't be now."

Her lips quivered. "Am I ever gonna see you again?"

"Come here," I said forcing her toward me. I wrapped my cold hand around the back of her neck. The warmth of her sent chills over me. I kissed her forehead and whispered in her ear. "This is not the end. I won't let it be. I love you, and I won't let them win, Aly. As long as you want to be with me," I confirmed, placing my hand over her heart, my eyes seeking hers. I couldn't read her, and I lifted her chin and kissed her.

She folded, leaning into me and kissed me deeply. "Jake, you're my everything," she muttered, breathless. Her hands reached up under my shirt and her cool fingers tickled my back. "But it's not possible, not now, and it sucks."

She pouted and backed away. My hands rested in hers.

She sighed. "I haven't paid attention to what you've been doing, you know, staying away from the Internet and all." She stalled, deliberating. "I can't stand seeing you with other girls, even if they're fans."

"I know how you feel," I replied, disturbed. "It's tough when you see and hear things."

My thoughts flashed to all the things that Rachel so conveniently informed me of. She was ever delighted to show me pictures of the goings-on at school. Even though I was keen to her game, the fact that Mike and Aly were hanging out remained intolerable.

I couldn't stand it anymore, and had to say something. "I don't have the same discipline as you do."

"What do you mean?" she replied, a little too fast. She released my hands and leaned back in her seat. A flash of fear registered in her eyes. "If you have something to say, Jake, just spit it out."

I fought to keep myself dispassionate, but she was trying to hide behind a surprising bravado.

I chuckled lightly, shaking my head. "Aly, let's be real here, please. Have you forgotten how much time I've had to myself?"

She huffed and her eyes narrowed.

I continued. "Whether you want to admit it or not, I know you've been hanging out with Mike. Whatever's going on between you two, it's just a tough pill to swallow. I don't care if you're just saying hello to him."

Aly looked instantly ashamed, blinking twice and looking away. My heart froze. Was there more to them than I knew?

"I don't know what to say, Jake. We're friends. He's not like he was when I first met him. It's just a normal relationship, like I have with everyone else." She shrugged and continued. "Where do we go from here?"

"That depends," I said solemnly, considering what to say next. "If you hadn't called. I would have left you alone, for the both of us. I'd just hoped that in the future, that maybe we'd have another chance. You know, like if the planets aligned or something. My feelings haven't changed for you, they're stronger than ever, but it just has to be different right now. If we wanna remain friends and have any future together, there has to be an understanding."

"About what?" she asked, perplexed. She shivered, pulling her arms close to her, and breathed into her hands. The temperature dropped suddenly as a light fog rolled in, filtering the outside lighting in the distance.

"Come here," I coaxed, reaching for her elbow. Even though our knees were touching. I wanted her closer. "Sit on my lap."

Aly wrapped her arms around me and buried her face in my neck. "I feel I'll lose my mind without you in my life," she admitted weakly.

"I know what you mean." I rubbed her thigh, wishing it were bare and not covered by her black cotton legging. "Wanna hear some new music?"

She smiled devilishly. "Yeah."

"You think we can get away with sitting in my truck?"

"Yeah," she sung excitedly, smiling from ear to ear and jumping up off my lap. "Don't you feel like we're getting away with something?"

"For the moment, we are." I grabbed her hand and pulled her to me. "Anything for you. I'd risk jail for you."

She stood on her tiptoes and kissed me hard. The warmth of her tongue on my lips sent a throbbing feeling through me. I moaned and kissed her deeper. Our lips stayed locked almost all the way to my truck, caution stomped out with each step. Feeling her warm skin beneath my hands, after all these months, nearly sent me out of control.

"Can't we go somewhere? I'll call Kyle and…"

"Aly, stop," I said. I gently pushed her hand away from my groin. "I'm sorry. I want this so bad, but not like this." My words seared with desire.

"Why? I may never see you again," she said, her voice cracked.

"That's not true and you know it."

I moved, cracking the windows that had become fogged from the heat and moisture of our breath.

I continued. "We'll do this again soon. Christmas is coming. I'll be home and you'll be out of school. We'll see each other then."

"You know how hard it's going to be, having you only yards away?"

"Yep. I live it every time I come home."

As long as the fire ignited between us when we saw each other, I would always keep her at the forefront of my mind.

I headed straight to my sponsor's pad. With all the forced therapy and counseling, I was now familiar enough with myself to know my cycle of downward spiral. Coming down from any excitement was always tough. After a gig or thinking too much about Aly and our circumstances always threw me towards popping a pill to take the edge off. I felt that blaze of blistering yearning in the pit of my stomach and needed someone to talk me down.

Amy had been through the wringer, and looked like it too. She never gave two shits about what she looked like. She was a throwback to the hippy days. She'd used LSD and everything else under the sun, and lived to tell about it. She'd been Dump's sponsor, too. She opened her door wearing some sort of an ornamental gold-colored, jewel-encrusted headband. She wore a light pink tank top without a bra. I never asked, but she had to be in her late fifties; her tits had seen better days. Sometimes I wondered if she dressed like that on purpose, to test me - as if she'd go change into something skimpy or revealing when I told her I was coming.

I concentrated on the headpiece.

"Hey, Ames," I said, not making eye contact with her.

I could feel her taking me in and I finally looked at her. Her thin, wrinkly arm ran up the doorjam as she leaned against it. She wasn't too surprised to see me.

"Why so glum?" her raspy voice questioned.

"Believe it or not, I just spent some time with Aly."

"Whoa shit, brother, come on in!" she sang out excitedly. She loved the drama of it all. "What the hell were you thinking, anyway? You know I'm supposed to report any wrongdoing."

Unconcerned, I replied, "Call the cops."

"You really don't mean that, because if you're gonna be an asshole, I will." Her playfulness disappeared with my smart comeback. "I'm giving you a chance here, Jake. Don't blow this."

"Amy, I'm sorry. I'm just at *that* place. You know."

"Sit. Want somethin' to drink? I'm gonna make coffee," she sang out in a gentle tone. "I know how you love you some coffee."

"Sure."

I sat down on her worn black leather sofa. Her pad was eclectic, to say the least. There were a hundred little figurines of owls of all shapes and sizes, wooden and metal. She painted, and there were canvases everywhere, all half-covered with her paint strokes. Not one of them was finished. Everything went along perfectly with her personality. She walked into her kitchen and I observed the nervous tick she had of raising her eyebrows and opening her mouth in a little 'o' then stretching it wide open, over and over again. It had to be the damage from her drug abuse. She could have been really pretty once.

"You think I'll always be this way? Feeling so empty without her? Me feeling so high and then so low at every turn?"

"Jake, let me put it to you this way, and I've said this many times. I think I'm gonna have to start beating you.

You have a talent. You have your music. You need to channel your demons into making music *with* you." She waved the empty coffee cup at me.

"That's what I've been doing. It's just tough. Sleeping is the problem. It's like I don't dream. I stay on the surface, hearing all the noises around me. My brain won't turn off. I think about all my dreams and how I want Aly to be a part of them. The future. She's the future."

She handed me a cup of steaming black gold and I took a sip.

Amy sighed deeply taking sips out of her bright aquamarine colored cup. "You're a good-looking kid, Jake. You have your life ahead of you. You should be having a good time. Experiencing life. You come here every time you come home from your touring and you feel empty. You say it's because you feel incomplete without Aly. I'm not so sure that's what it is. The quicksand of addiction is easily disguised, Jake." She blinked three times and took another sip. "You're staying on the surface because there are bigger issues than you and Aly."

What she said sent a shock through me like I'd broken a bone. "It's funny you say that."

"Why?"

"No one's ever put it to me like that," I muttered, shrugging.

"You're different than the other former druggies that come through here, Jake."

"I was never a druggie," I said, low and harsh. I was hell bent on not having a relapse. "I'm not gonna be like you, Amy. I popped pills; I didn't shoot poison into my veins and end up homeless by losing my family from a decade of hard-core drug use."

As soon as the harsh words left my mouth, I regretted them. Amy smiled softly and pushed aside a stack of magazines, placing her cup on the coffee table. Her face stretched out and she looked over her shoulder.

I huffed, agitated. She couldn't be serious about me being a druggie and placing me in the same category as her. "I'm sorry. I didn't mean it…"

"Sure you did," she interrupted. "The truth will set you free."

She looked over her shoulder again.

"Amy, do you know what you're doing? I mean do you know that you're always looking over your shoulder?"

Her face stretched out again.

I continued. "Do you know that you make faces?" I paused, rubbing my face. I wasn't trying to be a dick anymore. "I don't wanna be a druggie, Amy. I'm sorry. I know you're only trying to help."

I felt a lump form in my throat.

She leaned back, stretching her arms over her head, and her boobs stared at me. I looked away, not wanting to stare at her nipples that faced the ground. *Shit, why did I come here?*

"I'm aware of my nervous…behavior," she said quietly. "And no, you're not a druggie like me—a former druggie, let me correct myself—but we don't want you to become one."

I thought about what she said—"*staying on the surface.*"

"There's a bunch of stuff with my mom, you know, and my dad and my manager." I went on, retelling the story to

Amy, every small detail, so she would fully understand. "I try just to push it all back, the fact my dad was having an affair and the still unclear relationship between my mother and Notting. Because it really has nothing to do with me, right? Am I right?"

"Right. Those things have nothing to do with you. Jake, this is a slippery subject. Do you really even know the truth? Have you talked to your mom? Let me put it to you this way. What I've learned is, parents make choices and some put their kids first. Others, like me, chose something that meant more to them at the time."

"I didn't mean to bring this up to put this on you."

"I know." Amy stalled, rubbing her mouth, contemplating. "What I'm trying to say is, your mother did the best she could with what she had at the time, and even now. Maybe someday you'll be able to sit with her and discuss all of this. But in the meantime, focus on you, Jake. Don't let what your parents did or didn't do define who you'll become."

I gulped. The conversation was beyond deep.

Chapter 52

RACHEL

New Year's Holiday Bomb arrived with as much flare as ever, my last and final high school party. My house was decorated in silver and white. My mother was impressed with my selections of faux trees and lighting. She'd complimented me on the placement of my arrangements, and offered me to be her assistant at her next job for *The Screen Actor's Guild*. Working with her was something I thought would never happen in a million years. Things were looking up for me.

Dump and Sienna were the first to arrive and we chilled sitting at my backyard table. "So, you're not gonna believe this, but I met someone," I blurted out.

Dump slammed his hands down on the table's wooden surface so hard that the red cups hopped in the air. "Hallefuckinglujah! Can we all just move on now, finally?"

Sienna guffawed and elbowed Dump hard. "Stop it!"

"Ouch! Damn, darlin'," Dump smirked, glancing between the both of us. "That little Python of yours got some bite." He rubbed his arm a bit longer. "That's gonna be a bruise, you know."

"You deserve it," Sienna remarked, but then she reached over, rubbing the area she'd just abused. "I'm sorry."

Dump reached over grabbing his pack of cigs off the table, popping one in his mouth. "So who's the unlucky bastard?"

"His name is Scott and he lives in Palos Verdes."

"Really?" Sienna chirped. "What the hell? Did you just meet him? Like yesterday?"

I laughed. "No, I met him when I was with my mom at one of her events."

"So? Prey tell," Sienna begged.

"He's a valet."

Dump laughed. "I bet your mom loved hearing that."

"She did!" I laughed, too. "She was *such* a rotten crotch to him."

"And you weren't?" he asked.

"Actually, no I wasn't. It was kinda…unexpected. At first I thought, *as if, naturally*. But then, something just happened and I can't tell you what it was. The funniest thing of all, my mom thinks he's some loser, the help, but he's so not. His house is bigger than ours and his dad is some big shot. His parents make him work for everything. I'm never telling my mom. I want her to die a slow death thinking I'll fall in love with losers for the rest of my life."

We all laughed our heads off at the thought.

Jake finally arrived. His eyes roamed around, and I knew he was looking for Mike and Aly. I wondered what game he was playing, and how he could tolerate Mike being with Aly when he clearly was still in love with her. The whole thing seemed sick, more than anything I would have been able to handle.

Poor Mike – he really thought he had a chance with Alyssa.

The DJ's beats pulsed through me. I watched as my backyard began to fill with people. The six commercial-sized heat lamps placed around kept the growing crowd warm. Thankfully, my parents were on their way to their own New Year's Eve festivities, because I needed to calm down. I found one of my fringe friends all the more willing to knock back a shot of tequila with me.

I was nervous about having Jake and Scott in the same room and apprehensive about Mike and Aly. I searched the thickening crowd for any of them. A soft blow in my ear sent my hand flying back into Scott's face, and his beer sloshed out all over the place. I was so involved in my search that I hadn't realize he and his friends had arrived.

"Oh my God, Scott, I'm so sorry! I thought maybe you were some drunk d-bag trying to be cute!"

"It's cool." He held out his arms and tugged on the front of his jacket, trying to keep the droplets of beer from falling onto his pants. "Got a towel?"

"Yes! Of course I do, come on," I said loudly over the music. I could barely hear myself.

He towered over me, handsome and golden. He and his friends followed me through the crowd, and lo and behold, I finally spotted Mike. It was hard to recognize him with his new hair color. He was chatting up a new chick from school, Carina Herzkova, another underclassman. She was new to America, and barely spoke English, but she was supermodel hot with her ice-blue eyes, her long limbs, and long dark wavy hair. A tinge of insecurity ran through me. She stood out for sure, and I glanced back at Scott to see if he'd be checking her out, as sure as Jake would have been, but Scott was staring at me and smiled when our eyes met.

"You have a nice home," he said, leaning in closer and placing his hand on my back. His cold fingers pressed into my neck and it made me tingle.

A barrage of people kept coming by, saying *hello* and *thank you* and *what a great party*, I waved and smiled. Leading Scott into the kitchen, I grabbed a white dishtowel from the neatly piled stack next to the refrigerator and handed it to him.

"For your jacket. I'm really sorry, do you want some soda water?"

Scott laughed, patting and rubbing at the spots. "Nah, this jacket's had more beer and booze spilt on it than any other. It would feel neglected if it didn't have a little at each party." He ran his hands under the kitchen faucet.

I sighed, feeling a little nervous. "Thanks for coming."

"Of course. It was either some other party with people I see all the time or this, and well, this definitely seemed more interesting." His eyes flirted with mine, and my heart skipped.

I was about to suggest that we move into the other room, where there was more privacy, when Mike appeared. "Hey, what up?" He nodded to Scott and me. I was beyond irritated with his timing.

"Hey. Um, Scott, this is my friend Mike. Where's Aly? You know, Jake is here."

"Hey man," Scott said and extended his hand. Mike blinked weirdly at the both of us, like he thought it was odd, and ignored Scott's gesture for a moment. I admired Scott for trying. Mike quickly shook his hand. "Aly's on her way with Modern Family."

Scott glanced between the two of us, looking confused, and I decided to explain. "This guy who goes to school with us is gay and he's hanging out with some people we know, whatever.... And my ex's former girlfriend is now hanging out with Mike. It's confusing." Scott just shook his head and drank his beer as Mike rambled on, sounding like the shallow idiot I knew him to be.

"When Aly gets in here, you better find Jake and tell him he needs to leave," he said, leaning into me so no one else would hear. He was on something, I could tell, because his eyes were dilated. My insides grew stiff and I wondered if Scott was a partier like that. I watched Mike for a moment more closely and he took out his phone from his back pocket. "She's here. I'm gonna grab her."

I shook my head as Mike left us.

Scott came closer to me with a crafty grin peaking at the edge of his lips. He reached into his jacket and pulled out a flask. "Want some?"

"Absolutely," I said. I surprised myself by kissing him. His lips felt nicer than they had the first time. We lingered close for a moment longer and I reached over, grabbing the flask out of his hand. "I'll take a little of this, too."

"Are you gonna introduce your friend?"

Jake's voice reverberated through my ears and Scott turned to face him. I was in an altered universe and I could barely squeak out an introduction. "Hey, yeah, this is Scott Hutchinson."

"Sup, man. I'm Jake." He smiled mildly.

Jake barely looked at me, and at that moment, I realized that he surely would never be what Scott already was to me. Scott was one hundred percent into me, more than Jake ever was in our entire relationship.

"Wait, I know you. You're in that band. Rita's Revolt, right?"

"Yeah." A smile jumped to Jake's lips. "That's it."

"You guys played at my school last year when I was a senior at PV."

"Cool." Jake blinked and looked at me. "I'm looking for Bobby. He said he was here. Have you seen him?"

If thing's couldn't get more dramatic. "They're right behind you."

Then Mike and Aly came in the room from around the corner.

"Oh shit, here we go." I whispered to Scott.

Scott's eyes grew wide. "Jake's your ex?"

"Something like that, yeah," I murmured.

The tension in the room grew as Mike stared down Jake. Aly wouldn't make eye contact with anyone but Marshall. She was in way over her head, and I actually identified with her. I no longer saw her as the opposition. Jake ignored Mike, not an iota of an acknowledgement. He just stared at Aly and smiled smugly. "I guess this is my exit. You know, before one of you calls the cops and all."

"Yeah, you wouldn't wanna fuck up your probation," Mike snarled.

Jake turned a death stare onto Mike and pointed viscously in his face. "Fuck you, asshole."

Aly glanced at Mike and alarm filled her eyes. She grabbed his arm in a silent plea to let Jake's attack slide. I looked at Jake for his reaction, and his eyes narrowed on Aly's hand on Mike's arm. It was as if we were all in a bubble, frozen for a moment in time. I waited for someone to throw the first punch. Scott squeezed my hand, urging me to say something.

"I don't need this shit going down in my house, people." I tugged at Scott's hand and he held it tight as I led him away from the spectacle. We rounded the corner into an empty hallway. "I'm sorry. Maybe someday I'll share the entire story."

Jake came up behind us. "I'm outta here. Happy fucking New Year."

I gripped Jake's arm as he passed. "Please don't go. It's New Year's Eve. I'll talk to Mike."

"Rachel, I don't want to be here. No offense. I just wanted to say hey to everyone. I have another party to go to anyway," he said, pulling away from me.

"Really? Who's the lucky girl?" I teased him, not expecting him to really have anywhere to go.

"Eva James. She's having a party at the SoHo House."

My stomach hit the floor. It never occurred to me that Jake would ever have anything else going on. I told Scott I'd be right back and went searching for Mike to tell him that Jake left. I ran into him as I went out into the backyard. The music was thumping and he yelled in my ear.

"Did Jake leave?"

I nodded *yes* and regarded the crowd and their happy, drunk faces. I pulled out my phone and took pictures of the crowd. I turned, wrapping my arm around Mike's shoulder, pressing our faces together. "Say cheese!" I yelled, and the camera flash blinded me. "Where's Aly?"

"She went inside with Marshall." He shook his head. "You're sure Jake left?"

"Yes, apparently he's going to see Eva James! As in he's seeing her, he's going to her party!"

"The singer?" he asked, doubtful.

"Yeah!" I said enthusiastically.

"Thanks for the info." He paused, nodding, considering his next words. Mike leaned in closer to me. "Hey, can we use your room?"

I backed away and chuckled a bit. "Yeah, but for what? Who's 'we'?" I asked, curious. Wondering if he was gonna get high and with whom.

"Aly and I, so we can be alone."

"You can use one of the guest rooms," I directed Mike and turned to leave. I pushed my way through the crowd, looking for Scott. I decided I couldn't worry anymore about any of them.

Just as I found Scott and his friends in the same spot I'd left them, Sienna came through the door into the kitchen. "Rachel! Is your friend here?" She winked and strutted toward me.

I shushed her, frowning. "Stop it!" I giggled and looked over my shoulder to see if Scott heard her. "He's right over there, the tall blond." I pointed discreetly over my shoulder.

"Ahh," she said in a low voice. "He's cute."

"Yeah, he's so unconcerned about anything, too. Super mellow. I like him," I admitted. "Wanna meet him?"

I turned pulling at Sienna's hand and Mike stopped me. I sighed, irritated. Aly was standing behind him. "What now?"

"Where's the vodka?"

"Hold on," I said, rolling my eyes at Mike and then at Aly. She was too close to me and I didn't like it. "Come on."

I walked into the empty dining area and opened the hutch, grabbing the half-full bottle of Grey Goose vodka. I watched as Mike filled two red cups.

"Thanks," he slurred.

"Can you hurry?" I tapped my foot and leaned against the wall.

Mike stopped pouring, grabbed the bottle top from the dining table, and slowly screwed it back on. He stared long and hard at me as if he was mad at me. "You know, this whole thing was your idea."

I sighed heavily. "Are we gonna go through this again?"

He licked his lips and his face twisted wickedly, chuckling. He reached into his pocket and pulled out a little packet of pills. "This is it. This is the end. The story stops here. Sorry you didn't get what you wanted, but I'm getting what I want."

I expected him to pop the pill in his mouth, but instead he cracked it open, pouring its contents into one of the cups, and stirred it with his finger. "What are you doing?" I asked, troubled. I knew exactly what he was doing, but hoped I was wrong.

"It's just a little something to help her relax. She keeps telling me she's nervous."

"Mike, you can't give her that," I insisted. "She's already relaxed enough. She's drunk."

Mike tried to move past me and I stepped in front of him. He turned and placed the cups back on the table. To my horror, he pushed me against wall by my neck, breathing his boozy bad breath in my face. "I'm so sick of your shit, Rachel," he whispered, close to my ear and released me. "You fucking started this, with your whining and crying about Jake and how you wanted to get him back. Don't you fucking stand in my way."

He pushed me hard in the chest as he backed away. I stood frozen, afraid he'd come at me again. Not another word came out of my mouth as he vanished into the kitchen. I panicked, but tried to compose myself, wondering if he'd left red marks on my neck. I didn't want to make a commotion, but the tears began to swell and Sienna came through the doorway catching me in near hysterics.

"What the fuck did he do?" Sienna growled. She came to my side and handed me a cloth napkin from the dining table.

I dabbed the napkin under my eyes, trying to stop my tears. "He put something in the drink he made for Aly, and when I tried to stop him, he fucking nearly choked me!" I touched my neck. "Is my neck red?"

"Just a little pink. No one will notice," she said, turning my chin from side to side to get a better view. "He's really fucked up…"

"I don't want him to get more violent or something," I said, interrupting her. I moved to the doorway to see if I could spot them, and I did. Aly was sipping on the drink Mike made her. "Shit, Sienna, this is bad. I don't want this shit going down in my house."

"Dude, if you call the cops, your parents could get in trouble. You want me to go get Dump?"

I hit my fists against my thighs in frustration. "Why! Why the hell does shit always go wrong! I finally meet a boy, he's here and I should be with him! Not worrying about this shit! And that little life-ruiner…she's still ruining my life!" I yelled, gesturing in Aly's direction. "Are you kidding me? She shouldn't even be here."

During my meltdown, Sienna moved to the doorway and stood looking, watching for who knows what. "They've disappeared."

"Shit!" I ran to the other side of the dining room and ran into a bunch of people I didn't know. I caught Aly and Mike ascending the stairs. Aly was clearly being propped up by Mike as he helped her up each step. I turned to Sienna and my eyes said it all.

"Call Jake," She directed. "He'll take care of it."

"He doesn't give a shit anymore, Sienna. He's on his way to be with that Eva James bitch! You know…I'm just not gonna give a shit, this isn't my problem." I pushed past her, but she grabbed my arm.

"He does give a shit, Rachel. They've been seeing each other for months now, under the radar."

All the sound from the room disappeared and I felt like I was burning from the inside out. "What?" I shouted. Everyone in the vicinity looked at me, waiting to hear more. I yanked her up the stairs and practically tripped over group of girls I *didn't* know. "If I don't know you, you don't belong up here!" I growled, and pointed down the stairs. One of them whispered, "*bitch*." Under normal circumstances I'd kick their asses out, but that battle wouldn't be fought tonight.

"Rachel, I'm sorry, but Dump wants to stay out of it, and I…"

"I would never, in a million years, keep something like that from you." I shook my head in disgust. "Dump can stay out of whatever he wants, Sienna. You're supposed to be my best friend!"

"I didn't want to be an influence to this anymore." She shrugged, looking around uncomfortably. "We're graduating soon, Rachel. I don't need the drama anymore, and neither do you." Sienna's eyes flashed with sadness. "I'm sorry. I should have said something...but come on." She pointed anxiously at the door to the room where Mike and Aly were. "You have to do something. Mike's a loser, Rachel. Aly, no matter what, doesn't deserve this."

As much as I wanted Aly to swallow the most jagged horse pill ever, I knew Sienna was right. I had to do something. I took my phone from my back pocket and called Jake. He didn't answer, so I sent a text.

Chapter 53

ALYSSA

I was happy Jake left, but all I could think about was how beautiful he looked and how Eva James, of all people, would be all over him. Playing the game we'd made up was hard. It was difficult pretending the longer it went on.

Eva James. I never asked how she happened, and all I could do was either push it from my mind or dream up all the intimate scenarios that her and Jake would be in. I just knew it went on. I centered my mind on Mike and his qualities. His bright green eyes, even though they were glossed over from intoxication, pulled me in. I felt like I was floating. I'd hardly ever drunk anything but beer, and the vodka drink Mike prepared tasted refreshing. Before I knew it, the harshness of knowing Jake was spending New Year's Eve with someone else began to fade.

Mike's hands felt warm and soothing as our fingers mingled together. "How you feelin'?" he asked curiously.

His little smirk made my insides flutter. I wondered if I was starting to really like him. His skin felt like velvet under my fingertips. It felt so good beneath my hands I slid them up under his jacket and shirt, feeling his back. There were many qualities I admired in him, like his edge and brevity. He was self-assured and so different than Jake. Mike was a true rebel, not a fake one, like Jake. Not that Jake was exactly a fake, but people thought of him as a rebel because of their own perceptions, not because of facts. Nope, Mike with his homegrown tattoos and his ripped jeans and motorcycle boots. He was old school, like something out of a James Dean movie. I was curious about him, and wondered if he had other tattoos in places I couldn't see.

He wasn't gentle like Jake, but not rough either. He held me secure and deliberate. "You feeling okay?" he whispered kissing my cheekbone.

"Yeah, I feel excellent," I giggled. His lips were moist as they pressed lightly again on my neck. I felt instant guilt as I looked into his eyes. Not because of Jake, but because I knew he really liked me. I mean he had to, right? He made such an effort to hang out with me all these months. I could at least give him one night of making out. Jake was, after all, doing the same thing with Eva. The thought of her pretty face made my insides burn.

I kissed Mike for the first time. He felt bulky in his leather jacket. "Take this off," I said tugging at his jacket, slipping it off his shoulders. "Your skin is so soft." I kept rubbing the contours of his arms.

His tongue slipped into my mouth, mingling with mine. His motions were more aggressive than Jake's. I pulled away and he twirled me around and sat on the bed. He pulled me down on top of him. "You're beautiful. But you know that."

Huh? My brain fought between rationalizations and feeling things I'd not experienced. I was completely wasted.

His rugged hands rubbed up my back and down to my butt. Every squeeze felt intense and pleasing. His warmth enveloped me, and I playfully hit his chest and rolled off, lying next to him. "But I know that? What's that supposed to mean?" He didn't answer me.

I rubbed at the blanket beneath my hand. It was the softest blanket I'd ever felt. I reached up and touched Mike's face, feeling the rough stubble at his jawline. It felt like sandpaper as it brushed against my skin, so unlike Jake. I ran my hands through his hair and pulled his face to mine. I was wishing he was Jake and I kissed him, again. I felt heavier and heavier. Like I was melting. I wanted Jake. I wanted Mike to be Jake. Mike kissed me harder, more forceful. I tried pushing him away, but I didn't know if my arms were working. I tried to speak, and I didn't know if he was hearing my words.

I couldn't do this, unless it was Jake. I told him to stop, but it all came out jumbled. I felt fear rise inside me. I was too fucked up to let this happen, but I couldn't move. I felt tugging at my jeans, but didn't feel I had the strength to move. I couldn't open my eyes and I felt pressure on top of me and then voices, and yelling. Female voices. I tried to raise my head and everyone was floating. I tried to move and slipped off the bed, onto the floor. Someone picked me up and I struggled to stay focused when I thought I heard Jake's voice. There was more shouting, and two bodies went flying onto the bed and onto the floor. Glass broke somewhere, and more yelling echoed in my head. I collapsed at someone's feet and grabbed at myself. I didn't have a shirt on.

I didn't know where I was.

I woke up in my bed and froze inside when I saw my sister was lying next to me. My mouth felt like I had a wad of tissues stuffed in it. My tongue was as dry as a piece of cardboard, and my head throbbed like nothing I'd ever felt in my life. I moved to get up.

"Hey," Allison said softly. She rubbed at my arm and I fell back against the pillows. I began to cry.

"Oh my god, Allison." I sobbed and grabbed the pillow, stuffing my face into it. "I need water."

Allison got up and grabbed the small bottle of Arrowhead off my dresser, handing it to me. I unscrewed the top as the tears spilled down my cheeks. She sat silent, her brow knitted with concern as she watched me sip and cry. I sipped more and cried harder. I cried for at least five minutes with my head buried in my pillow. Finally she spoke.

"Do you remember anything?"

"Not really, well, kinda. Just flashes," I sniveled. "Does Mom know? What about Dad? Oh God, please…"

"Yes, they both know, and …" she paused, rubbing my leg that was buried under my covers. "Jake's in jail, again… and so is Mike."

"Oh my God!" I sobbed harder. "Jake probably hates me."

"No. He doesn't."

"Did you talk to him?"

"No, but Dad did."

The next few days were a blur of worry on my mother's part, silence on my father's part, and endless support from my sister. My dad barely said a word to me, other than asking if I was okay when he poked his head into my room. I couldn't even look at him. I wanted to die. My sister did most of the speaking for me. As far as I was concerned, this entire thing was my dad's fault.

Marshall was the only one I allowed into my room, and he told me every painfully embarrassing detail. *"Aly, it was the most insane thing I'd ever witnessed in my entire life…and then when I saw you being held up with only your bra and undies on, I just lost it… you had black eye-makeup smeared all over your face and it was just awful!"* He went on and on, and all I could think of was Jake seeing me that way, thinking I'd screwed Mike.

Seemingly that night, Nadine and Nicole arrived to the party after Mike disappeared with me. Nadine confronted Rachel when she'd heard rumors of Mike and me. Nadine pushed Rachel around and they began to fight, and Jake and Mike basically had a nuclear meltdown. He said it'd gotten so out of control. When he heard yelling about Mike drugging me and saw me nearly naked, he dialed 911. *"I didn't mean for Jake to be thrown in jail, too. I wanted Mike to pay for what he did to you…not realizing about Jake's troubles."*

A week after the most humiliating event in my life, my dad stepped into my room, all authoritative, and my barriers went up. "Alyssa, this has gone on long enough. Either you get up and get out of this room, or I'll have to send you to a psychiatrist."

Was there really no end to his bullshit control? "I really have nothing to say to you, Dad, and for the record, I do plan on going to school on Monday. Mom already made an appointment with some head doctor, so don't you worry,"

I informed coldly. "You can close the door on your way out."

He hovered for a moment and went to shut the door, but opened it again.

"One of these days, Alyssa, you're going to see that I love you very much."

As soon as I heard the word *love*, a lump formed in my throat. "Apparently love has conditions with you, dad, and I'm just not meeting them."

I couldn't look at him, but I heard him sigh deeply. He walked all the way in and shut the door, sitting on my bed. My dad looked beaten and overcome with sadness. My heart sunk and I felt the sting in my eyes. I looked away from him when I felt the tears coming.

"Alyssa, I had a long talk with Jake, and…"

"I don't wanna talk about him with you!" I yelled and buried my face away in my pillows. I felt him grab my foot. "Go away!" I screamed into my bedding.

He kept talking. "I just wanted to protect you from certain things, things that your sister had experienced. I believed that if I instilled certain rules and values, it would keep you away from trouble, and Kyle would think twice before getting into something that could potentially change his life forever. Your mother and I didn't get into things like this, Alyssa. Sure, we messed around, but it wasn't as complicated."

I slowly came around to being able to look at him, and by this time, my mom was in the room with us. She cried and told me how much she loved me, and how much she cared for Jake. I'd learned that my dad was actually the one that went to the police department to collect Jake after Marshall explained to him the whole situation of Jake trying to rescue me. My dad felt it was the least he could do to not get Kate or Notting involved under those circumstances.

My life would never be the same.

Chapter 54

JAKE

Time flies when you're numb. I could hardly believe I'd graduated high school. It all seemed so unreal, because I hadn't walked with my friends and classmates wearing our black cap and gowns trimmed in blue. I'd still yet to receive my diploma in the mail, and it'd been four weeks. You plan your life based on how it goes for the majority, but then you're the minority, which makes life seem tougher. I'll always wonder—if I'd lived a normal life, would anything have been that much different? I sat slumped down in one of Amy's black leather chairs and watched her fritter around her apartment in a white slip dress that was so sheer you could see her animal print underwear. I'd come to understand that's just who she was, a bohemian hippy, happy to be alive and sober. She was the only one who understood me at the moment.

I'd fallen off the pill pop wagon and got back on again. Six months had passed since I'd beat Mike unconscious and I was picking up the pieces, trying to hold my band together and keep my distance from Aly. We were finally signed to an independent label under the Universal umbrella and one of our songs had hit radio with a little bit of success, but with all that, I still felt like I was missing an appendage.

"What's the scoop? You headin' home today? I heard you talking that you were going to your mom's." Amy plopped down on the floor, placing her lunch plate in front of her. "You want some? It's turkey avo on wheat."

"I hate avocado."

"Yeah, well, maybe it'll do ya some good." She took a huge bite and waved her finger at me as she chewed. "You need to get tested tomorrow. Don't forget. This will be it. Then you should be off probation."

My stomach turned with excitement and I smiled. "Yeah, it'll be nice to have all that shit behind me."

She looked at me cautiously. "Is it really behind you? Don't screw with me. Can't con a conman, you know. I feel it, I see it, and there ain't nothing behind you yet."

Her question dug at me and I ignored it, getting up. "Ok, I'm outta here. Thanks for letting me crash, eat you out of house, and home and all that shit."

Amy looked at me thoughtfully and took a drink of her water, smacking her lips. "Take care, Jake. You've come a long way. You're 18, and you've been given a gift and too many second chances. You really need to put to rest the things that hold you down. Your wings have grown back. Fly away."

Amy's used all those words so many times. "I know, and that's why I'm making some drastic changes."

"What?"

I sighed, still unsure if I'd pull the trigger. "I'll let you know when I make the jump." I smiled cleverly and walked out the door.

I'd come to really care about Amy. She'd turned into the big sister I'd never had. Between her and Notting, they were my rocks. I was forced to move in with Notting to get away from Aly's next door presence, and I'd barely spoken to my mother ever since, mainly because she didn't have anything to say to me. In her eyes, I'd gone crazy, and she wondered what *she'd* done wrong. I'd had enough of hearing how my life choices were about her. I didn't think she'd ever change. I dreaded telling her of the band's plans.

After much deliberation with Notting and the band, we all agreed and decided a change would do us good, especially after the offer Notting was presented with. We were offered a huge European tour, and I was still in shock about it. I drove to my mother's to give her the news and to talk to Mr. Montgomery. Aly was still all I could think about. I loved her too much to sit by and watch her fail at things because of me.

A knock came at our door. Even though I knew it was coming, my heart stopped when I heard his rumbling voice. Aly's dad was there to talk to me. I crept closer to get a better listen. My mother was indifferent to him. I could hear it in her voice. *"You have real boldness coming over here, Frank."* She'd had enough of anything that had to do with the Montgomery's after all of his scalding insults toward her as a mother. She'd said it was all so unfortunate.

"Jake called me and asked me to come over."

"Oh, I see." Kate's voice softened. "Well, then. Jake!" My heartbeat went from 80 to 500.

I wasn't ready for this.

Mr. Montgomery towered over my mother. She disappeared into her bedroom without a word when she saw me turn the corner into the foyer. We shook hands. A few awkward second ticked by and I finally began blurting out what my plans were. I asked if I could speak to Aly alone. I reiterated to him how much I cared for her and that all I wanted was what was best for her.

He nodded pensively at me. "Good luck with everything, Jake." He shook my hand respectfully. "Come over whenever you're ready."

———

My mother stood with me at our front door. Her crinkled forehead matched mine. My hands were damp from anxiety. I hadn't laid eyes on Aly since I saw her looking beat up and stripped down at Rachel's house. I still wanted to kill Mike and was glad his ass spent a long time in jail, thanks to Mr. Montgomery and his inability to come up with bail.

"This is just a little blip in your life, Jake." She tried to reach out for me, but I backed away. I was still so annoyed with her about so many things. "You are so much bigger than all this. You'll see."

"Mom, stop with the pep talk." I walked out the door and crossed our lawns to deliver the news to Aly.

My insides were a billion colorful, squiggly lines as I made my way to Aly's house. I felt out of control, even though I was in the most control I'd been in a long time. It was as if my arm moved in slow motion when I reached out to knock on the door. Aly's dad opened it and he didn't say a word. He looked drawn and unhappy. He blinked three times before removing his glasses, and rubbed his eyes as if he was seeing things. He yelled out for Aly to come down. I instantly felt the surge, the energy that was only between Aly and I. She was getting closer. When she saw me, her eyes popped wide and she gasped. I gulped. I don't ever recall feeling like I could burst out crying, but I knew what I felt in my jaw and throat was burn of emotion.

Aly stood at the door looking disheveled, wearing pink ladybug pajama bottoms, typical Aly, naturally beautiful as ever. I wanted to punch at the air, at the frustrations of life. Her hair had grown so long over the year that it cascaded all around her shoulders and chest. She wrung her hands. "Um, this is kinda awkward." She whispered, looking over her shoulder. "What's going on?"

I sighed and got sick to my stomach. "I called your dad and asked if I could see you."

She breathed in heavily and nodded. She wouldn't look at me. She was silent, staring down, and I saw the tears begin to leak down her cheeks. I reached for her hand, pulled her out the door, and shut it. I wrapped her in my arms, tight against my chest. "Stop crying. Please," I said it for me more than for her, as moisture filled my own eyes. I gulped over and over again, trying to hold it back. "Hey…"

"I'm so sorry, Jake. I'm so beyond mortified. I didn't mean for things to go so far with Mike."

I couldn't control my feelings and cupped her beautiful, sad face in my hands, trying to kiss away her tears. "Hey, shush, we did this together. It's not your fault."

We stood holding each other as if we'd die if we let go. "I can't believe my dad let you see me." Her muffled words squeezed through the fabric of my t-shirt. I felt her warm breath at my chest and knew how quickly I'd get caught up again if I let myself. I knew I had to just tell her, but I struggled with the delivery.

"Hey, I'm here because I have to tell you something. It's good...and bad news."

"I want the good news." She said, sitting down at the wrought-iron patio table. She wiped her face with hands that sported blue glittering fingernail polish.

I tried to stay up beat. "Nice nails," I said, kicking her foot.

"Spit it out," she ordered quietly. Her eyes were red and bloodshot as they searched mine.

"The band is going to Europe. We've been offered a pretty big tour, and if it goes well, we'll stay there for a while and on the east coast, too."

She nodded passively. "I'm happy for you. I really am." She was cold, but how else did I expect her to respond?

"You know this is good for the both of us, right?"

"Does it really matter anymore? We've barely spoken in almost six months, Jake."

"It's not because I didn't want to, Aly. This is just as painful for me as it is for you."

She looked away from me because she knew I was right. "It doesn't matter anymore." She stifled her tears and pressed her hand hard against her pink lips.

"It matters to me, Aly. I love you. Everything that's happened good with the band is because of you..."

"Who are you going on tour with?" she interrupted. My stomach went into a ball. I was hoping she wouldn't ask.

"We're opening for...Eva James."

Aly's eyes narrowed in on mine and I felt the energy between us falter as if she turned it off. "You're sleeping with her, aren't you? You know what…" She stood up and paced, huffing. Her chest heaved with each step. "It doesn't matter. Because for some reason, you never thought of me that way, or you would have taken your many chances! Instead you choose some fucking…who knows what?! This is how you operate. You say you love me, but then don't have the balls to tell me you've been seeing someone else!"

I couldn't argue with her, because it was true. I'd been seeing Eva.

"You can't blame me for carrying on with my life! And I wanted to honor you, Aly! Your father already thinks I'm a piece of shit! But you know what? At least I can walk away from this knowing I loved you enough to care about it. You're fifteen, Aly." I stood up to meet her and she backed away.

"I know how old I am, Jake! You're a coward. After everything, why couldn't you tell me? I sit here and live my life day after day, thinking and looking forward that we're gonna be together, because of the things you've said to me…"

"We're still gonna be together, Aly." I yelled over her rant. She quieted. "If I could be with you now, I would."

We stood at odds. "Please, don't do this. Don't blame me for all of this. I never made any promises on timing, Aly. Everything I've said to you, I've meant. But I can't stand by and watch you be with other people and pretend that I'm ok with it, and I don't expect you to do the same. The whole Mike thing was a joke. I was miserable. Your father hates me. My mom hates the thought of us. We need to grow up."

"You're already fucking grown up, now, aren't you? You're a coward! You made me waste months thinking we'd be together! I should have known better!"

Aly and I went around and around in conversational circles about who was right and who was wrong, and rehashed every painful, pathetic moment, trying to keep score. I was exhausted, and I was over it.

"I can't do this anymore, Aly. I've gotta get out of here," I announced, defeated. "I'm sorry, but we're never gonna change, at least not now."

I stepped toward the gate and she came after me, "Jake, please don't go. Not like this." Her voice quivered.

I wanted to hold her, but I just couldn't. I had to be strong and walk away, or we'd never learn. "Aly, I love you." I left her crying and never looked back.

My mother must have been waiting at the door for me, because she was right there when I came through it. As soon as I reached her I began to cry. The deepest pain I think I'd ever felt coursed through me. I collapsed on the floor and the tears didn't stop for what seemed like an hour. My mother sat next to me holding me, rocking back and forth. She was crying, too, and for the first time, she said nothing. I looked up at the wall of black and white photos and searched through the blur of tears for the ones I'd added of Aly. The ones my mother never said anything about.

I'd be taking those with me to New York.

It was almost midnight, and I'd sat on my own bed for the first time in months. It felt odd being there, knowing Aly was next door and hating me. She'd text me several times and I'd deleted them. I couldn't stand reading them anymore, as every word whipped and seared me. The light flickered bright and then went dim from the TV, over and over again as the images danced around the screen. It reminded me of all the nights spent there with Aly. I sat like old times, strumming my guitar. The song that came out was our next radio song, a duet with a hired voice, and it was bigger hit that our first, and the most poignant. I wondered what Aly would think when she heard it.

<u>Talk About It</u>
So far away
This thing that we started
Has ended just right
You let me down
I never promised I would be the one
And it's over now

I don't wanna talk about it
I don't wanna think about where we ended
I don't want to think about you
And all of the things we could have been

You had my heart
It's so hard to keep it when we're so far apart
I need you still
And I wish we could change but I know we never will
I don't wanna talk about it
I don't wanna think about where we ended
I don't want to think about you
And all of the things we could have been

Ann Marie Frohoff

I don't wanna talk about it
I don't wanna think about where we ended
I don't want to think about you
And all of the things we could have been
I don't wanna talk about it

I don't wanna talk about it

Chapter 55

JAKE

Rolling, rolling, rolling. Time doesn't care what time it is.

I wasn't ready to wake up. My head was as thick as a brick. The stink of cigarettes mixed with Victoria's musky perfume tickled at my senses, and not in a good way. I rolled over moving away from the foul aroma that made my stomach turn. These Europeans I'd been hanging with were the smokiest bunch of people I'd ever met. I thought the Midwest of the US was bad, nope. These people smoked like their lives depended on it, like it wouldn't send them to an early grave.

I stared over the mess that took over my rented flat. Victoria's shopping bags, shoes and clothes were strewn everywhere. I wondered how her place looked and if it smelled of smoke as mine did. However faint it was, I hated it. I didn't think her smoking would bother me, but it did. It crept into every fiber and stuck to my skin like sticky invisible tar. It clung to Victoria's hair, too. Since I'd met her, she'd never had clean smelling hair, ever. It was always smoke-tinged, and now it was gross to me.

I couldn't take the mess anymore, or the smell of Victoria and her cigarettes. I had to pull my shit together and figure out how to get rid of Victoria. Let's face it; she'd been a quick fix to fill the void, and now I wasn't so sure the void could ever be filled. There always seemed to be something askew, gnawing at the edges. *What time is it anyway?* I wondered. It had been dawn when we arrived home. I reached for my Levis and dragged myself out of bed.

I'd met Victoria Wellington half way through our first twelve city European tour. We'd been together nearly every day since, for nearly two months. Or was it longer? Whatever it was, I'd had enough. Victoria was a friend of a friend of the headlining band. I spotted her leaning against the wall, smoking, near the backstage entrance as we were loading in. Her long hair and bare back caught my attention, and from behind I swore it could have been Aly as a blonde.

Victoria's bare back was facing me once again, her golden blonde hair splayed out across the pillow. It could have been Aly lying there, too. To the eye they were so similar in body type, but to the touch, Victoria was way softer. She didn't work out like Aly. I missed Aly's firmness. I missed her clean, sweet smell. I missed Aly's everything. It'd been months since I'd obsessed about her.

In fact, meeting Victoria was exciting. We connected instantly, and it was fun for a while, she took my mind off of Aly almost completely. Now there I was again, in that place I wanted so bad to vacate, my own *Hotel California ~ You can check out anytime you like, but you can never leave. I should tattoo those lyrics on me somewhere,* I thought. What the fuck was wrong with me?

I wanted to get back to New York. To get back into the studio and to the girl I'd been seeing there, Sophia. That would help, right? I really liked Sophia. She was nothing like Aly at all. We'd only gone on a few dates before I had to leave. We exchanged a few emails, all playful and never serious. That's what I needed. Nothing serious. Victoria mentioned one night she wanted to move to New York to try something new. *Ugh*. Really? I guess that's what those trust fund Euros do. They just floated where the wind took them. I was no longer going to fill her sails.

"Now, you know you could have someone else doing that for you."

Victoria's raspy voice startled me and I tripped over her red stilettoes. I knew those things could kill someone. Her accent reminded me of Notting. That's right, another reminder of home. I needed to return his call.

"Hey. Yeah well, considering I can't stand looking at all this shit anymore."

"I'll call someone right over..."

"No," I interrupted. "No, really, please, Victoria. Thank you. It's fine. I have a washer and dryer right down the hall. Um, it would help if you could gather your stuff up, too."

I wondered how that last part came across, but I wanted her to leave, even though she looked beyond sexy lying there with her perfect breasts peeking out through her hair. She stretched out her arm and rubbed the empty space in the bed.

"Come back to bed. You *must* not be feeling well. I could change, that you know."

I felt a pang in my groin.

"Yeah?" Who was I to deny myself one last romp with a willing participant? Dropping the basket, I made my way around the mess. The closer I got, the more I could smell the staleness left over from last night. Then an idea popped in my head.

"Let's take a shower."

"Look at you, something new." She hummed.

She slid out of bed and tossed her blonde mane behind her. Her lilywhite skin was flawless, and her pale pink nipples stood erect. I couldn't deny my physical attraction for her. "After you." I said, smiling and held out my arm directing the way. "Start the shower. I'll be there in a sec, the shampoo's out."

I knew exactly what I was doing, but I just had to get rid of the decay that agonized my senses. I wanted a clean, refreshing scent. I wanted something from home. I rummaged through a duffle bag and grabbed out an old bottle of Suave Strawberry Citrus Rush, Aly's signature scent.

I stepped into the shower, placing the bottle on the tan tiled bench. I took Victoria in my arms and kissed her, shifting around so the water's warmth would wrap around me. She released me and I watched her as she squeezed the pink-tinged gel into the palm of her hand.

She giggled. "Where did you find this?"

"It's just something I picked up along the way."

"Ah, mhmm." She smiled slyly, as if she knew.

I paused, not sure how to react to that. She lathered her hair into a thick bubbly helmet. Thank God she wouldn't smell like an ashtray anymore, and whatever else she thought smelled good. She moved me out of the way, rinsing her hair. I picked up the bottle and held it under my nose, closing my eyes. The most vibrant happy memories of Aly flashed in front of me. That was so long ago. Then I thought of how I left her, crying and broken.

"Darling, no," Victoria said softly, rousing me from my time warp. "Let me wash your hair."

She gently took the bottle from my hands. I watched as she drizzled more gel into her palm, then she began running her shampoo-caked fingers through my hair. "Tip your head down more. Here, sit down on the bench."

Victoria was only a couple of years older than me, twenty-one, but she was way more secure with her sexual being than any American girl I'd been with. I'd heard that European woman were way more sexually forward thinking, and now I believed it. Our first few nights, together she'd taken control. Until then, I'd never gone down on a girl long enough for her to have an orgasm, or at least I didn't think I had. There was nothing more arousing with anyone else other than being with Aly, and even then, Aly and I only stayed on the surface. Victoria was sensual, knowing, and slow-moving. She was tantalizing. She talked me through everything and explained exactly how she liked it. From then on, it only took me a few minutes to please her that way.

I sat with my eyes closed as she gently massaged my scalp. I opened them to her belly button, only a few inches away from my lips. Of course, I couldn't help but glance down. She didn't have one hair on her, smooth from a Brazilian wax job. That turned me on. I reached up, wrapping my hands around her tiny waist, and kissed her stomach. A soft moan escaped her. My hands roamed over her slippery, wet body, to her breasts and between her legs. I kept my eyes closed as my tongue played with her nipple. The strawberry scent was overpowering, and I fought to focus on Victoria, but Aly kept popping in my head.

"Jake, rinse your hair," her breathy voice prompted.

I stood with a hard-on and backed into the water, rinsing the suds from my hair. I felt her hand gently wrap around me and her lips pressed eagerly against mine. As much as it felt good, it was wrong. It was wrong in so many ways. Not only because I was going to ask her to leave, but I was turned on because I was fantasizing about Aly. I felt the guilt drape over me. Taking Victoria in my arms, I held her. I knew I shouldn't go any further. She kissed and sucked at my neck as her hands roamed my butt.

"Are you ok?" she whispered.

"No, actually, I'm not. I feel sick, like I'm gonna puke." Those same words, why do I always default to those words? Like I'd done with Rachel all those months ago?

She released me, looking up and taking my face in her hands. I was sick that she wasn't Aly staring back at me. I'd filled the air with her scent, and pretended for a second it was her. What an asshole. Victoria was beautiful and willing, and she deserved more. I felt like history was repeating itself. The whole Aly thing came out of nowhere. I didn't realize I'd be taken by the familiar smell. What an idiot. I wasn't over her like I'd thought I was. I'd convinced myself that thinking of her from time to time was just a normal thing, as I'd thought of all my other friends I'd been missing.

Victoria didn't know about Aly, and it wouldn't make a difference now anyway.

I sat on the edge of the bed, watching Victoria gather her things, folding and gently placing them in their designated bags. Royal blue Rag and Bone skinny jeans and a black and silver muted Iro blazer remained out. I was schooled on her fashion choices and their meaning as I shopped with her day after day. She hadn't wanted to go home since we'd met. She lived in the country, an hour outside of London. I wondered why she never wanted to invite me to her place.

"Victoria, I'm curious. Why haven't you invited me to your house?"

"Oh, I don't know…it's just been a thrill…to be in the moment, you know…I…" She trailed off. There was something that flashed across her face. She wasn't telling me everything.

We looked at each other for a long moment and she giggled nervously. She walked past me to her purse and took out a pack of cigarettes. "You know how it goes, Jake, reality is just…reality. My family is a little difficult."

She pulled a long, slim cigarette out of its pastel green casing and played with it between her fingers. I never noticed she had her nails painted a pale green color.

"Please don't smoke," I said decisively.

"You never minded before."

"I did, I just didn't say anything. The smell isn't something I can tolerate. I thought I could, but I can't."

She sighed deeply. "What else is there?"

I was surprised her question came with a smile and glint in her eye, like she was daring me to continue.

"There's nothing other than that." I shrugged.

"So it's a deal breaker?" She lit her cigarette and walked to the balcony, the white toxic cloud drifting out behind her. I watched it as it hovered there, and it made me mad.

I thought about it. It actually was. "Was there a deal?" I asked smugly. It was the first time I'd spoken to her like that. I'd never acted like a dick toward her, but I was no longer playful nor in the mood to be challenged by her. I wasn't gonna be some toy of hers.

She turned to face me and sadness filled her normally bright eyes. "I suppose not."

———

I sat in front of my computer, staring at the tiny pale yellow folders that stacked on top of each other in the saved area of my email. *Legal, Images, Rufcuts, Mastered, Drafts*— my eyes bounced from folder to folder, on and on, avoiding the one that read *Personal*. I don't even know how many months it'd been since Aly sent me her last and final email. I deleted all of the others except that one. I'd never had the heart to open it and read it. I guess now was as good of a time as any. I looked around my room as if someone would be looking over my shoulder or something, catching me doing something wrong. There was no sign of Victoria. It's like she'd never been there at all, with the exception of the faint smell of cigarette smoke. I wondered how long it would take before it disappeared completely. Would I be packed and gone before then? Would I take it back to

New York as a reminder that I wasn't able to let go of Aly, even with nearly a year apart and six thousand miles between us?

Tap.

My heart raced as I read the subject line. The reason I'd never opened it to begin with.

Aly Montgomery
To: Jake Masters
I HATE YOU, YOU COWARD.
I gulped.
Tap.

From: Alycatforever@gmail.com
To: Jake.Masters@gmail.com
Re: I HATE YOU, YOU COWARD

I hope you never come home. I never want to lay eyes on you ever again. You're a chicken shit coward, Jake. I never would have thought in a million years you'd blow me off in such an unfeeling and callous way. Have a nice life.

I'm glad I never said it back,

Alyssa

Then nothing else. Are you fucking kidding me? My heart raced even faster. She never did say it back. No matter how much I professed my love. *"I love you, Aly"*. My voice echoed in my head and so did her *always* response, *"You're my everything."* I'd finally gotten the balls to ask her why she'd refused to tell me she loved me. *"Don't you love me, too? I mean if you don't, then maybe this is all wrong."* She gave the most honest answer she could have given. *"There's so much against us. I don't want to say it and have it squished into the ground. You're my everything, ever since the beginning. Always."*

What was I supposed to do? She was right. Everything was stacked against us and it all came tumbling down.

The last time I talked to Aly's brother, Kyle, he said Aly was hanging with that Matt whats-hisface, Skateboard Boy. Of course she was. He was safe. I bet Mr. Montgomery was so fucking stoked. My stomach balled up. I looked at the clock. It was 10 PM and 6 AM in California. I had rehearsal in an hour. I needed to get going if I wanted to finish my laundry.

I stared at the screen. Should I reply, after all this time? Was she completely over me? I owed it to myself to find out, right? Especially after what happened with Victoria. Maybe Aly telling me to leave her alone, after all this time is just what I needed, the final nail in the coffin.

From: Jake.Masters@gmail.com

To: Alycatforever@gmail.com

Re: I HATE YOU, YOU COWARD

You're right. I am a coward. I don't even know where to start or if you even want to read this. I guess I'll leave it simple. Do you still hate me? Do you still never want to lay eyes on me again?

I'm still gonna say it. I love you, Alycat. I hope you've been great. I hope you're dominating volleyball. I hope one day that you'll be able to stand in the same room as me. Know that I left because I had to, not because I wanted to. For the both of us.

Jake

I hit send and stared at my screen as if she'd instantly reply, like an IM. I laughed at myself. It was, after all, only 6 AM there, but she could be up for school. Regret seeped in. I rose so quickly from my seat that the chair toppled over behind me. I picked it up and chucked it on the bed as hard as I could, watching it crash into the bedside table. Wineglasses shattered, and the linen-colored lampshade tore wide open when it hit the floor. Would it ever be over? Would she ever not be every breath I take? *Every Breath You Take*—I shouted out, *every move you make…I'll be watching you*. Fuck, there's another song. I sat on the sofa and pulled my guitar close to me. I placed my cheek against its cool surface. Should I do a cover? Should I do a remake of that song? Put my own twist on it? I began strumming, singing the entire song.

I played another tune and then got up and grabbed my notepad…

Best Years

We had the best years
Of our lives
But you and I will never be the same
September took me by surprise
And I was left
To watch the seasons change

It's been so quiet since you've gone
Everyday seems more like a year
Some times I wish I could move on
But memories would all just disappear

So many things I shoulda said when I had the chance
So many times we took it all for granted

I never thought this could ever end
Never thought I'd lose my best friend
Everything is different now
Can't we stop the world from turning

Looking back on better days
But we were young
We thought we knew so much
And now it seems so far away
I'm wondering if I was good enough
So many things I shoulda said when I had the chance
So many times we took it all for granted
I never thought we would ever end
I never thought I'd lose my best friend
Everything is different now
Can't we stop the world from turning
I never thought I'd have to let you go
Never thought I'd feel this low

Gone are all the days
When we swore we'd never break
Now I'm left here alone
Never thought this would ever end...

I finished the song in two hours. Exhausted, I chided myself for actually crying. What a pussy. I thought of Notting and my mom. This song was for him, too. He deserved more from someone else. My mom would always be stuck in the past, just like me. Her and I were both cowards. Afraid of letting go, as if the memories would disappear or some miracle would bring everything back to a happier time. I thought of my dad; I barely knew him. I thought of Notting, who was everything a dad should be. He would never have his own children because he'd waited for my mother, who never gave him any. Was she really that selfish? I didn't know what to think about anyone anymore.

Staring at my glowing computer screen, I saw that Aly replied. Why was I shocked? My hands went numb and my feet felt like they were cemented into the ground. I couldn't move.

Tap.

_____

From: Alycatforever@gmail.com

To: Jake.Masters@gmail.com

Re: I HATE YOU, YOU COWARD

Jake—Is this real or a dream? I guess I'll begin with I love you, too. I've loved you since the first time you touched me. I should have told you. I should have been real with you, and not listened to everyone else. I should have said it a million times and maybe things would have been different. I think about you every day, too many times to count and I hope you can forgive me for being so selfish not realize the gravity of everything going down. I don't think you're a coward. I think you're so much stronger than me. I do want to lay my eyes on you again and so much more. I hope you can forgive me for all my harsh words.

I love you.

Aly

_____

I didn't know how to react. Elation ran through me, along with fear and a slew of other feelings that I couldn't comprehend. My phone rang and I dashed over to it. Was it Aly? No. It was the guys, wondering where I was. I could never tell them that Aly professed love for me, finally. They hadn't heard her name in months. They had no idea the hold she still had on me. I sighed with relief. Finally, the void was filled, and the rough edges smoothed. I felt new. I had to call her. I had to hear her voice.

My hands trembled as I dialed her number. Really? It had to be the adrenaline. When I heard her voice, everything disappeared. Now, it seemed, the only thing standing between us was time and distance.

I never did make it to band practice.

Printed in Great Britain
by Amazon